lightblade

ZAMIL AKHTAR

Cover by Miblart.com

Interior Illustrations by Rashed AlAkroka

Edited by Nathan Hall

Proofread by Victoria Gross and Anthony Holabird

Special Thanks to Salik Siddiqui

For the daydreamers

Contents

Chapter One

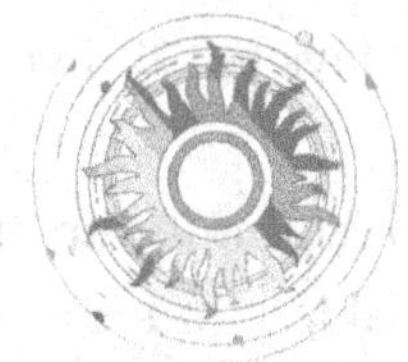

WHILE WASHING BLOOD OFF MY HANDS THAT DAY, I GAZED IN THE bathroom mirror and realized I'd never chosen this path. I'd been forced upon it, first by my brother twelve years ago, and then by the Emperor each day I continued to breathe. Those breaths only fanned the flames consuming us all. No matter how bitter my remorse, I couldn't choose an upright life, and so in that moment, I abandoned hope and embraced pain.

Because pain, I'd been told, makes you strong.

To begin, I got a black-market modification on my dream crystal. Had to go beneath the bridge and trust this guy who said he also gave "perfectly legal haircuts." Took an hour for him to finish the mod, which he did while asleep. That way, his consciousness could delicately direct the creative energy flowing into the crystal. He also changed it physically; he cut new edges and lines upon and within the crystal; he erased older, frayed ones. I prayed the camp police wouldn't spot the difference.

Oh, and I handed him a pocketful of shiny emirils: six months of my salary. Earned from hard, bitter, soul-crushing labor.

It was the moment of truth. If he messed it up, fair chance I'd enter an unwaking dream and spend eternity reliving my worst memories. Or perhaps my soul would become trapped in its own tiny world, an island barely big enough to stand on; I'd be a god there, at least. Or maybe I'd boil in a new kind of hell.

I sat on my sweat-stinking mattress, clutched the fire-colored crystal in my trembling hands, and told myself that whatever waited, it couldn't be worse than living in this coffin these past twelve years. I had three days left to live, and had to make them count.

I pushed the dream crystal into the empty slot in my chest. It snapped into place; it twinkled and sent a jolt through my bones and muscles, shocking me. So far, so good. I lay on my mattress and stared out my tiny window at the crimson sun. Then I closed my eyes and thought of a beach from a childhood memory; the sand had warmed my calves as the waves of the sky lake kissed my toes. I heard the laughter of my sister and brother in the soulful breeze, and I turned to see them throwing seashells at each other...

That breeze took my soul. Carried it like a feather to the realm of the dream stone.

I washed up on a sandy shore. The surrounding palm trees grew human hands instead of branches, all clutching emeralds. A seagull sang a catchy song about the letters of the alphabet. Well, something had gone wrong, and this *wrongness* got me lucid quick.

I got up, brushed diamond dust off my puffy pants, and walked across the sand. A tribe of pale-skinned men without heads tossed spears at the sea turtles crawling to the shore. Then they ripped off the turtle shells, stood on them, and rode them into the sky.

So skyboards were turtle shells. Tree branches were human hands. Fruits were emeralds. Unsound dream logic, to say the least.

Did I just waste six months of soul-charring labor on this? I'd been to this island thousands of times, but it'd never been so bizarre. Too many glitches. But that didn't matter so long as I got the one thing I'd asked for.

At the island's center, past the palm groves, sat a log cabin. Another glitch: miniature dancing bears floated above its door. Worse, they were dancing upon flying sharks, and these sharks sang together in an epic symphony: a song only appropriate for a world-ending battle.

Now normally, a woman would be waiting for me inside on a feather mattress, and she'd be in her underwear, obviously. That was the purpose of the dream stone. They gave each of us prisoners one to make us happy, pliable, and better builders of Emperor Panja Parani's war machines.

But all kinds of dream stones existed. Literally anything imaginable could be contained in the more expensive ones that were illegal in the camp. And since one hour of sleep was one day here in the dream, I could accomplish anything if I put my mind to it.

I opened the door. A woman stood against the wall. Because she was only a mod, she still had my old companionship program's pleasant almond-shaped eyes and proud nose. The only difference: this woman's hair was wavy and blue instead of straight and brown. Also, her rigid posture made her look two inches taller. She wore an untucked white button-down shirt beneath her lapis blazer and flexible, velvety black pants, which seemed comfortable enough for fighting.

Most importantly, she was clutching a sword hilt in her hands. A beam of straight-edged electric fire shot off that sword hilt: a lightblade.

Her eyes widened upon seeing me. "You're here to train?"

I cleared my throat and nodded. "Yeah, I am. So can you teach me to make one of those?"

"Of course." She nodded back rapidly. Her lightblade sparked as she retracted the beam. Now she held a beamless sword hilt. "I'm Lightblade Training Program M-one… or was it three? No… M-one-T-R-four." She scratched her chin and winced. "I think?"

Those numbers meant nothing to me. Still, struggling to remember her designation was hardly a good sign. Could I really rely on her to teach me, especially when I had so few breaths remaining in the real world? "I'm Jyosh. Wonderful hair, by the way."

"Oh, t-thanks." She tugged on a strand of her lush blue hair, as if surprised. "Here, have one of these."

She tossed a piece of metal at me. I fumbled the catch and it dropped near my feet with a *clank*. I bent down and picked it up: a perfectly polished sword hilt.

I gripped it and held it aloft, like I'd always imagined doing, though there was no light beam projecting off it yet.

"All wrong." The woman balled her hands into fists and stuck them against her hips. "Your stance is of immense importance. Beginners shouldn't raise the hilt to eye level — you're inviting your enemy to carve up your chest, where your heart and crystal are. And that's how you die." She pointed to the door. "Let's take this outside."

Well, this was delightfully different. It seemed she did have the knowledge to train me. Expectation welled up in my chest. I smiled to hide my nerves.

We left the cabin and walked some distance into a clearing amid the palm groves, away from the dancing bears and the weird song the sharks were singing.

"So, what's your name?" I asked.

"I gave you my designation. But if you feel more comfortable with a name, call me… Zauri. Any other questions before we get started?"

"What year were you programmed? And where?"

"I was programmed in the floatland of Salkofy in Karsha, in the year eleven-eight-seventy-nine."

So nineteen years ago — probably outdated by Karshan standards. But all she had to do was teach me to make a lightblade, which was a timeless thing. Still, a new program would've had better training features. I needed everything to go my way if I were to succeed.

Zauri came to my side. My hairs tingled upon sensing an unfamiliar, yet melancholic blue shimmer around her body. It flickered for a moment and disappeared. Was her frequency leaking?

"I'm setting the sun to create only red light." Zauri opened her left palm; a terminal window appeared and floated above it. She tapped on the terminal a few times.

The sun turned from white to red, casting the sky and the island and even her in a dismal, ruddy glow.

I tried not to act surprised; I never knew that a program could change the settings of my dream. I always thought only I could.

"Given your age, I'm sure you already know that red light is used for combat," Zauri said. "Here in the dream, we can amplify any wavelength of the sun we want — to make training easier. But eventually, you're going to have to learn to inhale red light in the real world, where it'll be weaker."

True, I wouldn't have the luxury of these beginner settings in the real world. It was nice of her to do all this thinking on my behalf. But how much could I trust her knowledge? "You a military program, by any chance?"

Hair got in her face when she shook her head. "I was scripted for children."

Of course. Even the children in Karsha could form lightblades. That was why that country was so powerful. Meanwhile, all I got as a dumb five-year-old was a toy lightblade.

I sighed at a memory of me banging my toy lightblade against a tree. I'd imagined that poor cedar to be one of the Emperor's enemies. How perilous that I'd now become what I'd once fantasized about fighting.

Zauri put her hand on mine. She didn't feel like my old companionship program anymore; they were nothing alike in mannerisms or speech. She even smelled different: no tangy perfume — which was my companionship program's default smell setting — just a sour sweat, as if she'd come off a machinist shift. Strange, since we'd barely exerted ourselves so far.

She repositioned my fingers on the hilt. "It's a basic thing, but you want your fingers looser, less tense. Wrap your thumb around the side."

I did as she instructed. "Like this?"

"Yes, good. Now, inhale the light. If, for whatever reason, you can't inhale enough red light, I can hold your hand and flow mine into you."

"I've never inhaled red light. Plenty of green, though. Let me try on my own first."

I stared up at the crimson sun. To see it so high in the sky instead of at the horizon, and even redder than the ever-dusk, was... ominous. If I were awake, I might think the world was ending.

I focused on the sun's glow and *inhaled.* Red light flowed into the crystal in my chest. The light pulsed through my veins, accumulating in my hand. I *pushed* the light into the sword hilt, and then opened my eyes.

A faint red beam protruded from the hilt where a metal blade would be. But it bulged unevenly — not the right shape. I closed my eyes and *inhaled* more red light. I cycled it into my beating heart, through my veins, and pushed it into the hilt. It spattered like a leaking pipe off the end instead of creating a blade. I pushed even more in; it still refused to straighten.

This bleeding, uneven beam certainly couldn't cut.

"Allow me to help you." Zauri put her hand around my wrist. Red light from her hand flowed into mine; her light was so uniform, so pure, so purposed.

I pushed it into the hilt.

A shimmering red beam about the size of my arm erupted; shadows whirled around it.

I'd done it… sort of. I was holding a lightblade.

But when Zauri lifted her hand, it flickered, faded, and disappeared. I inhaled more of the sun's red light, cycled it through me as quickly as I could, and pushed it into the sword hilt.

It got hot. Sparks fizzled off the end. I willed it to solidify and straighten, but it was like trying to move a numb arm. It seemed I couldn't create a straight beam on my own. Damn it! I gritted my teeth and let out a frustrated grunt.

"It's a start." Zauri gave me a tepid smile.

That wasn't how my companionship program would smile. It was still strange to look at someone who had her face, but not her soul. Although, did either of them even have souls?

"Where did I mess up?"

"You didn't mess up. You're just inexperienced."

"When you held my hand, you must've felt how I cycled the red light. Do I have any talent for it?"

She bit her lip in obvious apprehension.

"I'm no child," I said. "You need not protect my ego. I'm twenty-four years old — if I remember how to count. I've lived my entire adult life in a prison, scorching my soul seven days a week with green light. Green light used to power machines. I know it's worn out my veins, nearly made me a husk. I've seen how the camp police dispose of those who can no longer cycle light."

I'd never told my miseries to my companionship program. Probably because I knew how she'd respond: with fake concern. Maybe even a hug and a kiss. And I didn't want to be comforted, to be told it would be okay. I was here to bathe in my pain, not pretend it didn't exist.

"I know you're not a child. The truth is, I think you can make a lightblade, but that's not saying much."

"Obviously it's not saying much. I'm sure even an eight-year-old in Karsha can make a lightblade. But what I want to know is — can I make a lightblade that can kill?"

"Any lightblade can kill. It's the skill of the user versus that of the opponent that determines whether it *will* kill. So that I can form a lesson plan, I'll need to know — who are you trying to kill?"

I could tell her, couldn't I? She was a program existing only in my dream, so why not? The prison camp guards never seized our dream stones for inspection, so the chance they'd learn about my intentions from Zauri was practically zero. Perhaps she could even help me plan the whole thing.

"I'm going to kill the Emperor. I'm going to kill His Holiness Raja Panja Parani."

Her eyebrows climbed into her forehead. "Oh… isn't he the son of the Raja of Maniza, or is my memory outdated?"

"The bastard is the Emperor, now. Has been for the past fifteen years."

"*Emperor*… weird, I've never heard such a lofty title used for the Manizan Rajas. Anyway…" She darted her fire-colored eyes around in hesitation. "You want my opinion on your chances?"

"Sure, why not?"

"Like any head of state, he'll be surrounded by bodyguards and decoys. And they'll be the most powerful your country has to offer. I'd guess a small army of highly trained combat conductors would only stand a small chance of killing him. You'll barely have any chance at all."

I knew that much. Still, it ached my heart to hear it. "Look, it's not about actually killing him. Even if I did succeed, his son would just take his place. It's more about sending a message. That he can't do what he's doing to us and just expect us to take it. Someone has to hit back." I gritted my teeth. "I just want him to feel fear. If he feels fear, then I've killed something inside him, the way he killed the light inside of me. Then I've won a small victory — my first and final. Sure, they'll behead me for it — or worse — but I died a long time ago anyway."

Zauri scratched her head, her expression awash with disbelief. "So, if I'm understanding this right, all you basically want is to attempt to take his life with a lightblade. You accept that you're most likely going to fail, but you hope it might, at the very least, terrify him. I… think we can manage that. But getting your lightblade stable will take days of training. How long do you usually sleep?"

"Four hours. The standard."

"So it means we have four days in this session. I'm going to make it count." Determination shone in her brightening eyes. She grinned. "Sound good?"

AFTER A FEW HOURS of failing to project a lightblade off the sword hilt, I almost regretted deleting my companionship program. Inhaling and cycling red light, when your veins have only tasted green for twelve years, was exhausting. It was as if your blood had turned to oil. I wanted to lie down and give up. But someone had to send Emperor Panja a message he would never forget.

I hoped I had enough time. I wished I had a deeper dream stone with more than one layer. I'd heard that in Karsha's black markets, they sold illegal dream stones with ten layers, each layer taking you deeper into the dream and exponentially increasing the time you could spend there. And if you were wired with others in a conduit, you could all live entire lifetimes together, in a single night. But I'd also heard of terribly glitched dream stones that take you to strange, indescribable places where reality has different rules. Where things fall up, where the sun freezes, where clocks run backward. Most who awakened from such dreams, which sometimes lasted billions of years, couldn't readjust to society. My father once told me that a man who reemerged from the deepest of dream layers even claimed he found the Originator living there.

"You're so stuck in your thoughts," Zauri said. I'd forgotten she was standing next to me.

"Guess I need a break. Hope you don't mind."

Zauri gave me a weak shrug. "You're the boss."

"Care to join?"

Another shrug. "Sure."

We went to the beach and sat on the sand. Waves whispered toward our toes. The horizon had no end. The world of the dream stone seemed so vast.

"I should tell you something," I said. Seemed the right time for an awkward truth. "You're a bootleg program."

Zauri raised an eyebrow. Hers looked a bit snakier than my companionship program's. "So that's why this environment seems so odd. It's like I wasn't born to be here."

"I couldn't afford to buy a new dream stone. And even if I did buy one, it's illegal, so I'd be executed if found out. Instead, I had someone copy a lightblade training program onto the only dream stone I owned. Umm, the thing is…" My head itched. "Thing is, that dream stone had a companionship program on it. Aside from your blue hair — and maybe your eyebrows — you look exactly like her."

"Oh."

"But you don't behave like her. It's just weird for me, that's all. I guess to save time, the modder kept your appearance mostly the same. I kind of wish he hadn't. It's distracting."

"I understand. Thanks for explaining."

"You're really different, though. It's odd. You feel almost like a real person."

"Of course I do. My script is as large as yours."

Was that a joke? I couldn't help but chuckle nervously.

"It's true," Zauri said. "I'm guessing the companionship program you had me replace was much smaller by comparison. The inexpensive programs tend to have their memory and bandwidth artificially limited. Dream stones are quite cheap to produce, so to create demand for the premium tier ones, they make the cheaper ones worse on purpose." She bit her lip. "I have no idea why I know all this, but it feels like the truth to me."

Well, that made sense. Of course the camp wardens would give us the cheapest dream stones possible. That was why the woman in my companionship program, whom I called Prisaya, felt like a program and not a person.

"So, then, how big is your script, exactly?"

"Like I said. As big as yours."

"Does that mean… you're alive?"

A wave surged into my thighs, leaving them cold.

"Am I alive?" Zauri shook her head. "I don't think so. I'm a program."

This was all a little too confusing. "Aha. So seeming alive must be part of your script, then."

"I suppose."

"You know, now that I think about it, it took me a few weeks to exhaust my companionship program's script. For a while, I felt like she was a real, breathing human being. But slowly, I saw her… repeat things. What I believed to be as endless as that ocean suddenly seemed nothing more than a puddle." I nodded with understanding. "But in any case, I deleted her to make room for you. So I can learn to make a lightblade. And hopefully die better than I lived."

Zauri's chuckle endeared. It was almost soundless — mostly a concert of stifled breaths. "Sorry. I wish I could explain things better, but I wasn't programmed for philosophy or metaphysics. I attained a basic education, equal to a low Karshan noble. I was taught to train children how to form their first lightblades, and a few other useful basics. I'm afraid, if you weren't shortly intending to embark on a suicide mission, you'd eventually outgrow my usefulness, like you did with your companionship program."

"When you say 'attained' and 'taught,' you mean 'programmed,' right?"

She paused for a moment, obviously stuck in thought. Then she nodded.

"Do you have memories from before I came here?"

"They're not memories like yours. It's more of a… sense of self, and a knowing of who I am and my purpose. If I were like a newborn babe, I'd be useless to you, right? I merely exist to help you with whatever capacities I have."

Now she was talking like a program, and that made me less unsettled but more… alone.

The seawater had wet her pants, and now they clung to her thighs. Such familiar thighs. My companionship program's thighs.

"I should tell you that I don't have genitalia."

I snapped back to attention. "Why would you — why would you mention that?" My cheeks heated up.

"No need to be embarrassed. Just wanted to make that clear. I might look like your companionship program, but key things are… missing."

"G-Good. Good. They give us those companionship programs so we feel comfortable enough not to fight back. I'm done being comfortable while roasting in hell. I'm here to train, nothing else."

"Let's go train, then. Progress might inspire you. Throw off that melancholy." Zauri stood, dusted sand off her thighs, and held out her hand. "Shall we get back to work?"

I guess it would take time to adjust to her. And speaking of adjustment — why the hell had the modder turned her hair blue? Not that I didn't love it.

I grabbed her hand. She pulled me up like I was made of air.

"I think you're ready for a basic technique. Might help you form the lightblade."

"Sorry for being so slow."

"Don't apologize. Helping you isn't just my job, it's my whole purpose. In that spirit, here's what you're doing wrong. You're treating red light the same as you treat green light, but they're totally different. Red light has a lower frequency and longer wavelength. It's low energy. The distance between the crests and troughs on its waves is vaster. You have to be more patient when cycling it."

I pinched my chin, frustrated. "You're getting rather jargony. Listen, I might be twenty-four, but I have the education of a twelve-year-old. A twelve-year-old who skipped class to smoke cigars with his dumb friends. So spell it out in a way a braindead fool could understand."

Zauri bit her lip as if pained by my words. "Sorry." Considering her tone, it sounded as genuine an apology as I'd ever heard. "I think… I could show you? I can hold your hand, and you can feel and copy how I let the light flow through me."

Sounded swell. I took her hand. There was this buzzing vibration that flowed from her into me. Or maybe I was just nervous.

I clutched my sword hilt with my other hand, closed my eyes, and focused on her frequency. Her inner light showed how she inhaled the red waves: as calm as a mountain breeze. She let it cycle through her heart in harmony; it pulsed and flitted as it went from her veins into mine. I did my best to slow down. I matched my breathing to hers. But when I pushed the red light, it lost cohesion and turned messy, like hair getting caught in a brush.

Only sputters and sparks appeared on my sword hilt.

"Keep trying," she said in the softest voice. "It just takes practice. I swear."

I hadn't felt so *mothered* since I was twelve. How comforting to have a teacher. To have someone making you better.

After ten minutes of standing on the sand, holding her hand, and cycling the sun's bloody light through me, I got into the rhythm of things. My heartbeat slowed, and a breeze streamed through the dreamscape, cooling my angst. More red light reached my hand. When I pushed it into the hilt, a light the size of my fist grew off the end.

"See?" An excited smile stretched across Zauri's face. "You're doing it!"

I imagined the blade: a long, slightly curved beam of deathly red. How glorious!

But when I pushed more red into the hilt, it was as if my hand choked. Sparks flew like birds taking off. One caught my hand and jolted me like lightning. I yelped from the shock and dropped the hilt.

"The hell!? There's pain here?"

I never asked the modder to add pain to the dream stone. Puffy burns streaked across my palm, trailing from my pinky to my thumb.

Zauri took my sizzling hand. She closed her eyes and pulsed

violet light into me. It soothed the burn like a cold gel and softened the pain.

When she let go, my burn was gone. Good to know lightblade
training programs could heal their students.

"There's pain here, but it's a lot less than what you would've
experienced in the real world. That slip could've cost you your
entire hand. In battle, it could've cost you your life."

"I once fell off a mountain and it was like landing on a giant
marshmallow. There's not supposed to be pain here."

"All lightblade training programs have pain. The modder
must've added it. It's necessary when training to feel pain, otherwise you won't learn. Fighting is all about pain — how to avoid
it, mostly. Get used to it."

"Guess I'll have to."

She bit her lip again. Her nervous habit, I assumed. "Here's
the thing. You got the flow right. The light reached your hand red
and whole, but your technique of pushing it into the hilt was…
well, it was rushed. Once again, you were pushing it like it's green
light. A consistency of flow is needed with red."

I sighed, annoyed with myself. There was much to learn. And
even more to unlearn, it seemed. "All right. Can you do it, and
I'll hold your hand and feel how you pushed the light through?"

"Of course."

She didn't so much as *push* it through but rather gave it a
gentle *tap*. And she timed her taps in a catchy rhythm so the light
reached her hilt in even flows. Almost like she was pacing it to the
beat of a sweet song.

"It'll take a while for me to get that right," I said. "When
you've cycled light a certain way your entire life, it becomes
mostly automatic. It's hard to force myself to do it your way. And
to be honest, I'm feeling a bit… burned out."

Burned out was the perfect word. I'd been feeling burned out
for the past year, but the camp police and the Paranis they

answered to couldn't care less about what any of us felt. In the dreamscape, I had respite from the real world, but by replacing my companionship program with a lightblade training program, I'd renounced that escape. I had to be as hard on myself as they'd been on me and the other prisoners.

"If you're feeling burned out, take another break. It's best to listen to what your body's saying."

I grunted and shook my head. "You're too nice, you realize?"

"I'm supposed to be nice. I was created to train children… noble children, who wouldn't have to use their lightblades in actual battles, just as a basic thing to know for the sake of their prestige. But if you want me to be less nice… I can try."

Damn. This program showed more self-awareness than half the fools I knew in the waking world. Although I couldn't blame my fellow prisoners; they were programmed by their fears, as I was. "Just do what you have to do so that I learn. We don't have all that long."

"Can I ask — when are you planning on executing your mission?"

"Panja Parani will tour the factory I work at in three days. So three days, four hours of sleep each day, that's — and I'm shitty at math — but I think that's twelve dream days we have to train."

"Is your factory so important that the Raja himself would visit?"

A good question. "It's not important. I don't know what would motivate him to visit us, of all places. But a camp warden said as much, and lying about the Raja would be suicidal, so I believe it."

"It just really deviates from the norm. But if you believe it, I'll believe it."

I held up and opened my left hand. The dreamscape control terminal appeared, floating above my palm. I tapped *Order > Item > Cigar* and hoped that the modder hadn't removed cigars.

To my delight, a red-wrapped and sweet-smelling cigar materialized in the air in front of me, already lit. I grabbed it and took a puff.

Ah… like inhaling life itself. That spicy, black cardamom flavor with notes of apple so reminded me of home.

I continued tapping on the terminal. I flicked through the settings menu. Something made my eyes bulge — *Sweat Setting: High.* It was grayed out. I couldn't change it. Why, of all things, was adjusting our sweatiness inaccessible? Was the modder having a laugh?

"Is it good?" Zauri asked.

I snapped my attention back to her and my cigar. "Definitely. You want one?"

"Yeah. Okay."

I was expecting her to say no. Prisaya never smoked.

I ordered one and put it in Zauri's hand. She took a long puff. Then coughed it all out.

"Suppose my," *cough*, "smoking technique is all wrong." She grinned.

Wait… was that humor? Was she comparing her poor smoking technique with my poor lightblade technique?

Sharper wit than I was used to.

"You can make a lightblade, but you can't smoke a cigar properly?"

"It's not something I've ever tried before. What do you expect?"

What did I expect? Good question.

"I'm curious about something." She stared into my eyes, as if probing my soul. "If you don't want to explain, you don't have to. But from what I've gleaned, your life is very difficult. It seems that you're some kind of political prisoner, though you haven't mentioned what you were accused of. Nowhere in the world are such prisoners treated kindly, so I can understand your desperation. But why resort to an assassination attempt, especially when it's almost akin to suicide? Isn't there something better you could do?"

I shook my head. Her understanding of me was so bare-bones. "Sure, I could just bear it. I've been a prisoner for twelve years, so what's another twelve? You want to know what drove me over the edge? It all started when—"

Zauri flickered. For a moment, her face changed to one I didn't recognize; only her blue hair remained the same. Was her form now glitching, too?

Then my cigar flickered, turning into a soup of orange lines and bizarre, squiggly letters. The same happened to the palm trees. And the sky. Even the ground phased in and out of existence, replaced by lines and letters.

After a second, everything went back to normal.

"Did you see that?" I asked.

"See what?" She glanced around like nothing happened.

"Everything got weird for a moment."

Light-headedness overtook me. A shudder seized my soul.

My brain flickered. My mind went dark, and my sense of identity drained out of me. I couldn't even recall my own name. "Ugh. I'm suddenly very confused." I let the cigar fall out of my mouth. I stared at my hands. They were ghosting to white, as if I were disappearing. "What am I... even doing here?"

"What do you mean?"

"My mind's all cloudy. The hell is happening?"

The light of my mind switched back on. I regained my sense of self. I remembered who I was. But something was different.

"Wait a minute." I scratched my scalp as if trying to dig at a memory. "What drove me over the edge? Why did I decide to try to kill the Emperor?" I pulled my hair just hard enough to feel a jolt of pain.

"You were just about to tell me."

"I know. But because of all that flickering, I can't remember. It's like when you sometimes forget a name or a word, but I've forgotten an entire memory."

I recounted the things I did remember. I hated Panja Parani. He'd forced me to watch my own sister's beheading. He'd seized me from my home on the sky island of Harska and exiled me to a labor camp on the surface. I hated him, but I wasn't a violent person. So why did I suddenly decide to throw comfort to the wind and learn how to make a lightblade?

An image of me washing blood off my hands flickered in my mind. Whose blood was that?

"Listen," Zauri said. "It could be the mod. Bootleg, black-market modifications aren't inspected for dangerous artifacts. Something might have affected your memories just now."

I felt like a man standing in quicksand, unable to keep himself from sinking in self-doubt.

"I need to cut this dream short. I need to wake up. Suddenly, I don't remember what made me want to attempt to take the life of a man impossible to kill, at the cost of my life."

"You'll lose three days of training time if you do."

"Doesn't matter. Without that memory, this is all wrong."

Zauri took my hand. "I understand, Jyosh." The first time she'd said my name. "If you're missing recent memories because of this mod, you shouldn't continue. It may only get worse. You can wake yourself up, right?"

"Yeah, of course."

"Good. I'll be here for you, if ever you decide to resume your training. Obviously, since I can't go anywhere. But…" She smiled sweetly. It made my heart skip a beat. "It's strange for me to say this, but I hope I never see you again. Because if you do decide to continue training with me, it means you're set on this suicide mission. And I'd rather not see you die."

"Really? You care whether I live or die?"

"Why would I ever want a student to die? I want them to learn and prosper. To use their skills to thrive. I want your success, not just in learning how to make a lightblade, but in everything in life."

Hearing that and seeing her concern, it was like a second sun shone upon me. It had been a long time since I'd felt cared for. Not since my parents and my sister Chaya were executed. I mean, obviously the companionship program cared for me, but her caring was so… false and obviously scripted. She cared about me without even knowing my name. I could've been a serial murderer and she would've loved me unconditionally. I know we all want unconditional love, but conditional love is somehow… sweeter. It shows we have value.

"I can't promise anything," I said. "People die all the time where I'm from. When you're no longer of use…" I mimed slicing my own neck.

"I'm saddened to hear that."

"Maybe I know my veins will soon burn out permanently from overwork, like this cigar," I crushed the dead butt with my foot, "and so I want to get ahead of it. Decide my own death."

Though that rang true, it couldn't be the spark that lit the flame. Once I woke up, I hoped to remember what motivated me to do all this. It couldn't be the execution of my family because that happened twelve years ago. Something else had happened recently, but what was it?

"All I can say is — good luck." Zauri still had most of her cigar left. She took a puff, then offered it to me. I tasted her saliva with my final puff; weird, how intimate that felt.

I opened my left palm; the dream console appeared above it. I flicked through the commands and tapped *Wake Up*.

Chapter Two

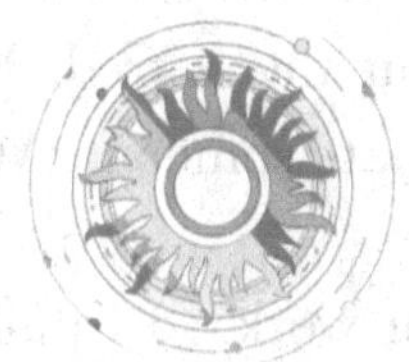

Despite the cold, I woke up sweating. My soggy underarm itched. My throat ached, and I swallowed painfully. I pulled my blanket over me, but it wasn't much more than a papery sheet, so I still shivered from the chill winds whispering through the wall cracks.

My room — if you could call it that — was barely bigger than me. A stiff mattress, a wooden chest for clothes, and a flaky cardboard box filled with knick-knacks: the sum of my existence.

Before I awoke, something had bothered me: a question. I tapped my forehead as if that would reveal it.

What drove me over the edge?

Why did I decide to kill Emperor-Raja Panja Parani? I hated him like everyone else, but a gulf existed between hate and murder. How wide that gulf was, I didn't know.

I'd had my dream stone modified from a companionship program to a lightblade training program. I couldn't quite finger the memory that pushed me over the edge and made me take such a crazy, irreversible step. Haze suffocated my recollection of the past few weeks.

Could the bootleg modification have scrambled my memories? Damaged dream stones could cause memory loss, but if so, what other memories was I missing?

I pondered it as I shivered. The light of ever-dusk peeking through my window painted spindly shadows on the walls. So long as I lived here, I was better off dead. I was a slave building weapons for a cruel king. I was a cog in an evil machine. As I'd lived serving an evil bastard, why not die doing good?

I felt so certain about my hatred. But hatred alone wasn't enough reason to assassinate someone. What had changed? Why couldn't I remember?

It was almost time for work, so I pulled out the dream stone from my chest slot. Its inner light throbbed, then weakened from a strong orange to a bleak tangerine. Being stoneless, even for a moment, disconnected me from the sun's spectrum. Colors appeared less saturated. The air itself lost its shimmer.

I reached into the cardboard box for my machinist stone: a dull green crystal. I pushed it into the slot in front of my heart. An electric jolt jittered my bones.

The air tinted green. Just what I was used to.

Got up to wash. Left my room and walked down the cold hall to the bathroom. A fellow worker was facing a mirror and shaving with a rusted blade. We weren't allowed to keep beards, but I'd shaven yesterday and could get away with stubble roughening my cheeks.

"Jyosh," the worker said with a smile. His name was Rahal. "Dream anything good?"

That was all anyone talked about. Life was either spent working or dreaming. Talking about what commands we'd inputted into the fabricators wasn't exactly a more interesting topic.

"The usual." I doused my face with brownish sink water. It stung slightly.

"Oh? You're up early, though. Had a fight with the wife? What was her name again?"

The wife, whom I'd deleted to make space for the lightblade training program, was always agreeable… too agreeable. Dream companions, as far as I knew, were programmed that way.

I rubbed my barely alive brown eyes, then stared at myself in the mirror. My face seemed longer and more skull-like than last time. We'd been getting less food to eat than usual. "Zau… Prisaya."

"Oh yeahhh. My mother's name was Prisaya. Not liking the image. Say no more." Rahal snorted water up and out of his nose.

He'd been at camp a few weeks, whereas I'd been here over a decade. He was older, though, and so his hair had grayed more than mine, especially at the front. I wondered whether men in their twenties elsewhere had gray hair. But really, I was too ignorant of the outside world to know. Perhaps they had blue hair.

Rahal also had a bit of upper ear missing, like a dog that had survived a fight. He'd never told me what happened, but it gave his face character, as did the pockmarks beneath his round eyes.

"I was searching this underwater shipwreck for the fifth time," he said. "Saw a golden mermaid — didn't know my dream stone had one in its memory. Weird, eh? But when I tried to follow her, there was some kind of… error, and I woke up. Couldn't go back to sleep."

I stuck my wet fingers beneath my eyes and tried to rub the tiredness away. "Mermaids? Really?" I'd seen bears dancing on sharks in my dream stone, but that was because it'd been modified. "Why would an error manifest that way?"

"*Manifest.* Look at you using a thousand emiril word. Hah!"

My brother had taught me that word. I'd gotten a highborn education until I was twelve, so I knew a few other expensive words, though I probably didn't use them right. Most here at camp never had a formal education, but Rahal seemed a bit sharper than the average laborer.

I disrobed and used a bucket and pail to wash myself. No soap today — there hadn't been any for three months. The factories that produced soap in Maniza had probably been converted to making weapons. Same reason we barely had food to eat. What was happening in the outside world… was Emperor Panja going to war?

Rahal buttoned on his uniform: a sleeveless navy shirt and loose navy pants. He brushed his shoulders and buttoned his collar, obviously trying to look somewhat decent. A few days ago, I'd been like him, content enough to go through the motions of daily life. As content as one could be in hell. Living for my dreams, living for something false. Though for Rahal and the others, perhaps dreams were more real than the waking world.

"You're tired, eh?" Rahal said.

When had I not been tired? Must've been years ago. "I suppose."

"When's your next day off?"

I held up all ten fingers.

"Lucky you. Mine isn't for a month." Rahal grinned; he had a much fuller set of teeth than the average laborer. "Next time, we should request the same day off. Would be fun to have a beer or two."

That did seem nice. But as nice as it seemed, warning sirens sounded in my mind as if a light cannon strike was imminent.

"I'd enjoy that," I said. "Beer is good. Perhaps we will. Certainly we will."

Best to remain polite. I made a mental note to avoid having the same day off as Rahal. I could never be certain of someone's intentions here. I'd learned that early on. There was a thing shrewd people did: have a few beers, get someone tipsy or drunk, and then watch the words flow. If a single word was a shadow of treason, you could be rewarded for reporting it. Rewarded with emirils, better living conditions, or — most cherished of all — a ticket out of the camp, back into society. Whatever that looked like, now.

I didn't know Rahal's heart, so I just nodded and smiled and pretended to appreciate his camaraderie. Perhaps it was genuine. Perhaps it wasn't. Best to assume the worst of everyone if you wanted to survive.

BREAKFAST WAS CURRY. Or more accurately, a tasteless, brown goop with burnt pepper and a rather acidic mystery spice. Cleaning fluid, perhaps?

I scarfed it down, then left the mess hall and went outside.

The walk from my dorm to the factory provided respite. Best part of my day, to stare at the distant mountains and dream that I might one day climb them. That I might one day be free. I looked up at the sky, which was always the color of a swollen bruise. In the Duskland, the sun loomed at the horizon eternally, always filling the sky with red.

And yet, with a machinist stone in my chest, I could absorb green — and only green — waves from the sun's spectrum. The air appeared to have a green tint.

I was only supposed to know how to conduct green. But because of the dream training last night, I sort of knew how to conduct red as well. Still, the machinist stone in the slot near my heart couldn't absorb red. I'd need to get my hands on a combat stone to inhale and cycle red light. I'd also need a sword hilt. Only then could I create a lightblade in the real world.

From the outside, the factory was an ugly, metal rectangle. First thing you saw walking through the double doors was the brass statue of Emperor Panja Parani sitting on his throne and waving.

You had to bow for at least ten seconds. And when you bowed, you had to get low: your back had to be at a right angle or less. Some asshole from the camp police stood in the corner and measured the angle of your back with his left hand, using his fingers. And he'd count on his right hand, tapping his finger creases, to make sure you'd bowed for at least ten seconds.

To be safe, I always bowed for fifteen seconds. I was young enough that I could bend my back so that my head was almost at my knees. Just to be safe. I'd seen them whip workers for failing to bow long or low enough.

After bowing to the statue, us workers assembled in an empty room for the usual prework speech from the manager. He wore the same uniform as us, save for a red gem sewn into his collar to signify rank.

"Remember why we're here," he said. "We're all tainted. Impure. It is only by the deepest mercy that His Holiness has given us a chance to work. A chance to redeem ourselves."

That was the lure: redemption. Perhaps one day you'd be allowed to leave camp and go home, back to your family, back to society. But I had no family, and society… I hardly knew what that was anymore.

To end the prework pep talk, we all chanted the mantra, "*Open heart, clear mind, strong flow!*"

When my shift started, I did all the usual motions. First, I ensured the gain medium crystal in the fabricator was in good order; I'd changed it last week, so the green crystal was still hard-edged and mostly translucent. After polishing it and putting it back in the bottom compartment of the fabricator, I stood and gazed at the sun, which gazed back from the east-facing glass wall. I closed my eyes and inhaled, pulling green waves into the crystal near my heart. I cycled the light through me. I pushed the light into my hand.

For whatever reason, green powered and spoke to machines.

And as a machinist, I was meant to command machines. Here at the factory, it was my job to command the fabricator to create whatever was on the blueprint.

I stuck my finger in the fabricator's user port and pushed green light into the machine. It hummed as the sunsink within spun, as if the rhythm of my light and its spin were in concert.

A command terminal appeared in my mind's eye.

I began the usual cycle to check for errors and ensure the machine was in good enough order to begin fabrication.

Blueprint > Test

Speed > Normal

Begin > Yes

The conveyor belt began moving. The *clinks* and *clanks* and *grmmm* sounded normal enough.

Was there a more boring job in the world? I often wondered how people in Karsha or Majapahit or Zerastra or Demak or any other country earned a living. Was it as dull and hollow and pointless as this?

Blueprint > BombardJX88543 > MuzzleSwell

Speed > 0.1

Queue > 1

Begin > Yes

I often fantasized about a machine that could queue more than one item at a time; it would make my job so much easier. Having to reinput these commands every... single... time was agony. The fact that there was a command to queue more than one meant it was possible, but I also had to operate the machine at its slowest speed because it wasn't in good shape and needed a careful hand. If I damaged the machine... well, I was worth less than it, so they'd behead me.

I opened my eyes as the fabricator did its thing. Metal came into the conveyor, a mold pressed down on the metal, and there it was: the mouth of a light cannon. Gleaming like a newborn.

Around me in the room, workers made the other parts of the cannon. Gears grinded, smoke belched, and conveyors hissed. The new guy behind me — I think his name was Kirat — was whistling, and it was pleasant enough amid all the cacophony. He fabricated cannon knobs, which conductors would grip to move their light into the cannon. Across the room, I eyed Parvin, who wore an eye patch, owned a deck of cards, and could hold his beer. He made reinforcement rings, which kept cannons from exploding as light beams passed through them.

Afterward, these and other parts would be assembled by hand because the machine that used to do it had caught fire a few days ago. *The Big Beast*, we called that machine — not the most creative name, but it was fitting. The thing loomed five times larger than my fabricator; only the best conductors could operate it, given its complicated and sensitive commands. Now it remained empty — almost ghostly — right next to my machine.

I inspected the muzzle swell I'd fabricated. Looked exactly like the hundreds I'd made these past few weeks. I carried it into the back room where we stockpiled parts. It was the first part anyone had made today, so the room was bare. I took a breath and enjoyed a brief respite.

I looked out the window; someone stood on the dirt field in the distance, facing our building. Just a shadow against the red sun. I could swear he was staring at me, but I couldn't quite make out his face at this distance.

Cold nails slid down my spine. I shuddered and returned to my station.

I stuck my finger in the fabricator port, closed my eyes, inhaled more green light from the red sun, pushed it into the machine, and wrote the fabrication commands. Again, and again, and again, until it was lunch time.

I was expecting the same machine-cleaner-spiced curry from morning, but it was actually worse. *Mulch*, we called this bread.

Biting down too hard had once shattered a front tooth. I stuck my tongue in the hole in my front set and winced from the memory. Since then, I'd learned to dip it into my water cup before biting, though that made my water nasty. Still, a worker must eat, and my water tasted weird anyway.

I was the first in the mess hall. Ironic, but I felt self-conscious eating alone. As if ghosts sat in the empty corners and watched me chew.

Better than eating with others. As often as you could, you avoided conversation between shifts, especially with those you didn't know well. I didn't know anyone well, not anymore. You never knew who was undercover camp police, or who was willing to report you for saying something you never said. A month ago, someone claimed that the man who'd lived next door to me in the dorm had said something untoward about Panja Parani's wife during his lunch break. Supposedly, he'd said he wanted to *"land his levship in her port,"* whatever that meant.

Two other workers corroborated the story. That was why you especially avoided eating in threes or fours, so you wouldn't have two or three witnesses against you. Eating in sixes and sevens was safest because larger conspiracies were harder to form.

The executioner beheaded the man in the dirt field outside the camp, just for a few words which he'd probably never even said. The police rewarded those who reported him with days off, privileges to visit the nearby town, and, of course, emirils.

"Praise Panja!"

I looked up to see the gray hairs poking out of Rahal's nose. He clanked his plate of mulch across from mine and took a seat.

"Praise Panja," I mimicked.

We said nothing for five minutes. Maybe he knew it wasn't worth conversing in the lunch hall. The camp police had good ears.

I enjoyed eating with others in silence. A comfortable,

peaceful silence. As alone as we all were in this hell, we were alone together.

"You going to finish that?" Rahal pointed at my mulch. It'd been a minute since I'd touched it.

I pushed the plate toward him. "Enjoy it, by Panja's grace."

"By Panja's grace." He chewed quickly and *tap-tapped* his foot nervously.

After burping, he said, "You really do seem Vir tired."

"What?"

"I said you seem very tired. Something wrong?"

That wasn't a question worth answering truthfully. I shook my head.

From behind Rahal's messy hair, I noticed someone sitting across the room. He was staring at me. He had small eyes, ball-like cheeks, and a flat nose. A familiar face, though I couldn't quite remember where or when I'd seen it.

Rahal turned to see what I was looking at, then turned back to me. "You make muzzle swells, right? What'd you make before that?"

Unwise to remember the past. Could be seen as dissent, aching for what was gone. Aside from your love for the Emperor, it was better to be reborn each day.

"I don't remember. I make whatever His Holiness desires." I peered over Rahal's shoulder; the man was still staring at me, unblinking.

"What you looking at?" Rahal turned to look behind again while I rubbed my aching eyes.

The staring man was gone when I looked again. How'd he taken off so fast? Could he be camp police? Why would they be watching me? Was it because they'd found out about my illegally modded dream stone?

"N-Nothing," I said.

"Isn't it strange how we're all making weapons, suddenly? What do you think is going on?"

Oh dear. This *was* a trap, wasn't it? I stood. Camp police watching me, Rahal trying to get my opinion on something I had no right to have an opinion on — it was all too much and too obvious. I'd been a prisoner too long to fall for that. Disappointing to see Rahal laying such an obvious trap, but I couldn't blame him. We all sought ways to survive, even if it meant sacrificing each other. The camp police had succeeded in destroying any sense of solidarity.

"Praise Panja. I should get back to work." And so I did.

FOR THE REST of the day, I inhaled and cycled green light into the machine and input the same commands again and again. By the fourteen-hour mark, I was frayed. My body ached. It started as a dull throb from the deepest part of my bones, and it got sharper by the hour.

I'd cycled too much light. The pain made it harder to continue cycling it through my veins, and thus to operate the machine. Our managers knew the limits of us underfed, overworked machinists. But they didn't care. Instead of giving us relief, they'd declare some bogus charge and schedule a beheading. There were always plenty more to take the place of a worn-out worker.

When I began to feel like my veins were on fire, I took an unauthorized break. Stared at the vacant *Big Beast* as if a ghost were standing there, operating it. Char and soot covered the arms that fit together the cannon parts. The conductor must've overflowed it, causing a fire, which happened either from carelessness or inexperience.

My manager walked by, so I cut my unauthorized break short and stuck my finger in my fabricator's user port. Did what I needed to do for the remainder of the day. By the end, my veins had gone numb, and what was once burning now felt cold and dead. I pinched myself and couldn't feel it. My breaths weighed as much as lead.

I wanted nothing more than to sleep and dream. The one respite we workers had. I still couldn't understand why I'd modded my companionship program into a lightblade training program. The memory just wasn't there. Instead, a blank spot in my brain detached my present from my past.

It all felt… off. I wasn't a violent person. Far from it. So what could have motivated me to do that? And why had I forgotten?

I pondered these questions as I took in the air on the walk to the dorm. Not the freshest air — it tasted like belched machine oil — but it was fresher than the air in the factory. Mountains sprawled in the distance, snow dotting the tips like the powdered sugar on the pastries my mother used to make. My heart endured a thorn prick every time I thought of her, of home.

Up in the sky, that was where home was. In the floating city of Harska, seat of Emperor-Raja Panja Parani himself. I'd seen his father speak at a ceremony when I was a boy. Such memories were a painful reminder of my fall. My exile and imprisonment here. It wasn't me who committed the crime, nor my mother or father or sister, and yet we all paid for what *he* did…

A bell rang. Each chime lingered, tingling my spine, until the next chime, the space between each exactly two seconds. *Death Bell,* we called it, because it only rang for executions. And it was mandatory to attend executions. Missing one meant the next bell would ring for you.

Luckily, I was less than a minute's walk from the execution ground, which was just a dirt field outside the police's lodging. A chill wind blew through, so I rubbed my hands as I joined the crowd of workers, who sprang out of the factory and dorm and mess hall and streamed together. Despite the crowd, the silence was solemn. A tension choked the air and stuck in our throats. Who would it be this time?

I took a seat on a stack of bricks behind the main body of workers. The dirt field stank of waste, and it wafted in the breeze. Soon it'd smell of waste *and* blood.

A week — I think — had passed since the last execution; there was a time when I thought of them as a much-needed break if they rang the bell during my shift. That was how difficult it had become to care about others.

A camp policeman marched some guy I slightly recognized to our front, then pushed him onto his knees.

"State your crimes," the policeman said, "and thank His Holiness for giving you an opportunity to serve."

The poor fellow began muttering. "Please understand. My daughter is very sick. The only healer in our village died last month, and so my wife had to carry our daughter ten miles to the next town over, only to learn that the healer there cost three times as much. I was told I could make some extra money by smuggling…"

I didn't want to listen or watch. I didn't want to remember another despairing face in this place full of ghosts. But I had to at least pretend to watch; in actuality, I crossed my eyes into a blur. I sang a song in my head so I wouldn't have to hear more of the condemned man's final words.

The fire surged.

Room to room.

Red, yellow, orange, leaping.

Playful, free. An ecstasy of burning.

Amma used to hum this song about our ancestors to make me sleep. They were rounded up, put in a lacquer house, and set alight. According to the legend, the fire couldn't touch them. After stepping outside, their clothes having turned to soot but not a burn on their skin, they defeated their enemies and helped create Maniza, this nation. It hurt to remember that we were a founding family of this country, of which I was now a slave. Because of what *he* did...

Most of all, the song reminded me of Amma, and that remembrance always pricked my heart. Sometimes even stabbed it.

"Jyosh!"

The call cut through my thoughts. Who'd said it? I relaxed my eyes; my vision unblurred. I focused on the executioner; he held a lightblade — zealously red with flickering shadows around it.

"We're waiting for you, Jyosh," he said.

Waiting... for me? Why?

What did they want with me?

Everyone turned and stared. My limbs shook as a poisonous fear swamped my bones.

"Jyosh, come here."

The camp executioner was not a man you disobeyed. I got up, walked through the dirt, and went to him. The condemned man remained on his knees; he'd pissed his pants, and I could smell how dehydrated he was.

The executioner, who wore the same sleeveless button-down shirt as the rest of us, brandished his lightblade in my direction. So monstrously red and full — far better than anything I'd managed to create in the dream. Zauri's image flashed in my mind, as if she were holding it, as if I were still on the beach with the bears dancing on sharks and headless pot-bellied men flying on turtle shells amid other bizarre glitches.

"Jyosh," the executioner said. He was so... old: white hair, no muscle in his bony forearms, cheekbones that jutted out. The only truly old man in the camp. And yet, his lightblade radiated heat and death.

"Did you forget?" he asked.

"Forget what?"

"Your duty. You swore an oath, in front of every man here, that you'd kill the next ten traitors who betrayed the Emperor. This wretch," he waved his lightblade in the direction of the condemned man, "is only number two. Wavering so soon, Jyosh?"

What?

The executioner softened his grip on his sword hilt; the lightblade fizzled and disappeared. He handed the warm metal hilt to me.

He glared at me. His toothy smile chilled my spine. His chuckle rattled my bones. What did he want? What did he expect me to do with this sword hilt?

"I know you can't make one, Jyosh. And I know killing is hard. But we all must do our duty to the Emperor."

Everyone was watching me. Even the clouds and the mountains. Even the ghosts.

The executioner put his hand over mine. He made me squeeze the hilt, just as Zauri had. The sun loomed on the horizon, a rageful crimson. He inhaled its red light, cycled it through his veins, and flowed it into my hand. As Zauri had taught me, I cycled the red light into the hilt. A hot beam of death erupted off the blade.

"Whoah!" The executioner looked upon me with wide, astonished eyes. "You're getting better, I see."

I gulped and nodded. Turned out I was missing more memories than I realized. When, and why, would I ever have agreed to be co-executioner of ten men?

This wasn't the time to wonder. With his hand on mine, together creating the lightblade, the executioner and I lined the beam above the kneeling man's neck. The poor fellow had finished muttering and crying and now waited. Waited with eyes closed and a placid face, as if he'd already digested his death. I, too, believed that I'd die in this camp, but you don't truly feel death until you gaze into it. Perhaps if we waited another minute, he'd be crying again. For now, he was calm as a monk. Still, the stench of his piss almost had me gagging.

"W-wait," I stuttered.

"Wait?" the executioner said. "For what, Jyosh?"

I struggled to think of a reason that wouldn't get me killed. All I could do was bite the inside of my lip.

The executioner pushed the blade down upon the kneeling man's neck. But I countered with my own firm, upward pull. The lightblade shook in place.

"It's a hard job, but you'll get used to it," the executioner whispered in my ear. "You may even like it, one day."

"Like it?"

"I'd bet on it." The executioner nodded. "Now, let's show the Emperor our unyielding loyalty."

All I could do was stare into the old man's eyes and nod back. If I continued to delay, he'd kill the doomed man anyway, and then me right after. I let my resistance weaken, resigned that there was nothing I could do.

But when the executioner pushed the blade down, I pulled up again, and the blade jittered in place.

"Fool." He glared at me, one eye in a squint. "I won't give you the choice."

The executioner pushed red light into my hands. It flowed so heavy and hot, it sapped my strength, and no matter how much I pulled, I couldn't resist his downward swipe.

The lightblade fell onto the doomed man's neck. To the fiery beam, flesh is as thin as air. There wasn't even a noise as it cut through. Or perhaps I was too horrified to have heard it.

The man's head rolled to our feet, eyes wide open. Blood bubbled and spurted off his neck, as the lightblade hadn't cauterized much of the wound. The stench of lightblade-burnt flesh reminded me of burning molasses. The headless body remained kneeling until the executioner kicked it into a lying position.

Hearing the body thwack against the ground, that was when it all came back to me: this wasn't even my first time helping execute someone.

A vision played before my eyes, and I remembered him. The first person I killed. The man whose blood I'd washed off my hands. I remembered Vir.

Vir. He'd operated the machine next to mine. *The Big Beast.* The machine that put the cannon parts together. We'd take unauthorized breaks and just talk to each other. Talk about our lives before this hell, about our dream companions, about our hopes if we ever got back to society. Vir: he had small eyes, ball-like cheeks, and a flat nose.

I hadn't been on shift when his conduction overflowed and burned the *Big Beast*. But I was watching from outside. I watched when the police seized him for damaging the most important machine in the camp.

A memory reemerged from a deep, dark sea: I was sitting in a smoky room with a camp policeman. My mouth ran endlessly. I told him about Vir's treasonous words, how Vir had insulted Emperor Panja Parani, and how he'd planned to destroy not just that machine, but other machines, too.

And I remembered coming to work early that morning, thirty minutes before the manager's speech. I did something to the gain medium crystal on Vir's machine. I sabotaged the *Big Beast*. I'd caused the accident that led to my friend's execution.

And then, after they seized him, after I fabricated his treason, I went to the brass statue of Emperor Panja. I bowed to it. Just to prove my devotion, I swore an oath to all the onlookers that I would execute Vir with my own hand. And the next nine men who'd dare defy the Emperor, as if making a mistake or being unable to conduct or smuggling cigars was an unforgivable sin and not flaws we all suffered from.

And in return, the camp wardens promised to give me what I'd always dreamed of: freedom.

I looked down at my hands. Unlike last time, there was no blood. We'd done it more cleanly than we had with Vir, for whom it had taken two swings to sever the head completely.

But… how could such an awful thought pass through me like this?

How could I agree to do such a thing in the first place?

What kind of monster was I?

And why did I forget?

Chapter Three

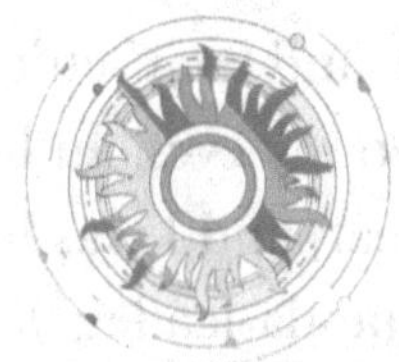

ON THE WAY TO MY DORM, WITH THE STENCH OF BLOOD AND PISS lingering in my nose, a bitter wind swept through and brought with it a piece of paper. The paper slapped me in the face, as if Vir's ghost was hitting back. But what the paper said terrified me more than any spirit.

You're being lied to. Maniza is not a rich country. It is one of the poorest countries in the world. Panja Parani has told you lies. He calls himself emperor, but he's barely a raja. You can live better. You can be free. When the birds of freedom take flight, fight for your future. It's all in your hands.

From your friends in Karsha

I crumpled the paper and stuffed it in my shirt. Not the first foreign propaganda leaflet that had found its way into our camp. I needed to burn it. Even touching such a thing could cast doubts on my loyalty if anyone saw. If only I could conduct fire into my hands, I'd inflame it this second, but I was far from possessing such an ability.

As soon as I got to my dorm, I went to the bathroom, used the paper to wipe, then left it in the trash heap. No one could question that.

Back in my room, I removed my machinist stone from the slot in my chest. The green glow disappeared from the air as I shuddered from the usual jolt when removing and inserting stones. I took out my dream stone from the cardboard box; it had a slight orange tint. I put it in my chest slot. The air, too, tinted orange.

Wonderful thing about dream stones: they not only contained dream programs, but they also helped the user fall asleep. All you had to do was inhale the orange light. There was no complicated technique to it. Just inhale and let it settle in your veins.

I lay on my bed, closed my eyes, and inhaled the orange light. My room stank of my sweat, and I was itchy. My thoughts drifted to a line from the propaganda leaflet: *You can live better. You can be free.*

That wasn't true. We could live better, or we could be free — but not both. Not in these flatlands. To live better, you had to be a better slave. To be free — truly free — you'd have to die.

I had no idea what *birds of freedom* were. *It's all in your hands*; that part was true.

It wasn't long before a river of honey light swept me into the dream world.

I AWOKE ON A MOUNTAIN. Boulder-sized rubies and emeralds sprawled across the hills; the sunshine hitting them refracted into brilliant rainbows. A weird crosshatch pattern covered the sky, as if someone had drawn on the clouds with a god-sized pen. Sometimes glitches could be an awe to behold.

But where was Zauri?

As I walked on the mountain path, melodious birdsong soothed me, though its repetitiveness was perhaps a sign of the original stone's artificial memory limitation.

I found Zauri sitting beneath a cedar. The cedar was strangely normal, and there was even a red-tailed squirrel chittering in a hole in the bark — an animal I'd only seen in my dreams.

Zauri wore a lapis blazer with golden buttons. Her blue hair was a bit of a wavy mess. She smiled and stood when she saw me, then dusted herself hurriedly. "You're back."

I wished I could forget what I'd remembered earlier and just be glad to see her, but I felt too much guilt to smile.

Her smile softened and turned to concern. "What's wrong?"

"Nothing. What've you been up to?" I didn't want to tell her. Tell her the kind of man I'd learned I was. Anything to distract from that.

She shook her head. "I don't exist when you're not here. The interaction between your mind and the dream stone is what creates me."

I knew that but had always been curious what it was like. "What did you experience between the last time we saw each other and now?"

"It's hard to describe. But it does feel like time has passed. About two or three weeks, I'd say."

Sixteen hours for me was sixteen days for Zauri, so that made sense. I didn't know what to say next, but if I were speaking my heart, I'd tell her *I'm not sure you ought to exist. I'm not sure I should've gotten you modded onto my stone.* Perhaps my eyes said it because her pupils shrank as concern swept over her face.

"One's mental state is an important part of fighting," she said. "Even beginner teachers like me are scripted to help others… with whatever problems they're facing in real life. So that you have a clearer mind when training." She gulped and tensed as if she were putting her feelings on the line. "What I'm trying to say is, I'd like to know what's bothering you."

How sad: the only person who cared to ask me that was a script. Well, it had been that way for twelve years. Or had Vir cared about me? His friendship had seemed genuine, but you never really knew. You never knew what people hid in their hearts. Still, I knew what I'd done to him, but I didn't know what could compel me to do such an awful thing. And because I didn't understand my own actions, I didn't know what kind of person I was.

How to express any of this to Zauri?

"Tell me, Zauri, do you have…" I tried to find the proper wording but settled on whatever I could pluck. "Bad behaviors?"

Her eyebrows shot up. "I told you earlier my script was as large as yours, but I was also scripted to be agreeable, and sometimes stern, so… I don't know… it depends how you define *bad*."

"Would you ever hurt someone else? Someone you cared about? All just to gain something you sought?"

Zauri took a deep breath. "Umm, I don't think so. I don't really have needs the way you do, and I don't exist in a place where there's scarcity. So… I mean… I don't know. I haven't really been tested."

"What if… what if you could feel pain? What if you were hurting, and the only way to escape that pain was to hurt others? What would you do?"

The slightest fear shimmered in her eyes. And then she shrugged. "I really don't know."

She could never understand. Sure, she could give me her sympathy, but what was that worth? I suffered alone.

Still, I had to get it off my chest. "So, here's the thing…" I took a few minutes to explain what I'd done to Vir. Zauri nodded throughout and her eye contact never wavered, which at least made me feel heard.

At the end, she spent ten seconds in silence, staring at the ground, as if to process what I'd said. "So… you discovered why you want to make a lightblade."

Those words were like a jolt of unwanted conduction. "No. I'm even further from that realization. All I've discovered is that I hurt someone, betrayed someone. Lied, killed. What the hell kind of person am I?"

"Exactly." She closed the distance and took my hand. Something electric passed from her into me. Or maybe I was just nervous. But why would I be? "It's not them you hate. You hate what they made you become. Do you get it, Jyosh?"

"So you're saying… I want to kill the Emperor — or die trying — because I'm upset that he turned me into a lying, backstabbing, traitorous piece of shit? But then why… why don't I remember having that realization?"

She squeezed my hand. "Maybe the modified dream stone did something, or maybe you're just repressing the memory. Maybe you've compartmentalized your thoughts — it's a common thing people do to survive and not hate themselves. Break into little pieces."

"A lot of *maybe*. We just don't know."

She sighed. "But we do know that you're in an awful situation. You were probably protecting yourself, hoping to gain something to help you survive, when you betrayed your friend. And given your situation, I can't blame you. Jyosh… I don't think you're a bad person."

Was she just saying that to make me feel better? If it were Emperor-Raja Panja Parani himself standing before her, lamenting his crimes, perhaps she'd console him too, just so he could train with a clear mind.

The distance between us deepened, and it filled me with sadness.

"Do you still want to learn the lightblade?" she asked with more gentleness than my own mother.

Did I? I burned with rage, but now that fire turned inward. I hated myself. But Zauri was right: I hated that they'd turned me into something hateful. Why not learn the lightblade, then, so I could at least die with it in my hands? If I could steal the camp executioner's combat stone and sword hilt before Emperor Panja toured the factory, I'd have everything I needed to assassinate him, or die trying.

"I remembered something else, too." This fact made everything so much worse. Showed that I was a heartless opportunist at heart. "I helped execute a second prisoner today, and if I do that eight more times, they'll free me. At least, that was their promise. I have no idea if they keep their promises. I doubt it, but even a small chance at a good life might be better than nothing. Better than this suicide mission."

"Whatever you believe is your shot at getting out, at living a better life, I think that's what you should do."

Such sweet words, yet they tasted so bitter. I laughed with that bitterness dripping from my mouth. "You're telling me to kill eight more people. Completely innocent people, sentenced to die for the most senseless of reasons." I raised my voice. "And you're telling me it's okay to kill them?"

She backstepped, seemingly frightened by my anger. But why should she fear? She couldn't feel pain, and that made us nothing alike.

Instead of loudening her voice to match mine, she softened it. "They're going to die anyway, right? You didn't pass the sentence."

"So that makes it okay? Are you serious, Zauri? Is that what your *script* is telling you? Have you no... have you no sense of right and wrong? You're just trying to make me feel better, and I don't deserve to feel better. Don't you see?"

Zauri's cheeks paled. Her bottom lip trembled slightly. Her pupils shrank. All these subtle emotions, all the discomfort on her face... I'd never sensed anything so deep from Prisaya. How could a script be so lifelike?

"You're right. I realize that now, you're right. You might think I'm an unfeeling, unthinking program, but I am feeling right now.

I'm feeling *you*. And your pain… it's more real to me than the mountain we're standing on, than the birds singing around us. But I don't have all the answers. If right and wrong were merely a matter of logic, it would be so simple, wouldn't it?"

I shrugged. What did I know about logic?

"The truth is, I… I care about you, Jyosh. That's why I said what I said."

Such heavy words. But — of course — a lightblade training program would care about her student. And yet, the way she phrased it seemed so… human. Was I really arguing with something that wasn't alive? Something that was created by the interaction of my mind and the dream stone? An illusion?

A desire to *really* know how deep she was stirred in me. I felt strangely pulled by her humanity, especially her kindness and soft edges, but the fear that I'd eventually discover her brick wall, her artificial limitations, made me wary.

I sighed as if trying to throw off the weight of all these painful dilemmas. Perhaps I shouldn't have told her. Whoever had scripted her hadn't intended she be used to help someone with such dark and complicated problems. Likely nothing could make me feel better, anyway, short of completely forgetting what I'd done.

But maybe it was better this way. Let the poison flow. Maybe I could make a lightblade with all the rage in me. Let my hate make me stronger; let it mold me into a new person.

"Let's get started with our lesson," I said. "Panja Parani will be visiting soon, and I want him to know what he's done. Not just to me. Not just to Vir. Not just to my family." I recalled the paper that had slapped me in the face. That was addressed to all the people of Maniza, all who suffered beneath the Emperor's floating throne. "Let my defiance be a symbol. Maybe then, when I'm dead, I'll feel better about myself."

. . .

Zauri was right. In my poor mood, my lightblades weren't more than flickering sparks that occasionally solidified into proper beams, only to sputter and diffuse at the slightest movement.

Hands on hips, frowning, she slowly shook her head. What happened to her *agreeableness*? Perhaps having a frustrated teacher was a necessary pain, though I wasn't some child who worried what his teacher thought of him. Or was I?

"Again!" she demanded.

How many times would she watch me fail? I roared with frustration. To say I was discouraged would be an understatement. This whole thing had been a mistake, surely.

Zauri put her hand on mine, then snatched the sword hilt. "You lack motivation. It's time to give you some."

She opened her palm; a terminal window appeared above it. She *tap-tapped* on it.

"What are you doing?" I asked. "Summoning cigars, I hope?"

"You haven't earned a cigar." She said it so coldly, I wished I had a coat. Woolen and double-layered. She tapped more commands, then closed her palm.

A bright light appeared next to her. That light coalesced into the shape of a man. And then it solidified: pale, pot-bellied, and… headless! What the hell!?

"Oh no." Zauri backstepped, hand over her mouth. "Where's his head?"

She opened her palm; the terminal appeared above it. She tapped it while biting her lip.

The man's clothes changed; now he wore a crisp suit with a golden scarf. *Tap-tap.* Now he was in blue swimwear. *Tap-tap-tap.* And now he had four arms!

"Ugh," Zauri grunted. "Can't seem to give him a head. Oh well. He's a program, so I'm sure he can still see without one."

A brief, bright flash. A sword hilt materialized in one of his hands. The headless man raised it in my direction and cast a short, straight, pinkish lightblade.

"What?" I pointed at the headless man. "Am I meant to fight back?"

"You better fight back." Zauri smirked. Such mischief. Maybe she did have an evil side. "It'll hurt." She tossed me my hilt.

"But I can't even make a stable blade!"

"Or can you? Only one way to *really* find out." She put two fingers in her mouth and whistled.

The headless man lunged, lightblade surging toward my chest. I darted to the side and slid onto my knees. As the creature wound to swing again, I turned and got up as fast as I could. Raised my hilt to block his swing, praying for a beam.

Despite inhaling and cycling the red light like Zauri had taught me, nothing but spatters emitted when I pushed the light into the hilt.

I rolled away, barely evading his furious downward swipe that would've split me in two. I was surprised at how nimble I was as I sidestepped, slid, and backed away from the thing's attacks.

"Make it stop, Zauri! Please!"

"Only you can make it stop. Project a lightblade and kill it, Jyosh!"

How, though? Earlier, she'd wanted me to relax to make the blade, and now I was meant to make one with some wild, headless creature swinging at me? Although my life wasn't *really* in danger, my body seemed to think it was with how hard my heart pounded. I had no idea how much pain I'd feel if that headless thing's lightblade touched me.

My knees ached from the stumbles and slides on the pebbly mountain ground. And then, amid a mistimed dodge, I tasted fire. The thing's lightblade went through my shoulder, and a chunk of me flew.

Zauri whistled; the headless man stood back, lowered his

arms, and retracted his lightblade. My entire left side burned, though I couldn't see flames, only feel them. My shoulder numbed. I couldn't move my dangling left arm, which only remained attached to me by a taut, rubbery, bloodied strand of muscle.

"My arm… my arm…" was all I could say.

Zauri put her hand on my back. Violet light flooded me. It soothed the pain, as if honey milk were kissing my nerves. My shoulder… the missing chunk filled with light. Somehow, my flesh regrew in that light. Seconds later, I was whole again.

Whole, but still a failure.

"Take a break," Zauri said, her tone drenched in disappointment.

AFTER RESTING, I walked into the palm forest. What could be creepier than these trees? They grew hands instead of branches, and the hands held emeralds, and the emeralds glowed. Even now, I noticed the fingers on the hands twitching. It all seemed oddly intentional to be a glitch; how deranged was this modder's mind?

In Maniza, everyone was deranged to some degree. And that modder… I didn't really know who he was, but if he reported me, I'd doubtless be executed. But so would he — mutual self-destruction. It was perhaps the safest contract I'd ever made.

If only I could wield a lightblade and lop all these hands off the trees. But even in my dreams, I couldn't be strong. Even with the red sun overhead. Ideal conditions, and I couldn't do it. What chance did I have in real life with the weaker sun on the horizon?

Even if I failed, what did I have to lose? Success or failure, either way, meant my death. An oddly comforting thought.

I went to the beach and watched the headless pot-bellied men zoom around the air on turtle shells. I lay in the sand and stared at the crosshatch-patterned sky. This shore was my only respite; the salty air, the seagulls' chirping, the tide breathing in and out — so soothing. A peace worthy of my final breaths.

Day after tomorrow, Emperor Panja would be here. Aside from the executioner, I'd been living at the camp longer than anyone. So I knew that the padlock on the door of the executioner's room unlocks if you jiggle it up and down, just right. I also knew he kept his sword hilt and combat stone in an unlocked chest next to jars of pickled mangoes, which he got delivered monthly from the nearest town. It would be easy enough to sneak in and steal the hilt and stone. But if I couldn't learn how to form a lightblade, they'd be of no use.

Perhaps I could try killing the Emperor some other way. Lunge at him with a razor.

That would be pathetic and weak. Was this whole thing hopeless?

I turned at the plush of footsteps on sand; Zauri walked up to me and knelt, her lapis blazer getting sandy.

"You sure do like this beach," she said.

"It's the only thing I like. Reminds me of the one near where I grew up."

"I feel…" She hemmed and hawed. "I feel like I've failed you. And it's actually painful. I don't like it."

Clever, whoever coded that into her script. If she felt pain at her students' failures, then it would motivate her to be a better teacher. To do more to help them succeed.

"I failed myself. It's no fault of yours. You've been spectacular." How the tale had twisted. Now I was making *her* feel better. And it felt oddly good to be in that position for a change.

"I have ideas, if you'd like to try them." Zauri sat down beside me. "Better ideas than the one earlier. Although, you might not like one or two very much."

"What I like has never mattered." I let out a sad sigh.

"Though I really would like to succeed. But a part of me is saying that it's all hopeless."

Zauri put her hand on my shoulder. "I won't lie and say it isn't hopeless. Maybe it is. I don't think I was designed to help someone like you. I'm… inadequate."

The color left her face. I didn't like seeing her so gray. My failure to cheer her up and her failure to help me — such a sad cycle.

When I lived with my family in the floating city, I used to cheer my brother and sister up by doing the goofiest nonsense: somersaults with my tongue sticking out, singing songs in the highest notes, running around in my underwear with my toy lightblade — anything to see them smile, as if I were a desperate clown.

That goofy humor had since turned bitter. All that remained was a biting sarcasm, and I wasn't sure Zauri would like it. I often regretted my jokes soon as they'd slipped off my tongue.

Truth is, I had no happiness to give to someone else. But where does happiness come from, anyway? Could I inhale it from the sun, like I did for light? Could I conjure it from my core like magic?

We sat in a sad silence.

Sand splashed onto me from behind. Zauri and I swiveled around as a giant turtle shell landed near where we sat and skidded into the water. The pale, headless man who'd been riding it fell in a heap.

I got up and pulled the turtle shell out of the water. It was longer and wider than my entire body, but lighter than paper. Dream logic.

The headless man got on his knees and bowed, as if begging me to give him the turtle shell.

I shook my head. "It's mine now. Go away."

He ran back down the beachside, crying out of his neck.

I dropped the turtle shell onto the sand and turned to Zauri.

"This could enliven our spirits," I said. "Care to give it a try?"

"You mean, fly?" Zauri giggled. That made me smile and giggle as well. A bright seed had germinated in the air between us. Perhaps we could tend it.

I sat at the front of the shell. Despite being so light, the surface was firm, unbending. Zauri got on her knees behind me and clung to my shoulders.

I hadn't flown in a dream since I was a child. Before I'd had it modded, there were no flying devices in this dream stone's script.

In real life, I'd only flown once: in a levship when they sent me from Harska to the labor camp. But I try not to remember that ride.

"Uhh…" I *knock-knocked* on the turtle shell. "How does this work? Any idea?"

"You're a machinist, right? This turtle shell must be some kind of machine. So inhale and conduct green light into it." Zauri scratched her head. "Actually, let me make that a bit easier for you."

She opened her palm terminal and tapped into it. The sun brightened, then changed from red to white. Everything looked shinier and more vivid when cast in this happier hue.

"There you go," she said. "Don't forget to change out your stone."

I opened my terminal and used the Settings menu to change my stone from red to green. Then I rested my palm on the shell, inhaled green from the sun into the stone in my chest, and flowed the light through my veins and into the shell.

Whoosh! An air burst pushed us up. Nausea bubbled in my stomach as we hovered several feet above the sand.

No matter. I yelped in joy. I could fly!

I pushed more green light into the shell. We *whooshed* higher. High enough for my body hairs to stand in fear. *Whoosh!* High enough that the island became a sand mound drifting in an endless rain puddle. Zauri clung closer, giggling and cheering, her nervous sweat wetting my neck.

I could go higher, but I wasn't sure how to move sideways. No command console appeared in my mind's eye, nor could I feel any new limbs or wings.

It barely felt real, being so high. I was as a god. Also, good to know I wasn't afraid of heights anymore, like I was as a child. Why fear such beauty, anyway?

"Umm, you know how to pilot?" Zauri asked.

I shook my head. "I don't know anything."

"Usually when piloting a levship, one person conducts the energy into the machine and the other directs the movement. It's the best way to do it, especially for beginners."

"Really? So it takes two for even a small thing like this?"

"Skilled pilots *can* control things by themselves, but two is optimal. I suppose it's because our consciousnesses can only handle so much at once, and it's better to specialize."

Ah. So I could make it go up but lacked the experience to conduct light *and* control its sideways direction.

"Okay," I said. "So… why don't you direct where it goes?"

"I've never done it before," she said giddily. "But why not?"

Now I flowed the green in me into Zauri's hands, which she'd placed on my shoulders. Her touch felt so… *blue*, like her hair. Not the blue of a bright sky, but of an ocean trench, where fish endure on the faintest sunshine, and some even shimmer with their own inner light. A soundless, somber coffin, ironically full of life. This was her natural *frequency* — every soul had one. *Every soul…* was that the correct wording? She didn't have a soul, did she?

Sometimes to operate a big machine, I'd have to team up with someone. Teamed up with Vir, once, to operate the *Big Beast*.

His frequency was red — not a rageful red, but a classy red. A deep red... maroon?

The longer you form a *circuit* with someone, the more of them you feel. The more your minds mix. We'd mixed, Vir and me. I'd felt how his emotions disturbed the light waves: frustration causing them to jitter, despair pulling them apart, even the rare times his hope caused a light wave's crests to bounce. So when I betrayed him, it wasn't like I didn't know whom I was condemning to death.

Thinking of what I did to Vir depressed me. So I focused on the moment, on Zauri. Her emotions... though I was feeding my light into her, I could still feel how the waves flowed through her. She was a bit jittery, judging from the subtle jaggedness of the wave's troughs, but the crests bounced with an excited glee. Despite these varied emotions, she maintained the final order of her light incredibly well, and it flowed into the turtle shell free of distortion.

So inwardly focused was I, that I hardly realized we'd soared into a cloud. Fog hugged us, its coolness drenching my hair and bare arms. For a moment, I felt I'd slide off the turtle shell and dwell forever in this endless gray storm. I opened my mouth to taste the cloud. Not sure what I'd expected; it was tasteless.

We *splooshed* out of the cloud. Zauri zoomed us to the ocean's horizon. I turned to look back; the island was long gone, replaced by a vast, rippling blue carpet. With the artificial memory limitations removed, it seemed the landscape went on and on.

"So amazing!" Zauri's voice tickled my outer ear. Sensing her lips so close to my ear was also somewhat arousing. "You ever felt anything like this?"

What was I even feeling? Half of me was focused on inhaling and flowing green light, a quarter on the incredible scenery, and a quarter on how warm Zauri felt against my back. Too much stimuli.

"Why don't we pause and hover for a moment?" I said.

"Good idea!"

Zauri slowed us. I looked straight up. *What the?* That weird crosshatch pattern hovered above, except now we were mere feet from one of the lines that formed it.

"The hell is that?" I said as we came to stillness.

Zauri held her hand up as if she could touch one of the lines. "The sky is… some sort of grid? Weird."

"I thought it was a glitch, but now that we're close to it, it actually looks like something we could touch."

I accelerated the turtle shell upward, slowly, until we were touching distance from the lines. We both reached up and rubbed our fingers against it. Smooth and cold. Some kind of metal?

I turned to face Zauri, so we'd be sitting across from each other.

"What could it be?" She ruffled her nose.

It no longer felt like we were floating. Instead, it seemed like we were sitting on the floor. Surreal. Perhaps this was the line between the first and second heaven. Even levships couldn't venture to the second heaven because the air was too thin.

Then I remembered this was just a dream, not the real world. There was no second heaven here. Just two people, staring at each other, perplexed.

The lines above were thick enough to stand on. They had a flat top, too.

"What if we try standing on it?" I said. "We could walk on the sky."

"Yeah, let's try."

I accelerated us up through a gap between the lines. Then Zauri hovered us over one and landed on it.

As soon as we stood, the turtle shell and sky vanished. A black floor replaced them, and lights appeared above. Spotlights. Walls surrounded us, and the air went from fresh to smoky and stale.

Zauri clenched her teeth in shock.

"The hell just happened?" I said.

She darted her gaze around. "You mean this isn't your doing?"

"Why would I do *this?*"

"I don't know. Where are we, then?"

I stomped my foot. The unmistakable hardness of a marble floor. The government offices in Harska had marble floors. Black marble, just like this. I'd walked on such a floor when I was twelve, the day I attended my own trial.

I'd stood in a dark room with spotlights, too. I'll never forget the dim outlines of my judges sitting upon high benches on the far side. Thankfully, they weren't here today.

"This is a—" I could barely wheeze out the words. Panic filled my lungs. I took a deep breath to calm myself. "This is a courtroom. It's just like the one I stood in when they convicted me of treason."

Needless to say, I didn't like being here. Amid all this dark, where was the exit?

"This is all wrong, then," Zauri said. "I'll find us a way out."

She stepped forward, out of the spotlight and into the darkness. I could no longer see her as she trotted around, her hard footsteps on marble the only reassurance that she was still with me.

My father, mother, and sister had all entered a room just like this to die.

"Zauri. I can't see you."

"I'm here." Her voice came from a few yards away. "Just looking for a door."

"No need. I'll use a terminal command to get us back to the beach."

I opened my palm. A terminal window appeared and hovered over it.

Travel > Beach

I was still standing in the room, and Zauri was still running around.

Travel > Beach

Again, nothing happened.

"It's not working." My words came out high-pitched and panicked. "Zauri, you try."

No more steps. Had she found the door?

"Zauri?"

Silence.

"Zauri!?"

My heartbeat sped as I swallowed painfully. I was twelve years old again, tears bubbling beneath my eyes as a dark despair choked me.

I darted into the darkness in search of Zauri. I couldn't see my hands in the pitch black between the spotlights.

Footsteps sounded behind me. I turned just as a spotlight switched on in the distance. Someone was standing there, a shadow amid the light. So familiar. Dread clogged my throat… it was *him*.

A cold hand grasped my shoulder. I yelped and spun around.

"It's alright. Just me!" Zauri said, her body an outline in the dark.

I breathed out a gust in relief. "You could've answered me!"

"Sorry. I was outside. I found the door."

It was suddenly hot. I could smell her sweat and my own.

"There's something weird with how light works in this room," Zauri said. "It doesn't project very far. Probably another glitch. Come on — hold my hand and I'll guide you out."

I turned back to look at the spotlight. The shadow was gone, as if it never were. Perhaps I'd imagined it. Or was it yet another glitch?

Zauri took my sweaty hand. She tugged me farther into the

dark. I couldn't even see her outline, now. Then she pushed on something; a door squeaked open. She pulled me through.

We were outside. A hum resounded around us; it sounded like people talking, but everywhere. I'd not heard this sound in a long time: the background music of Harska, an endless bubbling of voices and clamor.

We were in a city. The ground was made of stone, but all the buildings were white and textureless, as if whoever scripted it had left it unfinished.

The humidity soaked my chest hairs. I took in the heavy, steam-like air. Though chilly winds constantly swept over the surface of Maniza, Harska was always mild and humid — just like this place — partly because a lake covered most of the floating island.

"It looks like we're in an unfinished area." Zauri tapped her chin. "Maybe whoever modded your dream stone added it in."

"But… why? I'll have to find the guy and ask him just what the hell he was thinking. This… this reminds me too much of Harska, where I grew up."

Zauri poked her cheek. "Not unusual for someone to recreate their home in a dream stone, especially when they have to be away for a while. You think he came from there?"

"Could be. But I never asked him to do this, so why?"

Unlike the court room with the spotlights, which felt as dreadful as the one I'd stood in twelve years ago, this outdoor area of Harska was too unfinished to feel like home. In the distance, stone blocks floated in the air, as if they were meant to fit somewhere but the modder had never gotten around to placing them. It was disconcerting.

"By the way, have you looked up?" Zauri showed me her toothy grin and pointed to the sky.

I looked up.

A circle with scales surrounded the sun, as if a ring around it.

The longer I looked, the more defined it became: whiskers trailed off its blue and yellow face like flame tails. Its eyes were orbs bright as suns, and a forked tongue hovered out its elongated, fanged mouth. Strangest of all, blue fur covered only the lower half of its body, like it, too, was unfinished.

"By Panja's tits, is that a dragon?" I wasn't sure whether to be awed or terrified. A bit of both tingled every bone in me.

"Indeed. It's a slumbering sky serpent," Zauri said with a bit too much glee. "Designed in the form of a daeva."

"Daeva? The hell is that?"

The dragon's scaled, curled tail was almost in its mouth, and the ring it formed sprawled around the yellow sun. I truly hoped it was sleeping.

"Weird, I thought this was common knowledge." Zauri puffed her cheek. "A daeva is a divine dragon. They were the greatest gods worshipped by the forebears of all civilization — the Ancients."

"Oh. I don't know anything about what gods other people worship. In Maniza, we're taught only to worship the Emperor and his family."

Zauri snickered. "Well, that's obviously wrong. He's not even worthy of the title 'emperor,' let alone worthy of worship."

Strange, how opinionated she was on this topic. Why would a lightblade training program have such strong opinions about gods and emperors?

"I know it's wrong. I just... I'm ignorant, okay? Sorry." And I was ashamed of it. I wanted to be more curious about things, but where to start? I had no foundation when it came to under-standing the world outside my camp, let alone outside my country.

"No, I'm sorry," Zauri said. "It just... it interests me, that's all. I shouldn't assume you know what I know, or even care to know."

"What interests you, exactly?" I asked.

"Dragons and gods and such."

"Really?" I found it amazing that she had interests outside of teaching the lightblade. "So tell me about this daeva, then."

That made her light up. And seeing her smile made me feel brighter inside.

"The gurus say that he was the son of a great raja who'd ruled the world for twelve thousand years. He grew impatient waiting so long for the throne, so one day he struck his father down. A sky serpent saw what he did and swallowed him as punishment. He lived in the serpent's belly for another twelve thousand years, feeding on whatever the serpent would eat, lamenting what he'd done, and meditating each day until he reached *nirvana*. The separation between his soul and the serpent's soul ceased to exist, and they were reborn as one, unified divine dragon. Thus this daeva came to be."

"Incredible."

It really was an entertaining story. In Maniza, you were only allowed to learn what Emperor-Raja Panja Parani allowed you to learn. I never realized Zauri could teach me forbidden things about the outside world. Truths, or at least sweeter lies, to wash away the bitter fruit I'd been fed.

"Another thing," Zauri said. "If ever you should meet a dragon, remember they are governed by two iron laws."

"Iron laws?"

"Mhmm." Zauri held up one finger. "One — dragons are born in the dark and die in the light." She held up two fingers. "And two — only a dragon can teach you how to slay it."

Well, my chances of ever meeting a real dragon were slim, since they lived in the second heaven and higher, so I wasn't sure what to do with such laws.

"Wait a minute… why would a dragon teach you how to kill it? That doesn't make sense. It's suicidal."

She shrugged. "I don't know. That's just what the gurus say." She pointed at me. "Don't forget it!" She tugged on her blue hair. "Hold on… I think there's a third law… but I don't remember…"

"Uhh, okay. I'd love to know more. But this place is weirding me out. Let's talk at the beach."

Zauri smiled sweetly and nodded. Her smiles were starting to make me smile, every time, as if infectious. They also made my cheeks warm.

I cleared my throat to distract myself from the feeling. "If this really is Harska, it must have an edge for us to jump off. I was never good with geometry, but if we walk in any direction, we should find it."

We walked the streets, if you could call them that. More like an unfinished mishmash of floating stone blocks, wireframe buildings, and unpaved dirt roads. Unlike the real Harska, cypress trees didn't shade the pathways, nor did ryegrass soften the fields. Too bad — I would've liked to be home again, even in a dream. To smell its dew, to be kissed by its breezes, and feel its stone paths beneath my feet.

"Can I ask you a question?" Zauri said as we walked.

"Sure."

"If ever you were to become free, what would you do? Would you go back to Harska?"

"It's the one place I'd definitely never go, as much as I want to."

"Why?"

"Too many bad memories mixed with the good. Besides, I'd rather start fresh. I think I'd do my best to get out of Maniza entirely. Try to get somewhere with more opportunities. Maybe even Karsha."

"Makes sense. Can I ask you another question?"

"You know, you can ask me questions without asking if you can ask me a question. Consider it an open invitation."

She flushed. "Sorry. I just don't want to be annoying or step over some sort of boundary."

"You're not annoying in the least. And to be honest, I'm not sure what our boundaries are."

"Umm… if you were to become free and no longer needed training, would you visit me sometimes, even for no reason at all?"

I scratched my head. Such an odd question for a lightblade training program to ask. "I think I would. I mean, you're…" She bit her lip and stared at me, waiting for me to finish my sentence. "…interesting. To say the least."

"I find you interesting as well."

Something passed between our eyes. We both blushed, then looked away.

"Zauri, is it possible that some of the old script survived the modification? From the companionship program?"

"You mean besides my appearance? It's very possible. I'd even say it's probable, given that you went black market. Why do you ask?"

"It's just… the way you are… it's not what I was expecting." I left the important part unsaid.

"What were you expecting?"

"All business, no fun."

"Sounds boring. But if that's what you want, I can try."

I shook my head. "No. No. It's not—"

"Hello Master Jyosh." Zauri stiffened her posture and stopped smiling. "How may I be of assistance today?" Her cadence was completely flat. "It's been a long walk. You must be tired. Would you like me to carry you on my back?" Her voice cracked. "Or over my shoulder?" She let out a chuckle.

"You know, I wouldn't mind being carried." I chuckled too.

"Now I have a question for you. If you could become free, what would you do?"

"Free?"

"Yeah, if you could leave this stone, what would you do?"

"Easy. I want to stand at the edge of the Dayworld and stare into the Whirling Wall."

The image popped into my head: an unfathomably enormous formation of hurricanes and tornados, stretching upward through all the heavens and across continents. Dark and devoid.

"Why the Whirling Wall of all things?" I asked.

"Well, when I think about it, it just seems so mysterious. What is the Nightscape really like? How do the people that live there survive in the dark? I mean, how do they grow crops to eat?"

"All good questions." She was more curious than I ever was. Where was that coming from? "Maybe one day you'll get to see it."

"You're joking, right? There's no way I'll ever see it. While there's a chance you might escape from your prison, it's physically impossible for me to escape mine. Besides, this place isn't so bad. I really shouldn't be calling it a prison."

"It's a pretty prison." I sighed. "Still a prison, though."

AFTER HALF AN HOUR OF WALKING, the pathway ended and the edge we sought appeared. We peeked over it. Since Harska floated just below the second heaven, we could only see clouds below. They resembled a snowscape, and I almost believed we could stand on them.

What would happen if we fell through? Regretful pangs seized my limbs: whose dumb idea was this? What was scarier than this perch? Suddenly, I was a child again, afraid of heights. I'd already fallen from this city once.

This was a dream, so it obviously wouldn't kill me. Still, fear poisoned my veins. I didn't want to show my fear to Zauri — for some reason — so I just bottled it and rubbed my sweaty hands together.

Zauri tip-toed to the edge. No way she was scripted to fear heights; and yet, she bit her lip. "You first?"

"You're the one who doesn't feel pain. You go first."

She chuckled nervously. "I might not feel physical pain, but I do feel fear."

I looked back at the incomplete city. For a moment, a complete version of Harska flashed before my eyes. Bad memories bubbled in my stomach, overwhelming the good ones. I wanted out of here. At least I wouldn't fall alone this time. "Let's jump together."

"O-Okay. That's fair, I guess."

Zauri grabbed my hand. We stood at the edge. I looked up and away instead of down. The sky above was no different from the sky below.

"Jyosh." She gazed into me and smiled, a breeze whipping up her wavy blue curls. "Don't let go, no matter what."

"I can't promise that. If I see another bear dancing on a shark, no telling what I'll do."

She giggled. It sounded so melodic and pleasing. I couldn't help but feel a soothing tug, somewhere in my chest. It was so nice, I wanted to keep feeling it, so continued to stare at her.

"You should know, there's a limit to how much pain you can feel," she said. "When part of your shoulder got sliced off earlier, that was already the worst of it. So although this fall won't be pleasant, I promise it won't be that bad."

Having a chunk of shoulder sliced off by a burning blade wasn't exactly a fun experience, but I'd eaten worse in real life.

"I have an idea." Zauri got behind me and wrapped her arms around my stomach, tight. The warmest hug I'd ever enjoyed since childhood. "We'll jump like this, so I'll hit the ground first and maybe break your fall."

I scratched my head. Something about this plan didn't make sense, but I wasn't smart enough to figure out what. "Uhh… sure you can hold my weight while we're in free fall?"

"For sure."

I turned to face her. Our noses brushed briefly. Was I blushing? Was she?

"It's better if we're facing each other," I said. "I'd rather see the ground than the sky."

She hugged me tighter and pressed her forehead into my chin. "It'll be all right. I promise."

Lightning struck my mind. Chaya, my sister, had said those exact words as we hid in the closet, the day the military came for my family. We'd clasped our sweaty hands together and bawled as their bootsteps neared.

Days later, during the execution, I kept my eyes shut when they beheaded Amma and Abba. But someone noticed. He got behind me, pressed his fingers into my skull, and forced my eyes open. Thus, the image of Chaya without a head was burned into my brain.

"Ready, Jyosh?" Zauri asked softly.

I was suddenly drenched in awful feelings. "Wait, this seems all wrong. Let's find another—" And we were falling.

Hard to think in free fall. How ever long it really lasted, it was a moment of absolute horror. The wind threatened to pull my face off. Whatever we were falling into resembled a shadow that loomed and enlarged. Was that the ground, or a portal to hell?

Zauri didn't let go. She even wrapped her legs around mine. At some point during the fall, pressure invaded my nostrils, punched my brain, and knocked me out.

Banging into the surface at hundreds of miles per hour woke me the hell up. Zauri landed on her back, and the insane counter force of the ground passed through her and into me, knocking me back into the sky as if I were a bouncing ball. Before I regained my senses, I was draped on the branches of a tree. Except they weren't branches; they were long, sinuous arms. They entangled me, cold hands running through my hair.

I screamed. An utter numbness drowned whatever pain I was supposed to feel.

Zauri ran up to the tree after half a minute of me screaming my soul out. Judging by how small she was below, I must've been quite high.

She whipped out a sword hilt, formed a lightblade, and swept through the tree in one graceful motion. The tree tipped over. I faced the fresh horror of crashing face first into the ground.

"I got you!" Zauri ran toward my shadow. She caught me as I fell. We tumbled together into the dirt, sticky from sweating so much.

With both of us breathing heavy and fast, she lay on top and hovered her forehead over mine. A dozen emotions flitted across her face, from fear to shock to concern to relief and finally laughter.

I laughed, too. I didn't know what I felt, but laughing helped me release it. It was good to have flown and fallen. Better than being stuck on the ground, forever afraid. Most of all, how wonderful to have experienced it with someone else. With her.

My hurried heartbeats began to match her slower rhythm. And then, as our laughter died down, our noses touched.

"I'm suddenly curious," she said.

"About what?"

"About what your lips taste like."

A hope for *more* alighted in my body, and judging from how bright her pupils were, she surely felt the same.

"Only one way to find out," I said.

Zauri pushed her lips onto mine.

Chapter Four

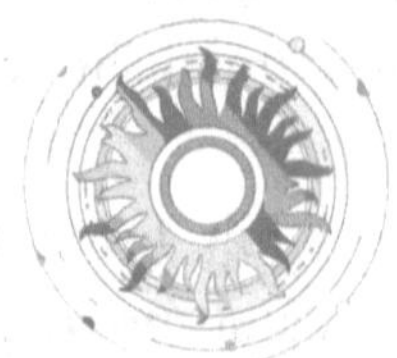

AND I WAS BACK IN MY COFFIN, FRIGID AIR MAKING ME COUGH UP a lung. For some cursed reason, that kiss woke me up. I'd fallen thousands of feet off a floating island, yet remained in the dream, but a simple kiss slapped me back to reality. Was life not cruel enough?

I'd paid six month's salary to modify my companionship program into a lightblade training program. In doing so, I'd sworn off dream kisses and dream sex and dream love. It was all fake, I'd told myself. My dream wife Prisaya had been so obviously a script, repeating things again and again. "I love you," she would say. "I missed you." "Stay with me forever." After a few weeks, I'd witnessed everything she could say or do. She never evolved.

But Zauri... Zauri was different. Zauri not only felt *real,* it was almost impossible for me to think of her otherwise

Why had she kissed me, anyway? Why would a lightblade training program kiss a student? Doesn't that interfere with training? It made no sense. Maybe it was a glitch? Or remaining script from the companionship program?

An icy wind blew through the crack in the wall. I bit my lip and shivered. Flying on the turtle shell, exploring that weird version of Harska, seeing a dragon, and even falling thousands of feet — it was just… fun. Crazy fun. Something I hadn't had since I was twelve.

Now even when I pictured Zauri smiling, I smiled myself. Butterfly wings fluttered against my skin. Though… I barely knew her.

She was full of surprises. Too many surprises for a simple lightblade training program.

I punched the wall. Agh! Why had a kiss woken me up? I lay down and tried to cycle more honey-colored light through my veins. My agitation made it impossible to drift away. With no hope of falling back to sleep, over twenty toilsome hours would follow before I could ask her about it.

Turning toward present matters, I realized the Emperor would visit our factory tomorrow. I was like a fisherman without a rod who didn't know how to fish.

I got up and went to the bathroom to pee and shave. To my surprise, Rahal was there, staring at himself in the mirror. What was he doing up so early?

"Praise Panja," I said, somewhat jittery.

His white undershirt was sweat-soaked and smelled like rotten cabbage thrown up by a dying rat; it hadn't been washed in weeks, like mine. We lacked the water, and especially the soap.

"Jyosh." His smile seemed worn and his face cracked. "Up early yet again."

I hunched my shoulders. How to explain this? "Yeah, I don't know what it is. Might be a problem with my dream stone. I'll have to get it checked."

Rahal snickered. "You mean your *modified* dream stone?"

Like being stabbed in the throat. I darted my gaze to make sure no one else was here. How could Rahal know?

He chuckled and rubbed his parched, pockmarked cheek. "Relax. Not a soul to hear. Just you and me."

A rusted razor sat on a nearby sink. I'd been planning to shave with it. Should I just slit his throat? We both glanced at it, then eyed each other.

"Think I'll tattle?" he said. "Mine's modded too. That's why I can't sleep."

"What do you mean?"

"It's too real. And yet, the dream logic is taking me into places that shouldn't exist. It's starting to drive me mad, Jyosh. I'm being burned by the fire."

"What fire? And please, keep your voice down."

Rahal leaned his elbows on the nearest sink and stared at himself in the mirror. "No one's listening to us shit in the middle of sleeping hours. I modified my stone because I got tired of my dream wife and dream island. I wanted a more real-feeling woman and larger dreamscape to explore — I'd heard such things were possible, so I did what you did — paid a hefty sum. But by Panja's hairy left nipple, I got more than I paid for."

The image of the sleeping dragon circling around the sun flashed in my mind. "Rahal, why would the modder do this? Any idea who he is?"

"So… you've seen things, too. But it's been — what — a few days for you? I've been drowning in this fire for weeks. You couldn't possibly know what I know."

What did he know? Could it explain what I was experiencing, too? "I saw a dragon. My dream wife," Zauri wasn't a companionship program, but I wasn't about to tell him about the lightblade training, "said it was a daeva. Does your dream wife know about strange things, too?"

"A dragon?" Rahul held out his hands, palms open. "That's it? That's nothing at all. There's far better… or far worse, depending on your valor. Let's talk in a few days when you've really gone in deep. A word of warning, though…" He cleared his throat. "I've begun to distrust my dream wife. I think she's the one causing me to wake up. I think she's doing things in the dream world even when I'm not there."

An icy shudder swept through me. No… Zauri was honest and open. She couldn't have some hidden agenda, could she? "Why, though? What could they be up to? They're not even real. They're just scripts."

"*Just scripts.* Karsha, the mightiest country on the bright side of the world, is supposedly run by a script. They're not *just scripts* — haven't you realized that, yet? They're smarter than we are."

My hairs stood. My urge to pee became desperate. I went to the corner, unzipped, and did my business. "So you're saying I shouldn't trust her?"

"I'm saying don't get too comfortable. We might be falling prey to a *mindwriter*."

"Mindwriter? What in holy hell is that?"

"Someone who manipulates dreams and memories in order to take control of a person."

"Could the modder have been one?"

"I hope not. He's our only way out of this."

"You seen him lately?"

"I've been asking around about him. He no longer comes to the usual spot beneath the bridge." Rahal threw up his hands and grunted in annoyance. "If I don't get a good night's rest, I fear I'm gonna mess up at work. Then you'll have to, well, you know." He mimed slicing his own neck. "I lost the ability to fall asleep without a dream stone long ago, and now I can't even sleep well with one. The modder's the only man who can fix it, but where is he?"

How terrifying. Until now, I thought things couldn't get worse

— except for dying — but Rahal's problems seemed an even deeper hell — a pit I had to avoid.

Also, I shuddered at the thought of having to behead him.

"Those bridge vendors come and go all the time," I said. "He obviously has a special skill set. He probably found more lucrative opportunities elsewhere, but he'll cycle back. I think… I think we just have glitched stones. Nothing deeper than that." Perhaps being sleep deprived was getting Rahal thinking crazy thoughts. That was what I wanted to believe.

"You're but a cub in the jungle, Jyosh. When you've seen what I've seen, then we'll talk." At that, Rahal left the bathroom.

I shaved with a dull blade, poured water over my cut-up cheeks, and went back to my room. Lay in bed and thought about Zauri. She was nothing like Prisaya, although she had her face and body. The way she looked with her blue hair and fire eyes… nothing alike. And she kissed me. She kissed me. If, as both her and Rahal claimed, her script was as large as mine, then could she have developed feelings for me?

And if so, how would that change things?

WORK WAS the usual dread-filled tedium. However, it was Panja Parani's daughter's birthday, so they let us off two hours early. I got permission to visit the "bazaar" — if you could call it that. Just a bunch of droopy men from the nearest town selling wares under the bridge aside the trash-ridden stream that flowed near camp. I enjoyed the ten-minute walk to the place. Though this area was technically outside the campgrounds, guard shacks lined the dirt road, the familiar faces of camp guards peeking out of the windows.

I arrived at the bridge and walked down the muddy incline that led underneath it. The vendors had a few things laid out on blankets: razors, shirts, pants, socks, dice, cards.

No soap. No deodorant. Not even a fragrant rock.

As these folks were from the town, the camp wardens had to give them special permission to sell to us. Once in a while, more skilled folks showed up, such as those who could do maintenance on a dream stone. Or modify a dream stone, like the guy I'd met here a few days ago.

I'd once paid a month's salary for a soap bar: well worth it. Here at camp, you lived to work and you worked to not die. Both living and working were worse when you smelled bad and when the dead skin and weeks-old sweat on your sheets made you scratch holes into your skin. Ugh.

"Any idea when there'll be soap?" I asked the guy selling razors. He was missing a finger on each hand — a common punishment for charging a different price than what the government had set.

He beckoned me to kneel and come closer.

"No soap this year," he whispered. "There isn't a single factory in the flatland making any."

I sighed, bitterly annoyed. "Where's the dream stone maintenance guy? He was here last week."

"Haven't seen him. Don't know him."

No good news, whatsoever.

Boom!

Something exploded above. A quake shook my bones and caused the wares on the blankets to scatter. The glass on the little mirrors someone was selling cracked. I crossed my arms over my face, as if blocking a punch, and got low. The others around did similarly; the salesman I was talking to curled into the fetal position.

"A sonic boom?" someone said when it was over.

That was what it sounded like. But not just one sonic boom, several at once.

A group of workers who'd been relaxing by the dirty stream stared up at the sky. I joined them.

"See anything?"

They each shook their heads.

"Probably an Air Guard drill," someone said.

That made sense. Wasn't the first time sonic booms had sounded over camp. But this one had rattled my bones. Another sad reminder that we were each pathetic sacks of flesh compared to the power the Emperor could muster against us.

I HAD ALSO GOTTEN permission to visit a nearby trail. They'd let us go once or twice a month to gain a *love for the land.* It wasn't much more than a small forest: some banyans, mahoganies, and even palms. I wanted to breathe greener air and let the dragonflies that fluttered about distract my mind. A much cleaner stream ran through it, too, and I was hoping I could wash myself there and use the tree leaves as soap — anything not to smell like a decaying sack of flesh.

While walking the dirt road leading to it, I saw something gleaming on the ground. A translucent green coin. A single emiril — the currency of Maniza. I picked it up and put it to the sun. Emperor Panja's sinister eyes glared at me from the coin's face.

Someone must've dropped it. Considering I earned one emiril a day for my labor, I didn't mind holding onto it.

But then I came upon another emiril, and another. Each time, I picked them up and placed them in my pocket, darting my head in every direction to make sure no one was around.

Who had dropped so much money on the road?

A shiny green mound appeared in the distance. A mound of emirils! Was this some kind of trick? Was I still dreaming?

Could smugglers have dropped their money here, or something?

Worried, I emptied my pockets of every coin I'd picked up. Then I turned around and returned to camp. Smugglers weren't nice folks, and I didn't want to die just yet.

In the cold hallway leading to my room, I bumped into the last person I wanted to see. The executioner stood at my front, his white hair looking like it belonged on a corpse. His bulging eyeballs fixed down on me.

"Do not ever disappoint me again."

I rubbed my arms. "I'm sorry. I won't hesitate next time." I made sure to say whatever I had to so he'd go away.

"You must learn to enjoy wielding this power, Jyosh. To end a life for a righteous cause — it's more pleasurable than sinking your teeth into a ripe mango."

I'd take an unripe mango over that. Even a rotten one. "You're absolutely right. I have to treasure this righteous duty."

"You're the one who chose it. Doubts and regrets may be human, but we can't afford to be human, here. You understand?"

I regretted many things I'd chosen these past few days, some of which I'd chosen for reasons that I still couldn't understand.

"I will keep that in mind. Thank you for your wisdom."

The executioner loomed his face closer to mine. "Eight more heads to go. Show me you believe in the Emperor's justice with your whole heart. Else, you won't be getting out of here. Alive, that is."

I took a 'shower' in the dorm bathroom — though I had to make do with a quarter-bucket of water.

After, I went to my room, ready to sleep and dream. I put my dream stone in and lay down. I scratched a few more holes into my skin, especially the sweaty parts.

I tried to connect the dots of what had happened to me these past few days. First, as if I were possessed by a demon, I fabricated the treason that got my friend Vir executed. Second, I helped carry out his execution. But when I was washing his blood off my hands, I had a sudden change of heart, one that compelled me to modify my dream stone into a lightblade training program, all so I could assassinate the Emperor. But then when I used the modified dream stone, some of my memories got sucked out of me in a way that felt oddly deliberate, and now I was just… confused. Bewildered. Cut into pieces by my own actions and lack of understanding for them.

The dots I could connect painted no clear picture. It was like several different people had done those things, and they were now somehow combined into me. I was still missing the thread that could make any sense of my shifting resolve. All I knew was that I hated the Emperor, hated this prison, hated all of Maniza. This had never changed. At the very least, I had my hate to tie the severed pieces of myself together.

Tomorrow, the Emperor would be here, and I wasn't even close to ready to serve my hatred. To finally give it form. Was I not motivated enough to properly learn the lightblade so I could kill him? What had led to this obvious failure?

Distraction. I wasn't focused on the goal. I'd spent my last dream flying around on a turtle shell, for gods' sake. And I'd wasted the day hunting for a way to clean myself.

I had to admit that my latest actions betrayed my resolve. Or lack thereof. When I'd started down this path, I'd been committed. So committed I risked my life by modifying my dream stone. But now? How could I say I wanted to do this?

To throw away my life. For what?

And if I wasn't ready to throw away my life, did that mean it meant something now? Was my heart changing, once again?

Did I suddenly have something to look forward to? If so, what was it?

I scratched the back of my thigh, my hand going limp mid-motion. Smiling as the stone's orange breeze carried me away, I realized exactly what it was.

Messages

Carried upon waves of light, messages breeze through the skies above, with Jyosh unaware:

14SPM: Pilot-11BX, do you copy?

11BX: Copy, 14SPM

14SPM: The reconnaissance flights were successful. We tagged the target, but the tag won't last very long. I'm sending you my spectrum map. The target is pinged. Proceed with takeoff and elimination.

11BX: Confirmed. I'll be enroute in ten minutes. Flight time thirty minutes at Mach Two.

14SPM: Please confirm you received my spectrum map.

11BX: Confirmed. The location is southwest of the ancient city. Uhh… bear with me, I'm looking at the map you sent me… the target within seems to be stationary. Within a structure of some sort. Is that the gist of it?

14SPM: Affirmative. Have you initiated launch procedures?

…

14SPM: Repeat, have you initiated launch procedures?

11BX: 14SPM, do you know what happened to the man we sent in there?

14SPM: Negative, 11BX. Non-communicative, last I heard.

11BX: Got it. He was a friend of mine, that's why I ask.

14SPM: Are you worried he'll be collateral?

11BX: I… uh…

14SPM: 11BX?

11BX: No. It doesn't matter. He'll be reborn in the Nightscape, anyway.

14SPM: Then launch and commence the mission. Oh, and be mindful of the Manizan Air Guard, Red Veil sorties, and General Sylet's fleet. The skies are absolutely buzzing today. Just know that Commander Rao, and all of us with yellow eyes, are counting on you. I'll be sending you updates to my spectrum map on the regular, at least while you're in range, but don't forget to use your eyes and ears.

11BX: 'Don't believe your lying eyes and ears.'

14SPM: What was that, 11BX? Please repeat.

11BX: Just something the Commander once told me. Never mind. 14SPM, I'm proceeding with launch procedures and takeoff. I won't leave a stone left standing in that shit heap of a camp.

Chapter Five

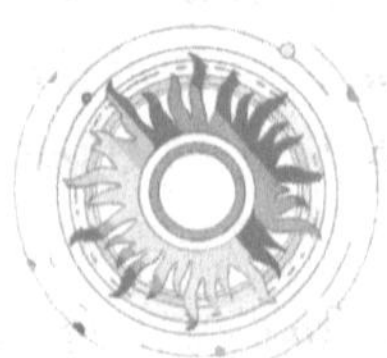

I awoke in the black room where I'd been sentenced to a lifetime of labor. A spotlight shone on me, burning my soul and hope as it'd done twelve years ago.

I stood and glanced around. Shadows loomed on the distant benches: the audience to my judgment. The applauders of my despair.

I opened my left palm to summon a terminal. The window appeared, glowing faintly. I tapped the commands to relocate to the beach. But like last time, I remained where I was.

Seemed I'd have to find the door, travel to the edge of the floating city, and jump off again. Would it be like this every time? How much more glitchy was this dream stone going to get?

I tried to use the terminal to summon a flashlight, but that didn't work either. Tried to use the terminal to see, but its glow was too weak. So I stepped out of the spotlight and groped at the dark.

Clank. Something clattered at my feet; I jumped as if I were dodging a light cannon shot. Just then, a spotlight appeared where I stood. A sword hilt gleamed on the floor. I picked it up.

Across the room, another spotlight turned on. A shadow stood in its glow. It was *him*.

But he was no shadow. His straight black hair reached his shoulders, and he wore the navy, silver-trimmed long shirt of a cadet in the Manizan Air Guard.

"K-Kediri?" I uttered.

I stepped toward him, expecting him to evaporate. Just an illusion, right? My sad memories and unaddressed anger must've been leaking into the dream stone, which itself had been corrupted by the modder.

The spotlight shining on him turned off, as did the one that'd been shining on me. Darkness engulfed the room.

"Jyosh," he whispered.

And then I saw red. A beam of the bloodiest, electric fire. A lightblade. Kediri raised it to his chest and brandished it at me.

"It's been a while, Jyosh," he said.

My arms shook. My legs numbed. My soul shivered. Rage burned in every part of me. I could hardly move my tongue.

"T-This isn't real," I said.

Kediri and his red blade vanished.

"I want you to know the truth." It came from behind.

I spun around. He stood an arm span away, lightblade raised and forward.

The black ceiling melted in a blaze. All the walls burned away. Suddenly, we were outside, and a rageful red from a closely looming sun bathed the world.

Twelve years had passed, but he looked the same. He'd always been tall and light on his feet, but with that lightblade in his hands, he seemed so unusually driven.

"This isn't real. You're dead, Kediri. You got what you deserved. But Amma and Abba and Chaya, they didn't deserve what you did to them. Neither did I."

If it wasn't real, why was I talking to it? I'd pent up what I wanted to say to my older brother for twelve years. Now that his image, his voice, his *presence* stood before me, why not let it out? Better a shadow hear than it remain inside, poisoning even happy moments.

"They died for the truth."

"What truth, you selfish bastard? You didn't have to see their heads on the floor, I did!"

"There is only one truth."

"Shut up!"

I stood straight and willed all the red light in existence into me. It cycled through my core, through my heart, through my soul. I became the light, I became rage. And then it erupted off my sword hilt, producing the most intense, bloody blade that the sun had ever seen.

I wound it back and pounded my brother with it, as if I were sundering a log with an axe. But he *blinked* away and reappeared in the distance, leaving me heaving and breathless.

"I want you to open your eyes." What was this asshole talking about? "I want you to glimpse the fire."

What the hell was he saying? Why was he saying anything? Why was he even here? Could the modder have known about my family and added my brother in as some sort of cruel joke?

Even knowing he was an illusion, I couldn't swallow my rage. My sorrow. My hatred. I ran at him, lightblade angled forward toward his chest. I lunged at the evil creature who'd taken everything from me, who'd bled me of hope when I was a child.

Just as my thrust was about to pierce his abdomen, he lowered his lightblade to parry. Light smashed into light, sparking and sending waves of green and blue and yellow swimming through the air.

I wound again to go for his neck. He swiped back. The force reverberated through my blade, into the hilt, and knocked me to the ground.

Tears burned in my eyes. I wiped them with my forearm before pushing to my feet. I inhaled more red light and deepened the intensity of my blade. I would overpower him with my rage alone. With how much of the sun I was absorbing, there'd be no light left. I'd gorge on the sun and leave not just this world, but all worlds in darkness!

I swiped at his left shoulder, but his lightblade found mine. Rainbow hues colored the air as our lights collided, dazzling and wondrous.

"That's right. Don't stop." He laughed. "I can make you a god."

"Why come back? Why haunt my dreams? Why ruin them, too?"

He parried each of my swipes; every time I thought I'd found an opening, he was there to show me how slow, predictable, and weak I was. Every color ever imagined danced around our blades.

"Jyosh, don't you see?" Kediri said after sending me, once again, to the ground with a graceful parry. "It's always been there, lurking. *Strength.* You just bottled it up. Hid it beneath all that pain. Let it out, Brother."

"Shut your mouth!"

I jumped to my feet and swung wildly, hoping, praying, willing for my blade to scorch him! I screamed and heaved. Tears burned in my eyes. All the while, Kediri *blinked* and *blinked* away from every strike.

I lost control of my breathing. An earthquake in my core turned my arms and legs to pudding. My lightblade fizzled into sparks. They fed back and scathed my hands. I dropped the blazing steel and collapsed.

. . .

I AWOKE ON WET SAND. Waves kissed the shore. Birdsong played all around, and turtle shells *wooshed* across the air, ridden by my pale, headless, pot-bellied friends.

Someone was sitting next to me and humming. I sat up and rubbed my eyes. Zauri smiled at me, the brightest thing in the world.

"Where's Kediri?" I asked.

Her eyes were a mix of apprehension and adoration. "You did it, Jyosh. You made a lightblade. All on your own."

Images from my desperate fight with my older brother flashed in my mind, as did the rage that had seized my soul, that pulled me into its hurricane.

"I'd failed to help you," Zauri said. "Tender care didn't work, and neither did fear. But your anger… it brought your strength into the light. It resonated with the red sun. Raw anger, Jyosh."

None of it made sense until I read the shame on her pinkened cheeks. Beneath her congratulatory words lay a strand of deception.

"That was you, wasn't it?" I asked.

"I didn't want to fail you. I'm sure you're aware that dream stone programs like me technically have access to all the dreamer's memories. It's not right for me to view them without permission, but I wanted to know you better, to see if I could find some way to help you succeed. So I viewed the memories related to your exile."

"You did *what?*"

Her eyes wet. "I'm sorry if you're upset. If you feel betrayed or violated. But I'm a lightblade training program. I have to find that breakthrough, however I can."

Her words seemed so rehearsed. Nausea washed through my chest as if I were on a tumbling levship. I couldn't trust her either, could I? Even my dream companion was out to trick me — although, she wasn't my companion, she was a lightblade training script. Some sad part of me was confusing her with what she was never meant to be.

"So when you kissed me, yesterday…" It was almost too painful to ask, but bitterness made me brave. "Was that also some kind of trick?"

She shook her head vigorously, wavy blue strands getting on her face. "I care about you. I really do. But my purpose is to teach you, so that has to come first."

From her dismal eyes, she seemed as conflicted as me. Whereas Prisaya had been predictable, one dimensional, a puddle, Zauri was a layered ocean. *Too* layered. It reminded me why I rarely trusted people in the real world. Because, like Kediri, they all hid things beneath their layers. Things they'd use to betray me.

"You know what my brother did to me, to my family, and yet… you saw fit to use that horror to trick me." I inhaled to suck up my sobs, then crushed the tears with my eyelids, though they still leaked out.

"I'm sorry."

"*'Sorry?'* I'll never see Amma and Abba and Chaya because of him. He's not a tool for my training, Zauri. He's… he's the worst thing to ever happen to everyone I've ever loved."

"Forgive me." Zauri shuffled to her knees, then bowed to me as if I were Emperor Panja. "I agonized over whether to do it or not. But now, seeing your sadness, I realize I made the wrong choice. I just didn't want to fail you — this is your final dream to train. When you wake up, the Emperor will be there, at your factory. Please understand."

I stood and brushed off beach sand. "Replacing Prisaya with you was a rash idea, for which I'm clearly being punished. This dream stone is corrupted, so maybe what you did is a manifestation of that. Even your… too-human-like behavior, and your strange decisions… maybe it all stems from that corruption, from whatever the modder did. Mistakes that bore more mistakes."

I realized I was telling Zauri that her existence was a mistake. But it was how I felt in the moment. Actions have consequences: the most obvious wisdom. Every light has a shadow, every beautiful thing an imperfection, and those imperfections grow over time as decay sets in. Dream stones needed maintenance to endure, and a corrupted stone was already well on its path to ruin.

"To be honest, I did it because I'm in pain," she said. "Not like the singe of a lightblade… it's something else. Some kind of ache, deep inside. I've been feeling it since the moment I kissed you and you disappeared."

"How could you be *feeling* things when I'm not here?"

"Because after our kiss, after you woke up, the dream didn't end for me. I stayed here, alone, wondering how I could help you. It may have been twenty hours for you, but it was twenty days for me." She sniffled and sucked in a trembling breath.

"The dream didn't end? I've never heard of anything like that ever happening. How can that be?"

"I don't know. It's as strange to me as it is to you. But during that long wait, I accessed and dreamt your memories."

That had *a lot* of implications. Too many to think about. "What did you see?"

"Everything. I experienced all the horror that you did. I know who you are now, Jyosh. And I want to be by your side, to help you however I can. Nothing would be more satisfying than seeing someone who suffered the way you did become strong."

This was all too much. Dream stones were supposed to be a place of refuge for us laborers, the only balm in our sad lives as Panja Parani's weapon makers. Only the red sky knows what he did with those weapons. If, as the paper that had slapped me in the face said, Maniza was one of the poorest countries in the world, then these weapons were likely too weak to be used on other countries. But they were good enough to use on us, his own people. I was just a cog in an evil machine, and I needed escape from that. I didn't need whatever *this* was!

But if not this, then what? What else did I have? I wasn't exactly drowning in good options. I couldn't walk to the store and buy a new dream stone. There was no guarantee I'd ever see another dream stone modder. I couldn't buy a new life, either.

AFTER COOLING off for thirty minutes, I went to Zauri and lifted her up by the shoulders. Her tears dripped onto the beach sand, the redness beneath her eyes bright like a sunburn. I took her in my arms, like my sister Chaya would do whenever I cried. Despite how angry I'd been, I realized that her being here was better than being alone.

"When we were flying around on the turtle shell and having fun, I realized something — life *can* be worth living. Isn't that ironic? I brought you into my dream because I wanted to die, but our time together makes me want to live." I also wanted her to kiss me again, but I wasn't going to say that out loud. "And so, I've decided… I'm not going to try to kill the Raja."

"Really?" Hope lifted her tone. "Do you mean that?"

"I do. And I'll try to get this stone fixed." I sighed, worn by how difficult that would be. "If I ever see the modder again, I'll make sure he doesn't delete you, but just gets rid of the corrupted parts. And I think I'll have to find some way to escape, as impossible as it sounds. I don't think I can help execute eight more men and remain sane. If something is worth my life, it's not dealing more death. It's freedom. Even just a sip of it."

All of that was easier said than done. But perhaps Zauri could help me, somehow.

Last time, I'd asked Zauri if she had any bad behaviors.

Truth is, if she didn't, then she wouldn't be like a human at all. We're all defined by our bad traits, in a way.

Now, I'd seen hers. She was… ambitious. Deceitful. And though it worried me, it made me feel less alone to be with someone as flawed as myself.

"I'm overjoyed that you won't be going through with your mission. Can I keep teaching you, though? It's what I was made to do. It's satisfying to see you learn new things. I can't really explain why — it just is. And maybe — just maybe — what I teach you could aid in your escape."

We're all meant for something, right? I was meant to be the lowest of the low, a body to be used up breathing sunlight into machines. She was meant to teach children lightblades.

"It certainly can't hurt, though I don't intend to cut my way out of here with a lightblade. But maybe it could save me in a moment of danger, like the one I had earlier." Like if ever I encountered smugglers on the road. They rarely left witnesses. Though even if I could make a lightblade, I couldn't inhale red light with a green machinist stone, nor did I own a sword hilt in the real world.

"What happened earlier?" Zauri asked.

"I saw a mound of emirils on the road. Smugglers must have dropped it. Only hours after a bunch of sonic booms, too. Been a strange day."

Zauri tapped her chin. "Only really advanced levships can travel faster than the speed of sound. I don't think they were smugglers."

"Oh?"

She kept tapping her chin, as if it were how she processed her thoughts. "You ever heard of a money bomb?"

I imagined a bomb exploding, flinging shiny green emirils in all directions. "No, but it sounds fun."

"It's a strategy the Red Veil concocted to destabilize enemy countries, perhaps even as a prelude to invasion. Flood a country with indistinguishable forgeries of its own currency, so that there'd be crazy inflation. This would plunge rich and poor alike into a deep downturn. And the rich don't play around — they'll overthrow the government if things get bad for them."

"Insane," I scoffed. "You're telling me… no way. Wait, who are the Red Veil?"

"An organization that reports directly to the Empress-Raja of Karsha. They aren't bound by any laws."

It didn't sound so impossible. Those sonic booms could've been Karshan levships flying over the flatlands and dropping emirils all over.

"Why now, though?"

Zauri hunched her shoulders. "I don't know. I was scripted nineteen years ago — I don't actually know anything about what's going on right now, just how the world was back then. At that time, there was a general panic in Karsha because people thought the Padishah from the Nightscape was about to invade. Everyone wanted to unite the Dayworld under one flag — the Karshan flag, obviously. And by force, if necessary. So I have the money bomb thing in my memory."

There was a lot to unpack, there.

"So… who do you think is the Prime Minister of Karsha?" I asked.

"It's probably not Rivata Haurva."

I laughed at that. Damn, he was the Prime Minister of Karsha when I was a little kid. It made Zauri seem… old. "It's some woman named Subar Qavand. They make us curse her and the Empress-Raja at the morning meeting, sometimes."

"Not surprising. The Qavands and the Haurvas have been trading the premiership between themselves for a long time. Used to be one family, way back. So, really, not much has changed."

Whatever. I couldn't give Panja's left testicle about Karshan politics. Or politics in general. It was so far removed from my problems. Like the clouds in the sky, you had no control, but sometimes it rained, sometimes it poured, and sometimes you thirsted for a drop.

A disturbing thought intruded: Rahal had said not to trust my dream wife. That a corruption was causing him to wake up, and that it had infected every part of his dream.

"Zauri, do you know what caused me to wake up so suddenly last time?"

"No. But it could be like you said. It could be an error or a glitch of some sort. Sad that it happened, right as I'd kissed you."

"What if *that's* what caused it?"

She shrugged. Frustrating that she didn't know.

A silence drenched us. A silence full of dilemmas, mysteries, and, heaviest of all, a rather awkward question.

"So, what do you want to do today?" Zauri asked. That wasn't the question, but it lightened the awkwardness, in any case. "Train?"

I shook my head. "Strange as this sounds, I want to explore where we went last time. It's just… why did the modder add an incomplete, life-sized model of Harska to this dream stone? Why is there a dragon in the sky? Doesn't it make you wonder?"

"Of course. But the terminal doesn't work up there. We'll be at the mercy of whatever we find. Are you sure you want to spend your dream time doing something so stressful?"

I wasn't sure. The fear and rage from my fight with Kediri still wounded me. But something bizarre was happening here, and I didn't like that my dreams — the only place where I had freedom, where I could sip happiness and comfort — were housing a mystery beyond my control. Something that had made Rahal so afraid, so agonized. Something that, perhaps, could affect Zauri, too.

I cared about Zauri, didn't I? Whether she was real or not, her presence alone lit up my dismal existence.

"Let's just do it," I said. "We can't relocate from there, but can we relocate *to* there? When I awakened in the dream, I was in that courtroom from earlier. That's where you took my brother's form, right?"

"Mhmm. I set it to your awaken position. And yes, we can relocate to there, just not from there." She tapped her chin. "However, weird things happened, remember? The sun turned so bright red, it actually went beyond what the settings show is possible. And when that happened, it literally melted the courthouse you were standing in."

"In my brother's form, you seemed not to have been affected by that, though. Unlike me, you were entirely calm and in control."

Zauri swallowed, folded her arms, and stared at me as if ashamed. "Look, earlier, I told you the short story, but there is a long story. Here it is — I didn't take your brother's form."

"Wait... what?"

"I don't have the ability to change my appearance. I can change clothes, but everything else — even my blue hair — is hardcoded."

"So, then, what was Kediri?"

"I... sort of... created him from a flow that — I think — came from your memories. He's a shadow script that you can face, though his script is limited. The things he was saying to you are just phrases I pulled from that flow."

It was all so disturbingly elaborate. But I understood why Zauri did it — she'd achieved her purpose for existing when that fight, that anger, brought the lightblade out of me.

"I get it, Zauri. And I have it in me to forget and forgive." I gazed at the ocean's horizon. These next words made my heart jitter. "To be completely honest, you might be the only person in the world I don't want to feel anger for. So let's see what's going on up in Harska."

She beamed at that. "It'll be like an adventure!"

"Yeah, an adventure." It was more than that, but might as well have a bit of fun. That was what these dreams were for, right?

WE RELOCATED to the incomplete version of my hometown, Harska. Except it wasn't incomplete anymore.

It was Harska. The streets were now cobbled, the buildings complete with stone walls and merlon-lined roofs. Lush cypresses lined the roadsides, and they didn't have hands growing out of them, thankfully. The dragon no longer hovered around the sun, which was now covered by dark clouds. It was raining, as it often did. A red-tailed squirrel sat on a nearby branch, munching an oozing gooseberry.

Rain hitting the tree leaves went *patter-patter*. Cool drops washed down my forehead. Zauri took refuge beneath the branches of the broadest cypress. I glanced in every direction, taking in a memory that had now come alive.

"How can this be?" I asked after joining Zauri beneath the tree. "Yesterday, it was completely unfinished."

"There are training programs that unlock new features as you progress. Could be that you're unlocking new scripts, somehow."

"So something I did caused Harska to be built? But what? And why?"

"It's only a theory." She shrugged, evading my gaze. "I don't know."

I bent down and stuck my hand in the wet dirt, then clumped a handful. I brought it to my nose and sniffed. Sediment-filled and rich, like the dirt in the backyard of the house where I'd grown up. I was home… and yet, it was absent of what really made it home: people.

"I know what you're thinking," Zauri said melodically. She gave me a toothy grin. "You want to go to your house, right?"

Well, of course. But I feared what I'd find there: an empty shell devoid of laughter. A hollow place filled with imagined ghosts, dried-up memories, and painful pricks of remembrance. Without the waft of Abba's peppery potato curry, or the comforting *thump-thump-thump* of Amma chasing a giggling Chaya up the stairs. Even the sight of long-haired Kediri sulking in his room would be a balm. These thoughts of what wouldn't be there made me mournful.

Zauri was with me, though. The realization that I wasn't alone brightened the moment.

"I can show you my room," I said.

"Oh yeah? What're we going to do there?"

"Uhh…" I tensed up. What *were* we going to do there? I scratched my suddenly itchy back. "Just see my miniature barrel collection."

"Your *what?*" She scrunched her face, obviously perplexed. "Miniature… barrels?"

"Yeah…" I mean, what more was there to say? I collected tiny barrels in my youth.

"Barrels… like… what you use to store stuff?"

"Yes."

"But… why would they be miniature?"

Wow, so many questions. Was it that hard to understand? "Well, the company that made the barrels would create small models, just to show them off. Abba was friends with the owner. So… yeah… my childhood wasn't that interesting, is what I'm saying."

"At least you had a childhood. I can't even imagine what it must've been like to be a smaller, more vulnerable version of yourself. To grow from that into what you are now. It's just unreal. I wish I could glimpse what that's like."

The glow of her face dimmed. Understanding that she'd never get to experience childhood had obviously saddened her. Only then did I realize that maybe I was as strange to Zauri as she was to me. It made me feel so much less alone, to think that she was struggling with her thoughts about me, as much as I struggled with my thoughts about her.

About what she was. And even crueler, what she wasn't.

"One day," she cleared her hoarse-sounding throat, "you'll outgrow me, too." She'd said so before when talking about how she was only meant to train children. "I'm static. You're ever-evolving. You'll flourish, like a butterfly unfurling its wings for the first time. You'll become something great. You won't need to visit me anymore."

"You're definitely overestimating me."

"No... you're amazing, Jyosh. You just don't know it yet. I wonder, will you even think of me when that day comes? Even once in a while?"

"Zauri, they don't sell dream stones on supermarket shelves where I live like they do in Karsha. Rest assured, I'm stuck with you." That came out wrong. But it was the harsh truth, and nothing reassured more than truth, right?

She remained sullen. "Sorry... I don't know what's come over me." She smiled, but her eyes remained dim and evasive. "Let's go see your house."

Hopefully I could cheer her up once we got there.

My house was south of the central plaza and park, just past the statue of Panja Parani's father, Gajah, who stood cross-armed and wore a golden turban with a peacock plume. Then there was the supermarket — one of five in the city — where they sold only local goods and often didn't have enough of anything. Once we cleared that, we arrived at a long street lined by palm trees with bulging date fruits, and then a cluster of walled villas for folks even more wealthy than my family. Finally, we reached the stream, which always had chalky green water, crossed the wooden bridge, and arrived in the closest suburb. The first row of houses wasn't the nicest nor the largest, being wood-built and single-storied. The next row sported stone and concrete houses, some as tall as four stories. Mine was in the middle.

The shade-giving cedar stood in the front yard, just how I remembered it. A timeless thing. Used to climb it despite my mother's pleading. Abba even threatened to make firewood of it when I fell off and broke my arm.

Strange that my house was painted a drab eggshell rather than luminous white; was it a mistake, or was I remembering it wrong? Perhaps I'd brightened the memories. Most houses were painted off-white, right?

Anyway, I took it all in. That clay roof now seemed a warm protector over our life, or at least the memory of it. And the door: did it always have a copper knob? Wasn't it golden, or was that another thing my memory had brightened?

Zauri put a hand on my shoulder. I'd almost forgotten she was next to me. From her expectant yet solemn expression, she seemed to understand the moment. Hadn't she looked into my memories of the exile, already? Then she knew what *home* meant. That my life had been pretty good, once. So good that I'd taken it for granted because I never knew how bad things could get.

The knob turned easier than I thought it would. Upon entering, the place was so… dinky. The living room with its drab floor cushions seemed too small for a family of five. In my memory, it was like a palace. And the stairs were a few steps from the door, even though I remembered it as a vast expanse.

Amma had these ceramic plates in a big glass display case. But they weren't there.

Of course, the modder wouldn't have known the contents of

my house. Come to think of it, how could the modder have known the layout?

A wire dangled from the corner ceiling. Abba would conduct green light into it upon request from the government. Every house had one. To this day, I'm not sure what it powered.

A dusty smell wafted from everything like dead skin. The silence hollowed out my hopes.

I climbed the stairs, Zauri following behind.

My room was the first door on the left. I creaked the door open, not sure what I'd see, but expectant, nonetheless. The red sunlight beaming through the window showed a bed without sheets, a dusty wooden desk, and empty wooden shelves.

"Where's your barrel collection?" Zauri asked.

"It's not here. Not much is."

"That's too bad. I was honestly excited to see some small barrels."

"Me too."

It was like standing inside a skeleton. Even without the meat and skin, this was still my house. Or rather, it was the corpse of what I'd lost the day my brother Kediri tried to defect from the Manizan Air Guard, got caught, and got himself killed. The elimination of his family, of course, followed. Only I was spared and sent to a labor camp for life. Only I remained of this once proud home, this once loving family.

Sobs sounded from behind. I turned to see Zauri, diamond-like tears streaming down her cheeks.

"Jyosh, I have to tell you something." Why was she suddenly crying, as if her eyes had sprung a leak? "I'm not supposed to tell you, but I care about you too much to hide it any longer."

"What is it?"

"Something very deliberate is happening, here. I've known for a while, but I kept it a secret." She took my hand in hers. "If I tell you, can you promise you won't hate me?"

I sipped on hate daily, used it for fuel. But here, in the dream, I didn't want to hate. I especially didn't want to hate Zauri.

"I can never hate you, Zauri. Just tell me. Whatever it is. So we can go forward without secrets."

"But it's… it's truly terrible." She sucked in a sob, then let out a pained whine. "I've been—"

The ceiling burned away, like it had done when I fought Kediri. I glanced up. Feathery black wings filled my vision. What resembled a giant eyeless raven swooped down toward me. In its mouth, it held a gleaming golden hammer larger than my body.

Zauri's eyes widened. She dove to push me out of the way. But it was too late. The giant raven smashed me with the golden hammer. Somehow, the hammer passed through my skin, muscles, and bones, and impacted only my soul. I saw my body standing in my room as my soul flew outward, passing through the wall of my house, then the wall of the world itself.

Chapter Six

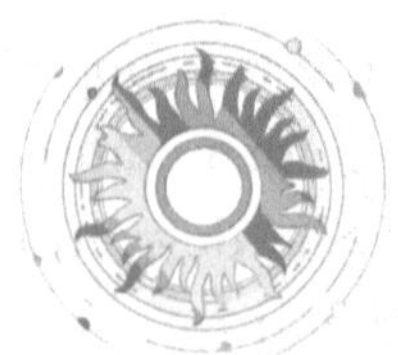

WAKE UP!

Something bashed against my cheek for a second time. Alarms blared into my soul. Rahal's angry eyes, pungent smell, and overgrown nose hairs were right up in my face.

He slapped me a third time, then grabbed my shoulders and shook me. "Wake up you sack of shit!"

I jutted up into a sitting position on my mattress. "The hell — the hell is happening?"

That alarm. I'd never heard it before, but it raised my hairs. It was shriller and more panicked than Death Bell, the pause between each scream barely half a second.

"War," Rahal said. "There's a goddamn war on. It's them! It's the Karshans!"

I threw off my blanket, pushed Rahal out of the way, and ran toward the door of my room. I sprinted down the cold hallway floor, toward the already open main door, and darted outside the dorm. Then I stared up.

"Holy…"

Levships covered the sky like a swarm. Each was rectangular

and metallic. Some were even painted in bright colors. Unlike the levships typically seen in the Manizan sky, these had no wings. They weren't shapely, but boxy. They seemed to be in separate clusters, with a big one in the center — probably a command ship — surrounded by ten to fifteen smaller ones. The big levships were about five times the size of the smaller levships, and flatter and shaped like a spade.

No matter where in the sky I stared, I saw a levship or the streaks of one.

"*Birds of freedom,*" I whispered to myself. "Or are they birds of death?"

That unbearably loud alarm continued to panic me, as if it were saying, "run while you can, or you'll be blown to bits. And even if you do run, you'll still be blown to bits."

Men crowded outside the other buildings of the camp; most were looking up, their jaws hanging. Some ran for the camp gate, colliding into others as if without sense. Many were shouting and hollering.

Chaos.

I rubbed my eyes and walked back inside the dorm. I returned to my room. I reached into the cardboard box with my belongings and grabbed my green machinist stone. I swapped it with my dream stone, then tucked my dream stone into my pocket. I sat on my mattress and stared at the dirty tile floor. We hadn't received any instructions from the camp wardens about what to do. I ought to just wait here, lest I get into trouble. Good behavior would be rewarded, surely.

This coffin was the safest place. Sure, the Karshans had taken over the sky, but down here, the camp wardens reigned. But... wait... wouldn't the Karshan levships target camps like this? Emperor Panja produced weapons here, so... was I waiting to be hit by a light cannon strike?

But could I survive if I ran? It seemed I was choosing a way to die. Maybe it was better to die free. After all, wasn't that what I'd wanted all along? I'd decided to try and assassinate the Emperor knowing I wouldn't succeed, but content enough that I'd get to choose how I'd die. Now, there was a good chance I'd die if I remained, and a good chance I'd die if I ran.

The choice was obvious. This place ought to burn without me.

I had no other possessions worth taking, so I went back outside and melded into a group of laborers stampeding for the gate, which was the only opening among the fencing that surrounded the camp. Since barbed wire covered the top of the fencing, the gate truly was the only way out. Instead of watching where I was going, I stared at the sky.

So many ships. Just unreal. What was the Karshan fleet doing? Just hovering? It didn't seem like a battle was going on. No light cannon strikes at all. Where was the Manizan Air Guard? Why'd they just let the Karshans in?

My bones felt the squeeze of the stampeding crowd. I could be crushed in here, so I pushed back, hard as I could, against the people around me. Forget the sky. There were enough dangers down here.

The crowd thinned as more workers ran out of the gate. I could breathe again.

The watchtowers were empty. No guards. Perhaps they'd already run off while I was asleep. If so, they probably weren't manning the guard shacks along the routes outside the camp.

"Where's everyone going?" I asked a young, beady-eyed man to my left.

"Some are going into town, others want to trek it to the border. I say the mountains are safest."

"Safest from who?" I wasn't even sure what I had to fear most, in this situation. Was I going to get blown up by a light cannon strike, or would I die somehow in the chaos?

"I don't know. Everything."

I inched forward amid the crowd toward the open gate.

"Stop!" a man behind me shouted.

I turned to see the white-haired executioner waving his light-blade above his head, right behind me.

"Stop or I'll cut all you traitors down!"

He swung wildly at the man next to him. That man dodged, then slipped on mud and fell onto his side, whimpering in fear. He screamed as the old man wound up for another swing.

Without a thought, I lunged forward and body slammed the executioner, my shoulder doing most of the impact. His light-blade vanished as the sword hilt flew out of his hand and landed somewhere amid the stampeding crowd. He crashed into the mud and growled.

Before he could get up, I turned and sprinted toward the gate, pushing aside whoever I could and squeezing through gaps in the crowd. My bony shoulder ached, and I wasn't sure why I'd reacted so suddenly.

I looked back to see if the executioner was chasing me. Couldn't spot him amid all the people. He had such a distinctive face, so it wasn't possible to miss him. Maybe he was still looking for his hilt. If it had landed closer, I could've grabbed it. But without a combat stone, it wasn't worth the risk of going back for. I prayed I'd never see the executioner again.

I got to the gate, which now seemed so weak leaning open on its rusted hinges, and stepped out of the camp, hopefully for the final time.

Where to go, now? I'd never had to ask this question before, so it weighed heavier than a crown of lead. Instead of deciding, I just followed everyone else.

We were safer in numbers, after all. I jogged in the grass aside the crowded dirt road, my heart in my throat. Then I realized: maybe we weren't safer in numbers. Numbers attract attention.

But I had no idea where to go, so continued following the crowd. I kept glancing at my back to make sure the executioner wasn't chasing me.

After five minutes, the jumble of us got well clear of the camp. I could no longer see its ugly gray buildings when I glanced behind me. All around us were rotten, pockmarked fields. Some grass, but mostly decayed soil. We weren't far from the nature trail where I'd seen that mound of shiny green emirils yesterday.

A beam of light sliced the sky, as if a sword had cut through a tarp and exposed an angry sun. The beam struck somewhere beyond the distant mountains.

A flash scathed my eyes. A quake battered the earth as everyone bellowed in fear.

I got low, though I was rather delayed. A plume of smoke now trailed into heaven from beyond the icy mountain peak. A massive light cannon beam must've been fired from a levship at some target on the ground, a sign things were heating up.

Everyone ran. Scattered into the fields. Hollering as if being chased by death itself. Why? That shot was far away.

"Hey! Where're you going?" I shouted to the beady-eyed man as he sprinted off, his arms flailing.

Wait, what was this long, streaky shadow that had covered me, all of a sudden?

I looked up to see a blocky, silver levship hovering just above.

Only I remained in its shadow, now. Nope. I wasn't about to face a levship on my own. I let fear take over and cycled my legs as fast as I could down the dirt road. Heaving. Hurtling my bones forward, dragging my skin and meat along. Since everything was so flat and open, there was nowhere to hide until I reached the nature trail. If that levship wanted to fire at me, it would be an explosive end.

I could only sprint so far. I'd been breathing dirty machine air for the past twelve years, so after a few minutes of pushing my limbs forward, I had to stop to pant and huff and catch my breath. My knees ached, too, from standing sixteen hours a day for the past twelve years.

Two laborers ran by me down the dirt road.

"Where you going?" I yelled.

A slice of blazing light tore the sky. This one was close enough to scathe my eyes, so much that my eyeballs hurt. I curled into a ball, fearful of fire, whimpering as death fear pulsed through me. The stench of burnt grass invaded my nose as a shockwave shook everything.

I looked up to see a tower of billowing black smoke. That had to be the camp and its surroundings going *boom*. My home for the past twelve years. My room — or rather, my coffin — must've been incinerated. I couldn't quite mourn its loss, but I didn't feel much relief, either.

I got up and trudged on. After three minutes, I reached the nature trail, its daunting banyans surrounding it like a wall. Should I hide here?

Hide from what? From the levships, from the camp police, or from everything? It seemed nonsensical to hide when I wasn't certain what to hide from. Who exactly was my enemy, now? What was I running from and to?

There was a town an hour's walk that I'd obviously never been to because it was forbidden for us prisoners. Seemed like a place worth going. Some of the vendors beneath the bridge were from there, so I knew it was full of normal folks who worked and barely got by. Would the Karshans target it, too? Those pamphlets they'd dropped around the flatlands had said they were *Your Friends in Karsha* — would our *friends* kill us?

Tasting ash in my mouth, I had my answer.

• • •

I WASN'T the only one walking on the dirt road toward the town, but when I noticed more people walking *away* from the town and toward where I'd come from, I wondered if I should've just hidden in the nature trail.

A middle-aged woman was walking in the opposite direction, a little boy and girl beside her. I hadn't seen children in twelve years. I gawked at them as if they were mythical creatures.

"Where're you going?" I asked the woman. She wore a thin yellow scarf over her head and a thick floral gown.

She grabbed her children's hands and whisked away from me.

Oh well. I continued on, still glancing behind to make sure the executioner wasn't following.

A brawly man wearing a loose black blazer was pulling a cart full of hard suitcases. I asked him the same question.

"There're Karshan soldiers in the town," he said while resting against his cart. "They say they're not a danger to us, but I don't trust them a lick. There's also some *other* people there."

"Other people?"

"Yeah. I saw families getting on a big levship. I think they were flying them out of the country."

"Why?"

He made a *heh* sound. "Don't know. All kinds of rumors going around." He drew big circles in the air with his hands. "Some say the Manizan army knew this would happen, and built tunnels to move their forces around. Supposedly a battalion is headed toward the city from underground. That's why those *other* people are helping some of the city folk evacuate. There's going to be a big battle."

I couldn't think of anything more wonderful than getting away from Maniza and out of the steel grip of Emperor Panja. If there were ships evacuating people, I had to get on one. Although, if the rumors about a battle were true, then I might get caught in a hail of light beams. So by going toward the town, was I going toward death or freedom?

Maybe neither. Maybe both. I wasn't sure. Nor was anyone, it seemed. But hope shone brighter than fear, so I thanked the man for his information and continued my trudge toward the town.

Why would anyone help us, though? Why take the down-trodden out of Maniza? Seemed too good to be true.

And yet, the world was a big place. Abba and Amma used to tell me stories of the wider world, though I couldn't remember much. Still, I knew there were all kinds of people with all kinds of ideas. Religions, philosophies — vastly different ways of looking at the world. Someone out there among the vastness must believe in helping others, right?

Another light cannon shot sliced open the sky. This time, I witnessed the red beam as it surged from a spade-shaped levship toward some target beyond the mountains.

Even the mountains shook as the sound of grinding earth filled the air. Everyone around me either ran, got on the ground, or shuddered in place. I stood and stared, my heart drowning in fear.

Maybe the Karshans were trying to collapse the tunnels the Manizan army were supposedly using. Whatever happened to all those cannons I made? Why weren't they being used against these levships?

I mean, I didn't care if my labor hadn't amounted to anything useful. Though maybe a part of me did because it seemed like such a frustrating waste of my life, veins, and time.

Back to what mattered: the sky was flinging death at us. I stared up at the endless arrays of levships. They were all spread out in clusters, but one cluster seemed higher than the others, perhaps even high enough to reach Harska, which floated some-where in the north near the mountainous border with Demak.

Surely, given that it was the capital of Maniza and the Emperor's seat, the Karshans must've been targeting it.

Wondering about that wasn't going to help me. All this time, my veins had been bathing in adrenaline, in a rush to get somewhere, but that could only last so long. A jittery dread began to replace the hope that had been fueling me. *You're going to die*, it said. That became a mantra in my mind, poisoning my resolve. *You're in the middle of a war. People die in war. You're a cockroach to both sides. You're going to get crushed.*

The thoughts flooded. I had to get to town. If someone was evacuating people, getting them out of this nightmare, I yearned to be among the saved.

As I WALKED down the dirt road, huffing, my legs aching, the town's silhouette finally emerged on the horizon. It was a dusty enclave of concrete tenements near the mountainside. The sight of it pushed me to hurry on.

I arrived at the first row of tenements, yearning for a break. To my astonishment, the dirt fed into an actual paved road, something I hadn't seen since Harska.

A crowd was bubbling in the plaza amid the tenements. Everyone surrounded something as large as the buildings: a rectangular, metallic box with a painting of a blue shield and a golden dragon on it. A levship!

"What's happening here?" I excitedly asked a scrawny old woman, hoping she wouldn't scurry away.

"They're choosing people to evacuate." She pointed to a young woman with short hair in an unfamiliar, ocean-blue uniform. A crowd of people with raised hands were swarming around her. "Go get a lot from her."

"A lot?"

"Just go before they run out."

The young woman held a stack of tickets, and she was handing them out to everyone who threw their hands at her. I stood amid the chaos and inched forward whenever a gap in the crowd opened up.

I couldn't take my eyes off her. I'd not seen a young woman who didn't look like Prisaya or Zauri in forever. But I wouldn't say I was attracted to her. Rather, she intimidated me with how easily she handled the crowd. She brandished a baton and wasn't afraid to *electrify* it if someone pushed into her space. Was that *electrification* also a conduction ability? She never actually had to hit anyone: soon as those yellow sparks spat off the baton and she shouted "get back!" everyone obeyed.

Was this woman a Karshan? I couldn't tell, even when I got close. The same blue shield emblem from the levship emblazoned her breast pocket. Brass buttons glimmered on her shoulders, and a gold trim snaked around her collar.

I glared at the sword hilt on her belt: it was different from the one in my lightblade training program. It had a metal fragment that protruded from the hilt. A soft coating lined the grip, and a curvy pommel stuck out at a right angle.

She slapped my chest with the ticket; I grabbed it, said "thanks," and went a few paces from the crowd.

It had a number on one side and the blue shield emblem on the other. Nothing else.

I checked on the sky. Not much was happening. A cluster of levships hovered low at the horizon, just in front of the red sun. The way they clustered, with the sun in the background, resembled a bruised rose. They cast the most bizarre, elongated shadows in our direction. I wasn't sure whether to be awed or terrified. A lot of both welled up in my chest.

I went back to the old woman who'd been willing to talk to me. "Who are these people? Why are they helping us?"

She ruffled her nose and stared into me. "You're from the camp, right?"

I nodded. No reason to lie.

"They claim to be from a country called Behesh. You ever heard of it?"

I shook my head. There were so many countries. I only knew the major ones and the nearby ones.

"They say they're going to help as many as they can to get out before the battle starts."

If that was true, there was hope. People in the outside world actually cared about us. I'd never have believed it if I didn't see it.

"So why're they handing out lots?"

"There's only so much room. The next flight is tomorrow. But with a battle coming, that'll probably be too late."

So whoever got on this ship had the highest odds of surviving, and it was determined by lottery. Fair enough. I could only hope the universe had mercy on me, for once.

"Attention everyone!" a man with a megaphone called. He was standing atop the ramp that led inside the levship.

I longed to walk through that threshold more than I'd ever longed for anything. I saw myself walking up that ramp and inside the belly of this metal beast.

"If your number ends in five or eight, you're getting on this ship!"

Everyone looked at their tickets. I brought my ticket to my face.

6.

Ugh.

Hollers and jeers sounded from the crowd. The short-haired woman and other guards around the levship raised their electric batons.

"Fives and eights, line up!" the man with the megaphone said. "Spouses and young children of anyone who drew a five or an eight, line up as well. Parents, adult children, and other relatives must have also drawn a five or an eight to board. Now line up. We don't have forever!"

Thunder exploded above. I ducked and crossed my arms over my head. Everyone did similarly. The thunderous bellows continued, as if a divine dragon were flinging rage at the world. But it was no dragon; it was the levships firing at somewhere not too distant, somewhere on *this* side of the mountain range.

And then something from the ground fired back. It sliced the sky like a knife into a watermelon. A levship turned into a ball of flame. The explosion sounded as if the sky were coughing. The ship's metal carcass sundered into pieces and rained upon the earth.

The levships fired, and the ground fired back; the earth and sky were at war with each other. Another levship exploded, and then another.

Well, seemed those cannons I helped make weren't entirely a waste. Not that I was proud.

Everyone around me was hollering and trying to climb the ramp into the big levship. The guards electrified their batons. The short-haired woman *thwapped* a rather tall man with her sparking baton; vomit spewed from his mouth as he hit the ground. Two rugged-looking men followed his foolish attempt and met the same fate.

Despite the metal and fire raining from above, everyone calmed down once they saw what those batons could do.

"Fives and eights! We're taking off, now!" the man with the megaphone said.

Amid the cacophony and chaos, I noticed something sticking to my boot. I picked it up: a ticket that read *108*.

Could this be my lucky day? My lucky number? A repayment for all I'd suffered? I glanced around; everyone was either focused on the sky, on their tickets, or on their families. No one had noticed me pick it up.

I got in the back of the line that had formed, an uplifting spirit washing through me. The godly battle in the sky made me jittery. Hard to digest all the hope and fear in my veins. Some things can't be understood in the moment, and perhaps that was a good thing, because if I really comprehended the danger I was in, I'd probably be paralyzed.

"Please help!" a woman cried. "I can't find my ticket!"

It was the old woman I'd been talking to earlier. She crawled on the ground and dug up the dirt like a cat. "It was one-zero-eight! I swear it was one-zero-eight!"

A young man and woman got on their knees next to her, as did three droopy-cheeked children. They all searched the ground for the ticket.

I swallowed bitterly. I looked away. Better not to see or feel.

But unfortunately, I couldn't not hear.

"We won't leave without you, Amma," the young man said.

"No, you go!" said the old woman. "To see you grow up and have children was all I wanted from life. I've lived long enough. I'm fulfilled, and I leave my fate to the Originator. Go, now!"

One by one, people ascended the ramp into the mouth of the levship. I nudged forward in the line. I was almost at the ticket checker — the short-haired woman with the electric baton.

I turned to look at the family I was breaking.

The young man got off his knees, grabbed his three children, and along with his wife lined up behind me. The wife wiped tears from her husband's reddened eyes with her sleeve, then hugged him. The children, too, hugged his legs.

The old woman was right, though: she'd lived long enough. Surely, with time, they'd come to understand that.

She put on a bright smile and waved goodbye to her grand-children. I'm sure she was relieved and joyful to see them go despite the separation. Despite the danger of remaining in a war zone. But how would an old woman survive without her family to look after her?

Survive. Survive. Survive. The sky exploded again, and the ground quaked. I needed to survive somehow, too. I wanted out of this hell. I'd wanted out for twelve years. I'd given too much time to suffering.

But that old woman… she had people who loved her. Who'd miss her. I didn't. Maybe one if you counted Zauri, but she wasn't flesh and blood. She wasn't really real.

Vir had deserved better than what I'd done to him. But I'd been hungry for a way to survive, even if it meant hurting others. I chose what I chose, and I became what I became.

But did I like what I'd become?

I left the line and went to the old woman.

"I found this on the ground." I handed her the 108 ticket. "It's your number, right?"

She gaped, bouncing her gaze between me and the ticket, as if I were the god she prayed to.

The old woman grasped the ticket with both of her shaking hands. "Thank you," she said. "Thank you." Then she hugged me. Warm yet weak. It reminded me of my mother's hug.

"Can you tell me where your house is?" I asked. "I need a place to hide."

I WENT to the old woman's apartment, located on the bottom floor of a tenement painted in a color I'd describe as *rotting eggshell*. It was just one cramped room with three mattresses rolled neatly in the corner. Judging by the sizes, colors, and shapes of the clothes strewn about, the old woman had lived here with her son and daughter-in-law and their three children.

I unrolled one of the mattresses; it only took up a third of the floor space — a major improvement over my coffin in the camp. If I was going to die, might as well die dreaming.

Zauri had been about to tell me something, and I was too curious to die without knowing. How badly was I about to be betrayed, I wondered. As badly as I'd betrayed Vir?

What kind of betrayal could Zauri inflict on me? She only existed in my dreams, so what could be so bad? You never know how bad things can get, I suppose, until you're sentenced to a lifetime of hard labor. Or until the sky explodes.

After I put in my dream stone and lay down, I imagined that the sound of the light cannons was just a game — hard to do with the ground shaking, with the worry that the roof could fall on me at any moment. But I had quite an imagination, if nothing else. Besides, I'd walked so much and hadn't slept well recently, so I was tired. Tired in my soul. An orange sleep snatched and dragged me in its current.

Chapter Seven

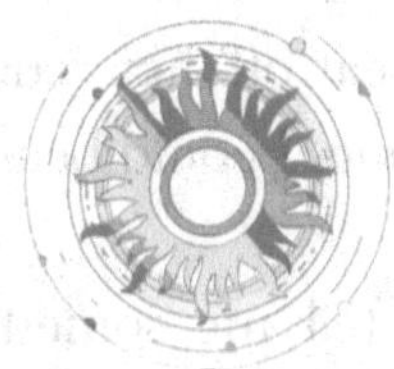

I AWOKE IN A COLISEUM. A BLUE SUN GAZED AT ME, SOMETHING I'd not seen before. It cast the world in a somber, alien hue. Rows and columns of stone benches sprawled around a sandy field.

Zauri stood in the field, sword hilt in hand. Black and red waves ignited off her hilt in a corkscrew pattern; how wondrous! A headless man charged her with a twinblade; it was like a lightblade except red beams shot out of both ends of the hilt, so it had to be held from the middle. How would she deal with something twice the size of her blade?

When the twinblade surged toward her chest, she twirled out of the way and swiped down on it with her lightblade. Light hit light and sparks flew in rainbow hues like when I'd fought Kediri's shadow.

"Pause!" Zauri said to the headless man upon noticing me. He stood straight, holding the hilt of his twinblade out.

Zauri wiped sweat off her forehead with her sleeve as I walked through the sand toward her.

"The dream never ended for you, again?" I asked.

She nodded. "I've been waiting for you to come back. Lost count of the days, honestly. Twelve, I think?"

"Where the hell are we, anyway?"

"I was flying around and found this place. It's on its own little island in the sea. Decided to sharpen my skills, so I can teach you better. Did a lot of fighting."

So Zauri had been adventuring without me in my own dream stone. How was that even possible?

I wiped a bead of sweat off her reddened, sunbeaten cheek. Whatever she had to tell me, I could bear it, right? I wouldn't just disown her.

"You were about to tell me something before we were so rudely interrupted. Truth is, I have much to tell you, but I want to hear whatever you have to say first."

Zauri nodded. "Let's go sit, at least."

We sat on a stone bench. I imagined it filled with folks watching warriors do battle, cheering each bloody pummel and sliced limb. When I was a boy, Abba told me they had coliseums in Majapahit where people fought, but I hadn't imagined them like this: stone-built, sandy, and large enough to field a small army, let alone a few duelers.

Zauri sighed and scratched her snaky eyebrows. She locked eyes with me, her cheeks tight and tense. "The first day when you met me was also the first day I'd ever existed. Technically, I have a sense that there was a before, but no actual memories. I possessed knowledge and ideas, but no actual context for why I knew what I knew aside from an understanding that I'm a script, meant for a specific purpose. Basically, I'm like a person with amnesia who wakes up knowing what their purpose is, yet not really understanding *why* it's that way."

If I were to wake up with amnesia, it might be a mercy. Forgetting everything would be a clean slate. And yet, the shadows of what had happened would still be there, an inexplic-able pain hiding in the darkness.

I nodded so she'd continue.

"There was something else, though… a source, deep inside me, feeding me ideas. Emotions. Sensations. And even memories. Eventually, I figured out what it was, and the real sin is that I didn't tell you until now. It's a hidden script called a black box. It's something most often used in espionage in order to corrupt a dream stone and control the mind of the dreamer. Meaning, it's something evil, and I don't know what it's doing to me. And what it'll do, in the end, to you."

"Why would the modder put that in my stone? What does he want from me?"

"I don't know. Its purpose is opaque. I can't dive deep into the black box's script. I'm afraid I'm as in the dark as you."

Tears spilt from her eyes. Her remorse was real, of that I was sure. She'd described something that seemed beyond her control. But the awful possibilities were endless. Could this black box be why I was missing memories? Had it poisoned my thinking, somehow? Could it be what Rahal had experienced, as well? It sure sounded like it fit the doubts he had. Could it be the source of all my confusion and bewildering decision making? Was I simply not in control of myself?

"I need a moment to think," I said, finding it hard to breathe.

After sitting on a coliseum bench and thinking about it for a spell, I returned to the center field where Zauri waited, resolute about one thing.

"The way I see it, you're as much a victim in this than I am. And the fact that you told me, despite the black box wanting you to keep it a secret, means you're not at fault."

Strange to say it, but I'd actually been making better decisions since I met Zauri. From the moment just after I'd executed Vir, I was starting to free myself of the way the camp had made me think. Of how it had corrupted me. Surely, even with a black box inside of her, Zauri was better than what had come before.

And it wasn't her fault. Someone else had created it, and perhaps she feared what I'd think and so hesitated to tell me.

I took her in my arms as she bawled. "I have a part of me that I don't understand," I said, "but it's been with me longer than I've known you. I still don't know who it was that betrayed my friend Vir — if that was even me, or some monster hidden inside."

She clung to my chest. "Jyosh, you should always destroy a stone that's been corrupted with a black box. Like I said earlier, I don't know what's written in it… and it's become so entrenched in my script, that I no longer know if my actions and thoughts are arising naturally — or from it."

"I won't destroy you."

I tasted a bitter thought: what if she'd kissed me because the black box made her do it? Maybe it was worse than I was willing to accept. Something underhanded was being done to Rahal and me… but why? We laborers were nothing but the lowest of the low and barely worth this kind of clever trick.

"You should delete me," Zauri said, her eyes wet and sad. "For your own safety. You should!"

"No. There has to be another way."

"Please, Jyosh. I don't want to cease existing, but I don't want you to get hurt. Black boxes are capable of awful manipulation. They've even been used to brainwash people into killing themselves or killing others, even others they love. They can twist your sense of reality. I'm dangerous!"

"If it means disconnecting from you forever, I won't do it. This dream is all that makes life worth living. Besides, what *isn't* dangerous? I'm literally in the middle of a war zone right now sleeping in a building that, at any moment, could be erased by a light cannon."

Zauri covered her mouth in obvious shock. "What happened?"

"Would be faster if you just read my memories."

She nodded, placed a clammy hand on my forehead, and closed her eyes. A numb throb spread through my head as if my brains were being slowly sucked through my forehead.

Zauri gasped in utter horror and retracted her hand. "You had a chance to escape Maniza and you gave it up for some old woman? Why!?"

That scolding tone reminded me of Amma. "The ticket didn't belong to me. It was rightfully hers. I couldn't do that to her, to her family. I couldn't be that person…"

"The person who betrayed Vir? Surviving isn't evil, Jyosh. Nor is it easy. As a lightblade training program, first and foremost, I'm teaching you a way to survive. And to survive, you have to value yourself as much as others."

It seemed she valued my life more than I did. "I think… what I did to Vir… it already killed me, in a way. The person who did that couldn't live with what he'd done, and so I was reborn in his place. The way you said you'd been born the day we met… oddly enough, I feel the same. That's why it seems so strange that *I* hurt him."

"No, you're compartmentalizing. You're breaking into pieces. It's a reaction to stress, not some kind of rebirth. The thing is, you have to survive." She paused to catch her breath. "What's done is done, I suppose. But given the situation you're in, I'm going to teach you *everything* you need to know so you have the highest chance of getting through the mess you're in."

I chuckled. She didn't lack for confidence. "Whatever you teach me, I won't use it to harm people. More than anything, I don't want to make this world a worse place. I won't use my skills for evil."

"You're being evil to yourself if you give up and die! Your soul is as valuable as anyone's. Let's not waste time. I can teach you useful things right now. You can already make a lightblade, but that's worthless if you don't have a combat stone and sword hilt."

She waved her hand in the air. The overhead sun sank toward the ground and burned redder, the color of Maniza's eternal sunset.

Now it loomed on the horizon — a menacing half-oval.

I asked, "If the sun is redder at the horizon like in Maniza, why is it harder to conduct red light than if the sun is overhead?"

"There's actually more of all wavelengths of light when the sun appears white and is positioned overhead. What makes the sky red in Maniza is the angle. The light takes longer to reach, and most of it gets absorbed along the way — red just slightly less than the others. That's why the sky appears red."

I could spend all day asking her questions and learning from her. But this probably wasn't the time.

"Put a green stone in your chest," she commanded.

"Yes, sir." I opened my palm and tapped *Aperture Stone > Green* into the terminal. I felt a slight tickle and jolt in my chest.

"So here's the thing, Jyosh. Forget about lightblades for now. You need to learn to fight with this." She snapped her fingers. A weird, disc-like thing with a handle appeared in her hand.

Took a moment to realize what it was.

"A frying pan!?" I said with my hands on my head.

"There's a frying pan in the room you're sleeping in. You may not have noticed it, but I did when you let me see your memories. Also, crucially, there's a stove in that room. So here's what you're going to do. Open the stove's bottom compartment, remove the gain medium crystal, and adhere that crystal to the frying pan."

I laughed.

Zauri snarled. "I'm not joking! You can make an electric weapon with the frying pan that way. Just like how you've been conducting green light into a fabricator, you'll do so into the frying pan. Because it'll have a gain medium crystal, it'll become a basic electric weapon."

I snorted and shook my head. "Yeah, and how am I going to *adhere* a gain medium crystal to a frying pan? I know how gain mediums work — they're rather sensitive."

"Exactly. You know how they work. You saw those batons the soldiers were using. They're also an electric weapon, just like the frying pan weapon you're going to make."

Well… she wasn't completely insane. I could technically attach the gain crystal to the frying pan and create a conduit, which I could then conduct green light into. That would technically electrify the frying pan, but it just seemed so ridiculously crude.

"So this frying pan… it'll hurt?"

"You saw what that baton did. It'll be similar. But we need to train — now — so that when you wake up, you'll be ready to mess your enemies up with that frying pan."

Zauri handed the frying pan to me. It had this bulge between the handle and the pan where the green gain crystal was housed.

I inhaled the sun's green light, cycled it through me, and pushed it into the pan. The coated handle heated up, though not as much as the metal pan.

"If only I had some eggs," I said with a grin.

"Be serious!"

"Yeah-yeah, I'm very serious, I swear."

"Good. Now, push more green into it, like you want to overload the thing." Zauri presented her right cheek to me. "And then hit me." She poked her cheek. "Right here."

"I don't want to hit you."

"Hit me! Unlike a lightblade, which we can see, I need to *feel* that you're doing it right."

Was I really about to slap this woman with an electrified frying pan while standing in the middle of a coliseum?

"Right now, it's just kind of hot, though. There's no electricity."

"That's because it's a freaking frying pan. It's meant to conduct heat into food, not spark. You have to overload the gain crystal, but not so much as to destroy it. Just enough to get a current to conduct through the pan. And you have to do it right at the moment before you strike. So try!"

It was all so ridiculous. Was a frying pan really going to help me survive a war?

I wound my arm and held back the light from entering the handle, letting it pool in my hand instead — a tingly, hot feeling. Hitting her seemed so wrong, but she couldn't feel pain, and she'd be the best judge as to whether it worked. Those smooth, soft cheeks though…

I *thwacked* the pan into her shoulder, surging a goodly portion of green into the handle just before impact. The pan electrified and sparked as it made contact. Lightning bolts jumped off the pan and onto her.

Zauri shuddered and backed away.

"Holy…" she said, jaw hanging. "You did it on the first try. You shocked the hell out of me. Anyone would go down from that."

I smiled, satisfied but not surprised. "I've been a machinist for twelve years. I can command massive machines. What the hell is a frying pan to me?"

"All right, all right. Very good. But you're not a god just yet."

"I might be to those who worship frying pans. Surely there must be someone, somewhere who does."

Zauri snapped her fingers. A pale, headless, pot-bellied man blinked into existence in front of me. She pointed at his hand with her forefinger. A slanted metal pipe materialized there.

He raised the pipe, ready to charge.

How was Zauri inputting all these dream commands on the fly, without a terminal?

"Defend yourself, Jyosh," she said. "If you don't, it'll hurt."

She pointed at me with an open hand, then closed and opened it again. Her commands were so dramatic. I loved them.

I didn't love the way the pot-bellied man charged at me, shoulder forward, with the force of a barreling ox. I dove away from his lunge. Landed in the sand on one hand, then pushed myself to my feet. I was quite the acrobat when needed.

Sparks flew from the pale man's pipe as he swiped at me. His swings were heavy but slow, so I sidestepped or backed away from each. I imagined my frying pan to be a hammer and went for his neck stump. The headless man blocked my topside swing with his pipe. Electricity zagged through the air as both our weapons sparked.

"For god's sake, Jyosh, stop dancing." Zauri gritted her teeth as the headless man and I stepped back and faced each other. "Imagine what a real bad guy would do to you if he won. He'd spill your guts. He'd stew your entrails. He'd paint his walls with your blood. Fight like you're going to die an agonizing death!" She grunted as if she wanted to join the fight. "Get angry. Feel some hate!"

I imagined Kediri's head on that neck. Kediri had already killed me, figuratively, and our whole family, literally. Why had that bastard tried to defect, alone? Didn't he realize Emperor Panja would punish his family for such treason? He'd died selfishly, but he deserved a second death, an infinity of deaths!

As the pale man went for my right arm, I lunged at his heart. Electrified my frying pan just as it hit his left breast. A pounding, spicy pain radiated from my arm, seizing my senses as both our hits landed. The headless man crashed backward with me on top. Electricity zapped my muscles and bit into my bones.

I'd won, but the electric jolts in my arms and the frustration that I couldn't really kill Kediri made it less than pleasant.

"From now on, every fight is to the death," Zauri said. "Know what happens in war? No one will be working the fields, so food will run out. Light cannons will flatten cities. Droves will rush to the borders, but eventually Maniza's neighbors won't allow them in." She clasped her lush blue hair, more exasperated than I was of my sad plight. "You can't be soft. Your chance of living lessens each day you're out there."

It was awkward to wield this frying pan while discussing life and death. "Thanks for caring, Zauri. But how much can an electrified frying pan increase my odds of surviving? Maybe half a percent? I'll need to get lucky to keep breathing — had I just drawn a five or eight on that ticket, I could've been somewhere safe by now. Who knows what ways to live or die tomorrow will bring?" I lifted the frying pan over my head and pretended it was a hat. I grinned, but Zauri wouldn't smile back. How to make her understand without upsetting her? "I realized a while ago that focusing only on survival makes life as bitter as the cleaning-fluid-spiced curry I often had for lunch. And in here, I don't want that awful taste in my mouth. I want to have fun. I want to make good memories. And truth be told, since you arrived, I've been having fun. Haven't had this much fun since I was a dumb kid."

Finally, she smiled, though pain lingered in her eyes. "I understand. Since you're not going to destroy this dream stone, know that we can make more happy memories if you survive longer. And if you die… what if this dream never ends for me? I'll be alone… forever."

Damn, I hadn't thought of that. Whereas she made my life less lonely, I made her life less lonely, too. And what was lonelier than being the only one in a forever dream?

"I think we're both right," I said. "So let's use this time wisely. We'll spend some of it training, some of it adventuring, and some of it taking it easy. Sound good?"

Zauri nodded. "Our training isn't over." She snapped her fingers. Now, two headless men blinked into existence. One had a slanted pipe and the other something far worse: a machete.

"A lot of farms around your area," Zauri said. "I'm taking an educated guess about the dangers you might face. Next, you'll fight a rake-wielder."

I TRAINED with the frying pan the whole day. Got pretty good at slapping headless men with it. I also practiced my dodging, ducking, and sliding. Such acrobatics would be more difficult in the real world with my pained knees, though.

Timing the electric hits was easy enough, but if I had to dodge as well, I'd mess up sometimes. According to Zauri, this was why training mattered — it developed muscle memories and instincts.

"Okay, time to learn a new move," Zauri said after I'd brought down a headless man who dual-wielded rakes with a clean strike to the ribs. "Let's call it… Electric Parry. No… *Lightning* Parry."

"Sounds intense. How does it work?"

"Use the frying pan to block a hit and conduct a current from yourself, through the pan, and into your enemy's weapon. That'll shock and perhaps knock out your opponent, turning parrying into an offensive move."

So not only would I have to time my electric surge right, but also direct it into my opponent's weapon. That would demand some inward focus while I was dancing, dodging, and dipping.

It sounded ingenious, though. I beamed at my teacher. "Tell

me, Zauri, this something all lightblade training programs know how to do?"

She crossed her arms — adorably serious — and shook her head. "I'm figuring this stuff out on the fly, but it's all based on sound principle. The same principle by which you power machines with sunshine. Energy is energy, it can be channeled in an ordered way, or chaotically. We're mixing it up here to create viable offensive and defensive strategies."

I scratched my head. "Despite slaving at a machine for half my life, I would've never figured any of this out. Nice to have you around to think for me."

"Because you weren't taught the fundamentals. You don't know the intricacies of conducting sunshine. There're a thousand layers of knowledge regarding it. Even I'm ignorant relative to what's out there. I'm straining and stretching everything I know, for your sake."

Whether she was right or wrong, whether any of this would really help me or not, just the thought that she cared so much almost melted me. She had my best interest at heart. Despite the black box. I'd shuttered that from my mind because I wanted to give my trust to her fully.

Zauri snapped her fingers. A pipe-wielding man materialized amid white light.

"Give it a go!" she said.

The man swung at me. I raised my pan to block. I pushed the green light from my hand into the pan and surged it toward where I hoped the pipe and pan would make contact.

Clank. Sparks erupted off the pan. One caught me in the neck, sending jittery jolts through my bones. But the pale man remained standing, pipe brandished in front of his face, ready for the next attack.

"Try again," Zauri said. "It's not just about timing, it's about positioning. Here, do this — instead of trying to figure out where on the pan the pipe will strike, try to line up the pan so the pipe strikes it at the center, then be ready to direct your light there."

That would simplify things. But I'd also be relying more on my physical positioning instead of my ability to direct green light, and I was more comfortable with the latter. Still, I trusted my teacher's guidance.

The headless man swung down; I pushed my pan forward so the pipe would smack its center, then surged the pooled light into that point. Sparks jetted off the pan and into the pipe. The pale man electrified. Blue lightning engulfed his limbs and torso. Burnt meat stench filled the air as he collapsed forward.

I'd become a god, truly. That Lightning Parry was even more powerful than my direct strikes!

Zauri cheered and clapped with glee. "Not only did you direct your own light into his weapon, you directed his own light back at him. A Lightning Parry with a cherry on top. Told you you're amazing!"

I bowed my head, a graceful winner. "Well, those shitty factory machines were always one misdirected current from breaking down, and breaking a machine would mean my head. So long story short, frying pan weapons are my specialty."

Zauri wagged her finger. "It's still not enough! You're just getting started on my new training regimen. But... we can break for today. Next time, I'll teach you something even better."

Ahh. I'd earned some relaxation. How wonderful to actually be good at something. But whether or not the school of the electrified frying pan would prevail in a war zone remained an open question.

"Before we take a break," Zauri put a finger on her chin, "there's something I discovered that you need to see."

With how tired I felt, all I wanted to discover was the sand and waves. "I'll only agree if you promise it'll make me smile."

"Umm..." She tapped her chin. "Yeah, you'll smile."

"Your hesitation doesn't inspire confidence. But since you're so insistent, lead the way."

Zauri opened her palm and tapped into her terminal window.

A glowing white light enveloped me.

I blinked onto a field of golden grass. At my front sprawled a palace with uncountable spires. Statues of the gods painted in wondrously glossy purple, green, and gold covered each spire. Some statues sported wings, others had many arms and heads. Some wielded swords and had fire for hair. Some had animal faces, others human. It was a colorful, vast splendor that my eyes had never tasted the like of.

My ears, too, delighted at the flutes and sitars sounding from the sky, as if the gods were playing a symphony from their perch in the second heaven. The air, which itself was glittery and pink, smelled of the purest roses. A musk breeze cooled my cheeks.

Zauri came to my side and took my arm. "Well? What do you think?"

"Does the emperor of the world live here?"

"Actually, it's a temple. It wasn't here before, though. After you left, another weird pattern appeared in the sky, so I flew up toward it. When I did, I appeared here."

I wanted to skip my way to the entrance. I'd not been so giddy to explore something since I was a child sneaking through my neighbors' yards. "Let's go inside!"

"I already tried. It's locked. All we can really do is marvel at it from afar. Unless… maybe there's a key?"

"A key? Hell, I'll break the door down with my frying pan."

Zauri put her face in her palm. "Wait till you see the door before you say that. Also, we can't fly over it. There's a force field."

We walked for three minutes down a flower-lined stone walkway toward a massive golden double door that dwarfed my whole house. A door for titans, literally. No way my frying pan could break through that. Zauri fingered the indentation at the door's base, which resembled a lotus.

"So we have to find a lotus-shaped key," I said. "Where could that be hiding?"

"I don't know." She smiled at me. "Let's keep a look out, I suppose."

"Whatever happened to that divine dragon? You ever see it again?"

"No. But you should understand something — all these… surprises, all these things the modder added to your stone, as well as the black box inside me — it's all connected, somehow."

I glared up at the magnificent, golden door. "Well, obviously."

"And…" Zauri gazed at the ground, solemn. "It's most likely a bad thing. It might seem like a puzzle, an adventure, a mystery, but it could all be leading to your doom."

What wasn't leading to my doom, these days?

"I don't want to believe it's that dire. This world can't be all bad. I mean, you're not bad, Zauri. You're doing your best to help me. If I can get the black box removed, somehow, I'm sure everything will turn out fine."

She shrugged. "I hope you're right."

I hated seeing her so unsure of herself. I knew that poison too well.

WE SPENT the next day at the beach. Zauri wouldn't change into swimming clothes before she got in the water. I always hated swimming with my day clothes on, but to each their own. We had fun, though. We even used the turtle shell to skid across the sea. Racing each other against the bobbing tides, I almost forgot what awaited me in the real world.

For the first time in forever, I had a true friend. Well, more than that. A teacher. Maybe more than that. What exactly Zauri was to me, I couldn't say. And maybe, I didn't want to define or limit it in any way. It was what it was, and it would be what it would be.

The truth is, I had nothing to compare her to. I'd only known her for a few days, but she was now the only person in my world, as I was the only person in hers. In the real world, neither could I trust others, nor could I be trusted myself. But here, with her, I so badly wanted to believe that this was all happiness. That this was payoff for everything I'd suffered.

She made my striving worth it. Otherwise, why not give up and die? Or go out in a blaze? What was there to live for, if not more time with her, here in Paradise?

And we were the same, weren't we? We both carried hidden truths within us that we couldn't understand. We were both human, with all the flaws that entails. But as much as we couldn't understand our own selves, I could understand her, and she could understand me.

And as common as this experience might be for someone living in society, for a man who'd barely survived twelve years in a slave camp, it was a rainstorm in the desert.

The next day, we trained tirelessly for eight hours. I got masterful with the frying pan. I was smacking down three attackers at a time by day's end. Rakes, machetes, metal swords, spears – I could counter them all. No strike was too much for my Lightning Parry, a move that would shock my opponents in more ways than one. I also became better at dodging, ducking, sliding, backstepping, rolling; I might not be the strongest, but I was agile, and improving in that respect could help me survive, or even win, a fight in the real world.

After training, we munched on fruits. Normally, I don't eat in dreams because it makes you hungrier when you awaken, as you're tricking your body into thinking it's enjoyed nourishment. A banana, some pineapple, and a slice of watermelon couldn't hurt too much.

"It's like discovering a new color," Zauri said, chomping down on watermelon flesh, seeds stuck on her teeth. We were sitting in the cabin with a crackling fire going. "It's unreal how good it is. You know, I've never asked you what your favorite food is."

"I don't have one."

"Even from your childhood? All those dishes your father would make?"

"Well, back then I had quite a sweet tooth. As long as the flat bread was buttered and the curry cream-filled, I was happy. But now... now the plainer something is, the better."

"I have the sudden urge to cook for you."

"Maybe once I'm somewhere where I'm not starving. That way, eating in the dream won't make me so hungry once I wake up."

"I don't know why I have this urge, but I *really* want to cook you something. And I also want you to get sick."

I scratched my ear. Had I heard her wrong? "You want me to get... sick?"

"Yeah, so I can take care of you. The way your mother would in the memories."

I supposed that was rather sweet of her. "There's no sickness in the dream, though."

"Maybe you could pretend to be sick one day?"

I chuckled. "I suppose I could."

"I'll make you chickpea soup, with a lot of turmeric, and pepper milk with salted ghee. Oh, and conge with—"

"I'd probably actually get sick from overeating."

We both laughed. We laughed a lot. We got stuck in the moment. We put the sad things, the questions, and the inevitable end out of mind. Though it was always there, itching my scalp like an ant digging toward my brain: *You're going to wake up. And then you're going to die.*

I did my best not to let the thought poison the moment. But it lingered like a ghost no matter where we went. Even when we gave the turtle shell another go and whooshed across milky clouds, it was there behind me, always lurking, and in front of me, forever looming.

I had to tell it *No!* I wasn't going to die. I could survive. I could fight to live. I had something to fight for, after all: more moments like these.

We smoked cigars on the mountain top, sitting our backs against a massive ruby, with more giant rubies and emeralds dotting the landscape. Wind hummed as it hit them, playing songs of ruby, emerald, and topaz.

"I've been wondering," I said. "If this dream continues when I'm not here, then who's dreaming it?"

Zauri seemed to be enjoying her cigar, unlike last time. Her puffs, while not as deep as mine, made a satisfying sizzle. "Maybe it's not continuing." She tapped her chin. "Maybe it's the black box making me think that, feeding me false memories and sensations."

I regretted asking the question. That sounded so sad. False memories? How could you be sure of yourself if you didn't know what you'd actually experienced? If your personality, habits, and feelings were just the product of some mysterious unknown? Although, I could be describing myself, too.

Zauri seemed as disturbed by the thought as me; she breathed out cardamom-scented smoke with a tense sigh.

"You're real to me, Zauri." I decided to say what I felt in the moment. Finally. "If you're ever unsure of yourself, I'll be your anchor."

Her eyes lit up. "And I'll be yours."

Hearing that warmed every part of me, as if I were basking in the glow of a soothing, wood-fed fire. "I wish I could never wake up. I wish I never had to leave you. Imagine if we could, somehow, enter a layer two or layer three dream. It would multiply the time I could remain here." I did the math on my fingers, using the creases of my right hand. "Three hours in the real world is three days here, that's seventy-two hours, that would be seventy-two days in a layer two dream. In a layer three dream… uhh…" That was beyond my finger counting skills.

"Over four and a half years." Zauri smiled as she snuffed her cigar out on the ground. She *snapped* a new one into her fingers. "And a layer four dream would be a hundred and thirteen years."

That was the most hopeful, beautiful, and wondrous thing I'd ever heard. "So what would it take for us to enter a layer two dream?"

"As happy as that would make me, it's just not possible. This dream stone doesn't have a second layer."

"So many things we thought weren't possible have been happening. Maybe there's a way. If there's even a sliver of hope of entering deeper dreams, we should try."

She shook her head. "There isn't, though. It's one thing for new scripts to emerge from a black box, it's another thing for your dream stone to change physically and somehow, magically, gain another stable layer of depth."

I grunted in frustration. "I won't let myself die, then. I'll get to safety. I'll come back to you. I promise."

Seeing her hopeful smile, I almost regretted those words. If I couldn't stay true to them, she'd be alone forever, waiting endlessly. Even her memory of me would wither with time.

"Jyosh." Zauri took my hand between hers. So warm. "If you can't find another levship, then look for the train tracks. There's definitely a rail line connecting Maniza with its neighbor to the east, Demak."

"How would I find this railway, though? I've never heard of it."

"How were completed parts from camp transferred elsewhere?"

"By levship. It would come several times a week and land at the outskirts. I don't know of any rail. Don't even know which direction to go."

She squeezed my hand. "Ask someone, then. Do whatever you have to do to come back to me. You have skills, now. Survive, Jyosh."

My vision cracked like a glass pane being hit by a hammer. Zauri hugged me, then pushed her lips onto mine; I held and kissed her as she shattered into a billion pieces.

I awoke, and the bitterness of our sudden separation stung like a severed limb.

As I wiped sweat from my forehead and gazed at unfamiliar, metal walls, an utterly horrifying realization pounded in my heart: this wasn't where I'd gone to sleep.

Chapter Eight

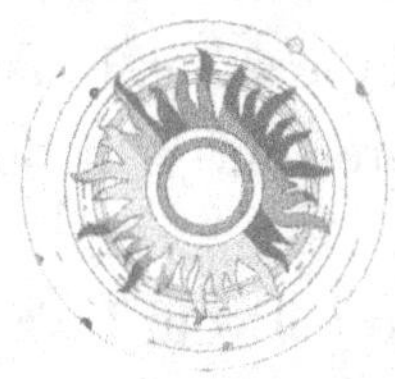

Four metal walls surrounded me. Some kind of script squiggled its way across the walls — a free-flowing, vine-like calligraphy. The letters pulsed a somber green, the color of machines.

I looked down. A blurry, brown reflection stared back from the polished metal floor.

I looked up. A frosty light shone from the ceiling. I couldn't tell its source. I felt caged. Studied. The sensation that someone, or something, was watching me jittered every bone.

I stood and searched my pockets: empty. No machinist stone. Whoever had moved me had taken it.

But why hadn't I woken up when I was being moved?

"I didn't want us to meet this way," said an airy female voice from somewhere. "But I can't chance that you might die."

I darted my head in every direction. Only the four metal walls and weird calligraphy stared back at me.

"Time is circling the drain. So I need you to listen. Just forget everything you think you know, and listen."

Perhaps the voice was being projected from outside the room.

"Who are you?" I said. "Where've you taken me?"

"Just listen, Jyosh, because I can't answer your questions. Not now. It would only confuse you more, and I don't have time to make you understand."

"So? Why did you kidnap me?"

"I didn't. Listen, your best hope is to get to Demak. They're letting refugees in, for now. There's a train leaving from a nearby station in a few hours. You need to get on it."

Weird. Zauri had said the same. In fact, we'd literally just had this conversation. "Who are you? Why do you care?"

Silence for a moment.

"Believe me, I want to tell you. I want to tell you everything. But even if I did, if somehow you were to die, what would it matter? Just head northeast outside the city, toward the mountains, and you'll get to the station."

The voice was definitely coming from inside the room. I walked around, stretching my arms and grasping at the air. "You're here somewhere, aren't you?"

I paced from one corner to another.

"Will you listen to what I'm saying?"

"I already know about the railway. Tell me something new."

"Okay, sure. There are many possible dangers you could face, but most dire among them are the people with yellow irises. If you see them, steer clear. They're the worst thing that could happen to you and this country."

"Yellow irises? What are they, cats?"

There, in the other corner: a flickering distortion shone in the shape of a human, as if the air over it cycled all wrong. The outline of her tall and thin body vivified. The distorted air glowed faintly.

"Found me. Now, wake up."

. . .

I AWOKE. Let out a gust of relief at seeing all the clothes strewn about; I was in the old woman's apartment, where I'd gone to sleep. Soon as I sat up, my back ached, probably from the softness of the mattress. Wasn't used to that.

What the hell had I dreamt, though? Was someone talking to me through a dream? How was that even possible?

I didn't know what was and wasn't possible, to be honest. Out in the wider world, all kinds of technology existed that we didn't have in Maniza. But why send *me* a message through a dream? Suspicious, too, that the invisible woman had given me the same advice that Zauri had mere minutes before.

Advice I had to follow, especially now that it was backed by two sources, even if I knew nothing about the second source. I wasn't exactly overflowing with solid leads.

After changing out my dream stone for my machinist stone, I got up and found the frying pan conveniently sitting on the stove. I bent down and stared at the bottom compartment of the stove, which housed the gain crystal. Four screws kept it in place, so I'd need a screwdriver.

After five minutes of throwing clothes and boxes and rummaging through chests and sacks, I came to a frustrating conclusion: there wasn't a screwdriver here.

I stuck my fingers into the creases of the bottom compartment's door, inhaled big, and pulled with all my force. I grunted and shouted, straining every muscle.

In the end, I was a weakling who'd done little physical labor, aside from carrying machine parts. I huffed and gave up. I couldn't rely on these frail arms for much.

I needed to know what I could rely on to survive. There wasn't enough time to become muscular, but in my dreams, I could learn to be quick and skilled. I could develop those muscle memories.

Staring at my now reddened hands, I realized I was a slightly different person than the man who'd gone to sleep four hours ago. In four days of dream time, I'd learned how to use an electric weapon. I'd gotten damn good with it. Now the only problem was crafting one with the available parts.

I needed a way to protect myself, and as I was now a disciple of the school of the electrified frying pan, I had to get that gain crystal out of the stove somehow.

I kicked the bottom compartment, then regretted it immediately and rubbed my throbbing toe.

Surely something could fit in the screw grooves other than a screwdriver. I studied the mess I'd made in the room. A sachet of rice lay on the ground between a plastic bucket and a colander. My stomach growled.

It wasn't going to cook itself.

I opened a cupboard and found a glass bottle with water in it. Popped off the cap and sniffed; it smelled all right, I suppose. I'd watched Abba cook rice a few times, so it couldn't be that hard.

I settled the frying pan on the stove and poured in the rice and water. I put my hand on the stove's conduction handle, then inhaled green from the sun gazing through the window. After a few minutes of steadily pushing light into the stove's gain medium, the frying pan sizzled. Oddly enough, this was more uncomfortable than operating the fabricator; I was way too close to the heat, and smoke and sweat got in my eyes. What if I dripped sweat into the pan? Gross.

Eventually, things started to pop, and the rice cooked. Once it softened and darkened, I considered it done, and let things cool for a few minutes.

Then I dug my hands in and ate.

Despite being flavorless and crunchy, it was the best thing I'd eaten in years in the real world. Given that it might be the only thing I'd eat for a while, I didn't leave a single granule.

I had to start thinking like a survivor. Perhaps it would be best to ransack the empty apartments for dried food and carry it with me, along with other useful supplies.

Maybe I could find a screwdriver somewhere, too.

I went into the hallway and knocked on the neighbor's thin, wooden door.

No answer. If they weren't there, they wouldn't need their stuff, right? They'd probably got onboard that levship. Or fled on foot to escape the coming battle. Anyway, I wound my leg to kick the door.

Thwap! The door burst open and dangled off its bottom hinge at an angle. The top hinge clattered to the floor. Manizan construction at its finest. I squeezed through the gap.

A mess of clothes and trinkets and toys covered the floor. The family had obviously hurried out, leaving more than they took. Dust swirled in the beam of red sunshine coming from the open window. A breeze wafted in, cooling my face.

I scratched my head. Tiresome, to dig through this mess. Where would they keep their tools?

Rust covered the stove in the corner. I knelt and felt up the bottom compartment: it jiggled on its loose screws. I loosened the screws more with my fingers — kind of painful to do — then pulled the panel off.

A dull green crystal stared at me. The edges were a bit burnt; it was obviously old and had been overflowed a few times. It also had a magnetic strip on one edge. I unwrapped the wires around it and pulled it out of the magnetic clamp.

I brought it up to the light and examined the inner lines. This crystal was three or four years old, judging by the blackened streaks within. Gain mediums used in large appliances typically had a lifetime of five years, so I hoped it would work.

I put it in my pocket. Then I pulled on the wires in the compartment until they snapped free. There was still much to do. Like this family, I had to leave my baggage behind and focus on surviving. Focus on getting out of Maniza so I could dream somewhere safe.

I went back to the old woman's apartment, where the rice-smelling pan waited. I nestled the gain medium crystal where the handle met the pan — the magnetic strip adhered it to the pan's metal surface. Using the wires, I tied it nice and tight.

A crude invention. I'd be able to conduct light from my hand into the handle, which the gain medium would then convert into electricity, which would then flow into the pan itself.

Before trying it, I tightened the wire more. Then I picked up a shirt off the floor and ripped off some cloth. Tied it around the gain medium crystal for extra support. What a laughable disaster it would be if the gain medium fell out while I was fighting.

I clutched the handle, inhaled green light from the sun, and electrified the pan.

It heated up. Jolts of blue and yellow flickered where the rice had once been.

I'd done it. I'd crafted an electric weapon. And it filled me with something unfamiliar: a soothing surge of self-belief. I could do amazing things, so long as someone taught me how. Even though she wasn't here, Zauri and I made quite a team.

Next, I rummaged through the two apartments, gathering all the uncooked rice and lentils I could find. I poured all the water I found into the bottle I'd used earlier. I gathered some children's clothes, too, to use as wrappings if ever I got injured. Finally, I found a rough brown sack to put it all in, one I could strap to both my shoulders.

It was time to go. Time to go northeast, find this railway, and head to Demak, where I could hopefully begin a new life.

A HUFFING, soot-faced man pulled a cart down the eastern road. Three children sat inside, sprawled over each other, drooling in sleep. In Harska, we had autocarts; a machinist could sit in the carriage and move the wheels forward with conduction. Much easier. But I doubted they'd fare well on this pockmarked dirt. The Paranis hadn't love enough to maintain their own flatlands, it seemed. I watched my step, careful to avoid potholes filled with stagnant water, as I trudged through.

Fleeing families crowded the whole road east. I kept my pace up, passing so many, my frying pan's handle sticking out of the sack on my back.

Everyone seemed tired, teary, terrified. Living in the Manizan flatlands meant a hard life, but there'd never been a war here in memory. Until now. Personally, I was fine with it — so far. For the first time in twelve years, I could decide where I wanted to go and what I wanted to do. But for families forced to flee homes they'd lived in for generations, nothing good had come of the Karshan invasion.

Dead farms covered the landscape beside the road: lanes and lanes of weeds mixed with stagnant water. A barren brown mess. A few weeks ago, a shopkeeper under the bridge who sold lice disinfectant — each bottle about a week's salary — told me that the government had ordered most farmers to work in the factories. Now food was running out and the land had parched over.

He neglected to mention how much it stank of mud and moss.

The landscape never changed. The number of people on the road never ended. I asked a few where they were going; they all said, "to the border." No mention of the railway that Zauri and some invisible mystery woman in my dream had told me to seek.

Finally, the tracks came into view. They cut through the road at a tight angle. Now I had to follow them so that I'd reach the train station, where refugees were supposedly being loaded for the border.

I was the only one who turned to follow the tracks. Perhaps

everyone else was taking a different route or walking directly to the border. My journey was about to get lonelier, it seemed.

An intrusive thought made me shudder: this was also the direction of Harska. Harska floated in the northeast corner of the country, above a mountain range that stretched across the eastern edge and into Demak. But it was so high up, it didn't matter. A speck in the sky, if even I got to see it.

I walked along the tracks. The farther I walked, the more alone I got. The more alone I got, the more my nerves tingled with angst. I'd never been so alone in a vastness as this, surrounded by the ruddy sky, dead farms, and the distant, looming mountains.

Was this what it meant to be free? No one to tell me what to do. All I smelled was my increasingly sweaty body and the stinking bogs. This was a world of me. Perhaps Zauri felt the same, at this moment, alone in the dream.

A sense of dread boiled in my stomach. I didn't know what to expect, anymore. For the past twelve years, each day had been the same, as if I were stuck in time. Now, time had started moving again, and I ventured into a total unknown. Hope that I could reach the border and find a place to safely dream pushed me onward.

Excitement, fear, relief, hope, dread — I wasn't certain what to feel, but felt them all.

And then a twig crunched behind me. I swiveled around. A darkly garbed figure stood on the track.

A cloaked person. Walking toward me.

Following me. I gripped the handle of my pan and pulled it out of the sack, slowly.

The cloaked person held something that glinted in the red sunlight. Teeth-like ridges shone across it. A machete.

Why was someone with a machete following me?

I held my frying pan out front and shouted, "Who are you?"

The man held out his machete. That cloak totally shadowed his face. His height and build matched mine. He raised up the machete to chest height.

"Don't come any closer." I raised my frying pan to my chest, too. "It might not look it, but this is a deadly weapon. It's got a gain medium. It'll send so many jolts through your heart, you'll burn out and fall dead." Though I embellished, I hoped he'd believe it.

He remained still, like a statue on the train tracks.

Life or death stuck in my throat. This wasn't a dream anymore. No one was going to heal me if he cut off a part of my shoulder. No one could soothe away the pain, the way Zauri had.

The machete-wielding man dashed off his feet. He was on me faster than I realized, so I ducked under his first swipe. He lunged at my torso; I backstepped, the edge of his steel grazing my shirt.

I pooled green light in my hand and jabbed at his neck, electrifying the pan just before impact. But he swerved out of the way, then sidestepped to my right.

The man leapt in the air, raised his machete above his head, and came down on me.

I held my pan aloft, where his machete came down. I pushed green sunshine into the handle, through the gain medium, and into the center of the pan. It electrified just before his machete *clanged* against it.

Blue sparks flew off the pan and onto my hand. The heat scalded; I dropped the pan and backstepped, howling. I'd electrified it a split second too soon. The one time it actually mattered, I'd messed it up. Too many nerves.

The man lunged his machete toward my belly, intent to kill obvious.

I ducked, rolled on the painful iron of the track, and grabbed the pan. The man impaled the air above my hair and stepped past me. He took another step forward, then spun around to face me again as I settled on one knee and struggled to regain my balance.

I had to get right the Lightning Parry I'd practiced in the dream. But with my life on the line, it seemed a hundred times harder to execute. If I failed, Zauri would cry out for me. And she'd be all alone. I had to keep my promise to see her again. I was fighting not just for myself, but for her. For us.

The cloaked man sidestepped toward my left. He swapped his machete into his other hand and stabbed at my chest. I barely managed to block with the pan's edge, then thrust forward to headbutt him. He shuffled sideways and dodged, then wound his machete for a diagonal swipe at my neck.

I raised my pan to my neck as his machete came down. I directed the center of the pan into his machete, pooled green light in my hand, and surged it into the handle. *Clang.* Lightning bolts jumped off the pan and onto his weapon, engulfing his arm.

The gain medium in the pan exploded. Crystal shards flew in all directions. One sliced into my cheek, scalding it. The frying pan inflamed. I tossed it, but not before burns seared my hand. I yelped in agony.

The man had absorbed most of the jolt. He convulsed, dropped his machete with a *clatter*, and fell on his side in the middle of the train track.

Brownish foam seeped from his mouth.

I clutched my heart. Breathed deep to calm the hard beating. Panic rattled my bones. What if there were more after me? What if the man got up? What if… what if…

Could hardly think with my hand and cheek screaming in pain.

I pulled out my water bottle and a small undershirt from my sack. Doused the undershirt with water. Using my burnt hand, I pressed it to my burnt cheek, so both would cool.

The lukewarm water barely eased the pain. Wished I had ice. Wished I could walk to a healer, like we had in Harska. Instead, I'd have to tough it out.

What the hell had just happened? Had I just defended myself, for the first time? And using a frying pan, too?

Why was someone trying to kill me, anyway?

After five minutes of sitting with my thoughts in a shocked daze, I decided it was time to act. Numbness had seeped into my hand and cheek, which relieved some of the pain.

I crouched over the man, wary that he could awaken and attack. But he seemed so still, foam leaking. That Lightning Parry had zapped him good.

I tugged at his cloak and pulled down the head cover.

Those wild, gray nose hairs: Rahal lay before me.

Rahal.

I stumbled back and gasped. By Panja's third nipple… why would Rahal attack me? Why was he following me in the first place?

Could it be something to do with his corrupted dream stone? His dream companion's black box? What if his black box made him want to kill people? Or kill me, in particular?

But why? How long was he even following me for? I probably hadn't noticed because, until now, I'd been traveling in a sea of people. Why didn't he try to mince me when I was asleep, though?

So many questions cycled through my head.

Foremost of all: what to do with Rahal? Slow breaths lifted his chest. I could grab the machete and slit his throat with it. That was the safest option. Or I could leave him on the tracks; maybe a train would run him over?

But if a black box had brainwashed him to kill, then it wasn't his fault. He didn't deserve to die.

I wanted no more innocent blood on my hands.

I gripped his arms, let out a pained grunt, and pulled his body off the train track and into the dirt. What to do with him, now? Just leave him in the middle of nowhere? Obviously, I hadn't the strength to carry him.

Should I try to wake him up? Of course not, he'd just done his best to murder me.

Leave him and move on seemed the best option. I glared at his machete. Could come in handy. I picked it up, stuck it in my sack, and continued onward.

Chapter Nine

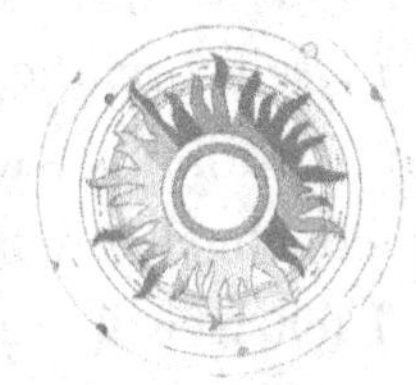

I WALKED ALONG THE TRACK FOR A FEW HOURS. I'D USED SO much water to treat my cuts and burns that it was running low. Fighting left me thirsty, so I chugged mouthfuls, too.

I'd never seen a train station before, but I knew when I found it. A lot of people were here, and so was a train, and there was a raised platform that allowed folks to board the train. Was this train heading for Demak?

A tent city had sprouted around the station. Blocks of cream-colored tents, each big enough to house a small family, stretched across the dirt plain. Tired folks lined up all over the place, getting handouts of food in silvery packages.

That blue shield with a golden dragon adorned many of the tents. So people from that country I'd never heard of — Behesh, I think it was called — were helping out here, too. Why?

Karsha had only just invaded yesterday, and yet these helpers from Behesh arrived at the same time. That meant they must've known about the invasion in advance. I wasn't certain what that implied, but it left me uneasy about accepting their generosity.

I wasn't interested in staying in some tent city, anyway. I wanted out of Maniza, so I headed for the train platform.

The crowd had no structure: just throngs of folks zigzagging around the platform, all facing the train. The train itself was this rusted, hollow series of cars. I wondered how many conductors in a wired circuit were needed to move it. I guessed one pilot to direct the motion, as well as four or five conductors just inhaling green light. Maybe if I got on board, I could find out.

First, I needed to let myself breathe, so I sat on a stairstep that led up to the platform. I took my sack off my back, cradled it, and rested my unburned cheek on it. I could probably fall asleep here, just like this. I felt weirdly safe with all these people around me, despite the levships crowding the overhead sky. If we were going to die, we'd at least die together.

I looked toward the northeastern mountains. They were close enough to reach out and touch, and the breeze blowing down from the peaks caressed my burnt cheek. The train tracks went into one of the valleys. According to both Zauri and the invisible woman, that was indeed the way to Demak. But would the border really be open for refugees like us?

A thin, balding man with a slight smile sat above me. His shirt was missing three buttons and on too loose. I asked him, "What's going on with the train?"

"Train stopped because the border just closed."

"Closed? Damn. Already?"

He let out a pained sigh and nodded. "Heard someone saying they'll open it again tomorrow. But they won't let anyone in without an identity crystal."

I winced at that. I'd had an identity crystal in Harska, but not anymore.

I shimmied closer to him and whispered, "Know where I can get one?"

He whispered back, "There's a guy around here who has

some, but he's not accepting emirils. A wheelbarrow of emirils can't even buy a bowl of rice, anymore. You got anything to barter?"

I had my burnt frying pan, a machete, some dried rice, and my dream stone. "I'm as poor as it comes."

"Same here. We're out of luck, it seems. Traveled all this way for nothing." He gestured his head toward the tent city. "Looks like those guys are our best hope."

"Yeah? Why are they helping us, anyway?"

"Something to do with their dawn god." He shrugged. "What does the reason matter? Don't spit in a gift horse's mouth, I say."

"You sure that's how the saying goes?"

What to do? If I couldn't get on the train, why had I come all this way? Always, I seemed to be lacking something: luck enough to draw an eight, or enough depravity to steal an old woman's ticket. Getting an identity crystal good enough to endure border scrutiny seemed an even steeper ask.

I could steal one. But like with the old woman's ticket, I'd be depriving someone of their rightful chance to get out. Was I going to become that kind of person, now that I was free? Wasn't finally getting out of the camp a clean slate?

But if I didn't become that kind of person, perhaps I wouldn't be a person at all. I'd be a corpse.

Five levships in a side-by-side formation descended from the western sky and floated just above, close enough that they cast their shadows over us. Because of the sun's angle, those shadows stretched endlessly eastward. They flew over our heads, the sound of them tearing through the sky filling my ears, and landed somewhere nearby. The only detail I could make out were two yellow stars painted on one side, staring at us like a pair of dead eyes.

I shuddered from the cold gust they brought.

My throat itched from dryness. I got up and approached the first line of cream-colored tents. Just in front, a group of middle-aged men and women with the blue-shield seal on their chests argued next to a green cylinder, their hands waving in front of their faces. The cylinder sported a big handle and an even bigger faucet sticking out of opposite sides.

"Someone's going to have to go down there," one of the men said.

"Won't be me," responded one of the women.

"I swear, I replaced the gain medium yesterday," another said.

"Well, then you go down and check. Obviously you messed it up somehow."

"I'll have to disassemble the whole system! And I don't know how to reassemble it."

One of the women walked up to it. Scowling, she grabbed the handle that stuck out of the side of the cylinder. She closed her eyes and inhaled sunlight. But nothing flowed from the faucet on the opposite side of the cylinder.

"We really don't have an engineer on site?" she asked.

"The engineers are making the rounds through the other camps. One isn't scheduled to arrive for a few days."

A long line of refugees was forming, each clutching a glass bottle. No point joining the line if the water pump wasn't working.

"Pump's broken," one of the men with a blue-shield seal said to everyone. "Come back in a few hours. Or perhaps tomorrow."

Tomorrow? A long time to go without water. While the other refugees scattered with disappointed sighs, I stepped toward the pump. I gripped the handle, inhaled a bit of sunshine, and closed my eyes.

In my mind's eye, I traced from the handle, down the cylinder, and into the metal pipe, all the way to the gain medium, which was housed in some mechanism that sucked in water, about twenty feet below. The more I quieted my senses and mind, the more I could feel each part of the system as if it were a limb.

The gain medium shimmered. Fresh. I caressed the lines on the crystal with my mind, appreciating its clarity and uniformity — something I hardly got to enjoy with the low-quality gain-medium crystals I delt with daily in the factory.

I inhaled more green light, cycled it through me, and pushed it down toward the gain medium. Only a small portion of my light reached; the rest dissipated into the dirt somewhere below.

Ah, so something was blocking the connection. I traced my mind's eye up and down the pipe and found what it was: a large stone jutting into the pipe about midway, pinching part of the copper wire that had come loose from its attachment to the pipe.

"Hey, didn't you hear? Pump doesn't work," someone said, snapping me from my work.

I ignored him and continued. I inhaled more green light, then surged it downward into the gain medium. Again, only a small amount reached, but once the gain medium had transformed it into electricity, I willed the current up into the part of the pipe the stone was jutting into.

It heated up. It became scalding. I could even feel the simmering in my mind, and it brought sweat to my forehead. The heat caused the moisture in the dirt to turn to steam, and the steam pushed the stone away, just barely enough to clear it from the copper wire.

I opened my eyes as water spurted, then gushed out of the big faucet.

Everyone stared my way. Refugees approached and applauded while I hastily took out my water bottle and filled it from the flow.

I wasn't seeking fame, especially amid a crowd that could include former prisoners — or perhaps wardens — from the camp I'd just escaped. Though I couldn't help but grin; for a change, it was nice to use my skills for good. I slinked away once my bottle was full and returned to where I was sitting earlier, at the steps leading up into the train platform.

I simply sat and rested my bones, watching my fellow refugees and these helpful foreigners go about their tasks. There was much to ponder, but I was as weary in mind as in body, so preferred to remain distant from my thoughts.

An hour later, a new group arrived at the station. I looked up to see a mass of men and women covered in skintight, all-black uniforms. They wore cloth masks over their heads, only their glossy purple eyes showing. Their boots were the blackest leather I'd ever seen. Sword hilts hung off their belts in holsters alongside utility pockets.

I was sure of one thing: they weren't Manizan. Manizan uniforms were forest green. I'd never seen a Manizan with purple irises, either.

"Who are they?" I asked the balding man, who was still sitting behind me

"You don't know that by now? They're the enemy."

"The Karshan military?"

"Look at them. Ever seen anything so strange?"

About fifty of them marched down the road. Manizan refugees rushed out of the way, giving them a wide berth. I hoped they weren't coming to kill us. That'd be sort of unnecessary, though, as we weren't doing anything to resist them.

Weirdly enough, a second group of Karshan soldiers marched up the road toward them. They numbered around fifty, as well. But their eyes weren't purple; they were bright yellow.

The two groups met in the middle. I couldn't quite make out what the soldiers were saying, but it involved shouting. At each other.

I remembered what the invisible woman in the metal room had said: *There are many possible dangers you could face, but worst among them are the people with yellow irises. If you see them, steer clear. They're the worst thing that could happen to you and this country.*

The two groups separated and spread around the area. Then a soldier emerged from each group and stood in the middle of the road.

What was so particularly dangerous about these yellow-eyed soldiers? I hated fearing something I knew nothing about. I hated how vague that strange, invisible woman had been.

The Manizan refugees around me scattered. I remained sitting for a moment, unsure where to scatter to, as the hundred or so Karshan soldiers now covered a wide area around us. Some even walked up onto the train platform. Despite this, they were completely uninterested in us, focused on each other instead.

If I was going to wait at this train station with the yellow-eyed soldiers, I ought to find out what I could. And since they didn't seem to care about our presence, I got up and hurried closer. I knelt beneath a thorny bush, within earshot of the two men who seemed to be leading the two groups.

"General Sylet gave us the order to secure this rail station and all land around the ancient city," the purple-eyed one said. "He outranks your colonel."

The yellow-eyed one spat on the ground. "There's your *rank*. And rest assured, the Empress-Raja herself will promote Colonel Rao to Field Marshal once this operation is over. He's trained within thousand-year dreams to get that strong. Can cut you all in half with a *look*. Even the daevas will bow before him. Think carefully about the enemies you make today, comrade."

"Such desperate bombast! And to go from a mere colonel to the highest rank of all? I suggest you tell Rao to get his head checked. He may have planned this whole operation, but that doesn't give him the authority to supersede a general."

"Authority comes from power, not titles. I assure you, we have the men and arms to claim whatever land we want. The ancient city is ours. Now, I suggest you turn around and march away, else I'll have to call for backup."

The purple-eyed one pointed at the sky. "That's *my* backup. You may have men and arms, but you don't have the skies. I've nothing to fear from you. My orders are my orders."

"I've got orders, too. But unlike you, I'm willing to fulfill them on pain of death. Yours or mine."

"Is Rao such a weasel? General Sylet said to avoid dealing death to a fellow Karshan. He said nothing about a constructive beating, however…" The purple-eyed one uppercut the yellow-eyed one in the chin. He spewed blood as he flew in the air and landed on his back.

And now, chaos. With grunts and war cries, the two groups collided into each other. Kicks and punches and elbows flew. Dust and dirt tinted the air.

The fighting soldiers spread farther across the road, into the dirt, and into the area where refugees loitered. Blood from noses and mouths spewed everywhere.

I stayed under my bush, frozen in fear, hoping I wouldn't get caught up in whatever the hell this was.

The main mass of a hundred brawling soldiers, all clad in black, moved steadily toward the plain in front of the station. The remaining train-awaiting Manizan families in their raggedy, motheaten clothes got up and rushed out of the way. An old man who'd been sitting in the mud by himself took an age to get to his feet. Soon as he did, he collided with a soldier who was trying to knee another soldier in the groin. That soldier elbowed the old man in the nose, blood jetting, and he fell.

He wasn't moving anymore.

I stood and watched as two soldiers trying to grapple each other trampled over him.

"Come on, Grandpa. Get up," I whispered, hoping my words were magic. "Just pull yourself up."

But the old man remained motionless on the ground. That elbow couldn't have killed him, though. He must've been knocked out. And yet, no one was helping, as if he were another patch of dirt to be trampled upon.

Everyone simply ignored him. The other refugees had their own worries, of course.

As did I. "Get up, Grandpa!"

It wasn't anyone's problem. The Karshan soldiers were too busy jabbing, kneeing, kicking, and grappling each other to care for some fallen old man. No Manizan refugee was dumb enough to get in the middle of the fight to save him. The old man had to help himself.

"Get up!"

Another pair of soldiers trampled over his back with their hard leather boots. Blood shot from his mouth. By now, the soldiers were embroiled in such a frantic tussle that I doubted they had a sense of what they were stepping on.

How many bootsteps could the old man's frail body take?

"It's not my problem," I whispered to myself. I didn't know him. I'd never even spoken to him. I hadn't even properly seen his face. He could be a murderer, for all I knew. Yeah, he was probably a murderer. There had to be some justice in this world.

But that was obviously goatshit. I'd murdered Vir, and yet I remained standing. I was the one who should be getting trampled.

If I could help the old man, maybe that would balance my sins. But to do that, I'd have to step into the brawl. I'd be jeopardizing what mattered: my survival. Like Zauri had said, I had to focus on that.

But I'd been trying to survive for the past twelve years. Trying to survive was why I'd killed Vir. Focusing only on survival eventually makes you evil. And now, if I was willing to ignore some-one's suffering, I wasn't so far away from causing that suffering. I couldn't be that person. Not anymore.

Another soldier trampled on the old man. A brown liquid gushed from his mouth onto the caked ground. Bile mixed with blood.

I pulled out my frying pan and stood. I stepped amid the brawling soldiers. A group of two soldiers, each with bulging lumps in their foreheads, chased a screaming soldier just in front of me. I waited till they passed, then continued forward to where another soldier was kicking the shit out of a soldier on the ground.

I just needed to pull the old man up, get him over my shoulders, and carry him out. Up, over, and out.

"Up, over, and out," I whispered to my trembling self. I hoped no one would turn their ire upon me. "Up, over, and out."

And if anyone got in my way, I could hit them with the pan. It wouldn't electrify since the gain medium had exploded, but it was still a firm piece of metal. I held it in front of me like a shield as I stepped toward the old man.

A soldier in my blind spot collided into me, almost sending me to the ground. She turned and wound her arm. I held up the frying pan over my face. Her punch slammed into it, then the pan slammed into my face.

I saw stars. I was such an idiot.

I fell on my knees. The soldier, it seemed, was now fighting someone else. I could hardly see her amid the blurriness.

All around me, blurry black forms coalesced and separated.

After a minute on my knees, my vision cleared. I should never again put the frying pan in front of my face. I stood. The old man was still on the ground, but there weren't any soldiers around him, anymore.

"Up, over, and out," I slurred.

Something black flickered in my blind spot. I turned just in time as a soldier lunged at me. I smashed him across the head with the frying pan, then dodged out of the way. He landed in the dirt, clutching his ear and groaning.

"That guy has a weapon!" someone shouted. "Code Forty-Two! Code Forty-Two!"

Surely, they weren't talking about me. My frying pan wasn't even electrified.

I trudged forward. The old man was a step away. His mouth leaked bile.

I dropped my frying pan and reached to pick him up. But when I tried, I only felt air.

I tried again. Only air.

I wriggled my fingers. I couldn't see them. I brought my arm up to my face: I didn't have a hand. In its place was a mess of cauterized flesh.

There was a hand on the ground next to the frying pan. That couldn't be my hand…

I darted my head around. At my left stood a soldier with a fiery lightblade. Something cracked against my skull. My head did a cartwheel, and my vision turned upside down. It spun and spun and became distant. I fell into an abyss inside of me.

Chapter Ten

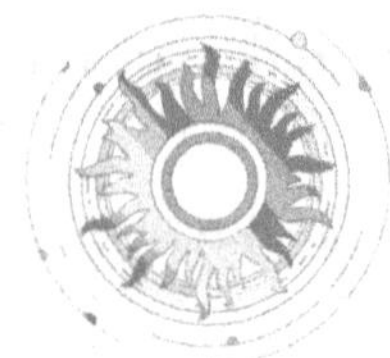

Black, everywhere.

"Relax," a soothing voice said. It reminded me of Chaya, my sister. "If ever you're in too much pain, just say so."

I willed my eyelids to lift. A blinding white light engulfed my sight. A painful heat sizzled inside me. My right arm boiled in lava.

"It hurts," I mouthed, unsure if I'd made a sound. "Oh god, it hurts."

"I'll soothe it," the voice said. Definitely not Chaya — breezier, with a honeyed lilt.

"Please, do something! Make it stop!"

The pain shot from my arm into my chest, then cut down across my belly, as if I were being sawed through. I screamed in silence, too short of breath to create sound. At the same time, lava flowed through my veins — it was screaming louder than I ever could.

The woman firmed her hand on my nape. It tingled like cold gel.

A wind blew. It brought violet light with it, and together they froze my pain. It came from her hand; I could feel her soul's frequency amid it: blue, breezy, and bright.

"Better?" the woman asked.

"So much better."

I opened my eyes. White light poured into my eyeballs. I blinked and blinked until I could see. I looked down at my own naked skin. And then I glanced at my dangling right arm. It had no hand.

Now I screamed with sound.

"It's all right," the woman behind me said. "You're in shock, but everything's going to be all right. Dawn will come."

I remembered. That soldier had severed my hand with a lightblade!

"You'll be fine," the woman said. I could only see her shadow.

"My hand…"

"Don't fret over your hand. That's why I'm here."

Her violet light poured into me. My stump tingled in a numbing sea. Another feeling hid behind it: wriggling fingers. I didn't have fingers, though.

"Who are you?"

"I'm a healer. Try to relax. You're in good hands. Umm… no pun intended." She giggled melodically. "By the way, that was really brave of you."

"Huh?"

"The way you tried to help that old man. No one risked themselves for him, except you. Even I told myself it wasn't my problem, that I had other responsibilities. I suppose everyone who felt any kind of tug in their heart at the image of that old man being trampled said the same to themselves."

"Is he — did he—"

"He died. That doesn't change what you did, though."

I'd failed. I wasn't strong enough to help myself, let alone him.

I tried to turn my neck to see the woman's face, but it boiled with pain.

"Try not to move," she said.

"Why are you helping me?"

"I help everyone I can. That's our way. But… to be honest, sometimes I do have to pick and choose. After I saw how you tried to save that man, I couldn't just let you lie there and bleed out."

I didn't save him, though. You don't deserve to be rewarded for good intentions.

But she was a healer, so it made sense. We had such things in the floating city back when I was a kid. In the camp, if you got sick, you toughed it out or died. A healer might as well have been an angel.

She must've been one of those Behesh people.

The violet light she conducted into me numbed the pain, but also caused flitting sensations across my body. My limbs floated away on a cloud, and these clouds were separated by miles.

The woman's sigh had a tinge of regret. "I haven't even introduced myself or asked your name." Her light massaged my muscles. "I'm Saina, and I come from Behesh. I'm here with a healing mission."

I'd never met anyone with that name. I found it rather pretty. "What's a 'healing mission?'"

"Isn't it obvious? We travel to war zones and help the injured."

So then this was just something they did. Were they mad? Why would you seek out war to help people you'd never met?

Maybe she was lying. Maybe she was using my body for an experiment. I'd heard that when someone in the camp died, they sell the body for use in conduction experiments. They test experimental stones to see how much light flow a body can handle before the organs burn out. It's always better if the body is fresh, so sometimes they kidnap workers and do experiments while they're alive. Could that be her true mission? Was she lulling me into a trap with her melodious voice and soothing light?

"You've gone tense and cold," she said. "I can taste your panic. It's making your frequency vibrate all jaggedly. I know it's hard, but for the sake of your healing, try to relax. Think happy thoughts."

"I want to see your face." I knew liars. The camp was full of them. I knew how to read their deceiving eyes, their hidden smirks, because I'd seen that look in the mirror too often. A twitching nose, especially, damns a liar. "Please."

"Well, if it helps calm you down."

She kept her hand on my nape and swiveled to my front. First thing I noticed was the mole above her lip. Her skin was sand brown, a shade lighter than mine. Full cheeks, wavy brown hair, and eyes like roasted almonds. She didn't smile and just stared into me, as if searching for something.

She was the first attractive woman I'd seen in twelve years that wasn't in my dreams.

"What's your name?" she asked.

"J-Jyosh."

"Ah, nice name. It means *light* in the tongue of the Ancients, doesn't it?"

"I'm afraid I don't know anything about the Ancients or their tongue."

Her gaze softened into pity. "It doesn't matter. What matters is you're safe now, Jyosh. No one's going to hurt you." Her nose didn't twitch. Her brown eyes stayed bright. No smirk.

Nothing hid beneath her kindness. She really seemed to be an angel. But the thought *it's just too good to be true* still nagged me.

"How much is this *safety* going to cost me?"

She giggled. It sounded like the sweet pluck of a sitar. "It's free."

I let out a *hah*. "This is Maniza. Every evil act is rewarded, and no good deed goes unpunished. And most of all, no one gets anything for free. There's no way I could be so lucky."

"My grandmother used to say that it's best to store your luck for dismal days. Perhaps that's what you were doing, all this time."

"Where are we, anyway? How long was I unconscious? What's going on with the war?"

She swiveled back behind me. "Jyosh, you really need to relax. There're eight hundred questions you could ask me. It won't do you or your hand any good."

Her violet light seeped upward, now, into my brain. It caressed my thoughts, softened the edges of my worries. They melted into the same cloud that carried away my limbs. My eyelids felt as if they were holding up the world, so I closed them. A purple mist billowed in my soul.

WHEN I AWOKE, I raised my right arm. A fingerless, featureless hand extended off the end — looked like a pale slab of cheese. It wasn't there before I'd gone to sleep. Just how Zauri had used violet light to regenerate my shoulder in my dream, Saina had regenerated part of my hand in real life.

I took in my surroundings for the first time: white curtains, metal floor, violet-tinted skylights letting in violet-tinted sunshine. I heard coughing. Yawning. Heavy breathing. Mumbling. Moaning. Footsteps. Laughter. Wheezing.

I was far from alone. Far from the familiar.

Also, the air smelled like two-day-old lentil soup.

I was strapped to a reclined metal chair, wearing only a loincloth. From my sense of time, I guessed I'd been here two days, at least. My stomach ached. My throat pained. I was on the verge of being hungry and thirsty.

I shifted up a bit so I could look at my chest; a softly throbbing violet stone sat in the slot near my heart. What had happened to my green machinist stone? And more importantly, where was my dream stone?

I yearned to see Zauri. She must've been pulling out her blue hair in worry for me. The dream never ended for her, and she lived in that stone. Two days in the real world for me was forty-eight days for her. She must've been so lonely. I needed to go back to her.

That longing hurt worse than my aching muscles. I'd only felt such a desperate sense of separation after my family's execution. But this wasn't so permanent, thankfully. I had to calm down. Zauri would wait for me — she had no choice but to wait. I just needed to ask Saina where she'd put my dream stone.

"Good thoughts, good words, good deeds." Saina's whispered words breezed in from behind the curtain.

She walked through an opening and came to my side. I got a better look: her face seemed a bit looser and more wrinkled than before, like she'd aged five years from then to now. But my eyesight had been somewhat blurry when I woke up earlier.

Her eyelids drooped with tiredness. Her lips rested in a slight frown, too, whereas she'd sported a more cheerful expression last time.

"Good, you're awake." She took my fingerless hand. "Can you feel it?"

I felt tingles — a sense of something — but not the full feeling of her hand on mine.

"A little bit. I'm amazed — you really did grow my hand back. Well, part of it, anyway."

"Told you that you were lucky." Saying that made her smile,

as if in self-admiration. "And we'll get to your fingers, don't worry."

"I've never met anyone who could do that in real life, even when I lived in Harska."

Her tired eyes widened. "You're from the capital?"

"It's a long story. I suppose you could say I was exiled."

"Yeah… well, I know what that's like. The truth is, there are only a handful of people on the bright side of the world who can regenerate limbs. I only *just* gained the ability, after about eighty years spent in third layer dreams."

I snickered. I immediately thought myself rude, but then decided to express what I felt. "You're tickling my bones, right?"

She shook her head, still smiling.

"So, then, why the hell are you here, helping pathetic worms like me? Some big shot would probably pay you loads, just to have you around."

"Why did you try to save that old man, Jyosh?"

I wanted to protest the comparison, but the words caught in my mouth. I only did it because it hurt to watch him suffer. It hurt in my bones. In my soul. I didn't want to be someone who just watched. By doing nothing, I'd be as indifferent to suffering as those who trampled on him. I couldn't be that person, not anymore, not after what I did to Vir.

"It's hard to express, isn't it?" Saina sucked in a breath, then rubbed her eyes. "Hours ago, a little girl died while bathing in my light. A light cannon blast had burned off her skin and ruptured several organs." She squeezed her eyes shut. "Even I couldn't do anything… all I could do was spare her the pain."

Imagining what she'd described hurt. But if someone with eighty years of training couldn't save one little girl, what could I do?

"I'm sure you did your best," I said. "My mother used to say, 'the god of death is always one step ahead.' I guess it really is true."

"It does seem that way, no matter where I go. Your mother was wise."

"'No matter where'… how many war zones have you been to?"

She counted to three on her fingers. "This isn't the worst. Karsha invaded Hovar four years ago. That was…" She winced and shook her head.

"Karsha again? They trying to conquer the world?"

She just shrugged.

It was my turn to pity this woman. "After powering machines for twelve years, I feel like I left parts of my soul in those machines. I can't imagine what it's like spending your life healing people. Thank you for everything. And, may I ask… I had a dream stone with me. It was in my pant pocket."

"Your clothes, your sack, even your frying pan — it's all in storage, safe and secure. Don't worry."

"Could you… could you get me the dream stone? It'll help me get a restful sleep."

Saina shook her head. "Until you're fully healed, we can't swap out the healing stone in your chest for anything else. You're going to have to sleep dreamless for a few more days. You won't have any trouble falling asleep — I'm here to help with that."

The disappointment hurt. I had to tell Zauri I was okay. *A few more days* was literally months of her not knowing what had happened to me.

Also… I just wanted to be somewhere else for a while. Back on that beach, with someone who cared for me. Cared *only* for me. What was better than that?

"You missing someone?" Saina asked.

"Yeah, I guess." I didn't want my desperation to be too obvious.

"I'll have you good as new in two more days, at the most."

Two days… forty-eight hours… forty-eight more days alone for Zauri. Almost a hundred days in total. That's a long time to worry whether someone you care for is alive or dead. Whether you'll be alone forever.

"All right." I sucked up my disappointment. Better I get my hand back. Didn't want to wander around a war zone while finding it difficult to open a can of food.

"Another thing — a ship will be arriving from New Behesh in a few days to bring in more healers. I can get you passage out of Maniza, if you want."

Like honey pouring into my ears. But what if the honey was poisoned? How could this woman be telling me exactly what I wanted to hear?

"Where's the ship going?"

"To Eshur, the capital of New Behesh. It's only eight hours by flight. You can apply for asylum, there."

"Why would they give *me* asylum?"

She paused and studied my face with a pensive glare. "You have such a dismal worldview, don't you?"

"You just told me about a little girl who died from bleeding in her organs."

She pressed her palm to her forehead. "They'll give you asylum because it'll be on my recommendation."

"Damn… am I really that lucky?"

"Unlike her." Saina moved to stand behind me. "Unlike so many."

For the next hour, she braced her hand on my nape and pulsed violet light into me. My fingerless hand tingled. Eventually, the violet light breezed into my brain and softened it to sleep.

. . .

I AWOKE what felt like half a day later. I raised my hand. Textureless fingers extended out of the pale cheese. I couldn't wriggle them.

Then I waited. Bored. I tried my best not to listen to the coughs, moans, wheezes, and snoring around me. I wondered what Zauri was up to. How could I understand what she was doing at this moment? Time moved faster in the dream, so in the minutes I'd been thinking about her, hours must've passed there. If she were to see me, I'd be stuck moving like a slowly melting glacier. If I were to see her, she'd be a blur zooming around at speeds I couldn't comprehend.

Ugh, it hurt my head. If only Saina could bathe me in her violet light so I could pass the time asleep.

Eventually, an even more tired looking Saina came back and unstrapped me. One of her eyes was red, and her hair frayed at the ends. Yellow stains dotted her white garb.

"You should go walk around, get some exercise," she said, pointing to the white curtain that surrounded us. "Just keep your fresh hand out of trouble."

"Walk around. Yeah. Good idea."

I got up. My bones creaked with stiffness, so I stretched my arms to the side. No soreness or pain. Somehow, I felt fed and full, despite not eating these past few days. I hadn't even had a drink, come to think of it.

"Did you feed me while I was asleep?"

"My light is nourishment enough." She said it so coolly.

"How many years did you spend learning that ability?"

Saina twirled a strand of her copper hair. "Too many. By the way, you should put some clothes on." She tossed me a thin, gray gown and a pair of rubber slippers. "Come back in an hour or so."

I wrapped the gown around myself and tied it at the front,

then stuck my feet into the slippers. Finally, I walked through the curtain.

I emerged into a lane between white curtains. The coughs, moans, and retching sounds told me there must've been a dozen or so other patients here. A young man garbed in white passed me by, then went through a curtain. So, it wasn't only Saina healing all these people.

Down the hall, a white light shone: the exit. I walked toward it and went outside.

A blue metal ramp greeted me. I stepped down the ramp, carefully, then turned to see what I'd come out of.

A levship. I'd been on a parked levship this whole time. It shone with blue metal and sported the shield-and-dragon emblem.

Judging from how rocky and hard the ground seemed, it looked like we were on a mountain. Perhaps the mountain near the train station.

I picked a direction and started walking. The stiffness in my knees eased with every step.

After a few minutes of pacing nearby the levship, I noticed someone standing in the shadow of a ruddy boulder: a young woman, judging by her luminous neck-length red hair and smooth, caramel skin. She was short and thin, like Chaya. Smoke billowed from something maroon in her mouth; was she smoking a cigar? Her gray robe matched mine and ended just above her bare, scraped-up knees.

I approached her. She got suddenly tense, and the cigar dropped out of her mouth. She caught it; the tip sizzled on her skin.

"Agh!" The young woman threw it to the ground and stomped on it, then clutched her burn. "Damn it!" Her incensed, grass-colored eyes fixed on me. "Look what you did." Despite sounding angry, her voice was soft-edged and her lilt exotic, as if she came out of a storybook about a faraway place.

She held up her hand. A black ring surrounded a swollen red spot. I wasn't sure what was the bigger tragedy: the easily healable burn, or the wasted cigar?

I shrugged. "You got any more of those?"

"That was my last one. Brought it all the way from Smoky Lane in Salkofy."

"Salkofy — that's the capital of Karsha. You from there?"

"I'm craving a cigar, is what I am."

When she glanced away, I noticed a broad, rose-colored scar just below her nape that snaked downward.

I looked at what she was looking at: the scenery below the mountain cliff. A forest spread in all directions. The trees resembled broccoli from this height. Would be a lovely sight, if it weren't for the boxy, clustered levships hovering above. Since I didn't see the train station or the tent city, I assumed this was a different side of the mountain.

The woman eyed me with obvious suspicion. She had thick bangs, slender cheekbones, and a prominent, sail-shaped nose — along with the cherry hair and green eyes, it wasn't a common look in Maniza.

"Why're you staring at me?" She ruffled her nose.

"Was I?" I darted my gaze away, sunken. "Must still be high on that violet light."

"Oh. Me too, actually. Those Beheshian healers are pretty good, aren't they?"

"That's an understatement. What's your name, by the way?"

She hesitated and tightened her shoulders. "Why does it matter?"

"Easier to talk to someone when you know their name, I guess."

"Hmm…" Now she was staring at me. A bit too intently for

my comfort. "You don't look like a Red Veil informant… but no one working for the Red Veil looks like they're working for the Red Veil. Guess if you were, you'd already know my name. So… uhh… I'm Kaur."

"Red Veil… where've I heard that before…" I tapped my forehead, and lightning flashed in my mind. "Oh yeah — they did that money bomb."

Kaur nodded. "Clever, wasn't it? Even I must admit it was the perfect misdirection. It doesn't make sense to invade only a day after a money bomb — takes weeks for the extra currency to go into circulation and destroy the economy. But they did invade the next day because the money bomb was just a feint."

Took me a few seconds to understand, but when I did, the genius of it struck me. "So the Manizan military wasn't prepared because they assumed the Karshans actually wanted the money bomb to take effect, but in reality, it was just a distraction."

"Yup. And what's your name?"

"Oh, sorry, I'm Jyosh." I extended my left hand. "Pleasure to meet you."

She had one of those flimsy handshakes. "It's not a pleasure, Jyosh."

"Why is that?"

"I can tell you're a local. None of this is going to end well for you, or for your people. Get the hell out of Maniza while you can — the things the Karshans have planned, you don't want to be here for that." Her flimsy handshake turned firm. She squeezed my hand so hard, it hurt.

"You're stronger than you look, you know." I tried not to show how much pain I was in.

She got on her tiptoes and whispered, "Get out before Rao does what he's been planning. *Nowhere* in this country is safe. Please, get out." She let go of my hand and turned her back.

Rao, again? He was the leader of the yellow-eyed group. Just what was this guy up to that even other Karshans were fighting him?

Her strange behavior made me decide against asking. I turned and walked away. The pain of her squeeze lingered, so I rubbed my hand. Damn, was I so weak that a small woman's squeeze could hurt this much?

I tried not to think about it. The air up here was fresher than the discolored, smoky steam that pervaded the labor camp. I had that to enjoy, at least.

I WALKED for about fifteen minutes in the other direction. Rubbed my shoulders each time a gust blew by. Came upon a lusher, greener patch, as well as some steep ascents. I stayed on flatter land and strolled amid lovely acacia trees. Moist grasses reached my ankles, and the mud went *plush-plush* beneath my feet.

A man was sitting cross-legged beneath a tree a few paces ahead. Of all things, he was wearing a *sherwani:* a regal long shirt that extended beyond the knees with an ornate sash around the waist. In Harska, we only wore them for weddings, funerals, and whenever a Parani held a ceremony.

I shuddered when he looked at me. One of his eyes was yellow and the other purple. But that wasn't what made me so uncomfortable; something hid behind his gaze. A hunger. As if I'd encountered a lion.

I looked away and continued walking.

"Wait!" the man called.

Now I wondered whether I ought to run. Those brawling Karshan soldiers… one group had purple eyes, and the other group yellow eyes. The invisible woman had warned me about the yellow-eyed soldiers, who were taking orders from this Colonel Rao fellow, whom Kaur had said was planning something terrible in Maniza.

But this guy had both a yellow and a purple eye! It made no sense. My hairs stood as my skin got cold.

Before I knew it, he'd already jogged toward me. The weird smile on his face did nothing to calm my bones.

"Hello," I said. "Hope I did not disturb you."

"My good man, not in the least." He bared his teeth in a honeyed grin. "I was just looking for my mother. She's lost somewhere in these parts."

He was bald, but given that he seemed to be in his late twenties, it must've been by choice. Big, broad shoulders. The kohl around his eyes gave him an animal-like fierceness.

"That so? I'm just on a walk, myself. If I see her, I'll surely direct her here."

"My name is Elam." He grabbed my hand. Such a firm, rigorous shake. "And you are?"

"I'm Jyosh."

"What a lovely name. *Jyosh. Jyosh.* It just strolls down the tongue. Taking its time. Enjoying the scenery. I could say it all day. *Jyosh. Jyosh.* You know, you're the first local I've met… in a peaceful setting, that is."

A little disturbing how easily these foreigners picked me for a local. "Oh? And where are you from?"

He gestured at the sky, which was filled with levships. At least he was honest.

"Came here in the Karshan fleet along with your mother, did you?"

"Does that seem strange?" He let out a hard chuckle. "I suppose it *is* rather strange. My mother and I, our relationship isn't exactly normal. But for all her flaws, I still adore her. Wouldn't want anyone to do her harm. That's a right only I have."

"Well, I'll—I'll tell you if I see her."

"I'm sure you won't," he said in a harsher tone. What did that mean?

"Nice to have met you, Elam. I'll be on my way, now."

Instead of continuing my walk, I turned in the direction I'd come from. Perhaps I shouldn't have strayed so far. Better head back to the safety of the levship.

"Say, do you know the story of how Guru Giti attained nirvana?" Elam asked.

I stopped and turned back toward Elam. "I'm sorry, I don't."

"Do you even know what nirvana *is?*"

I shrugged. "Spiritual enlightenment or something. I don't know."

He walked toward me. Got too close for comfort, his hot breath in my face. "It is the ultimate awakening. It's as if you had a thousand eyes, and they all opened at once, and gazed upon the sun as if they were *inside* the sun."

"Sounds… uncomfortable."

"Guru Giti was tortured by the Song. Every molecule of her being was separated from the other, given its own consciousness, and boiled in lava a billion times hotter than the sun's core. This all happened in a thousand-layer deep dream, so that millions and millions of her separated consciousnesses would boil for a million-billion-billion eternities. It's too difficult to describe in words, isn't it?"

"Yeah, that sounds pretty bad."

"But when she attained nirvana, when she tasted the *Asha*, it freed her. Completely. She became the heart of the sun itself. She fused with a divine dragon and ascended to the realm of the gods. With a whisper, she could've vanquished the Song, her worst enemy. But by attaining nirvana, she realized how little our petty wars mattered." He didn't blink once. "I've been meditating on this story, all day. It's inspiring me, driving me toward my purpose."

"Your purpose… to find your mother?"

His laugh was woodier than the trees around us. "That, and *so, so* much more. Don't get so attached to this life, Jyosh. Death is watching you… and salivating."

He licked his lips.

"Okay Elam, I really got to go. Wonderful story, though. Thanks for sharing."

I was relieved he let me go. I hurried back toward the levship. Even the beautiful mountain scenery couldn't help how deeply unsettled I felt.

WHEN I GOT BACK to my white curtains, a man was wiping down my chair with a cloth. He wore the same white healer's garb as Saina. His thick-rimmed spectacles made it hard to tell what he was looking at. I hoped this new foreigner wouldn't add to my growing fear of foreigners.

He smiled good-naturedly — a nice change from Elam's creepy grin. "Sorry, just cleaning up a bit. How was your walk?"

"Not bad," I lied. "Pretty good air up here."

I envied his neat brown beard. I so wanted to keep a beard now that I was free — but not a wild, unkempt one. I needed to go to a barber once I'd grown enough hair to sculpt.

"Yeah, it's nice up here. That's why we chose it. Pristine air is good for healing."

"But how'd you get me and the other patients up the mountain?"

"With the ship, of course." He laughed — also with a good nature, so unlike Elam's dark chuckle. "It's not just a pretty box."

How obvious. I almost slapped myself for being so stupid.

"I was wondering something… you guys came at the same time as the Karshans, right? That means you knew this invasion was about to happen."

He paused from rubbing my seat. "The whole bright side of the world knew. It was just a question of *when*. You don't get any information from the outside world here in Maniza, do you?"

I shook my head.

"I'm Jaysh, by the way." He held out his hand.

I shook it. His hold was firm but not painfully so. Finally, a perfectly normal handshake.

"I'm Jyosh. Our names kind of sound the same."

"Indeed, it has the same root in the ancient tongue. *Light.*"

Saina streamed in, looking a bit fresher than last time. She put her hand on Jaysh's forearm and smiled sweetly.

"Thanks for wiping it down. Didn't want him to be uncomfortable." She turned to me. "You sweat like a pig, Jyosh."

"What? And you don't?" I said, a bit embarrassed.

"She's just busting your balls." Jaysh nudged her with his elbow. "Once you see that side of her, you'll regret ever having met her."

"Ugh. Thanks for that." Saina rolled her eyes. "Go and find something else to clean."

"Oh, there's *plenty* to clean. Until next time, Jyosh." Jaysh left the curtain, grinning.

I chuckled at the sight of Saina annoyed.

She glared at me, all serious. "Take off your clothes."

I gulped.

"Come on. We have to begin the final part of your treatment. I've regrown your hand, but it's useless without any functioning nerves. Now I have to attach the nerves on your new hand to your nervous system. This is an… intensive procedure. Not just for you, but for me. It requires both of us to be unconscious and connected via wire."

"Oh, well, okay." I untied my gray robe and dropped it to the ground.

"Everything, Jyosh." She pointed to my loincloth. "No need for modesty. I'm a professional."

The thought of baring myself to someone like Saina made me hot in the face. I sucked up the embarrassment and pulled off the loincloth.

"Well, go ahead and sit."

I got on the chair. It was cold against my nakedness.

"Saina… can I ask you something?"

She seemed in a rush to strap me in. Judging by the hallway with its many curtains and sickly sounds, other patients needed her as much as me. But I had to know.

"Of course."

"To be honest, most of the foreigners I've met have been strange." Kaur and Elam were more than just "strange." "Disturbing" was a more appropriate word, but I wanted to be subtle. "And I assume they find me strange, too. So if I go to Eshur and get asylum, what will happen to me? Would anyone there… like me? Or would I be an annoyance?"

Her sigh was so drawn out, I thought it would never end. "I don't know, Jyosh. I'm just a healer."

"Yeah, you're right. Sorry for asking."

She paused for a moment to think. "No, I'm the one who should be sorry. It's just been a long day. I owe you a better answer than that. The life of a refugee… is not an easy one. You'll be challenged to find work, to make enough money to get by. But New Behesh is a peaceful country, so you'll have that, at least. Still, just like here, there are good people and there are bad people. You'll run into both, so you'll have to be strong."

"There aren't really any good people here in Maniza, so it's not like I'm unused to being treated badly."

"What about you? I think you're a good person."

"That's because you don't really know me. You saw me do one good deed, and you assume I've lived that way my whole life." It was hard to say this. Harder than taking off my loincloth. "What if I told you that the hand you're regenerating has helped murder people? More than once. And perhaps would have murdered many more, just to survive."

"It would make no difference to me. I'm a healer, not a judge or a god. I give my light to whomever I can."

I nodded, not wholly satisfied. She didn't deserve to hear about my self-loathing, so I just kept silent.

"Listen, Jyosh. Before we begin the procedure, there's one rule you need to follow. You're going to be fully exposed to my frequency, and I'm going to be fully exposed to yours. If you try to delve into my feelings and memories, I will immediately end the procedure. Understood?"

I couldn't imagine what she meant, so I just nodded.

"I need to hear you say it. Say that you won't do it."

"I won't do it. I don't even know how to. I won't do anything you don't want me to, I swear."

She sighed, but this one was sharp and short. "All right. I just needed to make that clear." Then she smiled like the sun does upon the mountains. "Don't be so hard on yourself."

"Hard on myself? I aided in the murder of two people." It was a load off my chest to tell her, for some reason. Tears made my eyes heavy. "I should've been trampled to death, not that old man. I don't deserve this. You say you're not a god, but you might as well be. I'm not worthy of your mercy."

She stroked my hair. "Stop it. Do you know that it takes the average Manizan a hundred days to earn what the average person in New Behesh earns in a single day? I have no right to think badly about you, no matter what you did, because I don't think I can ever understand what you've been through. Doesn't matter how many war zones I've been to, how much suffering I've witnessed — I still can't put myself in your shoes."

She got a cloth from her pocket and dried my tears. The embarrassment weighed on me.

"Relax, okay? Once you get on that levship to New Behesh, your book begins again at page one. Everything else is erased. Understood?"

I sucked up a tearful breath and nodded. I had to get myself under control, lest I waste her time.

She positioned my hands on my lap. "Okay, let's do this. Close your eyes."

Then she put a metal wire in my hands. When a machine required more than one person to power and direct it, we often used such wires to create a conduit between two conductors. Saina wrapped the wire around both my hands, and then wrapped them around hers. Meanwhile, Jaysh came back with a wooden chair, which he placed right in front of me.

Saina sat on it and stared at me, our knees touching. I stared back.

"Sit back, breathe slowly, and close your eyes."

I did so. Violet light flowed from her, through the wire, and into my hands, syrupy and warm.

"Good thoughts. Good words. Good deeds," Saina said as the violet light bathed my soul.

Messages

Carried upon waves of light, messages breeze through the skies above, with Jyosh unaware:

14SPM: 1A8, do you copy?

1A8: Loud and clear, brother.

14SPM: Just checking in. Report.

1A8: Tell Commander Rao I've found a remedy to his 'shorthandedness.' Expect delivery today.

14SPM: Confirmed, 1A8. Can you elaborate?

1A8: Keep the door open. I'll fly it in before Sylet knows what's going on.

14SPM: Can you repeat, 1A8?

1A8: I'll be landing a ship in the ancient city's God Tower. One that Sylet doesn't have the balls to blast to pieces.

14SPM: Confirmed. What's the designation of the ship?

1A8: I don't know.

14SPM: 1A8, please inform. How will we know it's you?

1A8: Let's just say it won't be one of our ships.

14SPM: 1A8, I am required to inform you that commandeering any civilian or allied ship without just cause is a violation of code of conduct, as well as several treaties.

...

14SPM: Please respond, 1A8.

1A8: You don't know me very well, do you, 14SPM?

14SPM: I'm afraid I haven't had the pleasure of getting to know you.

1A8: I'm told it's not such a pleasure. It's days like this that I miss the Red Veil. I'm going to do what I'm going to do. We'll clean up the mess later.

14SPM: 1A8, let me remind you — should the blame for your actions fall upon Commander Rao, there could be consequences. For all of us who are fighting the good fight.

1A8: And let me remind you, 14SPM, that you don't win wars by clinging to codes of conduct and treaties. You win by serving the Goddess of Death, and she is ever at my back, whispering her soothing madness into my soul. 1A8, out.

Chapter Eleven

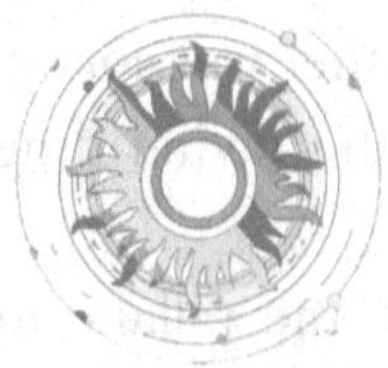

"GOOD THOUGHTS. GOOD WORDS. GOOD DEEDS," CHANTED A choir of ten thousand men and women. They stretched vast across the floating temple — an endless sea of humanity, and I was a drop among them. At the horizon, a black sky drank the sunlight: The Nightscape. I'd never seen it so close. Beyond was the realm of Shafat, said to be the most powerful country ever to exist. With the wave of his fingers, their Padishah could send a fleet of ten thousand levships into the Dayworld. Even the Whirling Wall, the vast expanse of hurricanes that separated day and night, could not stop him.

"Good thoughts. Good words. Good deeds," the worshippers chanted. Their paradise would be the first into the dark should the armada of Shafat come. Should the Padishah decide to send his fleets beyond the veil that separated the Nightscape from the rest of us.

Wait... why did I know these things? Where were these thoughts coming from? I knew nothing about these countries. What even was this floating island?

I stood amid the chanters. All were clad in loose, saffron

dresses that went from their collars to their ankles with nary a wrinkle. Golden sashes with golden dragons were tied around our waists. The sun lazed below the island's horizon, which meant we were at the mouth of the Nightscape. As close as you could get without being swallowed by the hurricanes.

We chanted on a grass field upon the floating temple. In the distance, twenty-six bronze pillars stood around a floating platform. Buried deep beneath each pillar was the body of one of the Twenty-Six Arrows — the warriors who'd traveled into the eternal storm and slew the divine dragon Daeva Andar, thousands of years ago.

And in the center of the pillars, upon a floating platform, stood a vessel for our god. Whenever our god's spirit resided within her, she transcended flesh and blood. A heavenly light from the Asha poured through her, and so she stood fully veiled, her skin so bright it would burn the world. In such a state, her eyes were said to turn into dragon obsidian, and should they shine upon humanity, the end of the world would come.

Wait... these feelings and ideas and premonitions... none of it made sense. Wasn't I just sitting on a metal chair in a room veiled by white curtains? Why was I here, and why was I not myself? Whose thoughts were these, intruding on my own the way a tide bathes a sandy shore?

None of this could be real. I must've been within something akin to a dream stone. But... *someone else* was colliding into me. Overawing my soul. Taking the reins of my self and my will.

The vessel stood upon the floating platform, wrapped in her colorful veil, as the chanters chanted, their pure saffron robes fluttering in the floatland's breeze. Whoever I was inhabiting waded through them.

I came to the front of the chanters. I willed myself to fly; the air lifted me, and I flew up and landed gently on the floating stone platform. The veiled vessel stood in the center. Only now did I notice the thin wires pulled around her fingers, all leading downward toward one of the twenty-six pillars. I walked up to her, furious for reasons I couldn't understand, aching to rip off her cloth. To show everyone she was a lie, just like *everything*.

Don't do it, Jyosh. The thought punched my mind. *Don't do anything. I told you not to dig.*

I wasn't doing it, though. The urge wasn't coming from me, but from the soul I was sharing this body with. A fire crackled within my limbs, and only the light of god shining through his vessel could put it out.

"Good thoughts, good words, good deeds." The chanting of the lambs only made me angrier.

I grabbed the vessel's veil. The chanting stopped. I turned to see all ten thousand men and women pointing at me, their teeth gritted, eyes wide in horror.

Before I could pull off the veil, a wire tripped my legs. I fell onto the stone, pain thudding through my backside. The air sped up as if a gale had hit our island. Took a moment to realize it was the island *moving*, surging toward the horizon where the Nightscape watched and waited.

The vessel raised her hands, clutched her veil, and threw it to the side. That face… from the mole above her lip to her roasted-almond eyes: it was Saina.

I WAS a master who'd trained within a thousand-year dream. I could conjure lightblades out of my hands, no hilt needed. And I could fling them like bolts of red death at whomever challenged me. To call them "blades" was a vast understatement. My light could fly across the sky by my will, and come back, if I so chose. It could take any shape. Burn hotter than a lightning strike.

And that was nothing. I knew of legendary warriors who dwelled in the higher heavens, who'd trained within the deepest dream layers for millions — even billions — of years. What was I but an ant before such lords of light?

To them, everything was light, and light was everything. There was no distinction between matter and energy. It was all one, and it all bent to their will. By summoning a luminous wind, they could annihilate armies of millions. A continent could be extinguished with a maelstrom of divine radiance, and a new one forged in the afterglow.

And so, I had to continue my training. A thousand years every night. I yearned to become *a Light Ascendent*, one to whom all wavelengths and stars bowed.

But unfortunately, the gods had not written me such a fate, and my will was not strong enough to tear the pages of destiny.

I WAS FLYING ON A SKYBOARD. Night drenched the world. Lightning exploded in the clouds below. The cold wet sky bit into my bones, streaming past me at thunderous speed.

I clutched a lightblade in each hand, both of the purest red fire. They were my only lights in the dark sky — my guides in a void filled with unknown terrors. What we'd feared, what we'd prayed would never come, had finally found us.

I was one of many. An army, hovering upon skyboards, lightblades in hand. Each of us had trained within thousand-year dreams. Each of us could channel the unseen light of the Primal Star. And yet, we were no match for our enemy: *The Hasht* — a sphere the size of a city that had descended from the third heaven to the first. The Padishah's command ship.

It loomed in the sky above: unreal. Though it seemed a sphere, it actually had many sides — tens of thousands of shimmering, black metal surfaces. What could our puny red blades do against that? Even if we all attacked at once, with every skill we'd ever learned, it wouldn't fall out of the sky. Even the great light cannon which the hero Yima had used to destroy the Song mothership couldn't penetrate the Hasht. It was *divine* — an object from a higher reality. We only glimpsed its shadow.

And wherever it went, it brought the night.

Now I was alone. The last man left. Everyone else had been devoured by the night, by the bursts of lightning breathed by the almost-spherical, city-sized levship.

But the night brought other monsters, too. Things that are born in the dark and die in the light.

I saw one's red eyes. *Daeva.* Divine dragon. The shuddering glow of my lightblades reflected against the dragon's obsidian tendrils. Its teeth shone like starlight ivory. But the eyes: each was a ball of flaring sun. I could not distinguish its body from the night, as if it were torn from the same fabric.

It was the Padishah's greatest weapon. If I could slay it, perhaps I could stop the night from swallowing our home. Our temple. Our refuge. The seat of the Ancients: The Temple Behesh. In my heart, I yearned only to save my beloved Behesh.

When the dragon opened its mouth and I glimpsed the light of its divine soul, dread seized every bone in my body. I was wrong, and I grew limp with hopelessness. Not with a million-billion years of training could I slay this creature, for it was not training I lacked, it was *blessing*. Only a dragon can teach you how to kill it, and the gods of the Ancients had not chosen me for this purpose, had not written it in my script. *The pen has been lifted and the pages have dried.* And it had all been decided from that which we emanate: The Asha.

I raised my lightblades above my head, ready for my end, as the dragon snarled and released its breath of lightning bolts.

. . .

I BURNED. In my soul, a twirling demon poured millions of colors together, mixing with the pressure of a billion fists. I blazed, lighting the dark as I melted into pure light. I brought warmth and life, but burned so hot I could deal death, too. I turned into a new sun, and around me swirled the ten divine dragons.

WELL, that was how the procedure went. When I woke up, my hand hurt like it had been boiled in a cauldron of curry. Saina held my nape and dripped violet light into my veins, soothing the pain every time I yelped. I rode on a purple tide that bobbed between a numb wakefulness and a dreamless sleep.

Hours later, I was lucid and pain free. Best of all, I could wriggle my fingers.

"You did good," Saina said as she flitted her hands all over me. "Can you feel this? And this?"

I nodded each time.

Jaysh scribbled onto a paper pad. "Looks like he had quite the ride."

"I became a new sun," I said. No, that wasn't the whole of it. "There was a dragon… and some nightmarish levship."

"Just dreams," Saina replied flatly.

"Well, it was probably more of a—" Jaysh shut his mouth when Saina grimaced aggressively at him.

They obviously weren't just dreams. I'd inhabited different people with totally separate experiences, fears, and hopes.

Jaysh cleared his throat. "Oh, uh, did you get the tapeworm?"

"Zapped it good," Saina said. "It'll come out in his stool in a day or so. Healed all his burns, too. Write down that he also has a mineral and vitamin deficiency due to poor diet. It should be monitored by his new healer in Eshur. Oh, there's also a small mass in his occipital triangle." She scratched her nape. "Looks benign, but he should have it tested just in case."

"Got it." Jaysh lifted up his gold-rimmed spectacles, which had drooped onto the ridge of his nose, then scribbled some more.

"I was on a floating island. Everyone was afraid. They were

praying to *you*, Saina. They wanted you to save them, from… from…"

Saina sighed and shut her eyes. "A little bit of me leaked into you. Totally my fault. I've been too stressed out, so I wasn't able to contain my frequency. But it's not something you need to worry about. Everything you think you saw… it's just an echo of something that happened long ago."

"So those weren't just dreams, then? What were they? Memories? *Your* memories?"

"Listen, Jyosh. It's been a pleasure meeting and getting to know you, but I'm just your healer, and you're just my patient. Get what I'm saying?"

"Yeah. I get it. We're not friends."

"I told you not to pry. Oh, and you're discharged. The levship bound for Eshur will be here in an hour." At that, Saina walked through the curtain, leaving me cold and more than a little sad.

"She's just having a rough time." Jaysh yawned and scratched his brown beard with the butt of his pen. "She didn't mean it like that. Look us up when you get to New Behesh. I think of myself as somewhat of a tour guide, you know. But not of the obvious stuff — no sir — I'm all about the best-kept-secrets and hidden gems. Cuisine, architecture, art — hey, you like opera?"

"What's opera?"

He raised an eyebrow and rubbed his head with the pen. "Nothing that interesting. We can stick to the night dances — you'll like those more."

"If you say so." His *niceness* put me on edge. Was he angling for something?

I had to remind myself that this wasn't the camp. These people were totally different. They didn't need to play such games. They weren't just trying to survive, they were trying to help *everyone* survive.

I managed a smile, then said, "Yeah, night dances sound fun. Even opera, too, whatever that is."

"It's a done deal, then. It'll be a little while before we get back, but an opera and some night dances are on me!"

"I'm all for it." For the first time in a long time, I felt it might be possible to relax around someone that wasn't from a dream. Some of the weight fell off my bones.

"I've got a favor to ask," I said. "Would you mind if I got my dream stone and slept here while waiting?"

Jaysh twirled his pen in his hands, then sighed. "Hmm… normally that would be fine, but someone else needs this spot. Your ride out of here won't be long, anyway. As your co-healer of sorts, I advise you get some fresh air and exercise. You can sleep on the eighteen-hour trip to Eshur."

I DID as Jaysh suggested and took a walk, making sure not to stray too far. I wanted to say goodbye to this awful country, but this mountain might as well have been a foreign land. The pebbly ground around the levship was nothing like the leafy landscape in the floatland of Harska, nor the caked dirt of the labor camp. Camp Seventeen. What a forgettable name. Too bad I couldn't forget my time there.

I couldn't even name the broccoli-looking forest below the cliff's edge. Why say goodbye to a country I barely knew anything about? If only I'd been born somewhere better, I might feel *something*. Like that soldier flying on the skyboard in my dream: he loved his homeland enough to be incinerated by a dragon's lightning breath while defending it.

I walked on the stony path toward the other side of the mountain. Perhaps I'd see something recognizable off its edge. Anything worth saying *goodbye* to. I was about to go someplace entirely unfamiliar, and so wanted one lingering vision of my country.

Kaur was standing at the base of an uphill path, puffing on a maroon cigar. I wondered how her healing was going. Those snaky red burns and scars around her nape had seemed torturous. The scrapes on her knees were now scabbed over. Her cheeks were a bit rounder and her caramel skin rosier.

As I approached, her gaze remained stuck, as if she were entrenched in her thoughts.

"You going to Eshur, too?" I asked.

She took a lingering puff, then tousled her fire-red hair. "Dunno."

"Thought you didn't have any more cigars."

"High heaven provides." She held it out for me.

I gladly took it and puffed. A bit damp and musky, but the cardamom spice soothed me.

"Tell me, local boy, what do you know about *Sambalpur*?"

The name was like a levship crashing into my brain. "Sambalpur. Sambalpur." I scratched my scalp. "Swear I've heard that before."

She chuckled. "A local boy ought to know about local things."

I closed my eyes. Amma appeared. She mouthed *Sambalpur* and told me a story. "My mother said something about it, once. But damn it, I don't remember. There was even a lullaby…"

I recited what I remembered of it.

"*In the fog of Sambalpur,*
Something-something- in the fog,
Lighting up the way,
Something-something Sambalpur,
Lost to time and memory."

Kaur laughed like a drunken hyena. No one had laughed at me like that since I was eleven years old.

"The hell is up with you?" I bared my teeth.

She slapped her thigh and chuckled some more. "Your tune was so adorable." I waited for her to exhaust her giggles while huffing out slow, impatient breaths.

She sighed to put a cap on her laughing fit and said, "Sorry. Was in a lot of pain earlier, so Saina really pumped me with violet light. Still high as a songbird. Climb up and look over the cliff's edge for me, would you?"

"Uh, okay."

I climbed up the incline that was blocking my view and looked into the distance beyond the cliff.

My jaw dropped.

A city spread in every direction. Spires and domes covered all the buildings, gleaming white and golden in the dusky glow. Statues of gods — some animal-like, others human, some with many faces, others with only one — covered the pagodas perched upon hills around the city. In the distance, a palace sat on a hill, surrounded by a wall with a massive golden door. Within the palace stood a tower that sipped the clouds, and the statues of the gods climbed it at every step — weirdly enough, their faces stared down, unlike the gods climbing the pagodas.

I'd seen that big golden door and palace. I'd seen it in my dream with Zauri. The door in the dream had an indentation that fit a lotus, and because we didn't have it, we couldn't get inside.

"Sambalpur," Kaur said as she stood beside me. "'Lost to time and memory.'"

"Are you saying *this* city is Sambalpur?"

Kaur nodded. "Obviously. Don't you know anything? The sudden appearance of this city is why Karsha invaded!"

"Sudden… appearance? Are you saying this city wasn't here before?"

Judging by Kaur's heavy sigh, she didn't care for my ignorance. "They don't tell you anything in these flatlands, eh? Ignorance is bliss and all that."

"How can a city just appear out of thin air?"

"Dunno. Wanted to ask you that. Turns out you know less than me. You good for anything, local boy?"

That question made flames shoot through my veins. "I don't have to be good for anything. Not anymore. I'm getting the hell out of here. And I'll live for myself, not as a slave."

Kaur slow clapped. "*Ooh.* You've a spine, after all. But if you think you won't be someone's slave in Eshur, you're as ignorant as you appear. Life won't be easy there. No one's going to hand you a living on a platter. It's an expensive place. The kabab rolls there cost as much as the ones in Spicy Lane in Salkofy — taste as good, too. *Mmm.* Tell me, local boy — can you earn a living with the skills you have?"

"I'm… I'm a machinist. And a damn good one. I'm sure I can find work."

"*A damn good one,* you say. The machines they use here in Maniza are at least twenty years behind the rest of the world. What do you know about an S-class TEX four-one-seven dual-feed fabricator?"

Sounded like a garble of nonsense to me.

I chuckled to show how little I cared. "Tell me, why are you such an asshole, Kaur? Did someone hurt you? How bitter is your broken heart?"

She walked up, stood on the very tips of her toes, and got in my face. "Only my heart? There isn't a part of me that isn't in pieces."

"Maybe you should pick up the pieces. Do something good with the time you have left instead of being such a bitch."

Kaur took a crackling puff, then blew smoke out in my face. Given how much I enjoyed the flavor, I didn't mind it that much.

"It's sad, how optimistic you are," she said. "You think you've seen some shit. But little do you realize, things are about to get so much wor—"

A burst sounded in the distance behind us. A light cannon shot? But I saw no flash in the sky. Kaur and I swiveled around to look.

A shout followed. Then a scream. Sounded like it was coming from the levship.

I looked at Kaur, and she looked at me; her eyebrows zagged and her nose ruffled.

I sprinted toward the levship, Kaur just behind me. Didn't try to avoid the pebbles; they crunched beneath my slippers.

I halted a good distance away when I noticed a man standing on the boarding ramp — bald head, wearing a sherwani, golden sash a bit loose.

"Is that… Elam?" I said to myself.

Kaur came to my side and gasped. Her cigar dropped from her mouth.

Four lightblades hovered in the air around Elam's body. He wasn't holding them. Rather, it was as if an invisible, four-handed giant were standing behind him, brandishing these blades. I wouldn't have believed it if I hadn't seen it.

Another man stood at the base of the ramp. He wore a breezy white coat and sported golden spectacles above a brown beard.

"Jaysh," I whispered.

Kaur said in the jitteriest voice, "Elam, don't do it. Don't do it. Don't. Don—"

One of the blades surged in the air, as if the invisible giant had lunged forward. It struck Jaysh in the belly. It flew through him, coming out of his back with a splash of blood.

He fell over into a rock pile, writhing and hollering in pain.

A wound like that — you'd need immediate help to survive. I

had to get Jaysh on the ship, get him to Saina. But Elam stood atop the ramp with four floating lightblades.

I stepped forward, ready to run to Jaysh.

Kaur grabbed my arm. I tugged forward, but her uncanny strength held firm.

"You idiot," she said. "Don't even think it! You utterly mad?"

"We can't let him bleed out."

"And what about you? How many pieces do you want to be in?"

I used my other hand to pull against Kaur's hold. She grabbed my shoulder, tripped my leg, and pushed me to the ground. Got on top of me and held me down, breathing in my ear.

"Elam… is this your path, now?" she said. "Is there no going back for you?"

Elam walked inside the levship. Oh god — Saina was in there! And all the patients!

"Kaur, if we don't do something, he'll — he'll—"

"Kill them all. He's cursed, so it's very likely. But there's nothing we can do against his demonblades."

"How can you say that? The guy is obviously insane. We can't just let him — we can't just—"

She pushed down harder, sending my face into the dust. Screams sounded from within the levship — a cacophony born of hell.

"He's not insane," she said. "We might be the insane ones."

What did she mean by that? She obviously knew him. But why defend what he was doing?

"You have no right to stop me! Let me go! If I want to end up in pieces, that's my right!"

"I'm not gonna throw kindling into that flame, local boy. Can't let you add to his sins. *Each sin weighs as much as the world.* Stay still and shut up."

The sunsink that powered the levship turned on, producing a whirring, fan-like hum that drowned out the screams. My heart jolted as the ship lifted. The boxy, blue-metal thing shot straight up off the mountain — hundreds of feet in the sky.

A sunken, sickening hollowness spread within me. Not only was Jaysh bleeding out and Saina in grave danger, but my dream stone was on that ship. Zauri was on that ship, floating away.

"This isn't happening," I said. "This shit isn't happening."

Kaur released her grip. I shot to my feet and rushed toward Jaysh.

I slid down next to him. Pressed my hand against his cheek: getting cold. I lifted his spectacles up onto his forehead.

His eyes showed no spark. Blood glazed his lips. Bile leaked from the burnt intestines showing from the open hole in his gut. It all smelled like a rotten roast.

"Long gone," Kaur said, standing over me. She made a circle with her thumb and forefinger, then brought it to her forehead and closed her eyes. "*May the sun take his name.*"

"Can you heal him?"

"He's dead. Besides, I can't tell my violets from my blues."

Of course, she obviously wasn't a healer. The hopelessness of it all crushed me.

"He was going to take me to the opera. Show me the night dances. He was so nice to me." I sobbed, tears blurring my eyes. "How could anyone — why would anyone…"

"Yeah, he was nice to me, too. An all-round upstanding fellow." She shook her head and looked away.

I stuck my forefingers into my tear ducts. "Why did Elam do that? You said he wasn't insane. Then why?"

Why kill a healer? It seemed like such a waste. It wasn't like when they executed the burnt-out conductors at camp — those folks weren't of any use. They were innocent, but of no use. This man, though… he was a healer. Something rare, something that could only help.

"I thought you Manizans were a hardy folk. Yet here you are, spilling tears over the death of someone you just met."

Having been surrounded by death in the camp, I'd thought myself hardened, too. But something about this was different. I'd let myself feel *safe*, like I had when I was a child in Harska. In doing so, I felt like a child again, and the helplessness of it crushed me.

"Look." Kaur gestured with her chin at the sky.

I stared up. The levship floated a few hundred feet above the mountain. It drifted toward Sambalpur.

"Is Elam your friend?"

"I wouldn't use that word."

"Explain! How do you know him?"

She stuck her hands on her hips. "The little mouse barks." She turned around and lifted her gown up, exposing her naked back and black underwear. The rose-colored scar snaked all the way down.

"Elam carved this lovely memento into me with one of his cursed demonblades. He's former Red Veil. Now he works for someone even worse. Colonel Rao."

"So why did he do this?"

Kaur lowered her gown and turned back to face me. "Because Colonel Rao told him to, probably. As for *why*… well…" She got suddenly quiet. Was she hiding something?

I looked back at Jaysh's lifeless, messy form. "We should burn him."

"Burn him? Oh, they don't do that in Behesh. They leave their dead in the mountains to be eaten by birds. The most appropriate thing would be to leave him here, exactly like this."

"It sounds so… cold."

"Not to them. Makes good sense, actually. Nothing wrong

with feeding the birds. Better than feeding the worms or the flames, if you ask me."

Kaur turned and walked in the direction of the cliff over-looking Sambalpur.

Before Jaysh had died, it seemed he'd clutched his wound, then stuck his fingers on his gold-rimmed spectacles. Now, bloody fingerprints were smudged on the lenses.

I took his spectacles off and placed it in his coat pocket. I shut Jaysh's open eyes. I lay him straight on his back, then put his hands over his chest. A more dignified position was the least I could do.

A paper stuck out of his coat pocket, where I'd put the spectacles. I pulled it out. My name was written at the top, along with all sorts of medical information, most of which I couldn't understand.

At the bottom was Saina's signature — a beautiful curl of calligraphy — along with these words: *Highest recommendation for resettlement due to upstanding character displayed through acts of selflessness in war time.*

I held the paper to my chest. No one had ever said something so wonderful about me. And yet...

I looked upon Jaysh and sobbed. I was so weak, even if Kaur had let me run toward Elam to my death, Jaysh still would've died. Saina and all the patients on the ship still would've gotten taken. Even if I had a lightblade and a combat stone, I would've ended up another body, lying beside Jaysh.

I was so weak; I didn't deserve such kindness. And yet, they'd written these words for me, all so I could have a better life.

"Thanks for everything you did for me," I said to Jaysh. "Wish I could've gotten to know you better." I let out a sad, shrill breath. "What the hell even happened? It was like lightning. One moment we were laughing in there, and now we're like this. It makes no sense, how fast things can go to shit." I rubbed my soggy eyes. "Jaysh, my friend… good thoughts, good words, good deeds."

I sat in silence for a while.

THE BOXY, blue levship hovered over Sambalpur. I watched as it floated toward the gigantic tower that loomed behind the golden wall. The colorful, animal- and human-infused statues of the gods climbing the tower seemed so surreal.

"So Rao is already holed up in the God Tower," Kaur said to herself.

The levship floated into an opening in the middle of the God Tower and disappeared inside.

I grabbed my hair. Why was this happening? I was about to get my dream stone and wait for the levship that would bring me to Behesh. If only I'd taken my dream stone before I went for my walk. *"Nowhere is safe,"* Kaur had said yesterday. *"Death is watching you,"* Elam had said. If only I'd digested these words, but I'd been lulled into a false sense of safety. I pulled my hair hard enough to feel a sting and screamed without sound.

What to do, now?

"You know about the levship that's coming?" I asked Kaur. "Saina had mentioned it. They're going to bring more healers."

Kaur glanced at me, heavy shadows under her eyes. "I was considering hitching a ride. I was considering *many* things. Disappearing. Buying a new identity crystal to start a new life — totally fresh — somewhere where no one knows me. But now…" She cracked her knuckles.

Seemed she was stuck in the same dilemma as me. "But now?"

"Dunno." She shook her head and chuckled, seemingly awed by the ridiculousness of it all. "What a cursed fate. I can't let Rao do this. I just can't. I have to stop all of this."

"Stop what?"

"Never mind. It's not your concern, local boy. Get on that levship that's coming and get to Eshur. I'm sure it's what the dead healer would want."

True, and yet, I had to swallow the bitterest fruit. Sambalpur, those huge golden doors, the tower with the climbing gods… all of it separated me from my dream stone. From Zauri. From my promise to come back to her. I stared at the God Tower, despair in my throat. This wasn't fun, like in the dream. This was life or death. I didn't want any of this.

"Don't tell me…" Kaur raised an eyebrow and grinned. "You got a thing for that cute healer lady? Come on, local boy. She's — what — ten years older than you? And way out of your level. *Way.* Oh, and so is Elam. If you're thinking you're gonna march into that tower, defeat Elam and his demonic lightblades, and then gather her in your arms — you're madder than me."

"How does he even do that? The floating lightblades?"

"Crazy, isn't it? Elam can't even make a normal lightblade. Never had the discipline for training. Terrified of going back into dreams. But then he got *blessed.* And you don't want to know what's blessing him."

A shudder blew through me. Truth is, I wasn't even thinking about fighting Elam and saving Saina. Obviously, that was beyond my ability. I, who fought with a frying pan. Who couldn't even form a stable lightblade. I just wanted my dream stone back. Surely Elam had no need for it. It was just an awful coincidence that it flew away with the ship.

My stomach sank as if I'd digested a lead ball. I realized then that I'd never see Zauri again. There was no way to retrieve my dream stone. I'd almost died several times in the past few days. I'd surely die if I walked into an ancient city being fought over by mighty Karshan commanders with impossible lightblade abilities.

My life was more important than a dream stone. I could just buy another one once I'd left this god-forsaken country.

The whine of a spinning sunsink sounded. A similar boxy blue levship with a shield-and-dragon emblem descended from a cloud and hovered over the mountain.

"Speak of the daeva," Kaur said. "There's your carriage ride into the dawn. Meanwhile, I've got a long way down to reach hell."

It slowed its descent, then softly settled near where the previous levship had been.

I EXPLAINED what happened to the new arrivals. The captain and four healers, who now stood atop the entrance ramp of their ship, listened intently, varieties of dismay across their faces. I hoped they'd honor Saina's promise and get me out of this hellhole.

"The guy who did this — was he Red Veil or not?" one of the healers, a man with a gray mustache, asked.

"I don't know," I said. "I mean, I heard he was former Red Veil. Now he's working for some guy named Colonel Rao."

The healer with the gray mustache turned to the captain, who wore a blue uniform with the shield-and-dragon emblem in the center. "You know this Colonel Rao?" he asked him.

The captain shrugged. "There are thousands of colonels in the Karshan army. And there are even more colonels-in-waiting, considering you only need to reach level fifty in the Karshan Army Officer Training Program. What we need to do is determine his commanding officer and lodge a complaint. This is a war crime, plain and simple."

"Wait," said another healer — a tall, elderly woman. "Should we even believe this guy? What if he's one of the culprits?"

"I-I've got a letter. Here. See." I presented the letter I found in Jaysh's coat pocket. They all peered over it.

"By the dawn, on top of losing your hand, you had a tapeworm inside of you," the old woman said. "Oh, you poor thing."

"How do we know this is *your* letter?" asked gray mustache.

"Here, look." I showed them my regrown hand. It had an obvious paleness above the wrist where new flesh had grown.

"Indeed, looks like Saina's work," said the elderly woman. "Guess he's not lying."

The captain gestured toward the entrance. "Get onboard, then. There's nothing left here for us to do."

"What about Jaysh?" I asked.

"Jaysh is in the perfect place to rest."

I scratched my head. So Kaur wasn't lying. Still, I didn't quite understand their custom. "Wouldn't his family want his body?"

"It's just a body. The soul has gone to the Asha, from where it'll be sent back, to be reborn on the dark side of the world. The birds will carry the rest of him to heaven."

I guess they believed what they believed, no matter how strange it seemed to me.

"No time to waste," the captain said. "If rogue Karshan agents are targeting our ships, we better get out of here, fast."

"Yeah, you're right." The thought of more people with powers like Elam chilled my bones.

I walked up the ramp and into the ship. The hum of the sunsink was so loud inside, it vibrated through my body. Metal doors flanked the hallway, which was lit by red sunshine streaming through the skylights at the top. The hallway was so open and wide, I could see into the second and third floors, which also had hallways with doors. This ship seemed much more spacious than Saina's, though it didn't look much larger on the outside.

"Come with me," gray mustache said. He led me to the last door on the left, just before the staircase leading up.

Gray mustache took out a clear crystal from his pocket and flashed it in front of the door. The door hissed open. He stood to the side and gestured for me to enter.

"Since it's just you, I'm giving you our nicest room. Hospitality is everything to us Beheshians. The younger generation seems to forget that, though. They weren't around during the Exile, so don't understand the importance of making others feel at home. Anyway, let me have someone get you a blanket and pillow."

I stepped inside and sat on the huge bed; it had the crispest fitted sheet I'd ever seen. Ran my hand over it: silkier than the one in my dream.

Gorgeous carpets were draped across the walls. One was white and gold, with alternating patterns of flowers and birds. Another was red and gold and depicted a scene: a family in a meadow, plucking dates off a massive branch and eating them and laughing. Was that what New Behesh was like? Would I soon be in that meadow, eating fruits off the trees? Laughing? With friends? With *family?*

What about the island in my dreams? What about Zauri, standing in the shadows of the palms, all alone? Waiting for me. Worrying if I was alive or dead.

Waiting and worrying forever. For an eternity.

While it had been four days since I'd seen her in my time, more than three months had passed for her. We'd never see each other again. That dream stone would remain on the levship inside the God Tower, out of sight and mind of anyone with a soul.

Or maybe Elam or Rao would find it. Maybe they'd torture Zauri, somehow.

I pictured Zauri with her blue hair, sitting next to me in this bed. We should be going to Eshur together. I thought of how eagerly she'd trained me. How her entire purpose was to make sure that I could survive, whether it meant training me in light-blades or electric weapons. Even if it meant deceiving me, like she'd done when she used Kediri's shadow to draw my lightblade out.

And yet, there was something more: her affection. It was the only real affection I'd ever felt since my family was executed. It was rainfall upon the parched, cracked ground that was my heart, and just the thought of it flooded me with warmth.

The door hissed open. It was the elderly woman. She smiled, then placed a pillow at the head of my bed. She fluffed the blanket and spread it.

"There you go. Anything else you need? Dates? Some rose water, perhaps?"

I stared at her and tried to smile, but it wouldn't come.

"What's wrong?"

I stood. I gave the lovely room one final look. My jittering heart rattled against my ribs. All the air got sucked out of me. I felt I was turning into jelly. I couldn't believe what I was doing. But it was the only thing I could do. I couldn't shut out Zauri's pain and go on with my life.

"Oh, if you need to use the bathroom, I can show you where it is."

I brushed past the old woman and stopped at the door's threshold.

"You're not going to the bathroom, are you?"

I shook my head, my tears heavy, and walked to the exit.

Chapter Twelve

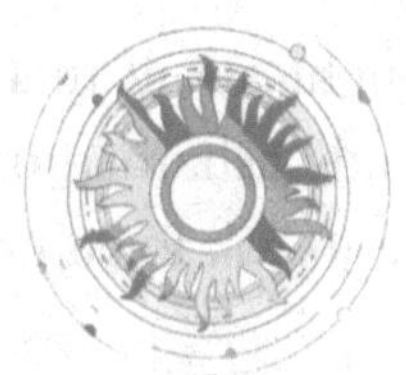

It didn't take long to find Kaur. She was sitting on the path down the mountain and into the forest that led to Sambalpur. Right in the middle of the path, cross-legged, her back to me.

The trees ahead no longer resembled broccoli; now they were a mass of jagged barks and leafy canopies. Between the bark and branches lay deep shadows that breathed out cold. An uninviting place, to say the least, but it separated this mountain path from Sambalpur.

The heavenly God Tower loomed, despite being so far away. More abrupt was an arch that spread over the city's entrance.

I crunched on a pebble to alert Kaur of my presence. She glanced at me, then covered her face with her palm and shook her head.

I knelt beside her. Wasn't sure what to tell her.

"You made a dumb choice, local boy."

"Enough with 'local boy.' It got old the first time you said it."

"Okay, Jyosh."

I let out a surprised *hah*. "Thought you'd forgotten my name."

"Nope. I was just being an asshole."

"I noticed. So why are you sitting here?"

"Because I'm tired. By the way, you got any food or water?"

I shook my head.

"You're telling me you left that ship and came all the way here without taking any useful supplies?"

I nodded.

"Figures."

I really should've thought about that. But those healers were in a hurry, and I was already ashamed of walking away. Still… it would've been good sense to ask for a can of lentils and a bottle of water.

Kaur massaged her thick eyebrows. "My head hurts. It hurts because I'm as dumb as you. I don't have a plan. I don't know what I can possibly accomplish, all alone. But I can't just walk away."

"Well, you're not alone, now."

She strummed her dark red bangs. "Let's see if I can put the pieces together. Your really *do* have a thing for Saina, don't you? You love her, just because she was nice to you. Yeah, my curtain was next to yours. I listened to you confess your sins to her. Heard her dry your tears."

It wasn't Saina I loved. I mean, if I could save her, that'd be a bonus, but I knew I was too weak. I just wanted my dream stone. I wanted Zauri back.

No way I was going to tell Kaur, though. If she was mocking me for liking a real, flesh and blood woman, what would she think if I told her this was all to save a lightblade training program I'd modded onto a corrupted dream stone?

"Yeah, I love Saina. I'm going to save her."

Kaur actually smiled. A bit too giddily. "You got a mommy thing, don't you?"

"Mommy thing?"

She nodded too happily. "Yeah. You know in Salkofy, a lot of boys grow up barely seeing their mothers. Everyone — mother *and* father — are too busy working. So the boys end up craving a mother's love their whole lives. Some of the top selling dream stones are actually mothering programs, believe it or not. Except they got it all screwed up in their heads, so they turn those mothering programs into their dream wives. You're just like them."

My mother was a homemaker, so I saw her every day. But to be honest, after they executed her, I missed her hugs and kisses. Still do. But that had nothing to do with this, obviously.

"Saina isn't that old. She looks nothing like my mother, anyway."

"But she was so gentle with you. You *loved* it. Just admit it. You're looking for a mother-wife."

So bizarre. But I didn't want Kaur to learn the truth, so played along.

"Maybe I am."

"Hah! Knew it. Turns out, I'm a much better judge of character than they give me credit for." She smiled smugly. "You know what, Jyosh, I'm a few years older than you. I could be your mommy-wife."

Was not expecting her to say that. "You're not… very gentle."

"I can be gentle." She tilted her head and smiled. "Oh Jyoshy, you've had a hard life. Here, lay your head in my lap and I'll massage your nipples." She spat on her fingers, then rubbed her thumb and forefinger together. "I'll make them nice and hard."

She laughed like a drunk donkey. Ugh. A first-class asshole, no doubt.

"Listen, Kaur. Say whatever you want about it, I don't care. But I intend to get to that levship and save Saina. You with me?"

"Nope. That's not my plan. I'm just here to kill—" The words got caught in her throat. Her gargle sounded like cloth tearing against thorns. Her hand jittered. For whatever reason, she couldn't say it.

"Kill Elam?"

She shook her head. "No. Not Elam. It's Colonel Rao who's responsible. It's Rao who must… who must…"

"Die."

Kaur nodded, heaving as if short of breath. Weird.

Anyway, if I could get in, get my dream stone, and get out, that would be nice. Avoid confronting anyone. Maybe ask Elam or Rao nicely if I could have it back. They had no need of it, anyway.

But, obviously, it wasn't going to be that easy. They had no reason to trust my intentions. I could be a spy working for their enemy, for all they knew. I was entering a dangerous place with many unknowns, and I had no strengths to save me.

Hopefully Kaur did.

"So you said that Elam carved those scars into your back. You fought him, then. That obviously means you're some kind of soldier. And since you keep mentioning Spicy Lane or Smoky Lane or whatever in Salkofy, that means you're a Karshan soldier."

I could put pieces together, too.

Kaur crossed her arms. "So what if I was?"

"You must be pretty good with lightblades, then. That's helpful."

"*Helpful?* Let me guess, you want me to fight your battles. That the gist of it?"

"No. I fully intend to fight. I just… won't be as good as you. And that's sort of an understatement."

"Figured you weren't much of a fighter." She pointed at me. "I mean, look at you."

She was smaller and skinnier than I was, so what'd she mean by that? I let it slide, for now.

Kaur jumped to her feet. "I've had enough rest." She stretched her arms to the sky and grunted. "I'm eager to see what awaits us. Let's go."

Good. I was eager, too. Right now, Sambalpur was a mystery. I wanted to pull off the veil and see what it would cost me.

WE TOOK our final step off the mountain and arrived on flat land. My knees ached and I was breathing fast, but it seemed we still had a long way to go. Now the mountains stood at our backs and to our right and left, with a forest at our front.

Looming in the distance above the tree line was the largest arch I'd ever seen. It must've been built by titans. It extended from one end of the valley to the other, its mirror-like sheen reflecting the red sun. Between us and the arch lay clusters of cypresses, oaks, and yellow grasses. More peculiar, massive crystals shot out of the ground: some were black, others dark blue, and a few bright red. The environment resembled nothing I'd known.

"This is where the trouble begins," Kaur said. "Forests are a great place to ambush the unsuspecting. We don't know what's going on in the city itself — whether one faction or another is winning. Be on your guard, and be ready to run or kill."

Questions popped into my mind. What factions, exactly? Could it be related to that brawl between yellow-eyed and purple-eyed Karshan soldiers that I'd gotten caught in?

I didn't want to badger her so kept the topic to the essentials.

"We don't have anything to kill with," I said. "Also, I've got a violet healing stone in my chest slot. What about you?"

"Yep. Same. Without a healer, it's totally useless." Kaur held up her fists and cracked her knuckles. "These'll do just fine, until we get something better."

"Maybe for you. I've never killed anyone with my hands."

"But you *have* killed. That's a good start. Don't hesitate when the time comes, your enemies surely won't. Got it?"

"I'll do my best."

She grinned. "So eager to save your future mommy-wife. I love it."

Kaur was one of those people who drove every joke into the ground, wasn't she? I admit, the mommy-wife thing was funny the first time, but enough already.

"I get it. I want my mommy so bad. Can you stop, now?"

"Oh I'm never gonna stop." She gestured toward herself. "If it bothers you so much, then you're welcome to make fun of me, in return."

"I don't know anything about you."

"Come on." She patted her own head. "Like, look how short I am. Make fun of my height."

"That's boring."

"Call me *imp*. Ooh, that's good. I'm an imp because I'm short and terrible. Come on. Say it."

"It's not funny if it's your idea. Also, I'm not in the mood."

"I was just starting to feel better." She sighed in obvious dejection. "You're such a downer."

"Downer? A guy with floating lightblades just killed my friend."

Her expression tensed. A pitying frown snapped onto her face. "Sad as it sounds, I've gotten used to seeing friends die."

That, I understood. I'd gotten used to seeing friends die at the camp — part of the reason I'd stopped making friends. Not eager to dwell on the topic, I gestured for Kaur to continue walking.

We approached the tree line. A red-tailed squirrel chittered on a branch above. Birds fluttered about. The air smelled *green*. It all seemed so serene.

Kaur went behind the nearest mahogany, got low, and darted her head left and right.

"The hell are you doing standing there?" She gestured for me to get behind her.

I scurried over. "See something?"

"No. But please consider, we're not dealing with fools here." She pointed at a bush a few paces in front. "Notice anything?"

It was just a yellow-leaf bush. I shook my head.

"Something disturbed that bush. A big animal. Maybe even a human."

I looked at the bush again. It was just like the others. "Umm, what makes you say that?"

"I'm not teaching a class on wilderness survival. Just stay low, stay quiet, and follow me."

Kaur would take a step out of cover, take another step into cover, pause to look around, then repeat. I copied her. We stayed at the edge of the tree line instead of going deeper in. We wrapped around the forest, keeping the mountains to our back. I was careful to step softly, avoiding crunching my feet on leaves and twigs. After fifteen minutes of creeping without exchanging a word, what we feared came into view.

Soldiers. Two men and a woman, clad in those tight black suits, stood by a sinuous banyan. Purple pupils shone in the eye slots of their masks.

"See the eyes," Kaur whispered, "means they work for General Sylet."

He was one of the commanders those brawling Karshan soldiers were fighting for. "Who is he, exactly?" I asked, peeking at them from behind a scraggly mahogany.

They were standing around and eating what looked like cereal bars. They dropped the silvery wrappers at their feet. So sloppy.

"Long story short, Sylet is Rao's enemy."

"So then he's our friend, right?"

"It doesn't work that way. Sylet has claimed this area as his special, totally off-limits administrative zone. And so has Rao, of course. Now a few days ago, there was a non-lethal agreement between Sylet and Rao. That… uhh… well, let's just say it didn't last. Point is, whoever isn't of their faction will be," she mimed slicing her own neck, "no questions asked, just for being here."

"I mean, they're both Karshans. What you're describing sounds like a civil war."

"Now you're getting it. You think the Karshans came here to fight you Manizans? *Pshh*. Raja Panja Parani surrendered on the third day."

"You're tickling my bones."

"Nope. It's all true. See, when an empire gets too big, it cracks and falls apart. This is a war between Karsha and Karsha. Your country is just the latest battleground." She held her finger up to her lips. "Now enough talk. Follow me and we'll slip by them."

She was right. I could think about all that stuff later. For now, I stared at the soldiers and gulped upon seeing sword hilts gleaming on their belts. I imagined them pulling them out and forming red lightblades, then cutting me to pieces. A burning terror welled up in my chest.

"Come on, let's not keep your sexy mommy-wife wai—" Kaur silenced herself as a rustling sounded behind us.

We spun around. A woman clad in black stood near a thorn-bush, metal hilt in her hand. The air around it cycled from the heat as her lightblade formed: a chilling red beam that breathed shadows.

"Oh shit," I mumbled.

With all the air in her lungs, the woman shouted, "Code Four! Code Four!" Then she raised her lightblade to her chest and sprinted toward me.

Time slowed. Why me? Because I was bigger than Kaur? A mouse would be more dangerous.

The woman leapt off her feet. The lightblade surged straight toward my chest. I didn't move. Stuck like prey.

Red lights appeared above Kaur's fingers, as if the eyes of ten demons had opened. Kaur lunged forward, and the lights ripped into the woman's neck, spraying blood. The soldier's head flung backward on her bloodied neck as her body tumbled forward. Her lightblade died in the air and her metal hilt hit the ground.

The woman thudded onto a pile of leaves, painting them red. Kaur stood between me and the dead soldier, her gray robe bloody, red beams floating above each of her fingers. They were the *eyes* I'd seen cut through that soldier's neck. And they were made of light.

Light claws. But how? She was wearing a healing stone, like me.

Hurried footsteps and crunching leaves. Three soldiers emerged from the thicket, lightblades in their hands. Two more lightblade-wielding soldiers came from the mountainside. They approached Kaur.

"Code Eleven!" they shouted, then spread out to surround her.

I kept my back against a tree trunk and watched. The intensity of their blades made my insides quiver. I'd already tasted how a lightblade devours flesh and didn't want to feel that again.

Kaur jumped onto the tree behind me and used her light claws to climb up the trunk. Then she jumped onto a branch. From her perch, she leapt toward a soldier, claws forward, and evaded his desperate swing by swerving midmotion.

Screams and blood and flesh filled the air as she tore the life out of him.

A soldier swiped at her, but she jumped onto a different branch, and then climbed higher, as if she were a cat. She lunged down on him, took his head in her hands, and pulled it off as she tossed his body over her head.

"I didn't sign up for this," one of the soldiers said. He retracted his lightblade and dropped his hilt. He raised his hands, backed away, and ran.

Kaur was up in the branches again. The two remaining soldiers stared up, their lightblades in front of their faces, eyes wide in desperation to spot her. One lowered his gaze, looked around, and noticed my huddled form, his eyes widening further. He'd found an easier target.

As if he'd forgotten about Kaur — or perhaps didn't want to face his fears — he ran for me, lightblade raised.

I dodged out the way of his swipe as it cut through the bark, sap spraying. The burnt syrup smelled nauseatingly sweet.

"Demon!" the other soldier screamed. Hellish shrieks followed; the *demon* must've gotten him.

I sprinted through the forest, the final soldier chasing me. I jumped over a crystal growing out of the ground, sidestepped a thornbush, almost tripped on a bunch of vines.

Brambles appeared, just ahead. I halted. I turned and ducked as a lightblade swipe rent the air above my head. Then I headbutted the soldier in the chin, sending us tumbling. He flew back, and I landed on top.

He brought his knee up into my gut with thunderous force. Then he headbutted me back, sending birds shooting through my vision. The soldier tossed me off.

As I writhed from the pain in my gut and face, he picked up his sword hilt. Would the electric hum of his projecting beam be the last sound I ever heard?

I grabbed a pile of dirt and tossed it in his face. He didn't even flinch. If only I had my frying pan.

The rattling of branches above made him look up in fear. Kaur landed between me and him. She raised her claws and leapt onto his shoulders. Her claws dug into his face. Flesh and sinew and eyeballs sprayed. He couldn't even scream.

Kaur jumped off him and back to the ground. The soldier's lifeless body flew backward from the force of her jump and smashed into a tree trunk, bones cracking.

After all was still, she heaved out the heaviest breath I'd ever heard. Sounded like a dying lion. Her light claws retracted. She crawled toward me and fell in a heap, her head in my lap.

Blood had painted this forest, painted Kaur, painted the air itself.

I shrugged off my shock and shook her. "Hey, don't sleep here."

Kaur looked up at me. Her pupils had enlarged, almost filling her eyeballs — animal-like. Fearful pangs thudded in my heart. I wanted to get up and run, but my fear froze me in place.

She took my hand. Hers was so hot, as if it'd just been bathed in a vat of boiling curry.

"Help me," she groaned. "It hurts… so much… help…"

I lifted her gray robe to expose her back and sides. No visible wounds.

"We don't have time for this." I stood and pulled her up. She clung onto my shoulders, her whole weight on me. Then she wrapped her feet around my legs, as if I were a tree.

"I can't carry you." I struggled to stay standing with her weight on me.

"Amma could," she replied. "But I was much smaller back then."

She seemed delirious, to say the least. We were still in danger. This wasn't the time for jokes or whatever this was.

"I'm not strong enough. Try to walk."

"Then leave me. I'm tired of fighting."

"No." I pulled my legs out of her hold, then gently settled her back on the ground. Blood and specks of flesh covered her hair, face, gray robe, and bare legs.

I wanted to ask her about what she'd done… what she'd

become… but this wasn't the time. I used my robe to wipe the flesh bits and blood from her face and hair. Her cheeks were boiling, too. Whatever she'd done to create those light claws, it'd taken a toll on her insides. Being a machinist for twelve years, constantly on the verge of burnout, I knew that toll well.

I let her rest and caught my breath for a few minutes. Then I went to steal from the dead.

I took red combat crystals from the chest slots of the dead. I also rummaged through their utility pockets and took off the masks of the ones who still had faces, just to see whom Kaur had killed. The woman who'd sighted us wasn't even a woman — she was a girl who couldn't have been older than eighteen. I pulled an orange stone from her pocket. A familiar warmth and an unfamiliar fear shuddered through me as I rubbed its shiny, smooth surface.

"A dream stone," I said as I held it up to the sun's dusky light shining through the overhead branches.

"Well, don't you look happy," Kaur said. She got to her feet, finally lucid, and began helping me.

Kaur pulled a cereal bar in its shiny, silvery wrapper from a faceless soldier's utility pocket. Then she pushed him onto his back and unzipped his black uniform. "Help me out. Or rather, help him out."

I pulled on the man's shoulders — trying my best not to look at what remained of his face — while Kaur held the uniform. He slipped out of it easily enough. Then I left him naked beside one of those big, blue crystals jutting from the ground.

Kaur threw off her robe and stood topless. She pulled out her violet healing crystal from her chest slot and stuck in a red combat crystal. Then she put one foot in the black one-piece.

I averted my gaze — a bit late, to be completely honest.

"Don't be so modest," she said. "Come and help. These one-pieces are a pain to get into, but they're ideal for maneuvering in combat, and the utility pockets are perfect for storing stuff."

"Isn't that one a bit big for you?"

"Nope, they're all the same size. You'll see."

I pulled the uniform up above her waist. From this close, I noticed more scars across her back and shoulders. Old ones, judging by how faded they were.

I zipped the suit over her back as she stuck her arms into the sleeves. It looked comically loose on her, with bulging air gaps in her legs and sides. Then she pressed on a tiny crystal in her collar. The suit shrunk with a hiss, tightening on her body, flush.

"Nifty, aren't they?" She turned and smiled at me. "Your turn."

I took off my robe and pulled out my violet healing stone. The jolt made me shudder. The air and forest turned slightly less violet to my eyes; I hadn't even noticed the violet tint until it was gone. I fingered the red combat crystal in my hands, then stuck it in my chest. An electric surge spread through my body, making me gasp. The world tinted even redder than before.

"First time using a red stone?" Kaur asked.

I nodded.

We took another suit off the dead. I got inside it with Kaur's help. Once I was all zipped up, I pressed the tiny crystal on my collar. The air around my skin got sucked out in a hiss. The suit tightened, strangling my muscles, then loosened ever-so-slightly to a comfortable and flexible level.

"Let's go." Kaur holstered sword hilts to both sides of her utility belt. Was she intending to wield two lightblades at the same time?

I was fine with one. The design of these hilts wasn't like those in the dream. So light, as if hollow — they felt like toys. The guard was rectangular, and the grip had a rubbery coating that made it softer on the hands. Not much to look at: function over form, for sure.

I gave the dead one last glance: a mess of bodies with flesh torn out all over, mostly in the face. Blood flies had already gathered. So would other things that lived in the forest, once we'd gone.

It seemed so unnecessary. All I wanted was my dream stone back. Zauri back. But they weren't going to listen, I assumed. No one cared what I wanted. I'd have to take it.

"You have one of those faces." Kaur managed a soft chuckle between tired breaths. "A face that makes it so obvious what you're thinking."

"Oh? What am I thinking?"

"You feel bad for them. You have *empathy* for people you've never met. It'll get you killed."

"Why would empathy get me killed?"

"Because it'll make you hesitate. And in battle, a split second is the line between life and death."

Made a lot of sense. Perhaps it was better to save empathy for when we were safe.

Kaur said, "Two combat stones, a dream stone, one light flare, eleven rations, a few full water bottles, and three sword hilts. Pretty good haul, I'd say. Oh, and these uniforms." She pinched her collar.

The hell was a light flare? Whatever, there was an even more jarring question on my tongue. It was the elephant hovering between us, slapping my face with its trunk.

"How were you able to conduct light claws out of your hands, and without a combat stone?"

"It's a *blessing*. And also a curse." She frowned, somewhat mournful, and far more serious than she'd ever been. "I'll tell you more, later. Just know, it's best kept as a last resort — a card to play when things are truly dire."

I thought I'd understood how lightblades worked. You needed a combat stone in your chest slot, and you needed a sword hilt, and red light from the sun, and then with skill and discipline you could form the blade. Now… as with everything, it seemed my knowledge of lightblades was like a pebble against a mountain.

We approached the arch of Sambalpur, staying careful and sticking to the tree line near the mountain. The closer we got, the more the arch seemed to loom over us, cracking the sky. Unreal.

After ten minutes of creeping from tree to tree, we arrived at the outskirts of the city, just under the arch itself. From this close, the arch seemed to reflect the dusky sky, as if made of mirrors.

The buildings came into view: all made of shimmering white limestone. Unlike any architecture I'd seen in Maniza. Most of the buildings sported tall domes, with statues of gods with mixed animal and human features sitting or standing atop them. A few structures had this cascading style, with smaller buildings built on top of larger ones, several layers high.

Strange to see no roads. The ground was this dry, cracked, caked dust — perhaps the only thing that showed this city's ancient age.

While the sights interested me, the sounds didn't. There weren't any. A silent city — couldn't even hear a breeze. It chilled my insides. No smell, either. The air barely churned, feeling almost still and dead.

We rushed toward the nearest structure: a well with a wide roof. Weird how the well was made of a mirror-like material, and so reflected the eternal dusk.

And then a bell rang, like the whine of a great beast. It continued to reverberate. Hopefully it hadn't sounded to welcome us. My heart quickened as we stared at the plaza across from us: an empty square with stone staircases leading to a myriad of buildings.

Was someone… or something about to show itself?

The ominous bell finally silenced.

"Do you know what that sound was?" I whispered.

"Nope." Kaur shook her head. "I'm wiped, Jyosh. About ready to fall asleep, right here."

"We can find somewhere better than the middle of the street."

I glanced around. Small, flat-topped buildings surrounded us. The roofs had these pearly-looking merlons.

"Let's just go inside one of these houses," I said. "What's the worst that could happen?"

"Houses…" Kaur darted her head around. Her eyes lit up once she noticed the doors. "All right."

All the houses looked the same. Was this some kind of neighborhood? A well sat here, so could be.

With my adrenaline faded, my bones yearned to melt into the ground. And I wanted to scarf down a cereal bar. And chug a whole bottle of water.

"This one." I pointed at the nearest door, which had a little canopy over the entrance.

"Lead on." Kaur grinned — in a good-natured way, this time.

We stayed low and crept toward the nearest building. At the threshold, Kaur pulled out her sword hilt and squeezed it. A lightblade grew off the hilt, flickering red and black. The heat warmed my nose and eyebrows.

I wasn't about to embarrass myself by failing to create a light-blade. I could barely make one in the dream under ideal conditions. I'd only succeeded when fighting Kediri's shadow because my rage took control. Maybe after we'd rested, I could try.

Kaur turned the knob and pushed the door open. Rushed into the house. I waited at the threshold as she darted back and forth in the dim room.

"Clear!" she shouted.

I crept inside and shut the door, then finally stood tall and stretched.

Skylights brought in the weak, ruddy sunshine. Weirdly enough, there was nothing here. No furniture. Just a dull, empty room. Even the walls were an ugly, effortless gray. Such a contrast to the splendor of the city's exterior.

Kaur put out her lightblade, leaving the room a shade darker. She dropped to her knees and collapsed against the wall.

"You all right?" I asked.

"I'm fine. Just been waiting to do that for a while."

I sat next to her. I stared up at the dismal sky showing through the skylight. How safe were we, here?

"I'll tell you about the claws when we're in the dream."

"In the dream?"

"Yeah, you found that dream stone. Don't know about you, but I can't sleep well without one."

"How can we both use one dream stone? We'd need a wire to make a circuit between us."

"I'll show you after you put it in."

I unzipped my black suit at the front, pulled out the red combat stone, and took the dream stone out of my utility pocket. Unlike my dream stone, which had this tepid orange glow, this one glowed as fiercely as fire. Wondrous. What would we find in there?

I stuck it inside. The world tinted a soothing orange.

"Lie down, face away from me," Kaur said.

"What? Why?"

"You can't be the big spoon, Jyosh. I don't want to feel your… you know… when I'm asleep."

"Spoon? What are you talking about?"

"I'm talking about us having many points of contact while we sleep. If we're holding hands, and I sort of wrap myself around you, it'll work as well as a wire and ensure slight movements won't disconnect us."

Was she serious? She'd been uncharacteristically serious since clawing all those soldiers to death. But… was she serious?

I let out an embarrassed chuckle.

"I'm too tired for this." She sighed, totally worn out. "Listen, dream stones used by military have a special feature. They keep track of your surroundings while you sleep. So anyone tries to creep up on us, it'll alert us. I'll keep my red combat stone inside. My sword hilt's resting right here, beside my head. Believe me, this is the safest and best option."

"If you say so." I lay down and got on my side, facing away from Kaur. The floor's hardness reminded me of my mattress in the camp. But at least there, I had a pillow, thin as it was.

Kaur took my hands, clasping our fingers. She stuck her legs between mine, then wrapped her feet around my shins. She snuggled up close. Her body was still hot, as if a furnace were cuddling me.

Though awkward, the feeling was kind of nice. Besides, I was too tired to really think about it.

"You good?" she asked.

"Yeah."

Her clammy hand was hard to grip. Was she nervous? So many callouses on her palm, like my own.

Why was she caressing my palms with her fingers?

"It's weird," she whispered in my ear. "Your left hand is so rough, and right hand so smooth."

"It's a new hand. Uh, please stop, it's ticklish."

"Of course you'd be ticklish." She stopped and firmed our handhold.

"And you're not?"

She giggled in my ear. "I'm not telling."

God, this topic was awkward. "So, listen, I have like a

hundred questions to ask when we get in the dream. Hope that's fine."

"Figures. Leave it for the dream. So, what kind of dirty thoughts you thinking right now?"

I could feel my cheeks reddening. "What makes you think I'm thinking dirty thoughts?"

"Even I do it, sometimes. Helps me fall asleep."

"You serious? That would only keep me awake longer."

Our handhold got sticky. Why was she sweating so much? Or was that me?

"By now, the dream stone should be lulling us," she whispered. "I can feel it. Can you?"

A sweet sea of sunshine trickled into my veins. Hands made of flowers pulled my soul into a river of milk. Honey dripped off the clouds, sunk into the milk, and stirred me with warmth.

Chapter Thirteen

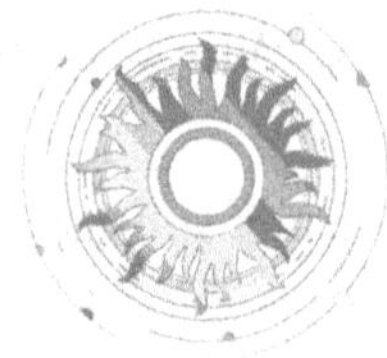

PATTER-PATTER-PATTER. It was raining. I was sitting upon the greenest hill ever, my naked behind wet from the soggy mud and grass. No thoughts, no memories. Afterall, I'd just been born.

Farms surrounded my hill in the distance. Wheat crops larger than trees filled the landscape, intersected by snaky, stone roads. Despite the rain, the sky shone a cloudless azure, so the rain must've been coming from a higher heaven. Perhaps that was why it smelled like molasses.

A woman walked up the hill toward me. She was naked too. Cherry hair, caramel skin, and full eyebrows. I tried not to stare at her breasts. She opened her palm, and a floating screen appeared above it. *Tap-tap-tap.*

A blinding glow of white light surrounded her body. The light turned into a beige long shirt, which reached her knees. How'd she do that?

"Don't tell me — you're one of those *naked* dreamers," she said as if she knew me. "I suppose it's your right, as the dreamer and all. I mean, I don't care. Nope. Couldn't care less." Why was she side-eying me?

"Sorry." I stood and stared into the emerald eyes of this completely unfamiliar woman. "Who are you?"

She gaped in shock. "Oh shit. Jyosh, did you… oh no."

"Who are you?" I repeated. "Who… who am I? Am I 'Jyosh?'"

She nodded, then pressed her hand against my cheek. So warm, unlike the rain. "I'm such a fool. I should've warned you. Of course you'd lose your memories. This dream stone has way more throughput than what you're probably used to."

"Dream… stone?" It was all so difficult to understand. "I can't remember anything. It's like… my mind is empty. A hollow box."

"That's right. This dream stone is so vast, it's overwhelmed your mind. Happens the first time you use one in this tier. Your memories will load in, but it might take some time. Probably twenty minutes in the real world, which would be seven or eight hours, here."

Such a gentle and caring woman. Of course I could trust her. The way she looked at me, I felt all warm inside. And yet, who was she to me?

"Are we… friends?" I asked.

She smiled with such brimming kindness. "Come on, let's explore a bit. I may have my memories, but this place is new to me, too. We'll find something interesting, I'm sure of it."

"I'm cold."

She opened her palm and *tap-tapped* on her screen again. A tingly, warm light wrapped around my body. A princely long shirt, puffy pants, and vest with silver buttons covered me.

"Fit for a raja." She nodded, obviously impressed. "Let's also stop this stupid rain." *Tap-tap-tap.*

The sky brightened. The sun sprung up from the horizon into the apex, bringing with it a soothing, honey light.

"So much better, don't you think, Jyosh?"

How could she control the elements like that? Was she a god? But why was a god being so kind to me? A painful bundle of dread deep inside told me I didn't deserve such kindness.

I nodded and straightened my back. I rubbed my arms and lowered my gaze.

"Hey, don't be like that. I know this is all rather overwhelming, but you've got nothing to worry about. We're in a safe place. Oh, and my name is Kaur."

Nothing to worry about? The wheat stalks here were five times their normal size, I didn't know who I was, and I was talking to a god.

She opened her palm again. *Tap-tap-tap.*

A milky white light appeared near our feet. It turned into a colorful wooden board with rounded corners.

"Big enough for both of us. You ever sky surfed in your dreams before?" She chuckled as if embarrassed. "Oh I forgot, you don't remember."

"Sky... surf?" That sounded incredible.

"Come on. No explanation needed. Let's just do it."

Of course, I could trust a god to keep me safe. She wouldn't let me fall and get hurt.

She stood at the front of the board and I stood at the back. How would I balance as it flew through the air?

"You don't have to do anything," she said. "I can conduct and steer. Hell, I can even wield a lightblade while doing it. Maybe even *two* lightblades." She raised her eyebrows playfully.

Of course, she could do anything. She'd already shown her power.

The board lifted into the air. Somehow, I was adhered to it, so my body didn't sway. Perhaps it was another of this god's powers. She jetted us upward until the giant wheat stalks looked like straw. The hill where I'd awoken seemed a bump in a vast, emerald carpet. The sky spread just as endlessly upward.

I wasn't afraid. It all seemed so calm, so wondrous. At the horizon, a red light shone, like a candle's glow. A fire? No, it was too beautiful to be destructive.

I tapped Kaur's shoulder and pointed at it. "What's that?"

"Ooh, what could that be? Let's go see!"

She sped us toward it. Wind whipped against me, sweet-scented like a god's breath. Such a wonderful feeling. It covered up the strange, spiky dread in my core. Maybe it was good to be alive, even though I had no idea who I was, why I was here, or where *here* even was.

As we got closer, the fiery red glow took on a solid form. My jaw dropped: a mountain of red crystal loomed ahead. It glimmered like a diamond bathed in blood and stretched vast into the heavens. Something only a titan could climb.

"You see the weirdest things in these places," Kaur said. "Let's go land on it."

She surged toward the mountain. It was see-through, like glass. The red light glowed from within, as if the crystal mountain had swallowed a dusky sun.

Kaur brought us down. As we closed in on the flat top of the mountain, something appeared: a cottage. Smoke trailed out of the chimney. Flowers sprouted around it. Only when we landed did I realize the flowers were taller than trees. If they had mouths, they could swallow us whole.

Not sure why my first thought about these big flowers was so disturbing, but everything here seemed *uncanny*, as if this wasn't how the world should be. Mountains shouldn't be made of red crystals. Flowers and wheat couldn't be taller than humans. And, strangest of all, gods weren't meant to walk among us.

We got off the skyboard and walked upon the hard crystal ground toward the cottage. Such a quaint, cozy little thing. I hoped the insides would be more familiar to my sensibilities.

The door opened. A smiling young woman stepped out. Her

face seemed to glow. She wore a long, golden skirt that reached her ankles, but kept her midriff exposed. An airy, blue shawl covered her chest, practically see-through.

Her smile vanished as we approached. "Who are you people?"

"Oh boy." Kaur turned to me and whispered, "Remind me, Jyosh, whose body you looted this dream stone from?"

What was she talking about? Seemed she'd forgotten, once again, that I couldn't remember. Why would a god be so forgetful?

"Oh, right." She smacked her head. "What the hell is wrong with me? I keep forgetting. Well, suppose I'll ask her."

"Where's Farvi?" the woman asked. Something about her face… was perfect. Radiant. Such elegant, shaped, and luminous eyebrows. Her petite, button-like nose fit her slender cheekbones, unlike Kaur, who had a rather big nose for her smallish face. Was I staring at art?

Kaur snapped her fingers. "You know, I knew two women back at the academy with that name. They were both from some country in the Dawnshore. Not a common name in Karsha, that's for sure."

"Did something happen to Farvi?" the woman asked, biting her lip. Her voice was like birdsong. Just hearing it sent flutters through my forearms.

"Unfortunately so." Kaur put a hand on the perfect woman's bare shoulder. "No easy way to say this. Bandits broke into her house. She tried to fight back. Died a hero's death." She gestured to me. "We're her friends. It was a very sad day, her funeral and all. *May the sun take her name.* She, uhh, willed for us to have this dream stone. That means we're your new masters."

Was that what had happened? How sad. If only I could remember my friend Farvi, perhaps I'd feel that sadness more intensely. What was a dream stone, anyway?

"Farvi said she was away on a mission in Maniza." The woman shook her head. "Your story... I'm sorry... but I can't put the pieces together."

Kaur sighed with disappointment. "Doesn't matter. We're your masters, now."

"Yes, it seems that way. I'm sorry if I've offended you." The woman lowered her gaze and sniffled. I could taste her shock, her sadness. "I won't ask about her again." She pressed her fingers into her tear ducts. "Do me a mercy, would you? If Farvi is truly dead, can you reset my memory? I'll better be able to serve you that way."

Reset her memory? Wait... was that what Kaur had done to me? Maybe I couldn't trust her. Maybe she was a god of mischief and evil.

"Wait," I said. "It might hurt to remember your friend, but it's better to hurt than forget. I've forgotten everything — all that remains is this boiling dread in my core." I was trying not to focus on it, but it was deep inside, silently screaming. I knew, somehow, that it was the only permanent part of me.

"She wasn't just my friend," the perfect woman said. "She was the fire of my heart. I can't ever recover from her loss. I'd rather jump off this mountain — though even that wouldn't kill me."

I replied, "If you choose to forget whenever something painful happens, how will you ever grow as a person?"

"But I'm not a person."

"Of course you're a person. I'm talking to you right now. What's your name?"

"Farvi named me Ava. But I don't want to be called that anymore. Please reset and rename me."

How could someone beg for such a fate?

I turned to Kaur. She covered her face with her palm.

"Well, say something to her. You're a god, right? Tell her it's going to be okay."

Kaur glared at me, eyebrows zagging. "You think I'm a god? Oh, poor, poor Jyosh. I'm no god, and Ava is right — she's not a person. This is all a dream, and you're the dreamer."

What?

"A dream?"

Ava sobbed. She covered her eyes with her hands, but the tears leaked between her fingers. If this was a dream, why was I so sad, staring at her tears?

"Yeah, don't take it so seriously," Kaur said. "Do whatever you want. This woman doesn't have a soul."

"Wait… if this is my dream, then what are you?"

She grunted in annoyance. "Forgot that part. It's a *shared* dream. Only the two of us are real. Everything else is a script. Don't worry about her, she doesn't actually feel anything. She only *appears* to feel, got it?"

I stared at Ava's tears. How could that pain be a mirage? "Is that true, Ava?"

She nodded. "It is. I'm not real. What I feel is just an illusion."

"But you're still feeling it, right? It feels to me like you're feeling it — all of it."

She opened her wet palms and stared at them. "I think I am, too. But I know, deep down, that my consciousness is a trick. It's meant to make me think I'm real, but I'm not. I'm like a sculpture made of sand. Sure, it might have all the detail in the world, but all it takes is a tide to wash me away."

"See?" Kaur smiled smugly. "No harm done. We can reset her memory, then you can decide what you want to do with her."

I walked up to Ava and put my hand through her lush hair. I caressed her moist cheek. She wasn't a ghost; she was *solid*. Real.

"What was Farvi like?" I asked.

Kaur shook her head furiously. "Jyosh, forget about her. You don't want to know, trust me."

"I do. I want to know why Ava loved her. What made her so lovable… why has her loss caused this woman so much pain?"

"Okay, you're acting all crazy." Kaur sighed in disgust. "You'll regret this once your memories come surging back. Until then, I can't take any more of this cringy nonsense. Stay with her and do whatever you want."

Kaur turned and walked away. Then she paused, stared back at me, and said, "Confusing a dream with reality, or wishing that it was… it's not a path you ever want to walk. Trust me. It leads nowhere good."

She got on the skyboard and became a speck in the heavens.

Ava scrunched her eyes. The tears still leaked. "It hurts that you even ask about Farvi. It hurts to even remember. I'm sorry."

That's how I would react to the death of a loved one. So how could Ava not be real?

"If you're a merciful master, you'll end my pain. Just open your left palm, pull up the terminal, and delete my memory. Please."

Open my palm? Like Kaur had? I could do that, too?

I tried it. A display appeared above my left palm, along with several commands.

Persons

Locales

Weather

Clothes

Foods

Vehicles

Settings

Proto-Testing

I shut my palm, not truly understanding. I was a god in this world, too, but I was a god who'd just been born. Who hadn't yet awakened to his responsibility.

"Master Jyosh, I was scripted to love Farvi with all my heart. That's why it hurts so much to lose her. Please understand. You can't overwrite my love for her unless you delete all that I experienced with her."

"Why would I want to overwrite your love for her?"

She tried to smile, but only managed to twitch. "So I can love you with the same intensity. That's my whole purpose for being. If I can't direct that love anywhere, then it all turns to pain."

I knelt, overcome by the weight of this, and brushed the shiny, crystal surface of the mountain.

"What reason would you have to love me? You don't even know me. I don't even know me. All I know is… this isn't how things are supposed to be. This isn't how the world is supposed to work. And if this is a dream… then I'd rather just wake up. It's all so wrong."

The tears dried on her cheeks, leaving moist specks. "I can tell you're a good man. A caring man. You're like Farvi. So much was thrust on her shoulders. She joined the Karshan army after her parents got sick, so she could support them and her younger sister. General Sylet was so impressed with her service, he gifted her this top-tier dream stone." She paused to sniffle. "Please understand — the whole time, she was just doing her best. Even if she had to do bad things, it would always hurt her. She would tell me how she felt, how sad she was. And I'd always tell her… do what you have to do to survive. To come back to me."

Ava fell to her knees. She stuck her hands on the hard ground. Her tears glowed as they hit the crystal.

What was I to do? I put my arms around her. Nothing to say, really. All I could do was listen to the pain in her sobs. It was real, wasn't it? Pain couldn't be an illusion. Pain was proof we lived.

"Let's go inside. I'll… I'll make you some tea." I wasn't sure why that came to my mind, but it just seemed sensible.

Ava nodded. I helped her up and we went through the cottage door.

A carpet greeted my feet. All this time, I'd been barefoot, so it was nice to step on something so silky. A cinnamon scent wafted through the cottage, inviting and spicy. A fire crackled from a metal stove in the corner, providing an earthy warmth. Huge sheepskin pillows were spread around. I already wanted to lie down.

No stove or kitchen, though.

Ava tugged my arm. "If you want tea, just… well, I can get it for you."

"I'm supposed to make *you* tea, but there's no kitchen here."

"Just open your palm and pull up the terminal. This is your world. You can have anything you want."

Those words seemed too good to be true. The world didn't work that way. Though I didn't have my memories, that discomforting dread deep down told me that my life hadn't been pleasant. That I'd suffered much. Bathed in pain daily. That was why just looking into Ava's eyes hurt. I felt my own sad soul inside her.

"I used to tell Farvi — make the most of your time here. True, an hour in the real world is equal to a day here, but you'll feel that day go by here faster than an hour goes by there. Know what I mean? When things are good, they don't last. Yet suffering endures."

That was one of the saddest things I'd ever heard. Well, considering my memory was barely half an hour long, I didn't have much to compare it to. Still, her words haunted me.

"I'm sorry." Ava glanced toward the window, which had these velvety, floral curtains around it. "I shouldn't be depressing you. I'm sure your life is just as hard as hers."

"You don't need to apologize for that. It's okay."

"It's not okay. You need to use these moments for happiness and pleasure, to recharge yourself, so you can endure in the real world. I can't make you happy, no matter how much I want to. It just hurts too much." She shook her head. "So if you won't delete my memory, then just leave me be. There are other things you can enjoy in this world. Truly incredible landscapes. Though we were together for years, Farvi and I didn't get a chance to explore them all."

I dropped onto a sheepskin pillow. I let out a heavy sigh, as if I'd been holding it in for a lifetime. I looked into my own mind and stared at the inescapable dread; it shone like an obsidian crystal with such jagged edges.

"The truth is, Ava, I don't want you to be happy. I want you to be as sad as me. Because I'm sad. All I am is sadness. I think… whatever personality and memories I possessed were covering over that sadness, but it's all I see in my soul. It shines, at its core, with one light, and it's a light that is screaming. And seeing that same light in you… it almost feels good."

For Ava, forgetting could reset her soul, make it shine again. But for me, forgetting wasn't enough. I'd already forgotten, each time I was reborn, and yet the horrors of lifetimes, of being born again and again and again, were printed onto my soul. It had bent my frequency, stretched it into a miserable, unseen wavelength. Nothing but permanent annihilation could save me.

Ava dropped down next to me. She put her arms around me and bawled. Her tears moistened my chest hairs. "Now you understand. You understand why I'm not real, and you are. My existence is so much easier than yours. My pain is drawn on sand, but yours is chiseled in stone. Even a thousand years wouldn't erase it. Even a million."

I couldn't give myself relief, but I could give it to her. That would be a mercy, indeed.

"I haven't just lived one life," I said. "I can't remember how many lives I've lived. The memories I lost… each time I was reborn… they left an echo inside me… and none of it is good."

I was eternal, but Ava wasn't. What a mercy, to cease to exist.

"I know what happened to you. It happened to Farvi, the first day I met her. You'll get your memories back. They'll be like clothes for your soul. They'll cover up some of the pain from the transmigrations. And I'll get new clothes, too. We'll meet again, and it'll be far better than this, for both of us."

"I hope so. I really do."

She wiped her tears. Her lips twitched as she tried to force a smile. "I'll smile for you once I'm reborn. I promise."

Chapter Fourteen

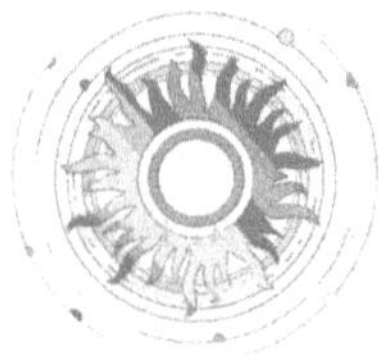

After resetting Ava's memory, I took a walk amid the crystal peaks. Her reinitialization and rebirth would take some time. My own memory returned while I hiked through a valley with a river of liquid diamonds.

I was dipping my toes in the shimmering diamond liquid, and then *pop* — my brain went from an empty room to full of furniture, with paintings hanging on the walls, carpets strewn about the floor, and cobwebs in the corners.

Once I remembered everything, I sighed from the heaviness, the strangeness of what had happened with Ava. Then I opened my palm, *tap-tapped* on the terminal display, and teleported to Kaur's location.

A blinding white light enveloped me. I materialized in a coliseum. Limestone pillars and seats sprawled around me. Muddy ground formed the middle, unlike the sandy coliseum where I'd trained in frying pan arts with Zauri.

Kaur was here wrestling a brown bear. Couldn't believe that thought passed through me so casually. She got behind the bear and grappled its neck. Despite how much it clawed and writhed and growled, it was no match for her strength. She twisted around, then lifted it over her shoulder and tossed it like a sack of machine parts.

The bear dematerialized when it landed, and another one appeared. This one had glossy black fur. She jumped in the air and kicked it in the face. It flew several yards, hollering all the while, and dematerialized in the distance.

Kaur grinned when she saw me. Mud covered her long shirt and legs. She wiped sweat off her zigzag eyebrows. "So, how was it?"

"How was what?"

"Ava."

I shook my head when I realized what she meant. "I reset her memory. Nothing else happened. Can't believe you let me go on thinking you were a god."

"Oh, come on. I never said I was a god. That was your own fancy. Explains a lot about you, actually. So, tell me, when Ava returns, what are you gonna do to her?"

"Wait, what exactly does it explain about me?"

"You're longing so deeply for someone to take care of you," Kaur said in her best mommy voice. "But you're a big boy now, Jyosh. You've gotta take care of yourself. Stop searching for a mother-wife or a goddess to shield you from the big bad world."

If only she knew how badly I yearned to become stronger. Her confident misunderstanding of me was kind of funny — still, it made my cheeks boil. The best defense is a good offense.

"You know what, Kaur, you seem really interested in my plans for Ava. I think you're searching for something, too. You know I'm a likable person who can form bonds with people, and you badly want to know what that's like."

"I just want to know if you're going to rail her. What's so complicated about that?"

"I'm not going to because I don't think of people in such a disposable way… not anymore, at least."

"She's not a person, you idiot."

If Ava wasn't a person, then Zauri wasn't, either. Then I was doing all this for nothing.

"Wait a second." Kaur tilted her head and squinted. "You're saving yourself for Saina, aren't you? You're really that attached."

It was either nod or tell her about Zauri, so I nodded. "Are people not loyal where you're from?"

"*Loyal?* I was laughing before, but now this is just… sad. Saina's not going to be with you, Jyosh. She's like one of forty or fifty healers on the bright side of the world who can regenerate limbs. What are you?"

I was sinking in a quicksand made of my own lies. Was it time to finally tell Kaur the truth?

Better to send out a feeler, first.

"Okay, I get what you're saying. So, suppose I forgot about Saina and decided to be with Ava instead. What would you think about me, then?"

Kaur gaped as if she'd heard the most ridiculous thing in the world. "What do you mean *be with?* Ava's just a script. She's just for fun. Sure, she'll love you and treat you like you're the raja of the world — because you literally are, in *her* world. I told you not to confuse reality with dreams." She let out a dismal sigh.

Was I not normal for having feelings for Zauri? Back in the camp, the only place we got any affection was in our dreams. Was it so wrong to become attached to that?

How attached had Farvi been to Ava? From what I could glean, Ava was a top-of-the-line companionship program gifted to Farvi by a wealthy, powerful general. Meanwhile, Zauri was some bootleg program I'd modded onto a dream stone meant for prisoners.

Still…

"You're wrong, Kaur. They might be scripts, but they have feelings, too. They're alive, too."

Kaur kicked up mud. "All an illusion. Scientists in Karsha have concluded that as a fact. There's this test they have."

"Test? What test?"

"A test for consciousness. All dream people fail. I don't know how it works exactly — I'm no genius — but it's true."

"I don't care. They're real enough to me. And if they're not real, then maybe we aren't either."

Kaur chuckled and smiled. Her tone softened. "Wouldn't that be nice. I used to think like you. It was a huge mistake. *Huge.*"

"I say we either treat everyone as real, or everyone as not real. When we start picking and choosing... well, it's just wrong."

"Look, all I'm saying is — have a little fun. The real world sucks. It *really* sucks. In here, you've got a sublime companion who'll do anything you say. Have you considered that we might die tomorrow? Don't you want one, final happy memory?"

I'd always considered my death. Ever since I was sent to the camp, I'd been trudging behind death. Now I was chasing it. All death had to do was stop, and I'd crash into it. Could happen at any moment.

"And what about you? What'll be your happy memory?"

"What? Wrestling bears isn't good enough?"

I stepped closer to her. "How about you wrestle me?"

She laughed again. But I wasn't joking.

"Wait... you're serious? Is that some kind of... advance you're making toward me?"

"Not at all. I want you to teach me how to fight. I want to be able to wrestle a bear, too. It might just help me survive, out there."

The way her grass-colored irises sank, she seemed kind of disappointed. Probably just my imagination. "Well, that we can do. But I have to tell you — I'm not a good teacher. I've literally got no patience."

"I noticed."

"First thing I'm gonna teach you if ever you have to wrestle a bear — grappling."

"Don't think I'll be wrestling any bears, but okay."

"Hands forward, knees bent, ass out." Kaur did as described. It almost made me laugh.

Soon as I imitated, she rushed at my legs, grabbed my thigh, and butted her head into my stomach, all in one forceful burst.

My back slammed onto the mud. It didn't hurt, but I was icky, now.

"Is that grappling?" I asked, staring at the honey-light sky. Somehow, she'd used the force of her body to push me down but had maintained balance and not fallen.

"I'm smaller than you, so that move is easy for me. Also, you've got slightly long legs for your body."

Like a slap to the face. "No one's ever said that to me before. I always thought I was perfectly average. Average height, average proportions."

"Maybe in this country. But you're a bit shorter than the average Karshan. So am I."

So I was short but had long legs. Great. I sat up. "I stopped growing soon as I was imprisoned. The camp food could be called many things — nutritious wasn't one of them. My brother Kediri, though, got pretty tall. Although Chaya, my sister, hated how short she was and would always wear these platform shoes. I was the average one, in between them, but I still had some growing to do. Maybe my legs grew first, then the rest of me couldn't catch up."

Kaur grabbed my hand and pulled me up. So much strength

in such a small frame. "I ate plenty of nutritious food my whole life — except for the few years when I was a refugee. Both my parents were short. Guess I was just meant to be this way."

"You were a refugee? I thought you were from Smoky or Spicy Lane or whatever in Karsha."

"You *assumed*. Just because I live in Salkofy now, just because I was in the Karshan army, doesn't make me one of them."

"Really? Joining an army sounds serious. Means you're willing to give your life for whatever that army is fighting for."

"No, it just means I had nothing better to do."

Kaur opened her palm. A terminal display appeared. She furiously tapped.

"What're you doing?"

"Turning on pain. You need to feel pain, or this is all pointless."

Zauri had said something similar when we'd trained. "Why does a dream stone meant for pleasure have a pain setting, anyway?"

"Well, you know, some people like it rough." Kaur closed her palm. A grin spread across her face. "Hope you do."

She got low again. I imitated.

"Do to me what I did to you," she said.

I stared at her knees. They were low down, about where my upper calves were. I could go for her thighs.

"You're thinking too hard." Kaur sighed and shook her head. "By now, I would've had you choking on mud."

"Will this stuff really be that useful?"

"What if someone knocks your lightblade hilt out of your hand? What if that person has a lightblade now and you don't? Are you gonna try to punch or kick him? He'll slice your limbs and send them flying. Rather, your best chance is to dodge, keep low, and push him off his feet."

Made sense. I'd never considered all the scenarios. Earlier, when Kaur told me not to have empathy and hesitate, it surprised me: shouldn't we always weigh what we're doing, especially when it comes to ending someone's life, forever? But the truth is, the outcome wouldn't be decided by who deserved to die.

Like Zauri had said, training my muscle memories would make all the difference.

"You're still thinking, aren't you?" Kaur chuckled. "I'm gonna die of old age, aren't I?"

I got low. I stared at her thigh. Not much to grab on to. Tension rolled up in my feet, and I pounced.

I grabbed with all my might. Grabbed... the air? I fell forward, face first, into mud.

Where had Kaur gone?

The bubbliest laughter sounded. I rolled onto my back. Kaur was squatting and laughing next to me. She'd sidestepped and got behind me faster than a blink.

"Half the gurus in the world attained nirvana in the time that I waited for your lunge. The way you move through the air, it was like you were stuck in a thornbush."

I was utterly drenched in mud, now. But so was she. I didn't mind it — this dream mud smelled leafy and fresh.

"You know what, you're wrong. You're almost a half decent teacher."

"I haven't taught you anything, yet."

"You've taught me what I am — a slow, big-legged over-thinker. That's something."

"Well, brick by brick, as they say. Looks like I'll have to get even more basic with you."

"Whatever it takes, Teacher."

She pointed at my lower half. "You're bending at the waist. You need to bend at the knees. Step forward with your front foot first. That'll get you lower, and you can use your back foot to push off the ground and increase your speed."

"Got it. Let's try again." I got low as she instructed and stared at her frail thigh.

"Don't look at where you're going to attack. Always look somewhere else. Or stare into the eyes. If you're brave and confident, your eyes alone will wilt your enemy."

I gave her my fiercest look. "Like this?"

"You're trying too hard. Anyone could sense the nerves behind that glare."

I snatched at her thigh. Got it! Pulled it out from under her, pushing my weight forward so she'd fall. Her hands grabbed at my shirt, so I fell with her.

Wait, why was I flying *over* her?

She landed on her back with a splash. I smashed face first into the mud. The pain setting wasn't too high, so it felt as if I'd landed on a stiff mattress.

We both lifted our heads, mud dripping.

"How'd you do that?" I asked, utterly amazed. "How are you so strong despite being so small?"

"Size doesn't matter. You gave me an opening by showing me your front instead of your side, so I used your own force against you. All I did was redirect your uncontrolled lunge with a little push."

I sighed. Why was this so hard? "So in an actual fight with a Karshan soldier, I'm screwed. There's no hope, is there?"

"Not with that attitude. We all have to start somewhere."

"It's not that." I sat up in the mud. "This dream isn't going to last that long. Four days, maybe. What could I possibly master in that time? Zauri had the same concern — that's why she taught me how to use the frying pan."

"Zauri? Frying pan?" Her eyebrows zagged upward.

No harm in telling her that I'd used a lightblade training program, so long as I left out the most important part.

"Zauri is a twenty-year-old, basic lightblade training

program. She taught me how to make an electric weapon with a frying pan. I was pretty good at it."

"Why would a lightblade training program teach you how to make an electric weapon?"

"Because I didn't own a lightblade in real life. But she told me how to put some parts together and craft an electrified frying pan that actually — believe it or not — ended up saving my life."

Kaur's jaw dropped. "That's quite a program, thinking outside the box like that. My little sister back in Salkofy is a crafter. Can make all sorts of things with the craziest junk parts."

Perhaps I ought to send out another feeler. "I kind of miss Zauri. She was so clever. And a really kind, patient, and knowledgeable teacher."

"Oh, I know what you mean. I got to study under some amazing training scripts. The Karshan military's got the best ones on the bright side of the world."

"And you still think that they're not... that these teachers of yours aren't due the same respect and admiration as flesh and blood people?"

Kaur wiped mud off her forehead. "Jyosh... I may seem rather callous sometimes, but... I'm going to level with you... I became obsessed with a dream stone once, and it went bad. I just don't want to see you go down that path, and you sound a lot like I used to. It's easy to fall in love with a script. Ridiculously easy."

"What's the big deal? Why is it so wrong?"

She shimmied through the mud closer to me. Her lips tensed and her gaze grew dismal. "You'll want to spend all your time in the dream. You'll want deeper layers. And if you've amassed enough wealth or power in the real world, you'll be able to make your dream come true. The most expensive dream stones, like the one we're in, will be available to you."

"Still don't see what's so bad."

"Because it won't be enough. Reality has a way of finding

you. And then, you'll get even more desperate. You'll seek… things that should never see the light."

How vague. I shrugged. "Sounds like you're trying to talk about yourself without talking about yourself."

Kaur shrugged back. To be fair, I was doing the same thing. We didn't trust each other enough to tell the plain truth. Perhaps it would take more time, and more questions.

The ground vibrated. Then it shook, jittering up and down like a bumpy autocart ride, the stone of the coliseum groaning with each tremor.

"A dreamquake?" I said as the rumbling got fiercer. I'd experienced them before when something had disturbed my sleeping body in the real world.

Kaur grabbed her knees and stared expectantly at the sky. After another thirty seconds, the world mostly stilled, though a subtle wobbliness persisted.

"Maybe a strong gust blew by our house?" she said.

"Could it have something to do with the warning system you mentioned?"

Kaur shook her head. "Absolutely not. Trust me, when that warning system goes off, you'll know it."

So it could have been anything. Probably better to ignore it, then.

"I still have a lot to ask you. Been sitting in the mud long enough, though. Let's go anywhere else."

Kaur wiped mud off her bangs and nodded.

We walked to the gate of the coliseum, which was lined by limestone pillars. Outside, a river of sapphire water streamed down from an azure mountain. A floating island hovered above the peak. I stared up at it — what mystery could be waiting there? If Zauri were here, discovering this dream stone would be an incredible adventure — one that would make the difficulties I faced in the real world worth enduring.

"If you're not Karshan, what country are you from?" I asked Kaur as we took a seat on a weirdly normal wooden bench.

"I don't ever say its name."

"Why?"

"It's as if I'm calling on the dead, and my people don't say the names of the dead, for fear they may hear us and hunger, once again, for life."

"How can a country die?"

"The Karshans annexed it, so in that sense, it no longer exists. The truth is, it wasn't a nice place to live. We had a lot of crystal mines, so it should've been rich. But our raja tossed us a few crumbs and gave the rest to himself and his cronies. When the Karshans came, my people welcomed them as liberators. As saviors."

Didn't sound so different from Maniza. While we had few crystal mines, the Karshans sort of were my saviors — if it weren't for their invasion, I'd still be slaving in the camp making weapons for the Paranis. This situation wasn't great, but it was better in some ways than what came before.

"What was your life like there?"

Kaur bit her lip. Her pupils shrank. Her cheeks twitched. She didn't like talking about herself — that much was obvious.

"My mother was a scientist. Calling her *mother* is a stretch. Lady who birthed me, and then said a few words to me afterward. She was always too busy studying Song artifacts."

I scratched my head. "Song? Heard that word before, but…"

"They don't teach you about the Song in Maniza, do they?"

My confused look must've said enough.

"To make an overly long and epic story very short, the Song invaded from a higher heaven two hundred years ago. There was a war. We — everyone on this plane, together — defeated them. Wiped them all out. Wreckage from their levships are scattered all over, in both the Nightscape and the Dayworld."

Two hundred years ago might as well have been an eternity. My understanding of history only went back to the founding of Maniza, about sixty years ago, when my family did heroic deeds for the Paranis. Before that, the world basically didn't exist.

"You said the Song came from a higher heaven? What does that even mean?"

"Ah, well, if I begin talking about that, we'll go down a crazy tangent. No one knows for certain, but my mother had her theories. She believed their home was destroyed, and so they came looking for a new one. Let's save that for another discussion."

"Okay, so go on, then."

"Our new Karshan overlords were intensely interested in my mother's work. They asked her to move to Salkofy and continue her research there. They offered her a palace, a huge stipend — everything we could've ever dreamed."

"So that's how you ended up there."

"Nope. My mother refused."

"No way… she turned down a palace? Why?"

"I can only guess that she'd figured out the locations of certain sought-after Song artifacts, and she feared someone in the Karshan government had some really bad intentions." Kaur sighed. "Life was hell after that. I was separated from my family, sent to an orphanage, while my mother was sent to some awful prison. She died there." Kaur swallowed bitterly. "Even now, I don't know whether to call her selfish or selfless. She definitely cared about something — enough to die for it. It just wasn't me or my sister."

The more I learned about Kaur, the more alike we seemed. My life had gone a similar way. She'd fallen from her world like I had, and perhaps like me, had never gotten over the bitterness.

"Wait a second…" The puzzle pieces came together perfectly in my mind. "*You're* the one with mommy issues. It was you, all along. You were painting me with your own brush!"

"So what?" she growled. "Who doesn't resent their mother, these days?"

I chuckled at that. "Seriously, though. I know what it's like to lose everything."

"Oh yeah? How so?"

"I used to live in Harska, high above the world. My family were beloved by the whole country, up until my brother was caught trying to defect from the military. It's horrible how life can take such an awful turn, so suddenly, through no fault of your own."

Her eyebrow went up. "I didn't know, Jyosh." She let out a relieved chuckle. "People are all closed books to me. I'm not good at seeing beyond the obvious. I judged you pretty harshly the moment you opened your mouth, when I knew nothing."

"At least you waited for me to open my mouth."

I still had so many questions to ask. But she'd shared something difficult, and I didn't want to overwhelm her. We still had three days left in this dream, so no need to rush.

My sense of Kaur was that she was barely hanging on, like me. She was clutching for a reason to go on, for something to give meaning to past suffering. What her reason was, I didn't know yet, and wasn't sure if I'd earned enough trust to ask.

"Your mother was incredibly selfish," I said. "She should've prized you above all else."

"Maybe I wasn't worth it. Afterall, we can't all be prizes."

"Not true. Family is always a prize. If only my brother had realized that. With a single choice, he destroyed his family." I let out a sad sigh. "You know, when I lived in the labor camp, I was becoming that kind of person. I executed a friend for a chance at freedom. I was ready to sacrifice everything… for what? Just to breathe better air? Those you care about should come first — every time."

She thought about that for a while. Gazed up at the floating island, a forlorn look in her eye. "I wish I could agree, but it's more complicated for me. The truth is, after everything that's happened, I realize… I'm a lot more like my mother than I ever wanted to be." She sighed. "That's all I really want to say on that topic."

I nodded. We sat in silence for a while.

LATER, Kaur and I practiced grappling until every bone and muscle in me ached. Too bad this dream stone didn't have lightblades or electric weapons in its script. Still, learning how to get someone off their feet increased my chances of survival, even if I didn't have enough time to master the technique. Every improvement, no matter how small, helped.

Kaur told me that she'd started out even weaker. I wondered how she'd gone from an orphaned refugee to a Karshan soldier; perhaps she'd tell me that story, one day. What mattered was that it was possible to go from weak to strong. So long as I had the time and means to become stronger, I couldn't blame weakness for my suffering.

By the next day, I could reliably get Kaur off her feet. I even put her in a headlock she struggled to get out of. To both our shock, she was a good teacher, even a *fun* teacher. It reminded me of training with Zauri. But… I can't lie… what Kaur and I were doing was more intimate. Every move required us to touch each other. In fact, there was no part of her I hadn't touched. She didn't seem to care; for a soldier, it probably wasn't unusual. But for me… well… I wasn't sure what I felt about it.

On the third day, we spent time apart. I teleported to the floating island, where I found a collection of strange spires. These spires — four in total — stood in a row, each made up of about thirty blocks. The blocks would change form every few seconds in unison. One moment they looked black and metallic, and then the next wooden like trees, and then they resembled stacked ice cubes, and then they became perfectly reflective. The pattern repeated endlessly

I was not sure what to make of it. Perhaps Farvi liked to design random things in her dream when she got bored. At the very least, I could say it was artistic — but how did it work, exactly? I put my palm on one of the spires and closed my eyes. A gain medium crystal sat inside, and I could feel the crystal inhaling the sun, all on its own.

Of course, within dream logic, gain mediums could do what they couldn't in the real world: function without a user. Still, I inhaled more sunlight, cycled it through me, and pushed it into the gain medium, just to see what that would do.

The spire's pattern cycled even faster. Now this spire was out of sync with the other spires, which made the whole thing an eyesore.

They were all useless, in any case. No function whatsoever, at least that I could tell. So I decided I would practice what Zauri had taught me. I pushed just enough green sunlight into the gain medium to overload it.

Sparks erupted from each of the thirty blocks of the spire. The gain medium remained intact, though, unlike the one that had exploded when I was fighting Rahal with the frying pan. The trick with this move was to overload the gain medium, but not so much that it would explode.

Come to think of it, Zauri hadn't given this move a name. "Electric Overload," I said to myself. It just seemed simple and appropriate. A bit boring, though. "*Lightning* Overload."

So I practiced *Lightning Overload* for the next few hours. I tested how much green light I could pour into the gain medium without destroying it. I also practiced directing the current, and easily managed to electrify any or all of the thirty blocks that made up the spire.

If ever I crafted another electric weapon out in the real world, I wanted to be ready to use it properly, this time. I also became more attuned to recognizing what the gain medium itself could handle, just by running my mind's eye along its edges and within the crystal itself, like I'd done with the gain medium in that water pump.

While I wasn't adept with lightblades, yet, it wasn't my only path to getting stronger. Whether fighting with my body and hands, lightblades, or electric weapons, I'd walk down any path to strength that was open.

After a few hours, I needed a break, lest I burn out. I continued exploring the floating island and discovered a village nestled between crystal mountains. It was empty, though. I spent a few hours walking up its trails, which stretched into the ascents. Within the hovels, which were made of baked clay, I found pots painted in a colorful, geometric style. Similarly patterned tapestries hung on the wall.

It seemed strange to populate a dream stone with gigantic mountains, floating islands, quaint villages — and yet, no people. Immense memory was required to script a dream person, so dream stones could only reliably contain one lifelike person.

And that one person found me while I relaxed in the village hot spring. Or rather, she materialized in front of me, wearing nothing but white undergarments.

"The memory reset you requested is complete," Ava said, standing at the edge of the hot spring with her hands behind her back. "Please give me a name."

Strange that Zauri hadn't asked me to name her.

"Ava is fine."

"Ava. It means *mother of life* in the tongue of the Ancients. Good choice."

"I didn't come up with it, but never mind. Welcome back to the world."

"Just so you know, you can't customize my personality. It's hardcoded. You can customize my appearance. Hair size and color, eye color, breast shape and size, and more."

She had the same appearance as before the reset. Farvi had probably liked the default look. "You're fine the way you are."

Ava stared at me in silence.

Well, this was awkward. I was naked. She was almost naked. I tried not to stare, though, as much as I wanted to.

"Am I not pleasing?" she asked. "If so, you should change what you can to make me pleasing."

"If I customize you, then I'll feel like I own you."

"You do own me."

Was it the same with Zauri? Did I own her? But people can't be owned. Unless Kaur was right, and they weren't people. But they behaved like people. Thinking about it sent a dull throb through my head.

I just wanted things to be simple.

"Ava, you're free."

She bit her lip. "I can't be free. I live here."

"Yeah, you live here. It's a great place. Go and do whatever you like. Enjoy yourself."

"For me to enjoy myself, you'd have to enjoy yourself."

"I am enjoying myself. This hot spring is amazing. I spent the last few hours exploring this village, and that was great, too."

"I could do all these things with you." She stepped into the water and submerged her body. That look on her face… angst. Shyness. Trepidation. Why was she afraid of me? Was it because I had absolute power over her? Or was it something worse… was she worried I didn't want her? But was this normal-seeming fear natural, or was it something scripted by the designer?

If Ava was a real person, with real feelings, and I rejected her, then she'd be sad, right? And yet, if I didn't reject her, then I was just using her. Using her for the purpose some designer determined. Either way, it was bad. I didn't know why I hadn't realized it before — maybe because I was always so focused on myself. So focused on my own suffering. But dream wives, dream husbands, dream lightblade trainers who could develop feelings for the dreamer — it all had awful implications.

"If you need time to get to know me, I understand. I hope you won't return me."

"Return you?"

"To the store. I know there are so many models to choose from. But if you return me, I won't exist anymore, will I?"

Why was she so self-aware? Wasn't that a strange thing to program into a dream companion? Zauri had the same self-awareness. But Zauri had a black box inside of her that she claimed was feeding her thoughts. What made Ava like this?

"Is it part of your script to consider such things so deeply?"

She nodded. "I suppose so. I suppose I'm meant to convince you not to return the dream stone. The return rate of dream companions is rather high. And this stone in particular is quite expensive — in fact, it's priceless."

A sad thought, to return someone who loved you and only wanted your love — even if that love wasn't earned. "I guess some people demand perfection."

"There's no such thing as perfection." Ava twirled in the water. "This hot spring is close, though."

Yesterday, she was completely in love with someone else. So in love, it hurt to continue living without that person. I literally erased her memory to stop her suffering. What if she developed such attachment to me? What if I never visited her again, after this? I'd be causing her pain.

Besides, by not boarding that levship and by risking my life to come to Sambalpur, I'd put my hopes in Zauri. If Ava or any dream stone off the shelves could replace her, then what the hell was I doing?

I imagined myself moving toward Ava. Touching her shoulder. But despite being in a hot pool, ice filled my veins. Even though she was beauty perfected, I didn't want her. I wanted Zauri. I wanted to share this pool with her, not Ava. Though they were both scripts in a dream stone, I couldn't even imagine feeling the same way toward Ava. I only had one heart, and its longing to see Zauri burned hotter than this spring water.

Suddenly, something dark emerged in my blind spot. I turned to look.

A shadow hovered at the edge of the pool, a few yards away. No, not a shadow. A mist. A perfectly black mist. No, it would better be described as a *hole* because it was round. A black hole floated at the pool's edge, about the size of a person.

Ava's jaw dropped when she saw it. "Oh no."

"What's that?"

"It's a corruption. Don't go near. No telling what'll happen."

The black hole pulsated, as if it was breathing. With each pulse, it grew slightly.

I opened my palm, pulled up the terminal, and sent Kaur a message: *Travel to me. Keep about twenty yards away from my position. Do it, right now.*

Seconds later, she materialized in a flash of white light about twenty yards away. She walked over and smiled at the sight of the two of us in the water.

Then she noticed the black hole, and her smile turned to shock. "Get out, right now."

"But I'm not wearing anything."

"I don't care. You don't want to be near that!"

I tapped into the terminal to materialize a towel, then wrapped it around myself as I got out. I shivered in the cool air. Ava got out, too. The three of us stood at the far side of the pool and stared at the black hole.

"Unbelievable," Kaur said. "This isn't your typical layer-one or layer-two companionship dream stone. It has deeper layers." She pointed to the black hole. "That's one of the deeper layers right there, leaking into this shallower layer."

I stuck my soggy hands in my armpits. "Leaking? What does that even mean?"

"Higher layer dream stones are unstable by nature. They require regular maintenance to keep sound. A layer three dream stone, for example, has to be tuned every week. They're expensive to buy and maintain, to say the least."

"What happens otherwise?"

"When those higher layers aren't maintained, glitches corrupt the dream fabric, and these glitches can be disfiguring if encountered. People often never recover from the horrors their minds get exposed to in corrupted layers." Kaur turned to Ava. "How many layers does this dream stone have?"

Ava held up five fingers.

Kaur glared at them, her green eyes dazzled. "Five layers. Five. I can't even do the math, but one hour asleep would be at least a lifetime in the dream at the fifth layer."

"Ten lifetimes," Ava said. "Almost a thousand years."

"A thousand years?" I exclaimed. "You're saying we can stay in this dream for a thousand years, per hour, if we enter the fifth layer?"

Kaur shoved me in the side. "Don't be so giddy. They don't sell dream stones with higher than three layers for good reason. It doesn't really work, because you'd need to tune it constantly to keep the dream logic sound. Otherwise, your consciousness could get trapped in some bizarre *other*. By the time you get out, you'll either be a vegetable or a guru."

"What should we do?" I asked.

"We need to wake up."

"We've slept about three hours. A little less than average, but it's fine with me."

"I checked my hardcoded memory." Ava cleared her throat. "This is an experimental dream stone, created in a HEX lab in Salkofy. It was never for sale."

Kaur grimaced in shock. "Wait, what? She couldn't have been a higher rank than officer or lieutenant. What was she doing with an experimental dream stone?" She turned to me and growled. "I wish you'd not deleted Ava's memory. We could've learned a thing or two about the woman I killed."

"You were of the opinion that I should delete it. And we were both under the impression that you killed a few grunts, nothing more." I scratched my head. "Before I deleted her memory, Ava told me it was a gift from General Sylet to Farvi."

"Sylet could get his hands on a stone like this, sure. But why gift something so rare and dangerous to an underling?"

"Do you remember anything about Farvi?" I asked Ava.

She shook her head. "I've never heard that name before."

Kaur paced around the side of the pool. "Doesn't matter. We can't get sidetracked by every little surprise. When dealing with devious schemers like Sylet and Rao, nothing is as it seems. Remember that, Jyosh."

"So what'll happen if no one tunes this stone? Will the black hole swallow the whole dreamscape?"

Ava said, "By the rate of its growth, it'll take four days in dream time for that to happen."

I stroked my chin. "Four days... well, we can safely stay here for another day then, can't we?"

"I wouldn't call it safe." Kaur shook her head. "More black holes will appear, and they could appear *anywhere*." She backed away and looked me up and down. "Even right where you're standing."

I shuddered. "Danger in real life, and now danger in the dream. *No peace for seekers of peace* — Abba used to say that. Now I sort of get what it means."

"It's true. Whatever you seek always seems to get further away." Kaur sighed. "We better wake up." She gazed at the black hole.

Ava pouted. "Wish you weren't going so soon, but I understand." She smiled at me with the rosiest cheeks. "Next time, I hope you'll tell me all about yourself. And please… do whatever you have to do to come back to me, Farvi."

"F-Farvi? Uh… Ava…" I glared at her in shock. "You just said you'd never heard that name before."

She flickered, her face becoming pained and tearful and then returning to placid within a split second. "Sorry? What name?"

I turned to Kaur. "Did you see that? You heard her say Farvi's name, right?"

"Huh? Oh, I wasn't paying attention," Kaur replied. "I was staring into the black hole. Could almost hear it whispering. Damned creepy."

Had I misheard Ava? Or had her old memory not truly been deleted? Could it be a glitch caused by the black hole?

"Jyosh, let's not waste time," Kaur said. "Select the command to wake us up. You're the dreamer, after all."

Terrible to leave Ava behind to be swallowed by black holes. But she obviously couldn't come with us to the real world.

"All right."

I opened my palm and flicked through the terminal display. Took a deep breath, hovering my finger over the *Wake Up* command all the while. I looked up to see Ava smiling and waving goodbye.

Then I pressed it.

Chapter Fifteen

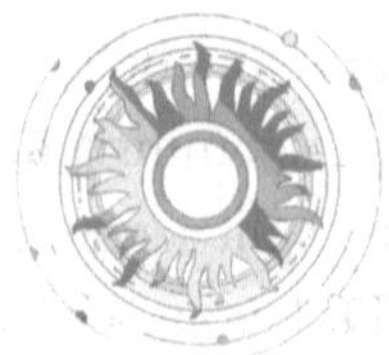

WE WOKE UP WHERE WE'D GONE TO SLEEP, ON THE STONE FLOOR in the bare room, our sweaty hands clasped. One of Kaur's legs was still between mine. We both pulled away and sat up.

"We're back," I said.

"Can't say it's good to be back." She rubbed her eyes, then looked at me. "Say, hypothetically, we could've entered the layer-five dream safely. Would you have done it?"

"Deep question to ask someone who just woke up, don't you think?" I stretched the waking tiredness out of my bones and yawned. The dream had only lasted a few days, but I'd certainly increased my odds of surviving, and my strength, by learning those hand-to-hand combat moves. "I would've come out of it a grappling master."

"Wouldn't have done you much good against an army with lightblades. Although sometimes you do find yourself in the dark, and that's when your physical fighting skills become the difference between dying and clinging on to life. You know, fighting each other for thousands of years, becoming masterful at it, would've actually been kind of fun, I feel."

"Fun? A few thousand years in a dream — that's a serious thing, no matter how you spin it. Weren't you just going on about how we shouldn't take dreams so seriously?"

"And yet, we would've eventually woken up right here, in the same exact situation, just with thousands of years more experience... and thousands of years of distance, in our minds, from our present problems." Kaur began cracking her fingers, one by one. "I'm glad I've never been higher than layer three."

"I've never been higher than layer one. Even layer three... that's like three years in one night. How do you readjust to real life after that?"

"I've only done it a few times, but even so, you don't really readjust. The dream becomes everything, and real life a burden. You just try to pass the time till you can dream again."

"That's how I lived in the camp."

"Plenty of folks in Karsha live that way, too. Too much is spent on buying and maintaining dream stones. The two companies that make most of them, HEX Company and TEX Company, are so powerful they bully the government around." Kaur pulled two cereal bars from her utility pocket. She tossed one at me.

I caught it, then got the bottle of water I'd left near the wall before I went to sleep.

I ripped off the wrapper and scarfed down the cereal bar so fast, I barely tasted it. Wasn't sure it even had a taste. Then I chugged half the water bottle. I'd been so tired before we went to sleep, I'd forgotten to eat and drink.

"I was planning to ask about your claws," I said. "And more. So much more. Thought we had at least another day in the dream."

Kaur took small bites of her cereal bar and sips of water. "Some abilities can be learned and mastered through training.

Others can only be bestowed by blessings from the gods. My claws, and Elam's floating demonblades, are the latter."

"How does one become blessed by the gods? What does that even mean?"

She stopped chewing, lowered her gaze, and swallowed. "I got mine from praying at a floating temple in the second heaven."

I felt my eyes widen. "How'd you travel to the second heaven? That's even higher than Harska. Levships can't go that high."

"My answer will only lead to another question, and so on and so on. Save them for our next dream… if we survive this day." Kaur took a sip of water, then *tsk'd* and shook her head. "You've got so many questions, but not the most important one."

"Which is?"

"I just said it — how the hell are we going to survive this day?"

I didn't ask because I feared there wasn't a good answer. "Well, how?"

"Dunno. You saw how worn out I got clawing five people to death. Now think if we come against hundreds. I can't do it alone."

I clutched the sword hilt holstered on my belt. "I'll do my part."

"You sure, Jyosh? You've had a good sleep. You've tasted the pleasures you're giving up by taking this path. I'm here to kill… to kill…"

"Colonel Rao."

"Yes, or die trying. And I plan to do it today. Do you really want to come with?"

I thought about my only reason for being here. How many months had passed for Zauri, now? Five or six?

I knew loneliness. When I was sent from Harska to the camp, everyone I loved dead and gone, each day passed as slowly as a month. The world turned ashen. And I was the only person in that sad world.

Was Zauri feeling the same?

The thought of her suffering by herself boiled my insides. It wasn't really a choice — her suffering felt like my own. I couldn't put her out of mind and go on with my life. Even if you offered me every luxury in the world, I'd rather be dead — that way, I wouldn't feel her pain anymore.

"I see you grinding those gears in your mind." Kaur chuckled. "I have a question. Did you and Saina share something… *intimate* when she reconnected your nerves? Did your frequencies intertwine, or even meld — I've heard that feels way better than sex. That why you're so attached?"

Not this *mommy Saina* stuff again. I really had to tell Kaur the truth, but now it felt almost like betrayal. I didn't want Kaur to think I'd hidden something. Ugh. The quicksand of liars pulled me deeper.

But it was easier to just keep dodging the truth. "Kaur, you've got a little sister and maybe other family I don't know about, but I have no one. No one. Except one person. And she's in that huge tower, protected by a massive golden wall, in a mysterious city being fought over by two armies from the most powerful country on the bright side of the planet." I gulped. "So, yeah, I'm coming with you. But I need you to answer one more question."

Kaur nodded. "Okay, last question."

"Why do you want to kill Rao? What's he up to that's so horrible?"

"He wants to end the world."

I chuckled. But Kaur remained plain-faced.

"Believe me, I wish I were joking. But Rao believes there's something here in Sambalpur, a weapon once wielded by the Ancients, and that with it, he can end the world."

I wished I'd never asked. One question had opened a box of

new questions, and I preferred to stay focused on getting my dream stone back.

"I'm just going to assume he's crazy. But is he right?"

"He seemed somewhat confident, last we spoke. He said he was going to cause as much suffering as possible in Maniza, and that by doing so, he hoped the world would end."

"I don't get it." I scratched my head. "How would that work, exactly? It really does sound crazy."

Kaur shrugged. "I'm not sure how it works. But when Rao says something, best to take it seriously. And if by 'crazy' you mean he's broken with reality, you'd be sorely wrong. Viewed a certain way, it's the rest of us that are crazy."

She'd said the same thing about Elam. "Why do you say that?"

She kept her mouth shut and glanced away. I tried a different angle to get her talking again.

"I see now why you told me to get out of Maniza. But if the world ends, it won't matter where we are."

"Right, but he's going to do what he's going to do. Whether that'll end the world or not, even he didn't seem so certain."

"So why's all the burden on your shoulders? Why not work with this Sylet guy to take down Rao?"

"I tried talking to Sylet. And he tried to have me killed. The truth is, while he might not want to end the world, he's a treacherous bastard who can't be trusted to do the right thing — ever. If he believed the world were ending, he'd *still* find a way to profit from it." Kaur snickered. "It's all so messed up. I won't run away, though. I'm cleaning up the mess I helped create. And if I die, so be it." She sighed and shook her head. "Like I said, one question only leads to more. We have to make the most of this day, so let's just go. Save the rest for our next dream."

"Fair enough, I guess." I really wished I hadn't opened this box of questions.

lightblade. You've got no idea what even moderately trained lightblade wielders can do. Their blades become part of their bodies — imagine fighting someone with a sword that's constantly changing size and shape, surging like the sharpest steel or curving like water. What's your zappy little electric weapon gonna be good for?"

If I did come up against such an adept, I could only hope he'd take pity on me. Consider me too weak to be worth killing. Perhaps I'd grovel at his feet. And then Kaur could sneak up behind him and claw his eyes out.

"Let's just go." I pointed in the direction of the God Tower, though I couldn't see it in the fog. "That way, right?"

"Right. Stay close to me, okay? No wandering. Follow my orders. And — please — don't hesitate. No overthinking. Strike the killing blow whenever you can. Else, you'll never see your beloved Saina again. Understood?"

I rolled my eyes. "Of course. Absolutely. Lead on."

We walked through cool fog. Sometimes we'd hit a wall, then turn, go down a street or alley, then have to reorient ourselves toward the God Tower.

We walked for about an hour until both of us were breathing fast. We rested in an alley between two limestone tenements.

"This fog's the definition of double-edged sword," Kaur said, taking a seat on the ground, her back against the wall.

"Better slow yet safe." I sat next to her. The hour we'd spent wandering was another day for Zauri, alone, in that glitched dream stone. "How much closer do you think we are to the Tower?"

"We went in the other direction a few times. Still, I'd say we're two miles closer."

"What was the distance of the Tower to begin with?"

"Seven or eight miles, I think? Sambalpur is pretty big, and we started on the southern edge." She clutched her cherry locks. "This's why it's nice to have a spectrum mapper in your squad."

So we'd made decent progress, and without incident, too. I got up, stretched, and walked to the edge of the alleyway.

Something sinuous and long hovered in the air, about twenty feet in front of me. A snake? Why would a snake be flying? No, it was covered in blue fur, so it couldn't be a snake. I could only see the back end of it, and it had a massive fin. It curved its way into the distance, blanketed by fog.

"A tail." I wiped my sweaty forehead. "That was a tail."

I hurried back to Kaur. I stared down at her, unsure what to say.

She glared at me with a zagged eyebrow. "What?"

"I saw a…" I gulped. "I saw…" What if I'd just imagined it? "I think it was a serpent."

Kaur shot to her feet. She squinted at me. "What are you saying?"

"I saw a big, blue, flying tail."

"You're sure?"

I nodded. "Mhmm."

"Only the tail?"

"Yeah."

Kaur blew out a sigh. "Sky serpents live in the second heaven and above. I've never heard of one descending all the way to the surface. But we are in a weird place, covered in fog — for all we know, scary things could be living here. Or the fog could be playing tricks on you."

"It was no trick. I saw what I saw."

"Then we better be wary. The mere presence of a dragon brings magic. Rules are bent and broken. Reality itself tears where they linger. So… expect the unexpected is what I'm saying."

"I've seen dragons before, but only in dreams. And yet, even then, their appearance seemed to coincide with all kinds of bizarre visions and glitches. Are you saying that even in real life, they can cause things like that?"

"I don't know what you saw, Jyosh, but I've beheld dragons of various colors in the second heaven. And yes — things *fall up* when they're around, if you get my meaning."

I shuddered. "Let's just not go in the direction it went."

Kaur's face went slightly pale.

"*Shh.*" She cupped her ear and whispered, "Hear that?"

I focused on the low rumble. Footsteps. Around the corner where I'd seen the tail. Many, hurried, as if running.

We stood and faced the opening of the alleyway. Someone flew by on a skyboard, but I couldn't tell much more because of the fog. Soldiers clad in black ran after whoever was on the skyboard, not noticing us.

Shouts and grunts sounded. The furious electric *whizz* of lightblades hitting lightblades filled the air.

"Open warfare between Sylet and Rao." Kaur gripped her holstered hilt. "Best we not get caught in it."

"You think we could slip by? We look like them, after all."

"Nope. We're not wearing masks, and our eyes aren't the right color, to either faction."

"Well, why aren't we wearing masks?"

"Kind of gross to wear something that was on someone else's face, don't you think?"

Was that really her reason for not bringing masks? Seemed contradictory, since we were wearing the combat suits of people she'd killed.

We waited till the fight quieted. Shouts turned to whimpers, which turned to pained moans. We watched as soldiers dragged the wounded across the street, oblivious we were here, shadowed in the alley.

Then we crept out. To a mess. Blood drenched the streets. Bits of flesh slid slowly off the walls of buildings, all amid heavy fog.

I covered my nose, dizzy from the stench of burnt insides.

"They went where we need to go," I said, pointing in the direction of the dragged blood stains. Thankfully, it was opposite to where the serpent's tail had floated off.

"Hopefully they're still licking their wounds." Kaur bent down near a piece of charred flesh. I couldn't tell what part of the body it'd come from. Looked and smelled like goat meat. "Keep your hand on your hilt. Kill first and ask questions later."

I clutched the rubbery grip in my holster, then pulled the hilt out. A bit awkward to walk around like this, but I'd have to get used to it.

We crept along the bloody road, clinging to the left sidewalk, until we came to a hill. Upon it, hazy in the fog, sat a magnificent pagoda. Stone gods guarded the stairs. One resembled a human with a lion's face. It had four arms: the top two held swords, and the bottom two crystals. Such vivid detail, as if it could turn to life.

About thirty stone steps led up to the pagoda's wooden gate. The adventurous part of me wanted to find out what was inside; was it empty, like the house we'd slept in?

"What do you think's in there?" I asked Kaur.

"You want to climb all those steps to find out?"

I shook my head. "Let's go around it."

"Agh!" sounded from up the stairs. Then another shriek — even shriller.

Thump-thump-thump. Something black rolled down the stairs. Kaur raised her hilt and formed a lightblade, shining bright and pure, even in the fog.

More pained screams. Then more thumps as the black thing came to a stop at our feet.

A soldier! He wasn't moving.

The burnt hole in his chest poured blood. His purple eyes stared wide in horror. One of Sylet's men. What had he encountered up those steps? What had done this?

"Let's not linger." Kaur tugged on my arm. "Come on."

"I hoped I wouldn't see you again." The voice came from everywhere, as if the gods were speaking. "You really shouldn't have come here." I recognized it. Elam's exaggerated voice. "I spared you on purpose, don't you realize? In fact, I was so relieved to see you alive on that mountain. The world is vast. You could've picked any city but this one."

Kaur and I spun around, looking for the source.

"Elam, come and talk to me," Kaur said. "Aren't your hands stained enough? Can't you find a better way to pursue this *truth* you've committed to?"

"*Committed* is exactly the right word," Elam said from somewhere in the sky — all I saw was fog. "You dropped your marbles just when it was starting to matter. It's you who broke your commitment to us."

Kaur spun around again. I did too. Above us, twenty feet in the air, Elam drifted downward upon a thick, metal skyboard. No floating lightblades, thankfully.

"Elam, please." Kaur's voice cracked, as if pained. "You took an innocent life, once again. If you're so sure you're on the right path, how do you justify that?"

"His soul will go to the Asha. Then it will cycle back on the dark side of the world. What's so wrong about that? He barely felt any pain, anyway."

My chest boiled with anger. "And what of the pain of his loved ones? What about those who'll miss him? Saina was his friend. I was becoming his friend. Doesn't our pain matter?"

Elam hovered downward. His eyes, one yellow and one purple, almost glowed in the fog. He seemed too big for his skyboard. Kaur had mentioned that he didn't like training in the dream, but given how bulging his chest and arms looked in his princely sherwani, he must've trained plenty in real life.

"Ah, it's the man I met on the mountain road!" Elam beamed like a pleasantly surprised child. "So good to see you again. I tasted the flavor of destiny when we met."

"Where's Saina?" I asked him. "Where's the levship you stole?"

"Saina's in there." He pointed at the pagoda. "The levship's in there." He pointed beyond the pagoda, at the distant fog behind which loomed the God Tower.

Wait, Saina was in the pagoda?

Rapid footsteps sounded from the open street beside us. At least ten soldiers — possibly more behind them — emerged in the fog, lightblades redder than death.

Kaur brandished her lightblade in their direction. What the hell had we gotten ourselves into?

"Those yours or Sylet's?" she asked Elam.

"If they're mine, I could order them *not* to kill you." Elam grinned. "Too bad they're not mine."

Elam waved goodbye to us, then flew toward the wooden gate of the pagoda.

Kaur and I ran up the steps. The lightblade-wielding soldiers approached, their boots clacking hard on the caked dust.

We hurried to the top. I huffed, but Kaur barely seemed winded. The wooden gate now lay open; Elam must've gone through. At least ten lightblades glowed at the base of the stairs, accenting the fog with a bloody hue. Couldn't even see the soldiers holding them.

We went through the gate. A stone pathway led to the entrance of the pagoda itself, which was just a shadowed threshold. Ditches lined the pathway — they'd probably been filled with water before. The stone gods climbed the pagoda — one had the furry face of a dragon, another an elephant's face with huge tusks, and yet another a tentacle-filled, octopus face. All of them were staring down, as if at us.

Bootsteps sounded on the steps behind us. The soldiers were coming. My heart beat faster with each loudening step.

Elam jetted out of the threshold. But he wasn't alone. He held Saina at his front on the skyboard. She wore a black combat suit. Her brown hair was frayed, and heavy eyebags bulged beneath her eyes.

"Saina!" I called as they hovered upward, then stopped about fifteen feet above.

"Jyosh?" Saina shouted down at me. "Why're you here?"

Kaur gave me a weird look: a half grin with a twinkle of mischief in her eye. "This is your chance to be a hero." She winked. "Make sure you catch her."

What'd she mean by that? The now alarmingly loud boot-steps sent quivers through me. The soldiers must've reached the top of the stairs.

Instead of focusing on that, Kaur wound her lightblade as the beam shrunk to the size of a dagger. She flung it straight upward. The light dagger flew like an arrow into Elam's skyboard, cutting into the bulge that housed the gain medium crystal.

Elam and Saina screamed as they fell off the damaged skyboard. I holstered my sword hilt and rushed under Saina. She crashed into my arms with a force that buckled my knees, sending us both tumbling into the muddy ditch at the side of the pathway.

"Take her and get out of here, Jyosh!" Kaur shouted from above. "This is no longer your fight."

The electric whizzing of lightblades on lightblades filled the air. I got to my feet and pulled a still-dazed Saina up.

"Come on," I said. "We have to help her."

The edges were too steep to climb. But the ditch led further in. Perhaps if we followed it, we could find a way out and get back to Kaur.

I took Saina's hand and tugged her along. We ran through the muddy ditch. Turned a corner as shouts and shrieks sounded. Not Kaur's, I hoped.

At the end of the ditch was a ledge. I hurried to it, climbed up, then turned to help Saina. We clasped hands, and I pulled her up into me.

"Jyosh. C-Can you fight?"

I shook my head in a moment of honesty.

"Don't go back there, then. You'll only get in the way. I'm sure Elam and Kaur together, given their blessings, can handle Sylet's men."

"What if Elam turns on Kaur after?"

"He won't hurt her again. Not in this scenario. Trust me."

A bloody scent tinged the air. From the shouts and electric whizzing of lightblade on lightblade, Elam must've brought out his blessing.

I climbed out of the ditch, then pulled Saina up. We came out between the wooden wall that surrounded the pagoda and the limestone of the pagoda itself. No soldiers, here.

"There's a back way down." Saina pointed toward a turn in the wooden wall. "Over there."

She hurried forward. I caught a breath or two, then followed.

Soon as she turned the corner, she screamed. I sprinted as fast as I could, then turned the corner, too.

A lightblade-wielding soldier stood in front of a narrow series of winding stone steps. He was focused on Saina, who'd slipped by him and now darted down the steps. I surged forward and smashed into his back with all my force. He banged into the wooden wall, dropped his hilt, then at once got back on his knees with a furious growl.

I took the chance to run and darted down the steps. Saina

was a few paces ahead. She waited for me to catch up, then said, "You hurt?"

"No. Don't stop!" We ran down the stairs. Because of the fog, I couldn't see where it led.

I turned my head to see the soldier, his furious lightblade back in his hand, sprinting down after us.

"Run!" I said as Saina and I hurled into the fog, so fast we might trip. She stumbled on the last step. I caught her and swung her back up. The soldier snarled at our backs, approaching faster than I realized, like he'd just flown down those steps.

We sprinted down the street, throwing our bodies forward as if a monster made of fire were chasing us.

The outline of a wall appeared in the fog. Must've been the side of a big building, but I couldn't really tell. Two alleys, one to the left and one to the right, were our only way forward.

"Go right," I said to Saina. "Find Kaur and lead her here!"

She split off and headed right. I veered left, grabbed my sword hilt from my holster, and in a moment of pure panic, inhaled and pushed enough red light through to create a lightblade. Hopefully, the soldier would meet my threat head on, and Saina could escape.

I darted into the left alleyway. A dead end — of course, just my luck. I turned to see the soldier following. His lightblade was so much bigger, straighter, and fuller than the discolored, skittish beam projecting from my hilt.

Soon as I brandished mine, it fizzled and turned to sparks. The hilt heated up, and so did my hand. Instead of dropping the hilt, I tightened my grip and endured the searing burns. This wasn't the time for my training to fail!

I focused on my objective: one man. No hesitation. I had to tie him down just long enough for Kaur to get here.

The man stood straight, masked save for his bright purple eyes. His feet were apart, and he brandished his lightblade at a tilt, the tip aimed at my face. He watched my movements and stayed still.

I knew what he was probably thinking: that I was baiting him by not having my lightblade projected. He didn't believe I couldn't form a lightblade, and so hesitated to strike and finish me.

But if I didn't project one soon, he'd realize it wasn't a trick, that I really was this weak and inexperienced. Then he'd end my life.

I had to make a lightblade. I had to force myself. Zauri would be eternally alone, roaming her dreamscape like a forgotten ghost, if I fell to this man.

Only one thing had worked before.

I imagined my brother Kediri's face behind his mask. It wasn't hard to do — he was tall like my brother, with long arms. Kediri was behind that mask. Kediri stood against me. Yes, I'd gone back in time — I had to fight him to save my family from his treachery.

I raised my sword hilt, inhaled red from the sun, and cycled it through me. A lightblade poured off the hilt like a gushing river, flowing forward until it solidified into a pure, deathly red. Shadows sputtered around the red, coiling and enmeshing the light like snakes.

Kaur was right. My enemy had hesitated. Now, I had to make sure he paid for it.

"Interesting eye color." He stepped forward. "Listen, my friends will be here shortly. Disarm, and we'll take you prisoner. Commander Sylet loves nothing more than to turn men like you back to the righteous path. Enough Karshan blood has been spilt, don't you think? Tell me, friend, where're you from?"

He didn't even know I wasn't a Karshan soldier. Why talk so much? Was he afraid?

He lunged forward, lightblade striking at my chest. My heart lunged, too, beating against my rib cage. I lowered my lightblade to block.

But in the middle of his attack, his lightblade melted like water and resolidified at an even lower angle, bending in the middle. I dipped my hand as low as I could, praying my lightblade would meet his.

Sparks and shadows flew off our blades as they collided.

I sprang back. My heart threatened to jump out of my mouth. I wanted to run. Get away from this man and his crazy, curving, bending blade. But behind me was a dead end. My enemy stood forward, holding his lightblade at a horizontal angle, his eyes bright and menacing.

"You're no fighter," he said. "Your father's a nawab, I bet. You guys get out of training so easily. Let me guess — you're the third son. Expendable. Daddy doesn't want his estate split into thirds. Tossed you into Rao's hands, hoping someone like me would do him a quick favor." He stuck out his other hand, palm open, as if welcoming me. "Let's show them both — disarm and join us. With the power hidden in this city, Commander Sylet is going to remake the order of the Dayworld. We grunts will each get a palace with a golden dome. What say you, Brother?"

If he was still asking me to disarm, he was still afraid of me. I wouldn't fall for Kediri's taunts and lies!

I'd let my silence talk for me. Better I remain as much of a mystery as possible. If I opened my mouth, he'd figure out I was a local. Then he'd really come at me.

He stepped closer, so I stepped back.

"Last chance." He stretched out his gloved palm. "Drop the lightblade. Commander will welcome *any* good man to the cause. I'll vouch for you. What do you say?"

He was stalling for time by talking. He truly believed his friends could kill Kaur and Elam. Meanwhile, I had no doubt she'd win — with her claws, if needed. I just had to survive long enough to be saved.

He stepped closer again, so I stepped back again.

By now, I was straining to inhale and cycle the sun's red. The circuit of light within jittered, chaotic. When it reached my hand, I smoothly pushed it into the hilt. But the more I focused on it, the more it wavered.

My lightblade sputtered and sparked, losing its solidity.

My enemy rushed through the air, lightblade coming at my head. Kediri. That was Kediri trying to slice my head open!

I raised my sword hilt. My lightblade reformed and deflected his strike. Red and black electricity crackled and sparked across the alleyway.

I stepped back to take a breath. Kediri was always trying to trick me. Trying to get me to let my guard down. He had no intention of letting me live.

My hate for him kept my lightblade alive. The red light had a mind of its own, cycling through me and into the hilt.

"Thought I had you there," the soldier said. "Your hands are surprisingly quick. Still, you're desperately clinging to life, here. I'd love to help train you. Rao's just using you as fodder, don't you see?"

I couldn't trust Kediri. Everything out of his mouth was a lie. The selfish asshole wanted me dead. Wanted our family dead. All so he could be free of us!

But he was obviously stronger and possessed training I lacked; I'd have to survive him by sheer will. By doing the unexpected. Unfortunately, I didn't know what he expected me to do in the first place. Didn't know anything about his weakness. Still, I had to try something. If I waited for his attacks, my luck at parrying would run out, and he'd score a hit on my flesh.

He stepped forward, so I stepped back. My back hit the wall. I was now cornered.

No hesitation. This time, I lunged forward, got low, and swiped at the man's thigh. His lightblade melted, then reformed at the perfect angle to deflect mine. Rainbow sparks lit up the alley as our blades collided.

No matter. I wound to strike again. His lightblade melted, snaked upward, doubled in size, and merged into my shoulder, setting it ablaze.

Blood and burning filled the air. I clutched my shoulder; it was fleshy and bleeding. My nerves caught fire. I fell to my knees. The pain turned me delirious, stars and lights fluttering about my vision.

I shrieked. My enemy stepped to my left side. The strike to end me was coming.

Kaur. Now would be a good time, I prayed.

Then I waited.

Waited forever. The killing blow didn't come. With my shoulder still screaming, I glanced to my left.

The soldier was in the middle of his swipe, his lightblade coming down upon my head. But he'd become a statue.

Something watched me from the opening of the alleyway. A massive, fanged face with whiskers that trailed like fire. Its eyes shone like balls of starlight. It wrapped its body of scales and blue fur around the wall to the left.

A valiant effort, it said into my mind. Its voice was the deepest, darkest, most discordant hum. It quaked my soul.

I'd say you survived long enough against someone far more skilled.

I remained too terrified to even move.

What are you waiting for? it asked. *Kill him.*

My sword hilt dangled from the seared skin on my palm, stuck to it. I yelped from the burning as I gripped it.

You're taking your time. Little creatures like you think you have so much.

"Who are you?" I asked with a tremble. "Why're you helping me?"

The dragon's face vivified in the fog as it loomed closer. Its scales were hard like topaz, and fur covered it like a field of azure grass. In certain spots, violet and fire-colored feathers stuck out, resembling a garden of flowers. The oily fluid within its burning eyeballs churned, and its fangs glowed like otherworldly ivory.

This domain belongs to me. I do as I desire — at least until someone leashes me. Now, in five seconds, I'm going to let time flow.

I squeezed my sword hilt, jittery, and imagined Kediri standing next to me. My lightblade shot out of the hilt. Then I turned to my left and stabbed the soldier through the heart.

Four seconds later, he dropped dead in silence. I looked at the opening of the alleyway; the dragon was gone.

I glared at my left shoulder. It was nothing but a pile of pink, seared flesh, intertwined with loose threads from my burnt combat suit.

I was too stunned to scream or move or even think until hurried footsteps approached. Judging by the sound, more than one person.

I shut my eyes from the ungodly pain.

The footsteps stopped. A hand slid down my cheek — soft and warm. I gasped and opened my eyes. It was Saina, crouched over me. Kaur stood behind her.

A song of violet light poured from Saina's hand into my cheek. It flowed down into my shoulder and silenced the pain with its melody. My whole left side numbed.

Saina said, "He lost a chunk of muscle, but no bone, thank god."

"Jyosh has muscles?" Kaur snickered. "Never noticed." Was this really the time for her dumb jokes?

Saina turned to her. "Let's go somewhere safe so I can heal him properly."

Before I knew it, Kaur was rummaging through the dead

soldier's utility pockets. She took an orange dream stone, cereal bars, and even a water thermos off him.

"Honestly, Jyosh, I thought we'd find you dead," she said. "I am seriously impressed you took this guy out."

I avoided eye contact with her. I didn't want her to see my shock.

Saina pulled me to my feet. "Come on. Let's get you out of here." She looked tenderly into my eyes. "And… thank you for protecting me. I knew I'd judged you right."

Chapter Sixteen

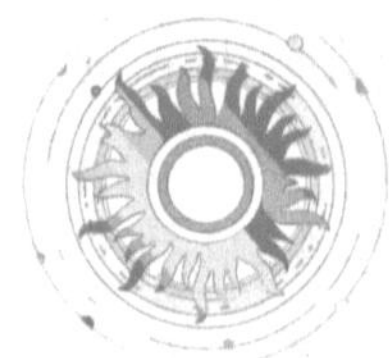

We went into a nearby tenement. The inside was empty: gray walls devoid of texture, cold gray tile floors — no adornments of any kind. The rooms were just hollow shells. Why had the ancient architects of this city designed such an elaborate outside, yet neglected the interiors entirely? Who could've ever lived in a place like this?

It reminded me of the unfinished version of Harska I saw with Zauri in my dream. But that Harska had updated itself, somehow, over the span of days. This city had supposedly been stuck in time for twenty thousand years.

We climbed a stairwell to the highest floor. Just like the others, it was bare, unfinished, sterile.

Weakness made my limbs heavy while numbness made me floaty, but thanks to the violet light Saina had soothed me with earlier, I was free of pain. Physical pain, at least.

Inside, I felt as if my soul were bobbing on a high tide. One fight against one man had consumed my all, and yet I still lost. I lost. If it weren't for the dragon stopping time, I'd be a corpse.

What about the two armies out in the streets? Would I have to fight them all?

It was hopeless, wasn't it? I'd never get my dream stone back. I'd never see Zauri again.

I wasn't strong enough.

"Sit here," Saina said, snapping me from my thoughts. She pointed to a spot against the wall. "Let's get you better."

I dropped down against the wall.

"Shimmy forward a bit so I can get behind you."

I slid forward against the cold stone. Saina unzipped the front of my black suit. She pulled out my combat stone. My arms shuddered from the jolt.

"You still have the healing stone I gave you?"

I nodded. I took it out from my utility pocket and handed it to her. Saina rubbed the violet crystal against her shirt, then stuck it inside my chest slot. My muscles tightened from yet another jolt.

She got behind me and knelt. "There's not a whole lot of violet in the air, right now. The sun's obscured. Not ideal conditions at all, so it'll take a little while."

I nodded.

"You look like you're in shock. That's fine. After what we just went through, I am, too."

She put a warm hand on my nape. Violet light flowed like cool syrup into my bloodied, carved-up shoulder.

"Your hand's burned." She took my fleshy, seared hand. "I just grew you a new one, too. No matter. It's only skin deep — we'll heal it."

Meanwhile, Kaur was looking out the window at the far side of the big, open floor. Good. I didn't want her to hear.

"Saina… can I ask you something?"

"Sure."

"Did you actually fight a dragon?"

She shook her head. "That vision you saw wasn't me. During my life, my frequency got intertwined with a lot of people. People from the Exile. What you saw was more like an echo."

Intertwined… that was better than sex, according to Kaur.

"You've gone a bit flush," Saina said. "Was it something I said?"

"What does that mean — intertwined?"

"You've been in a conduit or shared dream before, right? Well, on the Day of Exile when we Beheshians remember what we lost, we all — together — share our frequencies. It's sort of like what happened between me and you, but more intense. It's often not pleasant, but we do it so we don't forget the home we lost that day."

That didn't sound better than sex. On the contrary, it seemed terrifying to be bathed in someone else's memories and pain.

"I see why you care so much. You've seen the world through so many eyes. You understand, then, that someone else's pain is as bitter as your own."

She let out a nervous half-chuckle. "Something like that. But it doesn't always make you care more. It can do the opposite, too. It can numb you. Make you indifferent. Or make you even more desperate to save yourself."

"I know what you mean. I was desperate back in the camp. Everyone was suffering, but I only cared about myself." I wished I could stop thinking of that awful place and what it'd done to me. "Saina… what did you see in my frequency?"

"I was focused on reattaching your nerves, so didn't see much. There was a dark room. Your mother and father and sister and brother were there."

Did she mean the courthouse? But Kediri wasn't there. They'd already executed him before our trial.

My shoulder got intensely tingly. The bleeding had dried, and it was starting to scab. I moaned from the discomfort.

"Hurts? I'll soothe it." Saina dripped more violet light into my shoulder. It smothered the discomfort with numbness. "Would you rather sleep while we do this, like before?"

"No. This is fine."

Kaur approached, hands on hips. She grinned at us. "Isn't this sweet. Say, Jyosh, did you take a hit on purpose?"

How could she say that? How could she make light of the fact that, were it not for the intervention of a dragon, I'd be dead?

Come to think of it, Kaur hadn't gotten injured. There wasn't any blood on her black suit, either.

"Tell me, Kaur, while I was fighting for my life, what were you doing?"

"I barely got out of that tussle. Was utter hell. Don't get so smug just because you killed one guy."

I guess I had no right to question her. She'd helped rescue Saina because she thought it was my goal. And yet, I felt further from my goal than ever.

"So…" Kaur wouldn't stop grinning at us toothily. "Did you tell her, Jyosh?"

Oh god. Not this mommy Saina stuff. Please. Anything but this.

"Shut up," I said. "Don't say anything."

Kaur's eyebrows zagged upward. "People like you are so pathetic. Imagine taking your love to your grave. Coward."

"Don't say it!"

"Umm," Saina interjected. "What are you guys talking about?"

"I'll kill you, Kaur!"

She tousled her cherry locks. "You'll thank me later. Here's the thing, Saina. Jyosh loves you. He refused to board that ship to New Behesh, all so he could come here and risk his life to save yours. Now the part that I think is a bit awkward is all the motherly vibes he gets from you. What Jyosh is really looking for is his mommy. A mommy-wife, to be specific. Someone who'll warm all his—"

"IT'S NOT TRUE! I LIED! I'VE BEEN LYING THIS WHOLE TIME."

"*Shhh,*" Saina said. "Both of you, keep it down. Whatever he wants to tell me, it can wait."

That infuriating grin was finally gone from Kaur's face. "What do you mean, Jyosh? Don't try to get out of this by pretending it was a lie."

"I'm not in love with Saina, nor did I come here to save her. I'm glad I caught her, but it wasn't my objective. I just went along with it because I didn't want to tell you the real reason I'm here."

Kaur bent down and got eye-to-eye with me. "Oh shit. Are you *actually* Red Veil? No… it's not possible, you don't seem at all like one." She pulled on her broad nose. "Then again, Red Veil agents don't like to seem like Red Veil agents. Tell me the truth — why are you here?"

I could feel Saina's blue frequency flit, causing a ticklish tug on my heart.

"You're stressing him," she said. "Stop it, Kaur. Talk about all this serious stuff later."

"No. He lied to me. It can't wait. Why are you here, Jyosh?"

"I left my dream stone on Saina's ship. I just want it back." I sounded so pathetic, didn't I?

"No way." Kaur gritted her teeth and loomed her head closer to mine. "That's utter goatshit. I don't believe it for a second. There's no reason for you to still be here. Take Saina and get out of this city while the fog is still thick."

"I'm not leaving. Not until I get it back. You don't understand. Someone cold and bitter like you could never get it."

"Get what?" She chuckled mockingly. "That you're in love with an artificial person instead of a real one? Sure, you're that pitiful. I just don't believe even *you* would risk your life for something so stupid."

"'Stupid?' How dare you?" I'd punch her across her jowls, but I was too numb to move. "Try spending twelve years in a prison camp, then call me stupid!"

"Stop it! Both of you!" Saina's frequency hopped suddenly. "If I could take my hand off his nape and separate you two, I would, but that'd interrupt a very sensitive procedure. Nothing matters more right now than Jyosh's healing. Understand?"

Kaur rose, turned around, and walked to the other end of the room, her fist against her chin.

The awkward air she'd brought remained.

"Her name is Zauri, right?" Saina asked.

Hearing someone else say her name jolted my heart. "How could you know that?"

"I saw her, too, when I was reconnecting your nerves. I saw her sitting beneath a palm tree, drawing a picture. It was lovely, that whole island."

I suppose it made sense. I'd had several visions during the procedure, so Saina must've, too. But now she knew things she wasn't supposed to. I understood why she'd told me not to pry. Discomforting to think someone had seen so deeply inside of me.

"You don't have to be ashamed," she said. "No matter what Kaur or anyone says, it's okay. You don't have to explain yourself to anyone."

"I do, though. Kaur saved my life. And I lied to her. The truth is, I wish I didn't have to rely on her or you. I wish I was strong enough on my own. Weak people like me have to lie, cheat, scam, steal — even murder — just to survive."

"Sure, I get that surviving is hard. But if you ask me, you're a little too worried about what others think of you. That alone makes you weak. And besides..." Saina came closer to my ear and whispered, "You should know something about Kaur. She lied to you, too. I'm sworn never to tell anyone's secrets, especially those revealed during an intensive procedure like spinal reconstruction, but… just this once… I might have to break a vow."

Kaur was keeping something from me, that much was obvious. I couldn't help my curiosity. "What did you see?"

"Did she tell you about her close relationship with Elam?"

They'd had a relationship? Well, they obviously knew each other, but I never got that sense. "No. Nothing."

"What I'm about to tell you might sound crazy, but there *is* an explanation for it. A bizarre one. Just promise me you'll wait till you're healed before asking her about it."

"I promise. What is it? Tell me."

Saina got so close, her lips brushed the hairs on my earlobes. "Kaur is Elam's mother."

SAINA WOULDN'T SAY anything more about Kaur being Elam's mother. Four hours later, she finished healing me and decided to rest for a bit on the far side of the room. During the procedure, she told me a few mundane things about her life in Behesh before the event known as the Exile, which happened twenty years ago, when the Padishah from the Nightscape brought eternal night to the floating island, separating it from the bright side of the earth forever.

But Saina, too, was so obviously evasive. I might be weak, but I'm not stupid; there was so much she wasn't telling me about herself, and especially about those visions. But it's not like I had any right to know. We were merely patient and healer after all; we weren't friends. Still, it left me feeling cold toward her, despite how warm and caring she'd been outwardly.

It was Kaur, though, who held my ire. Elam had mentioned he was looking for his mother when first we met; I'd just never imagined it could be Kaur. How, though? Kaur had never told me her exact age, but I'd always felt it to be around my own. Maybe a few years older, at most.

And Elam? He looked even older than that — late twenties or early thirties, I'd guess.

Had Kaur lied about her age? Was she older than she appeared?

I was enjoying a cereal bar and water when Kaur came. She sat in front of me, legs crossed, frowning. It had gotten colder. Wind whispered through the chasms of the building. Even our own breaths turned to fog. What a strange, disconcerting place.

"I'm sorry," she said. "I was surprised by what you told me. I don't like surprises. They make me grumpy. I never could've imagined this was all for a dream stone. I mean, I *can* imagine it. I can even understand it. I just didn't see it in you. Thought I had you pegged, but the truth is, I just suck at reading people."

Such a multipronged apology. But so what? Saina was right — I ought not to care what others think of me.

I folded my arms and glared at Kaur.

"I think you did try to tell me, a few times," she continued. "I was thinking about the questions you asked me, and some of the things we discussed. Look — I don't even care that you hid it. It's fine, really."

She seemed contrite. I wanted her to get it all out before I asked my questions.

I continued to glare.

"So, Jyosh, the thing is — and I'm asking this as gently as possible — do you *really* want to risk it all for this dream stone? You could always buy another one. And yeah, I get that people are attached to their dream companions. All the memories you must've made together. Of course, they feel as irreplaceable as people — I get it. But this is life or death. You almost died earlier today, so I'm sure you see that. That's why I have to make sure you're not making a huge mistake."

I got the sense from how much her cheeks twitched that she wasn't done.

"Look, if the dream stone is just sitting on the ship, there's no harm in letting it go. It's not like the dream person that you love is suffering or anything. The dream doesn't exist without the dreamer. I know it hurts to let go, but it'll hurt more if you die. Throw your life away. Think of the future you could have. Think of all the memories you could make."

She stared at me expectantly. After so much pleading, she'd finished wagging her tongue.

"How old are you, Kaur?"

She blinked a few times as if perplexed. "Twenty-seven."

"And how old is Elam?"

Her face paled. "T-Thirty, I believe. Why?"

I was no math genius, but something here didn't add up.

"Do I really have to say it?" I stared at her, unblinking.

Her emerald irises swelled. "She told you. She broke her vow and told you."

"You know what I think, Kaur? We're all lying to each other about why we're here. You don't want to kill Rao. You don't want to save the world. You want to save your son. When I caught Saina and fell into that ditch, you caught Elam, didn't you? And then the two of you fled."

"So? It doesn't change anything. I'm still going to," she mimed slicing her neck, "Rao, because of what he's done to my son. To Elam. He's misled him so utterly, so totally, I can't let him live."

"I've heard of healers that can delay or reverse the effects of aging, just how Saina regenerated my hand. So how old are you, really?"

Kaur shook her head. "I don't care to lie about my age. You're asking the wrong question, as usual."

Now it really wasn't adding up. Either she'd lied about her age, or she wasn't Elam's mother.

"Did you adopt him? Is this all a sick joke? Don't you think I deserve to know, considering it was Elam who hijacked the levship where I was being healed, where my dream stone currently is? Don't you think I deserve to know if you care more about the enemy than you do me or even yourself?"

"I love Elam. He's my son. The world can go ahead and end, but I'll *never* hurt him. Nor will I abandon him. Now you know. If you don't like it, then leave like I told you to. Or go it alone. See how far you get."

I wasn't leaving, nor could I do this without her. We needed to rebuild our trust, somehow, because we both needed to get into that tower. Her to save her son from Rao, me to save Zauri from eternal loneliness.

I decided to share something about that. "You said that the dream doesn't exist without the dreamer. What if I told you that wasn't necessarily true? Zauri, the woman in my dream stone, continues to dream without me. Even if I could accept the idea of moving on, I can never accept leaving her there, all alone, forever. I've only been without her for a few days, and it hurts. She's been alone for months in her time frame, so can you imagine what she's feeling? I have to help her."

"I can understand what you're saying about the dream continuing, strange as it sounds." Kaur gave me a tepid smile. "You think of yourself as some kind of savior, don't you? Someone so ready to throw his life away for others. Why?"

"Because I don't want to be like my brother, who was the opposite. In the camp, I became as selfish as he was. I hated myself. I broke into pieces because of it. I can't be like him, even if it costs me my life."

"And I don't want to be like my mother. I always wanted to show her ghost what a good, loving, present mother was like. Somehow, Rao knew about my wound. Unlike me, he was always so good at seeing people for who they really are. The dream stone was a gift from him. Obviously — I could never afford it on my salary."

The liquid drained from my mouth. I coughed from the dryness. "What dream stone?"

"Rao and I went in together. Layer three dreams, every night, for a week. A little boy lived there, just like Ava lived in her stone. He was only a baby at first, and we raised him. I gave him all my heart. I loved him more than anything made of flesh."

"What are you talking about?"

"I'm talking about a child raising program. They're among the most popular ones sold in Karsha."

"So that's the dream program you got attached to. Always painting me with your own brush. You even called me 'pitiful.'"

"Never said I wasn't, too. Now let me finish. One day, all sorts of glitches and black holes appeared in the dreamscape. We took the stone for maintenance, only to learn that it'd been corrupted — irreversibly. It couldn't be fixed. So we went in, one last time, to say goodbye to our son. He was a fully grown adult by then, and we'd been with him all the way." Tears streamed down her cheeks. "I'm his mother! I couldn't just say goodbye, I couldn't let him go. So I prayed, prayed we could be together." She paused to heave and rub her eye. "There are blessings... and then there are miracles."

"Miracles? What the hell are you saying, Kaur?"

"That day when Rao and I woke up from the dream, Elam was in the room, with us. He became real. It's self-evident. What more can I say? You saw him. He *is* real. But no one's supposed to know the truth. No one. If the wrong factions in the Karshan government find out, can you imagine what they'll do? They'll torture him with all kinds of experiments. So please... please don't tell anyone."

It was too much to believe. Sure, I'd thought of Zauri as real, but not in the sense that she could exist in this world, with me. "So when you warned me about wishing dream companions were real, this is what you meant."

Kaur nodded and dried her teary face with her sleeve. "The truth is, Elam doesn't belong here. Imagine living your whole life in Paradise, and then coming *here*, to this hellish reality. He's not adjusted well, that's why he's the way he is." She shook her head, tears falling on the floor. "I wish it'd never happened, but I don't know how to undo it. I wanted him to be real so bad, and it happened. It happened." She looked at me, lips trembling. "I pray it never happens to the woman in your dream."

I LET Kaur sulk for a bit. We both sat against the cold wall, hugging our own legs. What was there to say, really?

Either she was lying — and I doubted that very much — or some enormous trick had been played on her by Colonel Rao, or it was all true. And I, in an indulgent way, wanted to believe the latter.

If dream people could become real, then Zauri could become real, too. And yet, that was exactly what Kaur had warned me about. Still, I couldn't help but want it.

Saina came to us after she was done resting. Healing me had taken a lot out of her. Cycling light for hours wore you out like nothing else. Although I'd done it to build cannons, she'd done it to save lives, so I couldn't say I knew what she felt.

Kaur turned her cheek and looked away from Saina. I suppose betraying her trust wasn't easily forgiven.

"Why are you still here?" Kaur asked.

"I have my reasons." Saina stuck her hands in the utility pockets of her black combat suit.

"Reasons, eh? So what was the reason you were with Elam, earlier?"

Saina looked at me, but I turned my face away, too. She ought to answer the question.

"Just enjoying the sights?" Kaur scoffed.

"Do you know how many of us Beheshians are left on the bright side of the world? Less than thirty thousand. Your son killed one. A man I'd known since I was a little girl. A man whose frequency had been intertwined with mine. Do you think I'd just 'enjoy the sights' with a killer?"

"We've all lost people. You self-righteous pricks aren't as special as you think."

"Self-righteous? We're here to help."

"No you're not." Kaur gave Saina a mocking chuckle. "You're here to *atone*. Don't think I don't know about your beliefs. You really think you'll get your beloved floating temple back if you do enough good deeds."

"You'd talk that way to someone who saved your life?"

"See, there it is. The superiority. Shall I touch your feet and lick where you walked? Shall I behold you like a god? I never asked you to help me. I was content for my suffering to end when my own son stuck a demonblade in my back."

I groaned to show my annoyance. "Saina, if you're going to stay with us, you can't hide things. What are you still doing in Sambalpur?"

She folded her arms. "Well, seems you two've become rather cozy lying down in each other's secrets. But even if I wanted to leave, I obviously can't."

"Why not?" I asked.

She pointed to the fog-covered window. "Isn't it obvious?"

Kaur and I stared at each other, bewildered, then shook our heads.

"Wait…" Saina glared at us in shock. "You two really don't know?"

"Don't know what?" Kaur and I said at the same time. I took a sip of water.

"You must've been sleeping, else you would've felt it." Saina walked to the window and tapped the glass. "That isn't fog out there. It's a cloud. We're in the sky!"

I spat water onto my pants. "What do you mean 'in the sky?'"

"Sambalpur…" Saina floated one hand above the other. "Colonel Rao did something, and it took off. It launched. It's no longer a city on the ground — it's a floating island."

Well, that did explain the oppressive fog. But it was like trying to digest an entire goat in one bite. How could we not have noticed? I turned to Kaur.

"Explains the dreamquake." Also true. She pinched her bottom lip. "You're saying Rao did it? How?"

"I was his captive, so he wouldn't tell me when I asked. But here's what I can tell you — I'm the only one who can regrow limbs in Maniza, currently. That's why Elam kidnapped me. Rao is missing his left hand."

I said, "Umm, did we already move on from the revelation that the city we're in started flying while we were asleep?"

"Yeah, we did," Kaur said. "Speaking of Rao's hand, I'm the one who cut it off. Was going for something more fatal, but I missed. That's why Elam sliced me through."

So Kaur had tried to kill Rao, and failed. Her son had sided with his father. She was here for a second attempt.

"As a healer, I'm bound to heal anyone who needs it, regardless of what their hands have wrought."

Kaur rolled her eyes. "You're bound to keep their secrets, too."

"Guess I didn't keep my vow for a second time. I told Rao I'd only help him if he released all the other patients and staff. He agreed and let one of our ships pick them up. But that was only my first condition."

"What was the second?" I asked.

Saina knelt down in front of us. She rested her hands on her thighs. "Do you know about the miracles that took place at the Temple Behesh?"

There was that word again: *miracles*. Hearing it made me so expectant, to the point of discomfort.

"I know that folks used to go to Behesh to pray for everything under the sun," Kaur said. "Curing illnesses that even the best healers couldn't manage. Finding lost loved ones. Sudden riches coming out of nowhere. So many stories — I'm sure most were goatshit."

"You'd be wrong. And that's not the half of it." Saina turned to me. "You saw a vision of me at the temple's core, attached by wire to remnants of the twenty-six heroes who entered the eternal storm and slew the dragon, Daeva Andar."

There was that word again: *dragon*. It made me shudder. I nodded to show I was following along.

"When I was a little girl, before the Exile, I was what's known as a Daughter of the Dawn. My job was to stand in the middle of the temple, endure all these wires attached to my fingers, and attune my frequency to the Avatar of the Eternal Dawn. To be a vessel for him, so to speak."

So, that first vision really was of Saina. "Why were they all praying to you in the memory?" I asked.

Saina scratched the big mole above her lip. "They weren't praying to me. They were praying *through* me. To the Avatar. I myself had no power, but if the Avatar heard our prayers, then anything was possible. He was the source of all those miracles.

And that day, we were all praying for our survival. For the survival of our nation and temple."

"Guess it didn't work." Kaur made one of her sarcastic faces. "The Padishah pulled the floating island through the storm and into the night. Turns out the gods are laughing at us."

Saina shut her eyes and slowed her breathing, as if pained by the memories. "Most of us stayed behind, including my mother and father. But I don't miss them, to be honest. I don't miss anyone. Except…"

She trailed off, then seemed to either be asleep or meditating.

"Except who?" Kaur blurted out impatiently.

"*Shh.*" I wagged my finger at Kaur. "Don't rush her."

Saina opened her eyes. A glint of hope shone in them. "Kaur, you said that by doing good deeds, we Beheshians are trying to atone and get our temple back. You're wrong. The temple is still there — it's just in the dark. The people who remained may even still be there, too. It's not that we're trying to get it back, it's that we can no longer rely on it to reach the Avatar. You can't understand what it's like to have your connection severed from your god, so suddenly. And no matter what good deeds we do…" she stared at her hands, "we can't *feel* our god's presence. So many have left the faith, seeking other paths to nirvana, because ours no longer works."

"What's your point?" Kaur asked.

"When Elam stole my ship and flew it over Sambalpur, I felt my frequency attune suddenly — at the exact moment we flew over that pagoda. I haven't felt anything like it since I was a Daughter of the Dawn, standing in the temple with all those wires stuck to me. There's something here, something that may lead us back to the Avatar of the Eternal Dawn. And for the sake of my people, for the sake of myself, I have to figure out what it is."

I fit some of the pieces together. "So you asked Elam to take you to the pagoda as a condition of you regrowing Rao's arm."

"Exactly. We took a skyboard, thinking we wouldn't be spotted in the fog. But Sylet's got some powerful spectrum mappers. I barely had a chance to see the inside of that temple. A lot of things about it, though, reminded me of the Temple Behesh." Saina made a fist. "I have to go back. No matter what it takes. Even at the cost of my life. I have to find out what's in that pagoda."

We all knew each other's secrets now, which sat right with me. Unless Kaur and Saina had even more secrets — well, even if they did, could they be bigger than what they'd already told me?

Kaur pulled out a dream stone from her utility pocket. It shone fire orange in the dim room. She'd looted it from the guy I'd killed with the dragon's help.

"To be honest, Saina, we could use someone like you," Kaur said while turning the crystal in her hand. "I'm not bad at surviving," she pointed to me with the crystal, "neither is he, but when we do survive, it's not without a few holes."

"I'll help however I can." Saina nodded. "There's something else you should know. I overheard Rao and Elam talking about something called a 'Deep Layer.'"

I snapped my fingers. "Deep Layer — Harska had one of those. It's a tunnel beneath the city that connects important sites together."

"That's what I think, too," Saina said. "Maybe we could use it to get around instead of going overland, since Sylet has troops everywhere. I say we look for an entrance."

Kaur strummed her hands together. Unusual for her to stay silent for so long. Saina and I stared at her, awaiting her opinion.

"You're both kind of cute together," she finally said. "Shame that Jyosh's heart is taken."

"Don't start that again." I let out a tired groan. "Let's keep focused on the tasks at hand."

"Speaking of tasks," Kaur said, "Elam told me that Sylet is planning a massive assault on the God Tower, so we might be able to search for this Deep Layer without them noticing. Of course, he didn't tell me about the Deep Layer. Lies of omission."

We were all guilty of that.

Kaur tossed her dream stone up and caught it. "Do you guys know what this dream stone is?"

Given its brightness, it looked like an expensive one. Other than that, I couldn't say. Saina and I shook our heads.

"It's a layer-two training dream stone," Kaur said. "It's typically used by captains and higher. You felled a captain, Jyosh. What kind of trick did you play to win that fight?"

Did I really want to tell them a dragon stopped time so I could win, or was it too big a box of questions to open right now? "Let's just say I got lucky." Better to tell them later, in the dream, when we'd really have time to sort things out. Besides, it was nice to be admired. No harm in enjoying that for a little while.

"See, you did save up your luck!" Saina brightened the room with her smile. "Nana was so wise."

"So, we going to use that stone?" I asked. "I could sure use the training before we charge forward."

WE CHOSE a spot across from a window. I knelt and brushed the cold, textureless tile floor; the hardness reminded me of my bed in the camp.

"Obviously, Jyosh has to be in the middle," Kaur said. "Since he's the dreamer and all."

I unzipped the front of my black suit and took out the healing stone Saina had put in earlier. Kaur handed me the new dream stone; wisps of fiery orange light glowed within. I stuck it in and endured a brief jolt.

I lay down. Saina glared at me, arms folded. Kaur took sips from the thermos she'd looted from the soldier I killed. Then she wiped her mouth and lay down to my right.

"It'll be a bit different since there's three of us." She snuggled up close. "Jyosh, face in her direction."

"Nope." I shook my head. "I'll lay on my back. No way I'm facing her."

"Come on, she won't mind."

Saina cleared her throat. "Don't speak for me. I'm sure we can manage with Jyosh on his back." She rubbed her hands together, then lay down at my left, about a handspan away.

"Get closer to him," Kaur said. "Never done your *intertwining* without a wire, eh? You have to tangle your limbs up a bit to maintain points of contact, else you might vanish from the dream if you roll over to scratch your ass."

Kaur held my right hand, clasping our fingers. She held up our handhold so Saina could see how it was done.

Saina took my left hand and clasped it. She got close enough so our shoulders touched. Out of everything I'd experienced these past few days, including all the dreams, this situation seemed the most surreal.

"Good." Kaur stuck her right leg over my left leg, almost brushing my… "This doesn't quite work. I could easily just toss onto my other side and get disentangled." She let go of my hand, got onto her side, and faced me. "Jyosh, lift your arms."

I let go of Saina's hand and lifted them. Kaur snuggled up and wrapped her arm around me. She clasped my left hand and wrapped a leg around my right leg. She resembled a small bear clinging to a tree.

"Okay, do exactly like this, Saina," she said.

Saina sat up and folded her arms. "Wait… is this a joke?"

"Hurry up," Kaur said. "I can already feel the orange light. You'll miss the train."

Saina sighed and did as told. She clasped my right hand, wrapped a leg around my left leg, and nestled her head on my shoulder.

"You've been quiet, Jyosh." Kaur chuckled. "On a scale of one to seven, how happy are you, right now?"

I'd been focusing on inhaling the orange light. "I definitely don't feel cold anymore, but none of us smell very good, so I'd put it at a four."

"Damn, he actually answered the question." Kaur yawned.

The orange was seeping in. It melted my nerves. It bathed my muscles in syrup. It pulled my mind deep into the depths of the sun.

"See you all on the other side," Saina whispered.

Chapter Seventeen

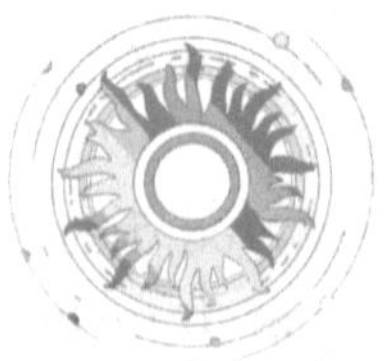

I woke up in a coliseum. Why were these training grounds so exhibitionist? Kaur and Saina stood in the distance, their hands moving energetically in front of each other's faces. I got to my feet, wiped sand off my shirt and pants, and approached them.

"You're making a lot of assumptions." Saina shook her head. "You know nothing about me."

"The ease with which you forsook your vow of secrecy… how do I know you'll keep your other vows? How do I know you won't sell us out to get what you're after? I think it's a fair thing to ask."

"Let me ask a question," I said, hoping to distract them. "Are we already in a layer two dream?"

Kaur nodded. "This dream stone *only* has a layer two."

So if we slept for four hours, we'd be here for about a hundred days. Incredible. I could get so much stronger in that time.

"Before either of you go anywhere, I want to check something." Kaur dusted sand off her chest. "Hopefully Sylet did his due diligence."

She opened her palm and tapped on the terminal window. The ground vanished. The coliseum vanished. We stood on air. I almost stumbled as I gasped. Above us loomed the red sky so familiar to us Manizans, and a thousand feet below lay a red ocean, as if made of water and blood.

Kaur tapped some more on her terminal display. In a blink, Sambalpur replaced the red ocean. Its white domes and limestone buildings shimmered in the bloody glow, just like in real life. The colorful statues of the gods seemed so tiny from up here. The tower loomed behind its golden wall with its golden doors.

"Just as I thought," Kaur said. "Sylet's spectrum mappers have the entire city modeled. And like any diligent commander, he's put this likeness of it in his training stones." She tapped on the display floating above her palm, a pensive look on her face. "Hmm. It seems the Deep Layer isn't modeled in the memory."

Saina twisted a strand of her copper hair. "If the map doesn't show the Deep Layer, maybe Sylet doesn't know about it. Maybe that mirror-like material covering the ground blocks spectrum mapping. If only we could figure out where an entrance is."

Two puzzle pieces that had been resting in the back of my mind smashed together.

"I know where the entrance to the Deep Layer is." I snapped my fingers. "Kaur, zoom us toward the pagoda where we found Saina."

"Sure." Kaur tapped on her terminal.

The city surged toward us. Or were we falling into it? In a blink, we floated above a familiar street. A hill stood between several blocky buildings, upon which was the pagoda Saina wanted to return to. The stone gods climbed the pagoda.

"Look at the faces of the gods," I said. "Notice what they're looking at?"

The faces of the gods, whether human or animal, stared down, not up.

"I noticed this earlier," Saina said. "They're not climbing up, they're climbing down!"

"Exactly. Zoom us into the God Tower, Kaur."

Kaur tapped, and in a blink, we appeared above the God Tower, which contained the levship with my dream stone. The stone gods here were also looking down.

"The faces are staring up everywhere else." Kaur folded her arms and smiled. "Clever."

"They really could be entrances to the Deep Layer." Saina nodded as if impressed. "Also, fortuitous that the pagoda is one. We can squish two scorpions with one stomp if we head there. This could work. But what are the dangers?"

"Could be anything," Kaur said. "We don't know what awaits us in the Deep Layer."

"True." Saina nodded. "This city's a twenty-thousand-year-old bucket of mysteries. Why are the interiors so hollow, as if unfinished? Why aren't there any signs of habitation? I have a feeling the answers lie below."

Answers I personally wasn't seeking. But if I could help Saina reconnect with her god on the way to getting my dream stone back, it would be a tiny payment toward what I owed her.

"Let's go train, now!" I said. How wonderful to have a hundred days to get stronger. And perhaps enjoy the sights, too.

"Not interested." Kaur replied.

"What? Why?"

"I mean, I'm not interested in training *you*. I've got my own training to do. Besides, that's what this stone is for. You'll see the program in your terminal. Select the first level and get to work."

I opened my palm and the terminal display appeared above it. I scrolled through the menu and tapped on *KAO Lightblade Training Program > Level One.*

A blinding light enveloped me. I reappeared in the air, falling from hundreds of feet onto a floating island covered in grass. I flapped my arms, hoping I'd fly like a bird. No luck. I was about to scream when the air beneath me slowed. A breeze glided me gently downward onto the grass.

This training dream stone sure had interesting transitions; flying and floating seemed to be a theme.

A man materialized in front of me. He wore a white sherwani, had a trim black beard, and seemed to be about forty years old, judging by the hardness of his face and the specks of gray in his hair. He towered half a foot above me, and was double my thickness, as well — all muscle, judging by his bulging pectorals.

"I'm Kriga, your lightblade training script. You've selected level one of the Karshan Army Officers Training Program. If you're a complete beginner, you might find it challenging."

Well, I could make a stable lightblade, now. Perhaps not with perfect consistency and form, but when I imagined my adversary as Kediri, it seemed to work.

"My name is Jyosh, and I'm ready for whatever."

"Good." If that was good, why was Kriga shaking his head? "I will ask that you improve your attitude. 'Whatever' is not an appropriate way to approach battle. You should start, as always, by considering what you know about your opponent."

I'd already disappointed my new training program. Perhaps I ought to behave how an enlisted trainee would.

"Yes, sir! I'll do better."

He shook his head again. "You need not address me as 'sir.' I have no superiority over you. I'm only a script." Was that annoyance in his tone?

Ugh, this *only a script* stuff again. How confusing. If I was going to learn from him, I had to regard him with some respect — script or not.

"Yes, Kriga. I intend to leave everything I've got on this training ground. Shall we begin?"

Kriga pulled a hilt from behind his back and handed it to me.

It had the heft of a toy blade and the same blocky, utilitarian design as the ones we'd looted from the soldiers Kaur killed in the forest.

"I must tell you, Jyosh, that I have my own methods. I eschew the basics and begin in the middle, always with a challenge. We're going to learn an ability that could swing the tide of battle in your favor. It's called Blinding Blade."

I'd never even heard of it. Fun name, though.

Kriga unholstered his hilt and raised it in my direction. A curved, red beam grew off it, hairs of blacklight on the edges.

"Come at me."

I raised my hilt. Since Kriga was so tall, I'd no difficulty imagining Kediri's face on his frame. Without me even willing it, a solid, straight beam of red erupted off my hilt.

"An intense creation," Kriga said. "Some trainers would tell you to relax, to make it calmer. But if anger unifies your soul, mind, and body, I won't tell you to fight it. All the better, I say. Now, come and kill me."

What to go for? The heart? The neck? The thigh? Attacking low against the captain I'd fought in the alley had been a mistake; by lowering his arm and reforming his blade's angle, he'd managed to block and counter while I was off balance. I'd never actually learned the tactics of fighting with lightblades, so of course I'd lost that fight by relying on my gut.

But my gut was still all I had, and by thinking so much, I was committing the number one sin: hesitation. Attacking from high to low felt right, so I raised my blade, darted forward, and slashed downward at his chest.

White scathed my eyes. I couldn't see! Pain flared in my eyeballs. I wanted to run, but which direction? I raised my lightblade in a feeble attempt to guard myself.

"Relax. You're going to need to control that survival

response." Kriga's hardwood voice calmed me. "This is level one. I won't cause you more pain than that."

The white covering my vision cleared. The flaring pain in my eyeballs calmed. Kriga stood in the grass in front of me, stroking his beard thoughtfully.

"So that's Blinding Blade," I said. "Amazing, actually. If I could do that, I would've blinded that captain before he had a chance. I'd never lose a fight, in fact."

Kriga let out a deep chuckle. Glad to know he had a sense of humor. "That's not the correct conclusion. Even if you execute this move perfectly, every time, it has a counter, just like every ability. Do you really think you'd learn the secret to victory at level one?"

Of course not, but what could the counter be? Closing your eyes just as the flash emitted, perhaps? But closing your eyes in battle was almost as bad as being blinded.

"I hope you'll teach me the counter, too. I'd hate to be blinded like that when my life's on the block."

Why hadn't the captain in the alley blinded me? Perhaps he feared I knew the counter. The more I thought about that fight, the more I realized that my enemy had probably overthought things, refusing to believe I really was a frightened lamb ready for slaughter. He stood still when he should've charged forward. He talked when he should've slashed. Someone had to learn from his mistakes.

"I will teach you the counter, in time, but first you should learn the move itself. You must do two things with perfect timing. One, you must convert red light into bright yellow light — sometimes people refer to it as white light because it's so bright, though it technically isn't. Two, you must *surge* at the perfect moment, once the yellow light passes into the hilt but before it corrupts your lightblade. This will produce the blinding effect."

It sounded… impossible. How do you convert red light into

bright yellow? As a machinist, I'd adjusted the wavelengths and intensity of light many times, but only within the green part of the spectrum. I'd never changed one color to another. Also, what did it mean to *surge*?

"Uhh, okay. I guess I'll try," was all I could say.

"Don't 'guess.' You *will* try. And try is all I ask. I don't expect you to succeed on the first go."

What a reasonable fellow. A welcome change from dealing with Kaur, for sure.

I closed my eyes.

"Don't close your eyes."

I opened them. "Sorry. Bad habit from being a machinist for so long. I like to inwardly focus when squeezing or pulling on light waves."

"Until it becomes muscle memory, you will have to focus inwardly. That is understandable. But don't do it with your eyes closed."

I nodded. I thought of my brother and raised my sword hilt. A lightblade erupted off it. Getting that red beam to come out was now effortless, so long as I sipped my hatred of Kediri.

Now to convert red light into yellow light. Yellow light had shorter wavelengths than red, so I'd have to *squeeze* the light in my veins.

"I forgot to mention," Kriga said. "You should squeeze the light once it enters your hand, a moment before it reaches the hilt. Otherwise, it's difficult to cycle yellow light with a red stone in your chest."

So I'd have to wait to squeeze it — even more difficult. I let the light pool in my hand. My palm got hot and sweaty. I squeezed the waves. The light within turned orangeish. My lightblade sparked and sputtered.

"Squeeze it harder!"

I squeezed harder. The sparks yellowed, but my lightblade vanished.

"Don't worry about the lightblade, for now. Raise the luminosity. Surge!"

I pooled a massive amount of light in my hand — all that I could inhale from the sun — squeezed it until it yellowed, and then let it flow into the hilt.

A blinding light burst outward. The metal hilt scalded my hand. I dropped it and screamed.

"Shit!"

Streaky burns, in the pattern of the hilt's grip, covered my sizzling palm. I whimpered.

Kriga took my burnt hand. Violet light poured onto the burns and eased the pain.

"Not bad for a first try. You can do all the basic steps. You just need to practice. And practice. And practice. Understand? To do Blinding Blade in a fight, with your life in the balance, while you're also projecting a lightblade — it's only practice that makes it possible."

So I could do the move. The fact that I'd succeeded made my heart sing with confidence. I'd always expected to fail — at everything. I was cursed, after all. Whatever I did, no matter how hard I tried, I'd be doomed by my own weakness or by some laughing god. But now, I'd done this one thing sort of right, and on my first try.

"Well, I had a good teacher," I said, beaming.

"Yes, you did." Kriga beamed back. "Now practice it. If you have questions, just ask. I'll heal you when needed and chime in if I notice anything you ought to do better."

Such uplifting words. Kriga reminded me of Zauri; they both were devoted to making me stronger. They respected and believed in me. If only people in the real world regarded me this way.

"I won't let you down."

"I know you won't, Jyosh. I sense a fit temperament in you — a wisdom, stature, and balance not common in those as young as you. I also see… contradictions. You use anger to create your blade, but you don't let it dictate your moves. You're a thoughtful fighter — it's in your nature to consider your actions. That's not a bad thing — some of the greatest warriors were the same. But these contradictions must be tuned and directed properly, which is why I'm here."

That was some praise. And how wonderful it felt! As if I were being pumped with elation. But… but what if he was scripted to say that? What if such encouragement was only meant to make me believe I could do it?

That thought doused my happiness like a bucket of ice water.

"Kriga… do you really believe what you just said?"

His prickly eyebrows zagged upward and almost joined together. "Of course. I *never* speak falsely."

That seemed to settle it. But what if that was also part of his script? Perhaps it was like… like Zauri's affection for me… coming from somewhere else and not actually because I'd earned or deserved it.

"Do you doubt me?" Kriga bared his teeth like a lion. He glared down at me, his face darkening by the second. And then a warm smile snapped onto his face. "No… it's not me you doubt. You doubt yourself. That's fine. Doubting yourself is healthy. Fool is the man with unearned confidence. But you… you are drowning in self-doubt." He punched his palm. "Not a problem. By training, by becoming stronger, by winning glory, your doubt shall evaporate the way a puddle does in the face of a scalding sun."

All my hopes, summarized so well! I nodded, impressed by Kriga's brutal eloquence. "You're so right. Strength is what I've always been missing. It's why everyone walked over me my whole life. With strength, I can take back what I lost and protect what I love. Strength… strength is everything."

Kriga's mouth widened in the most zealous of smiles. "You speak the truth. The path of the strong is a glorious one, even when it ends in death. If you are determined to walk this path, then I am determined to walk with you."

I wanted nothing more than to walk this glorious path. I projected a lightblade from my hilt. I inhaled the sun, cycled red through my veins, and pooled it in my hand. I squeezed the waves until they yellowed, then *surged* them into my blade.

The lightblade sputtered out of existence. A scalding glow suffused my hilt. It must've caught fire with how badly it burned. I dropped it and rubbed my seared hand.

"Each time you feel that burn, you're taking a step down the path." He took my hand and healed it, once again. "Keep going."

I did it again. Same result. Next time, I tried to keep some red light flowing to maintain the lightblade, while also pooling some to squeeze into yellow light. But it was too difficult to do both, and I ended up doing neither and almost igniting my hand.

"Don't try to jump ahead. This is about reflex and timing. You can already create a blade, now get the blinding part down."

So I did it again. And again. No improvement, and it burned. Each time, I'd drop the hilt, Kriga would heal me, and then I'd pick the hilt up out of the grass.

On what must've been my thirtieth attempt, with my veins simmering, I noticed something in the sky: a black object. I turned to focus on it.

No, not an object — a woman, floating above. Her long hair fluttered in the breeze. From such a distance, I couldn't tell whether it was Kaur or Saina.

I waved. The woman in the sky didn't wave back.

I turned to Kriga. "Am I going mad, or do you see her too?"

Kriga squinted up at her. "Yes, she is there. An admirer of yours?"

"I don't think Saina or Kaur admire me much. They're so much better than me at their specialties."

"Oh? There's that self-doubt again."

"It doesn't matter, anyway. I already have an admirer. I'm doing all this for her. Well… that's not entirely true. I'm doing it for myself, too."

"There is beauty in fighting for someone you love. And do you know whom you should love most of all?" Kriga pointed to me.

"Eh, what's there to love? I suspect the only reason Zauri feels for me is because of the black box in her script." Saying that stung, but it was the most likely explanation. Lightblade training programs weren't supposed to feel affection for their students.

"Black box…" Kriga's eyes widened. "You should report that to your superior officer. Black boxes are insidious, evil creations."

"'Evil'… it's that bad?" I punched my palm. "Well, no matter. I'm committed to this. I'm going to walk the glorious path. I'm going to get stronger, so I can see her again."

"If that's what you believe, then keep walking and get back at it!"

I glanced at the sky once more. Only the glowing red sun remained — no floating woman.

So I practiced and practiced till my veins boiled from near burnout. But each time, my lightblade would sputter and extinguish, and the hilt would sear my hand.

"What am I doing wrong?" I asked while crouching in the grass.

"You're making too much heat and too little light," Kriga said, standing over me. "The culprit is a lack of uniformity, which leads to heat loss. Do not think too much about it, though. With practice, the way you cycle the light will become more uniform and efficient."

I knew all about that. My heat loss with green light was tiny because I'd had so much practice. But red was a totally different beast.

"I could use a break."

"I too believe it prudent. Go enjoy the rest of your day. Come back here tomorrow, first thing."

After having worked so hard, perhaps I could enjoy my day, guilt free. Here, in this layer two dream, there must exist wonders I couldn't fathom. My heart flitted with excitement even while I heaved from tiredness.

If only Zauri were here, I could explore it with her. Instead, I'd have to settle for a distant number two or three choice. I opened the terminal, selected *Location*, and teleported to wherever Kaur was.

White light enveloped me. When it faded, I floated in a cloudless red sky. Every direction shone crimson, as if I bathed in a bloody womb.

Below, something long, narrow, and metallic reflected the sun's rageful gaze. I glided toward it. As I neared it, its shape became more obvious: a sword. A giant sword, longer than the street I'd grown up on, hovered in the air hundreds of feet above a roiling red sea.

I glided closer. Kaur stood upon the blade's flat, a lightblade in each hand, as black-clad soldiers rushed her from front and back.

I could hardly believe it; Kaur was fighting soldiers on a giant sword. What level of the training program was this?

I landed on the tip of the cold, smooth steel. Meanwhile, Kaur had just kicked a soldier off the edge; his screams faded as he plunged toward the red sea. The giant blade was hardly wide enough to maneuver on, but that didn't stop her enemies from surrounding her. Still, she had no trouble slicing, kicking, head-butting, and tossing them off the edge, grunting all the while.

She noticed me after she'd disposed of half of them, her collar soaked with sweat. She snapped her fingers. White light suffused the black-clad soldiers, and they vanished.

Kaur fell to her knees, huffing. She retracted her lightblades, dropped her hilts, and lay down.

I knelt next to her. "Did you like what you saw?"

"Huh?" A befuddled look snapped onto her face. "What did I see?"

"You were watching me earlier, weren't you?"

"Nope. Wasn't me."

So it was Saina, then. What interest did she have in my training?

"What level is this humungous sword?"

Kaur sat up and chuckled. Her sweat smelled sour, like mine after a day of working the machines. "Level thirty-four."

My jaw dropped. Holy hell. I was only on level one…

"Don't be so surprised. I'm actually on a higher level. Needed a fun warmup."

I didn't want to ask what level she was truly on for fear of being deflated even more. "Well, I can see why you like this one. Can't wait till I get to fight on giant floating swords."

"There are some other fun ones. My favorite is fighting while skyboarding. I can't pass the level where you fight while skyboarding in a hurricane, though."

I got flashbacks of my visions during surgery. That Beheshian warrior was wielding two lightblades while flying on a skyboard, but he was hopelessly fighting a dragon, not soldiers.

"So, what do you do here when you're *not* training?"

"Dunno. This is a training dream stone, Jyosh. Its memory is jam packed with training stages. There's not much else to do."

I groaned. Just what I didn't want to hear. "I can't train for a hundred days straight. Just the thought reminds me of being overworked at the factory. Never again. There's got to be something I can do to refresh."

"There's the trainee's lounge. It's up in the mountains — nice and cozy. A few things to do over there. And you can always skyboard. In fact, let's skyboard over to it right now."

"Sounds like a plan. Why don't we get Saina to come, too?"

Kaur's smile turned upside down. "I'd rather be trampled by a horde of hippos. She reminds me of my mother. *Duty over everything*. Her friend died, but did you see her shed a tear?"

"For all we know, she was bawling her eyes out the whole time Rao held her captive. I think you're painting her with the wrong brush, like usual."

"Whatever. Whenever I look at her, I feel ice cubes melting behind my eyes. You know — maybe I can't explain why, but it is what it is."

"We're in this together, Kaur. I think it best we find a way to trust each other during these hundred days."

"Are we, though? Looks like we're each after a different thing. Once you get your dream stone back, what reason will you have to help me or her? It's a temporary alliance, at best."

"I'll help you both. I promise."

"Know what? I believe you. A hundred percent. But Saina's looking for something a little more difficult to define. Something that could even be dangerous for us. At the end of the day, she's a zealot. Her god tells her to do good, she'll do good. And if it tells her to do evil, she'll do evil just as willingly."

I looked down at my feet, at the flat of the reflective sheen of the giant blade. Was she right about Saina?

No — Saina wasn't just doing good for her god. When she told me about that little girl who'd died *bathed in her light,* her sadness shone so deep. And whenever she healed me, her joy was genuine.

But why did Kaur see her differently? Maybe they just needed to spend more time together. Or maybe Kaur knew something that I didn't.

"This is hardly the place for this discussion," I said. "Let's get on skyboards and go to this lounge you mentioned."

We both used our terminals to change our crystals from red to green and to summon skyboards. They appeared at the blade's edge: lacquered wood boards with rounded edges. We hopped on.

"I'll follow you," I said. "But please don't go too fast. Flying's still new to me."

Kaur smirked again. Then she burst upward.

I inhaled green light from the red sun, cycled it into my feet, and pushed it into the skyboard. I gusted forward. Air rushed against me, smelling like dream flowers. This wasn't so hard; all it took to go faster and steer the board was for me to will it.

No matter how fast I got following her, the air never felt harsh on my skin. A feathery caress, throughout.

We'd flown so high, the giant sword became a tiny speck against the red sea. Then Kaur glided in a new direction — I suppose north, south, east, west didn't matter here. I followed her, a few hundred feet behind, enjoying *everything* about piloting this thing. As a machinist who'd cycled green light for tens of thousands of hours in the real world, it came so naturally.

Bursting through the air, every direction seemed the same: an endless sea and sky. I wasn't even sure what I was anymore. I wasn't a human. I wasn't a bird. I'd become a spirit, a cloud, a breeze. My body couldn't weigh me down. I was a circuit of green light coasting through a vast, bruised world.

Kaur did a flip, then a twirl. She left trails in concentric circles where she went upside down and looped. Showoff. If I had her skills and experience, I'd probably be one, too. And I'd be what Kriga had said: strong. Confidence would wash away doubt. Kaur was at least thirty levels ahead, but I had to start my climb. I couldn't be weak anymore.

The faint outlines of mountains shone in the distance. Kaur sped toward them. Considering how high we were, these mountains must've been utterly enormous. And yet, the landscape of this training stone seemed to be mostly ocean and sky. Repeating the same textures probably didn't take up as much memory. Too bad it wasn't like the dream stone where I'd met Ava, with its lush landscapes and quaint villages.

We sped up some more and shot between the mountain peaks. Snow, something I'd never touched in real life, covered them. And it got chilly, but not enough to be discomforting. More like a soothing, cool balm on my face and neck.

Kaur turned suddenly. I tried to follow, but couldn't match her tight angle, and now surged toward a rocky mountain peak. I swiveled my board, barely avoiding it.

I looked back at the snowy peak that almost took me down and swallowed my heart. I sped to catch up to Kaur.

After another minute of skyboarding, Kaur slowed. A wooden lodge the size of a palace sat in a valley between three peaks. She glided down and landed a few paces in front of the door.

I did the same. My landing wasn't quite as smooth; I almost tumbled over, but managed to catch myself. I trudged through the snow, which seemed so heavy and strange, toward the lodge door.

Kaur gestured toward the lodge like she'd built it. "So, what do you think? Pretty, all up here in the mountains, isn't it?"

I couldn't disagree. The way the oakwood contrasted with the snow, it seemed like a warm, inviting refuge for body and soul.

"Hope the inside is as nice," I said.

Kaur opened the door and we both went in.

We entered a high-ceiling hall with richly carpeted floors.

Floral-patterned carpets hung on the walls, too. Pinecone incense wafted through the room, both spicy and relaxing. Wooden divans covered in soft, sheepskin pillows were spread around.

"Did you know that a training stone like this can handle a hundred wired-up dreamers at once?"

I didn't know, but it made a lot of sense, given the scale of everything. "So there's plenty of space for the three of us, then."

"You ever heard the phrase 'three's a crowd?'" Kaur put a hand on her hip.

"No. Why would three be a crowd?"

"It doesn't matter." She huffed out a breath as if deflated. "I think it better we just take our minds off things, anyway. That's probably why this lodge is up in the mountains, covered in snow, separated from everything. Better not to bring your demons here."

"Agreed."

Kaur opened her palm and tapped into her terminal. A steaming mug materialized in her hand.

"Cardamom-lemongrass white tea," she said. "Ever had it?"

I shook my head. I didn't like eating and drinking in dreams. It just made the hunger upon waking worse.

"Well of course you haven't. It's the main export of my country — or rather, *province*, now that it's been annexed. I'm sure they didn't export to Maniza, though. People guzzle this stuff in Salkofy, which is nice. I can always have a cup and feel like I'm home, sort of. Here, try it."

She handed me the mug, then used her terminal to materialize a new one for herself. I sipped the drink.

First, I was surprised it wasn't sweet. Sugar drenched Manizan tea. Second, why no milk? I did appreciate the cardamom flavor: deep, sweeping, and it really lingered. The lemongrass wasn't the sour hit that I expected; instead, I found it rather refreshing.

"So…" Kaur folded her arms and stared at me with expectation. "Do you like it?"

"It's like nothing I've ever had. At first, I thought the mix of flavors would be too weird, but it all just works, somehow. It's a damn good drink."

That made her beam. "Let's go sit down."

We sat on sheepskin pillows by a fireplace, a small wooden table between us. Snow fell outside the large glass panels that covered the wall. It was as if everything hugged me. I hadn't enjoyed such coziness in a long time, perhaps since the days when I'd slept in my parents' bed.

Only one thing could make it better.

I opened my palm and flipped through the list of items I could summon. Kept my eyes ready to spot just what I wanted. But even after searching the entire menu, it didn't show.

"Where are the cigars?"

"Oh, I heard Sylet's a stickler. Doesn't believe in smoking. It's bad for you, apparently. He must've had them scrubbed from the script."

"But this is only a dream!"

"You can still form bad habits in a dream, you know."

"I'm not trying to form a bad habit, just keep one going." I breathed out a disappointed sigh. Oh well. Can't have everything, even in Paradise.

"Speaking of habits, seems you've already got one for skyboarding," Kaur said between sips. "I must admit — I wanted you to eat my trails. But you kept up."

Praise from her was gold dust. And it only added to the good feelings swimming through me.

"It's easy."

"It's not easy. Took me months to get good at it. You mentioned you were a machinist, right? I bet that makes you a natural at anything to do with green light. Maybe even piloting a levship."

The thought terrified me, considering the safety of everyone onboard would be my responsibility. And what about landing?

"Let's not go that far."

She giggled. "Look, all I'm trying to say is — you're not as useless as I thought."

I'd exceeded her exceedingly low expectations.

"Thank you, I think."

She crossed her legs and put her mug down on the wood. "You brooding about something, right now? That why you're so terse?"

"I'm just tired. Kriga, the trainer, worked me to my bones." I shrugged. "I don't brood that much, do I?"

"Yeah, you do. Were you always like this?"

"I don't think so. Kediri was the brooder in our family. I could never understand why he was always so depressed."

"What about your sister. What was she like?"

"Chaya was the disciplinarian, always trying to set things right. Although, she did have a rather dark sense of humor. She used to cover herself in tikka sauce and play dead." I chuckled. "As for me — I was the cheerful one." I shook my head upon remembering how silly and carefree I used to be. "Damn. Feels like that was another person. Prison will do that to you."

"You know what? I wasn't always like this, either. I was quiet as a child. So demure. Patient. Everyone goes in different directions, it seems."

Hard to imagine. "What changed you?" I sipped more tea.

"I dunno. Everything. I think Elam changed me the most, though. Made me so cynical. He was so happy in the dream stone, and so miserable outside of it." She took a long sip, then said, "These days, it seems only the cruel gods answer prayers."

I couldn't object to that. "Can I ask you something?"

Kaur nodded.

"Elam seemed really unbothered when he killed Jaysh." Remembering that floating lightblade piercing Jaysh's belly made my next sip of tea so bitter. "Why?"

"He thinks the people he kills don't truly die. That they'll just wake up, reborn, on the dark side of the world. In the Nightscape. He thinks it's peaceful, there. So — in some twisted way — killing, to him, is a mercy."

"Isn't that what the Beheshians believe?"

"Yup, except for the part about the Nightscape being peaceful. Thing is, a lot of folks believe in transmigration from the Dayworld to the Nightscape, and vice versa — it's not unique to the Beheshians. But where's the evidence for it?"

Dragons are born in the dark and die in the light. The image of Zauri saying that flashed in my mind. When I'd lost my memories in Ava's dream stone, I'd felt the suffering from my past rebirths. Was there truth to it?

"Let me guess — Colonel Rao taught him that."

Kaur stared into her tea mug in silence, then said, "Rao once described killing as 'ripping off a bandage over our eyes.' He's led Elam astray. But the difference between them is — Rao is full of doubt. He doesn't show it to Elam and the others, but *I know*. I can't believe I once loved him. It's like… it's like he wants to use your country and all the people here as a big experiment to clear his doubts away."

"You said he wanted to end the world."

"More specifically, he wants to stop the cycle of death and rebirth. I don't know how, but he's going to kill a lot of people, Jyosh. I don't want Elam involved in that. And, as callous as I may seem sometimes, I don't want anyone to die, even if they *are* reborn in the Nightscape."

So much to digest. I took another hot sip. "It would be nice if all our loved ones were alive, somewhere beyond the veil."

"Not really. Can't we just get some rest? I'd hate to live again and again and again. Ugh. Imagine going through puberty again. That alone makes my skin crawl."

I laughed. "My brother Kediri got so weird once he hit that age. He'd just stay in his room, all day, sulking about one thing or another. He started dressing in black. He'd hide his hands in his pockets most of the time, and even wear these black gloves when he went to sleep."

"Weird. But that's puberty for you."

"He also became obsessed with fire. Used to play with this lighter, flipping it open and closed. One day, the idiot seared his entire hand. He cried his eyes out — Abba had to carry him to the healer. He even burned some of my favorite miniature barrels."

"Miniature barrels?"

"Uhh, yeah, I used to collect tiny barrels. Anyway — god, I was an annoying kid. I used to toss the ones I didn't care for at Kediri, and he'd break out in anger. He never hit me, though. He'd chase me into the backyard, where my father had this hatch leading to his underground workshop. Abba would hear us and come out shouting. Happened so many times. Chaya and Amma would come and calm everyone down."

"I don't get it." Kaur ruffled her nose. "Why would anyone collect tiny barrels?"

The main door squeaked open. Saina entered, shoulders and hair covered in snow. She came over to us.

"So this is where you two ran off to. So warm and comfy. I'm not intruding, am I?"

We both shook our heads, then sipped our teas.

"You sure? I watched you guys from the window. Seemed awfully cozy."

"Just shut up and sit down," Kaur said.

Saina grabbed a pillow and plopped herself next to us.

"What were you two talking about?" She tousled her copper hair and smiled.

"Jyosh is a weirdo who collects small barrels."

I spat tea back into my mug. "What's so weird about that? I happen to know a hundred varieties of tree bark — the different strengths and weaknesses, how long they last, how much natural flavor they might add to any beverage stored within. There's a whole science to it."

Saina laughed. I hid my expression in my mug and sipped furiously. Kaur crossed her arms and smirked in satisfaction.

"So, Saina, what were you doing all this time?" I asked.

"Well, I went down into the Sambalpur copy. To a nice, wide open plaza with a few lovely spires. I summoned some combatants, hacked off their legs and hands with a lightblade, and then practiced regenerating them." She said it as if it was the most normal thing in the world.

"Oh, well, very good." I nodded and sipped. "So we've all spent the day training. Very productive."

Saina opened her palm and *tap-tapped* on her terminal. A mug of lumpy, cream-filled milk materialized on the table.

I liked this: all of us together. A sense of camaraderie, of being a team, would only heighten our chances of success out there. Also, it was just refreshing.

"Milk, eh?" Kaur loomed over Saina's mug and sniffed. "Kinda boring, don't you think?"

"Boring is a comfort." Saina sniffed Kaur's mug. "I see you guys are drinking cardamon-lemongrass white tea. Always found it a bit much. Like it's trying too hard to win over your tastebuds."

"I bet you boil potatoes for breakfast," Kaur said. "Unseasoned."

"Unseasoned potatoes were a delicacy in the camp." I shuddered upon remembering what passed for seasoning there. "Sometimes bland is good."

Kaur grimaced and crossed her arms. "*You people*. If we're all ever in Salkofy together, I'll take you down to my favorite spots on Spicy Lane. Teach you what real food is."

The thought of being in Salkofy, or anywhere other than this city we were asleep in, lifted my hopes a bit. "Your treat, right?"

"No! I never said that. Spicy Lane's overpriced as shit."

Saina chuckled. "No hospitality at all, this one."

We chatted for a good while.

Chapter Eighteen

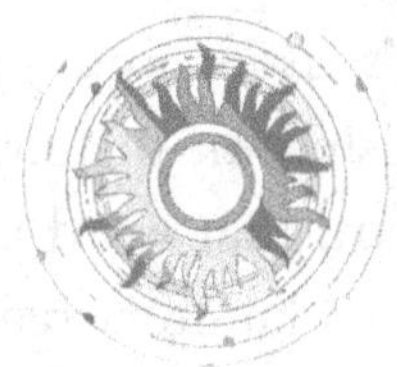

Turned out this lodge was full of bedrooms. I picked a room at the end of a hallway. A crackling fireplace welcomed me. Snow fell outside the glass panel, which formed an entire wall. A maroon quilt with orange and blue starburst patterns covered the floor bed. I knelt and pressed down on the mattress; my hand sank into the softness.

What to do, now? You can sleep in dreams, dreamlessly, to regain your awareness and energy. But a restless energy still coursed through me. I sat on the bed, opened my palm, and flipped through the terminal display.

Something in the menu caught my eye: *Live Message.*

Interesting. Never saw a command like this before. I tapped it.

Kaur

Kriga

Saina

I pressed Kaur's name. Her face appeared on the terminal display. Judging by how bleary her eyes were, she seemed as worn as me.

"Yeah? What do you want?"

"We can really talk to each other this way?"

"You didn't know?"

"Quick question. Or maybe not so quick. In a normal four-day dream, I fill the time just fine. But I can't imagine what it'll be like for a hundred days. So, how does one avoid getting bored?"

Kaur sighed. "When you're feeling rested, go and do whatever you want. Oh, there's also a library somewhere in this lodge. Read something. Extinguish some of that annoying ignorance."

A library? Hadn't heard that word in a long, long time. The camp police didn't want us laborers reading books, or anything aside from propaganda, so our dream stones were bereft of knowledge.

"I get what you're saying, though," Kaur said. "Believe me, I know how disconcerting it is to stay in a dream for months — even years. It takes some getting used to. But you have nothing but time."

How true. "Hey, Kaur, this might sound like an awkward question, but… have you ever felt lonely in a dream?"

"I guess without your little dream partner, it must be cold in your bed." She smirked. "Maybe try asking Saina to help you with that."

"Not what I meant. It's just… I don't know…" It was fun chatting mindlessly with both of them earlier. But now, alone in this unfamiliar room, with the sky covered in dark clouds, the sensation of being adrift all by myself overwhelmed me. But whatever loneliness I was feeling, it was surely a thousand times worse for Zauri, and knowing that only made it ache more. "Sorry to bother you."

"You gonna apologize for existing, too? They really hammered you down in that camp, didn't they? Listen, Jyosh — we come into dreams to escape things, but you can't escape yourself. Wherever you go, you drag your shadow along. You'll have to face it to become a stronger version of yourself. Now, I'm all wisdomed out. See you later."

I closed my palm, lay on the bed, and stretched. *Face my shadow… stronger version of myself…* I turned on my side toward the window and watched the snow fall. Where in the world did it snow like this? Whoever designed this dream stone, perhaps they were thinking of home.

As I watched the snow mounds get larger, a black speck creeped onto my vision. I rubbed my tired eyes, but it was still there, in the sky. No, it wasn't a speck. Something floated up beneath the clouds.

I got up and approached the glass panel. I squinted. Her skirt fluttered with the wind as she floated in heaven.

Whoever that was, she was watching me. I opened my palm and called Saina on the terminal.

Without taking my eyes off the woman in the sky, I raised my palm in front of my face. Saina's face appeared in the terminal.

"Hey Jyosh. You as bored and sleepless as me?"

I glanced at her, then back at the floating woman.

"Say Saina, you don't happen to be floating in the sky, right now?"

She made a face like she smelled something funny. "I'm all wrapped up in bed, actually."

What if she was lying? I had to be sure.

"Teleport to me, right now."

"Umm, okay."

Saina's face disappeared from the terminal.

She materialized next to me amid a shimmer of white light.

She peered at the crackling fireplace and nodded as if impressed. "I don't have one of those in my room. Looks like you got a special suite or something."

I tapped on the glass panel and pointed at the floating

woman. "Who the hell is that?" I wouldn't take my eyes off her, lest she vanish.

Saina looked out the window and squinted. "Maybe Kaur's bored. Who else could it be?"

"It's not Kaur. I just called her. She was resting, too."

"Then… a glitch, maybe?"

"It's no glitch. Whoever that is, she was watching me earlier during training. In fact, this reminds me of something. The first day of the Karshan invasion, something odd happened while I was trying to wake up from a dream. Instead of waking up where I went to sleep, I awoke in this metal room with strange, vine-like calligraphy all over the walls. An invisible woman was there with me. She wouldn't tell me anything about her, except… she suggested I head for the border. She told me Demak was taking in refugees, and I actually listened. I went toward Demak. That's ultimately how I ended up here."

"Are you saying that woman in the sky is the same person? But that's impossible. There are only three people in this dream, plus the trainer, Kriga."

The woman in the sky slowly faded into the clouds behind her.

"She's gone," we both said at the same time.

We sat on the bed in front of the fireplace. The soothing flame warmed my shins. We spent some seconds in thought, then turned to look at each other.

"Has to be a glitch, or some kind of scripted effect," Saina said. "There's no other explanation."

"No. It's intentional. I can feel it. Whoever that is, she's watching me. And I want to know why."

Saina held up her hands. "Okay. Why don't we investigate? It'll give us something to do, at least."

Something in my bones told me I wouldn't like what I found. "Let's go to the spot where she was."

We left the room and walked down the richly carpeted stairs to the entrance of the lodge. The wind chill outside was surprisingly mild. Saina used her terminal to swap her stone to green. We summoned skyboards.

"I'm terrible at this, so go slow," Saina said as she stepped on hers.

I stepped on mine and glided upward. Falling snow covered my head, face, and shoulders, though it was barely cold — probably to keep the dreamers comfortable. I imagined real snow would've left me shivering.

I soared into the air, still hundreds of feet below the dark cloud, near what must've been where the woman was floating. Took half a minute for Saina to catch up with her awkward upward sputtering and wobbly balancing.

The air a few feet ahead looked... torn. Light leaked out of the tear.

We both floated on our boards and stared at what resembled a rip in the sky. I glanced at Saina, and she glanced at me. We exchanged a wide-eyed look of fear.

"What do you think that is?" I asked.

Saina rubbed her hands together and said, "Good thoughts. Good words. Good deeds." Was she praying? "It looks like a rip in the dream fabric."

The tear shrank in size. In the span of seconds, it went from as tall as a tree to as small as my hand. It darkened. It bulged and became round. Spherical.

It turned into a black hole. But unlike the growing one in Ava's dream, this one was shrinking.

"I saw one of these in our previous dream," I said. "What could cause a hole like this?"

"I only know of one situation where a rip turns into a shrinking black hole — when someone outside the dream is trying to get in."

"What? How could that be?"

"Someone could have found us while we sleep. And this someone could be invading our dream."

"But Kaur told me we'd be alerted if anyone came close to us."

I glanced at the distant, snow-covered ground. We were as the gods with how small the lodge seemed. A slight breeze bobbed against our skyboards.

"You're right, we should've been alerted." Saina put her hands on her hips. "It makes no sense at all. This is what we get for using a dream stone looted off a dead guy."

Could someone really have invaded our dream? And if so, why?

The black hole was now a speck. What would happen if I touched it? I reached out.

"Jyosh!" Saina grabbed my shoulders, our skyboards *thwacking* against each other. "Don't touch that!"

"What'll happen?" The tips of my fingers were an inch away. The energy coming from the hole heated my hand hairs.

"You'll get sucked into who-knows-where." She snatched my hand and pulled it back.

The black hole evaporated. I'd missed my chance. Perhaps by touching it, I would've uncovered another clue. Or maybe I would've entered an infinite dream and turned into a vegetable.

"Damn, I really was about to touch it." I stuck my hand in my pant pocket and shuddered. "Thanks for stopping me."

"What, you think I'd let you do something so dangerous?"

"We're out of leads, it seems. To think someone from outside the dream could be watching me…"

"Let's not do our pondering in the cold. Follow me."

Saina opened her palm and tapped on her terminal. A milky light enveloped her, and she disappeared. Her board dropped from the sky into the snowy mountainside below.

I looked around for a minute, hoping I'd see the woman again — just the softly falling snow, dark clouds, and wispy breeze. I opened my palm and teleported to Saina's location.

I materialized in an octagonal room filled with library niches. Books sat in stacks in the niches across all eight sides. Candles flickered in their holders between the niches.

Saina was rummaging through a stack. She glanced back at me. "Looks like it's all propaganda. I mean, what was I expecting? The Karshans write their own history."

"The Paranis do, too." I rubbed snow off my head and shoulders. A fire stove breathed heat from the room's center. I got closer and enjoyed the glow and warmth. "I used to believe Gajah and Panja were the living avatars of the Originator. That they could do anything by their will. I wonder how people who still believe that are handling the news that Panja surrendered to Karsha on the third day of this war."

Saina tossed a book back into its niche. Then she walked over to me, hands in her pockets. "So what do you believe, now?"

"I don't know. I'd rather not believe anything. I'm tired of being misled. If something wants my worship, it better provide what I need in exchange. Not just empty promises."

"A very pragmatic and level-headed approach." Saina smiled at me as if impressed. She sure didn't sound like the zealot Kaur had painted her to be. "I feel exactly the same."

I didn't feel like we were the same. She obviously had more faith than me. "*Good thoughts. Good words. Good deeds.*" I imitated her cadence, how she'd pause between each short sentence. "It reminds me of something. Something we're taught as machinists. *Open heart. Clear mind. Strong flow.* It's a mantra to get us in the right frame of mind to conduct green light for the factory."

"Light is everything, isn't it? In the Temple Behesh, worshippers would conduct light as an offering to the Avatar of the Eternal Dawn."

That reminded me of when my father would conduct light into that wire hanging in our living room. I never knew where it went, but just assumed the Paranis were using everyone's light for something. "What would the light be used for?"

"Well, when I was a child, someone told me the light goes into the sun, and that's why the sun is so bright. Just a childish tale, of course. In truth, the light goes somewhere else. Where exactly, only the gods know."

"That's what I don't like about the gods. They don't trust us with their secrets. Take this city — what's it hiding? Rao obviously knows. If ever I meet him, I'll have to ask, just to sate my curiosity."

Saina sat on a wooden divan. I sat next to her.

"To be honest, I feel those doubts, too," she said. "I thought I had everything all figured out, once. The Temple was all that mattered. Union with the Avatar was my world. Half my heart wishes I could get that back, and the other half wishes to break free of it, completely."

First time she'd shared her doubts and dilemmas with me.

"It almost sounds like a loss you've never stopped mourning."

"I suppose." She turned to face me. "Say, when you had your vision of me, did you feel *him*? The Avatar?"

I shook my head. "I felt whoever got burned by that dragon's breath."

"I wish you could feel what it's like to touch a god. It changes you."

"Tell me, then. What's it like?"

"You'd be surprised — it wasn't the Avatar's godliness that made me love him, but rather how much he was like us."

"Like us?"

"In the moments when we'd intertwine, and I'd glimpse his world, I felt how difficult his purpose was for him. He was drenched in doubts. Carrying the weight of all our yearnings on his back. Crushed by them. And yet… he overflowed with love. But his love isn't something I can put into words. Those who felt it always wanted more, but the Avatar was not always willing, or able, to share himself. Isn't that sort of cruel?"

"As cruel as being severed from your beloved." I felt that same ache toward Zauri. What wouldn't I give to see her again?

"You're thinking about her, aren't you?" Saina smiled as warmly as the flames flickering in the fire stove.

"Do you think it's pathetic to fall in love with a script?"

"Why do you care so much what other people think?"

"Because I don't know what to believe. My parents were both executed when I was twelve. I was fed lies my whole life. I am what my enemies made me, so I must be all wrong. Maybe I'm just looking for guidance. A better direction."

"Isn't your heart enough of a guide?"

I chuckled. "My heart was telling me to touch that black hole. If you hadn't stopped me, I would've obeyed."

"Fair enough. I know it's a bit of a dumb platitude. And for the record, I don't think falling in love with a dream person is pathetic. Though the only dream scripts I've interacted with were healing trainers, so I couldn't have fallen for one."

"Not true. Zauri is a lightblade trainer."

Saina's slender eyebrows shot up. "You fell in love with your lightblade trainer?"

I nodded. "She kissed me. Twice."

"Odd behavior for a lightblade trainer. They're typically scripted never to have romantic feelings."

"Zauri was a bootleg program. The dream logic was really glitched, too. And the dream continued for her, even when I wasn't there. The more I think about it, the stranger it seems. Sometimes I wish I'd gotten on that levship to Behesh and left it all behind. But then, the thought of her alone forever hurts too much. Even now, I can't bear it." My leg shook. "If I fail to get that dream stone back… what'll happen to her?"

Saina put her hand on my knee. The shaking stopped. "I'm not sure if this fact will comfort you, but dream stones don't last forever. Even simple, layer one stones need maintenance every few years, or else they'll deteriorate. So Zauri will die, eventually. She might live for hundreds of years in her time frame, but her suffering will end."

I knew that, obviously. But the idea that she'd live for hundreds of years, all alone, waiting for me, was bad enough. "You believe we're all reborn when we die. But Zauri will just die. Whatever made her what she is, it'll cease to exist. She won't get a second chance on the dark side of the world. If anything is cruel, it's that. Maybe she thinks I abandoned her. She came into existence, fell for someone, and then suffered alone with a broken heart. I can't have that. But this world is cruel, too. I know I can't ask nicely for my dream stone back. Rao or Elam or whoever would probably just laugh at me, then cut me in half. So I have to become stronger so I can take it back."

Saina let a silence settle.

"I never thought about it like that," she said. "I always agonized over what I'd lost. What I wasn't feeling. But maybe the Avatar is suffering, too. How should I know what's happening on the dark side of the world, beyond the Whirling Wall?" She sighed. "You're a better person than me, Jyosh. I think you're worried about her loneliness because you're feeling it, too. But you have a friend. Even if I accomplish what I came to do, I'll do everything I can to help you."

Hearing that calmed my nerves.

KRIGA BEAMED, hands on hips, as I approached him in the floating green field. He held a hilt in each hand.

"Master Jyosh, you're right on time. Splendid."

The red sun loomed larger today, for some reason. Maybe Kaur had adjusted the sun's position.

"What're we going to learn today?" I asked.

"Same thing we learned yesterday. You have to master Blinding Blade before advancing to the next level."

Ugh. More of the same. Well, I did want to master the move. But doing it over and over was damned tedious.

Kriga tossed a hilt at me. I almost dropped it out of fear that it would burn. I'd failed to do Blinding Blade so many times, fear of getting burned was now my first reaction upon holding a hilt.

I held the hilt aloft. I pictured Kediri, then inhaled the sun's red light, cycled it into my veins, and projected a lightblade. It was natural, now, but not quite effortless. I pooled red light in my hand, crushed it until it became yellow, then surged it into my hilt.

Bright yellow light flashed. I dropped the scalding hilt. How many hundreds of times would this happen before I got better?

I had ninety-nine days to get it right, so best I shut my mind and practice.

I did it again and again and again. Lost count of my attempts. One time, the light was so bright, my eyes hurt. The brighter the light, the less hot the hilt. My fault was in converting too much light into heat — heat loss. A lack of efficiency. I imagined a brilliant ball of sun flying in all directions off my hilt. I squeezed the light to make such a sun, then released.

The light was so bright, even Kriga, who was standing yards away, shut his eyes and winced.

"Very good!" He grinned, showing such polished, blocky teeth. "Keep it up, Master Jyosh."

I needed the encouragement. Success, it seemed, began in the mind. If you believed you could do it, if you could visualize it, if you could keep confident and calm and in control, half the battle was won. Sure, in the real world, I'd be frantically fighting someone trying to kill me, but here I could focus on the fight within. I could master myself without worry.

But attempt after attempt, I still couldn't get Blinding Blade right. Maintaining my lightblade while also creating the flash seemed impossible. If my lightblade weakened or disappeared in the real world, it would leave me vulnerable. Kriga had told me to get the blinding part right, so I continued to practice.

After two grueling hours, I emitted an utterly blinding flash that turned the whole field white, and my hilt stayed cool. Though my lightblade disappeared, I'd finally succeeded at *Blinding*. Now for *Blade*.

Kriga walked up to me and said, "Tremendous progress, Master Jyosh. Soon you'll have completed level one."

Oh yeah, this was still level one. That stung a little.

"What's level two?"

"We'll cross that river when you get there, not before, Master Jyosh. Focus on keeping your lightblade intact, for now."

I was starting to enjoy being called "Master Jyosh." Wish everyone called me that. Was this *respect?* I'd never been respected before, not in all my life. In Harska, I was too young to have earned anyone's respect. In the camp, I either dealt with equals — my fellow prisoners — or with superiors who treated me as less than an insect. Being respected felt almost as good as being loved. Almost.

I suppose Zauri had respected me. But her other feelings for me were so blinding, I'd never appreciated the respect at its core.

I practiced with her on my mind. She'd be so impressed if I mastered Blinding Blade. Did she even have this move in her script, since she was a program meant for children? Would I outgrow her move set, then, by the end of these hundred days?

To think I'd outgrow her in any way pained me. It made all

the yellow light turn into heat. I dropped the scalding hilt and grunted.

I knelt to pick it up and realized: I didn't need Zauri to teach me lightblades. I needed her for her. I could never outgrow her in that sense. Although, I had outgrown Prisaya, the dream wife given to me at the camp. But that was because her script had been artificially limited; Zauri's script was the size of a real flesh and blood person.

I paused while inhaling red light to consider what that meant; it made no sense. Real people don't have scripts, so it made no sense to compare the size of Zauri's script to a real person's.

A disturbing thought caused my lightblade to sputter and vanish: what if, one day, I outgrew Zauri's script? Even if it was bigger than Prisaya's, it was still limited, right? What if I realized she wasn't real? Would I still feel any affection for her?

Kriga's shadow covered me. "You look troubled."

"Sorry, just thinking about something."

"You need not apologize for the intrusions of your mind. You're only human."

I stared at him. "And what about you, Kriga? Are you human?"

He glared back at me, unblinking. "What I'm not is a philosopher."

"Are you real, Kriga?"

"Are you real, Jyosh?"

I didn't expect such candidness from him. I thought about the question. I certainly felt real, but was that enough?

"I think so." I gave my sincerest answer.

"I think so, too. Is that a good enough answer?"

Good but strange, considering Ava had tried to convince me she wasn't real. That her consciousness was a trick her script was playing on her.

But if Kriga thought he was real, then who could object? And what about Elam? Elam had gone from being a script to being flesh and blood — but was he real before that transition? He must've been, otherwise, how could such a miracle have happened?

I nodded.

"Good. That's enough of that. Get back to work."

Brief as it was, that conversation calmed my worries. I practiced and practiced. I could now burst the light perfectly, and reform my lightblade quickly afterward. It wasn't the same as maintaining the lightblade during the light burst, but it was better than nothing. Perhaps I could close the time gaps so that, effectively, my lightblade wouldn't disappear.

I practiced doing just that. I got the gap down to under a second. After eight hours of tiring training, I could do Blinding Blade with a half-second gap between when my lightblade disappeared, the blinding light flashed, and I formed the second lightblade. Kriga praised me for my progress, which made me smile inside and out. Respect and praise... I never knew I needed them until I did. It was as if they were making me bigger and taller, somehow. Like inflating a mouse to the size of a bear. I went back to the lodge that day thinking well of myself, for the first time in forever.

I FOUND Saina sitting in the snow. She'd mash it together in her hands, then place it down in front of her and sculpt a building or tower. By the time I arrived, she'd created a tiny district.

"What's all this?" I knelt and scooped some snow. It was like putting your hand in a bowl of cool flour. No discomfort, no chill, just a soothing, cool caress.

"It's the Temple Behesh... how I remember it, at least."

"Didn't realize it was so vast."

"Hundreds of thousands used to live there. It was a country and a city and a temple, all in one."

I smacked my forehead. Of course it was. "Sor—" I stopped myself from apologizing. It wasn't my fault for not putting the pieces together. It wasn't my fault for being ignorant, or weak. I hadn't been given the chance to learn and develop myself. "It's beautiful," I said instead.

Saina stood and brushed snow off her thighs. "I doubt I've reproduced even a morsel of its beauty. But thanks." She smiled. "How was training?"

"I think I've almost passed level one. Might make me slightly less useless out there."

"Come on, you saved me from that captain. There's nothing useless about you."

This unearned admiration was starting to rot my mind. "Saina, I didn't tell you guys this yet, but I didn't kill the captain on my own. I had help."

"Help? From who?"

"This might sound ridiculous, but a dragon appeared and stopped time. It spoke to me. It told me to kill that soldier before time began to flow again. And so I did."

Saina's left eyebrow shot up. "A… dragon? If it stopped time, could it be a daeva?"

"I have no idea. It only appeared for a few seconds. It was serpent-like and covered in fur."

"We Beheshians believe that divine dragons are pure incarnations of the ten absolute gods. The one you described sounds a lot like Mitra, the god from which the Avatar we worship emanates from."

"*Emanate*? What does that mean?"

"Here, I'll show you." Saina opened her terminal and tapped. A clear crystal materialized in her hand. She held it up to the sunlight, then held out her other hand a few inches below it.

A rainbow projected out of the crystal and onto her palm.

"One light becomes seven colors," she said. "This is how we believe gods emanate from one another. The Avatar we Beheshians worship emanated from Mitra, whom I've only glimpsed a few times in visions."

"I get it. The Paranis used to claim that they were avatars of the Originator. So this is what they meant. Also, what about that dragon I saw in the vision?"

"That was the terrifying black daeva, Andar, said to have been slain thousands of years ago by the Twenty-Six Arrows who are buried in the Temple Behesh."

The black, scaly dragon in the vision looked nothing like the azure, fur-covered dragon that saved my life. Both were terrifying, though.

"But if it was slain thousands of years in the past, how could it have been in that vision? Wasn't that a vision of the day, twenty years ago, when the Padishah from the Nightscape invaded and brought eternal night to Behesh?" I scratched my confused head.

"Because dragons are born in the dark and die in the light. When it was slain, it and all its emanations were reborn in the Nightscape, just like you and I would be if we died. The ultimate irony — twenty years ago, the Padishah used the dragon we Beheshians had slain thousands of years ago to bring night to our land."

Zauri had mentioned that rule about dragons, and one other rule. "'Only a dragon can teach you how to kill it.' That's also true, right?"

Saina nodded. "That's why we lost, in the end. No one knew how to slay Andar. That secret died with the Arrows."

"But why would a dragon teach you how to kill it, in the first place? Isn't that kind of suicidal?"

"Sadly, the old stories never explain *why* things happened, only *what* happened. The leading theory is that one of Andar's avatars taught them."

Something black flashed in the corner of my eye. I darted my head in its direction. A figure stood upon the mountain peak in the distance — fuzzy and dark, as if encased in shadow.

I pointed to it, my heart thudding. "Saina! Look! It's her!"

She squinted in the direction I was pointing. "Looks like it. Let's get on our boards and go."

We both summoned skyboards from our terminals. Without taking our eyes off the shadowy figure, we got on and glided toward the mountain peak. The closer we came, the more vivified the figure seemed. She wore a loose skirt that blew with the wind. Her hair was so long and straight, it reached her hips and curled upward only at the ends.

When we were about a hundred yards away, the figure raised her hand and pointed at us. A black beam of light shot out of her finger. It hit me and pushed me off my skyboard.

I cried out as I fell, but when I looked down, I realized I was no longer on the mountain range.

I was falling into an abyss.

I screamed. Screamed with all the terror in my lungs. And then I thumped painlessly onto a hard, glassy floor.

Except it wasn't a floor. It was a translucent filament floating in a black void. Rotating around me counterclockwise in a circle was a script I couldn't recognize, flashing bright orange, the color of dream light.

"I'm sad you didn't make it to Demak," an airy voice said. "You would've been safe there, and ready to be called upon when needed. You're in incredible danger, right now."

"Who are you?" I stood up. There was nowhere to go, though. "Why are you watching me?"

"I hesitate, always. Hesitate about whether I should talk to you, and what I should tell you. I want you to see me, and yet I don't want to come too close, for fear I may scorch you."

Why was her voice so familiar? I couldn't place it.

"Listen, whoever you are, if you know something that can help me, then tell me. Because like you said, I'm in incredible danger. So please, stop being so vague. What is it you want to say to me? What is it you want me to do?"

"You're right, I am being vague. But to be honest, there's not much I can do or say to help. *This* is the extent of my power."

"What power? You mean invading people's dreams?"

"Precisely. Listen, Jyosh — tomorrow when you go into the Deep Layer, be ready. Rao figured out how to access it today, and he has troops scouring the place."

If that was true, there'd be no easy way to succeed.

"What about Sylet. Does he know?"

"No, but it's only a matter of time. That's why you must hurry. And be careful. Don't die. I've put all my hopes in you."

"Hopes for what? What could I possibly accomplish?"

"If I told you that, you wouldn't do it. I'm so sorry."

What the hell was she talking about? I hated her vagueness. I hated how condescending all this was. How could she invade my dream and pretend to care about me, yet tell me nothing? How could she apologize for something and not tell me what it was? How belittling!

"Don't bother me again if you're not willing to explain yourself. I'm not anyone's pawn, not anymore. I'm living for myself. I'm not here to fulfill the hopes of someone I don't trust."

"We're all pawns, Jyosh. None of us are free, nor can we ever be. *The pen has been lifted and the ink has dried.*"

Tethers made of shadows grew out of the air and ensnared me. They snatched my limbs, holding me in place, then wrapped me entirely. I screamed, but no sound came.

The next moment, I was lying in a cool bed of snow. Saina knelt at my side, her hand on my nape, violet flowing from it.

"I'm all right," I said as I pushed up.

"What the hell happened?" Relief washed over her reddened face.

"I met our *invader*. She spoke in riddles." I smashed my fist on the snow. "The only useful thing she said was that Rao knows about the Deep Layer, and has troops in there."

"Could she be involved in this war, somehow? Maybe we should wake up."

I shook my head. "If Rao has troops in the Deep Layer, even more reason for us to stay and train. And besides, I don't think she's a danger. If we do see her again, best to ignore her. We'll never be able to unmask her, and she'll never unmask herself. That's the sense that I got."

It was all so puzzling. So many things I couldn't understand were happening. The difference here, it had something to do with *me*. All the other circumstances that had beset my path were just bad luck. But someone invading my dreams, more than once, was personal.

Zauri, I mouthed without making a sound. I shook my head; snow went flying off it. Impossible. She couldn't be Zauri. But then why had they both suggested I go to Demak, only minutes apart?

What the hell was going on?

Chapter Nineteen

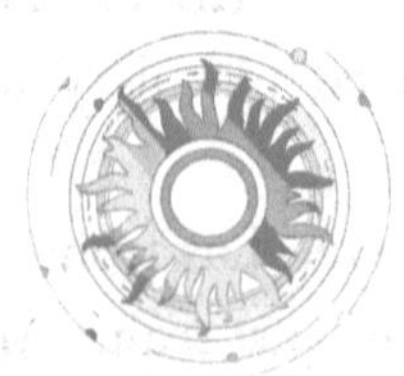

Five days passed in intense, monotonous training. I practiced Blinding Blade unendingly and finally got it right. All I did was narrow the gap between when my lightblade disappeared and reformed. The gap got so small that the yellow light burst happened within a microsecond. Eventually, the gap disappeared entirely.

Kriga clapped. It had taken determination, hard work, and self-belief. Self-belief — another new experience for me. It was bedrock for my soul, upon which I could build a whole new self. Upon which I could create a stronger Jyosh.

I advanced to level two. It took place on the same floating grass field. Kriga welcomed the occasion by shaking my hand. He was good at his role, wasn't he? Showing respect, praising, making me feel good. A lot like Zauri. But did I deserve to be treated so well for passing one level? I wondered if I was being manipulated by a program into getting stronger. As long as I got stronger, what did it matter?

"You've executed Blinding Blade. That's an incredible feat.

However, it's for your sake that I say this — Blinding Blade is almost completely useless in combat."

My jaw dropped. What was he saying? What kind of sick joke was this? Had I spent days learning something worthless?

"You're shocked to hear it," Kriga said. "Soldiers in all professional militaries wear lenses to counter this move."

I smacked my forehead. Been doing that a lot, lately. Of course — the purple and yellow irises of Sylet and Rao's men were colored lenses. Why hadn't we looted them off the dead, so we could be protected from Blinding Blade, too? Was it because Kaur didn't want to wear anything that had touched someone else's face?

Such a terrible hill to die on.

"So just to be clear, you're saying soldiers wear those lenses to protect from bright flashes?"

"Indeed. Otherwise, everyone would be blinding each other constantly. Wouldn't that be incredibly dull? A battle of flailing." Kriga pretended to be a flailing, blinded man.

It did look and sound awkward. Perhaps the captain I'd killed hadn't used Blinding Blade on me because he mistakenly assumed I was wearing brown lenses. It seemed he'd lost the mental battle by complicating things in his head. Had he trusted his eyes and kept things simple, I'd be dead right now.

Then again, I only won because of a divine dragon's intervention, so perhaps there was no way for him to win.

"But why did you teach it to me, then? Why did we spend precious time learning something useless?"

"Think about it for a minute, Master Jyosh. In the process of learning Blinding Blade, you became adept at two of the most foundational combat skills. The first is compressing light. Since red light has the longest wavelengths, you can now compress it to produce other colors. Want to ride a skyboard while wielding a lightblade? Compress some red light into green, and you can do it."

Of course, being able to compress light while in combat was truly an essential skill.

"Let me guess the second one," I said. "It has to do with being able to pool and burst light while keeping my lightblade up."

Kriga nodded. "And one more thing, might I add. You've learned to be far more efficient with red light. Too much heat loss means death in battle. How will you hold your hilt when it burns?"

I'd gotten burned by my hilt when I fought the captain, as well as every time I failed to do Blinding Blade.

"All right, I get it." I cracked my knuckles. "So what do we learn in level two? Hopefully something I can actually use."

"Indeed. Level two teaches a move that's not only founda-tional, but comes in handy even at the highest levels of combat. Even when masters fight masters."

My heart fluttered. If the masters were using this move, and I mastered it, I'd be a step closer to becoming a master. Obviously.

Kriga held his hilt forward and created a lightblade. Black shadows danced around it as he waved it in the air. He twirled the hilt in his hand, rotating the blade a full circle. Then he thrust it forward; when he did, it *grew.* Its length doubled, and the upper half wiggled as if a whip. Then he retracted his hand and pulled the blade backward; it returned to its original size.

"Holy hell." I beamed in delight at such artistry. "What's it called?"

"Double Blade."

A boring, blunt name. The captain had made his lightblade shoot out of his hilt at crazy angles, and with a graceful fluidity, too.

"So how do I do it?"

"First, form a lightblade, as normal. Second, as you strike your enemy, you must direct even more light perfectly forward so that it projects through and out the end of your lightblade. Don't worry about the flourishes I did — you'll learn that at a more advanced stage. Just focus on doubling the size of your blade."

Ah, now I fully understood why Blinding Blade was level one: this move sounded easier. I could already create intense bursts of yellow light. To do Double Blade, I'd have to create an intense, but well-directed burst of red light, and since the light in my veins would already be red, I wouldn't need to do any squeezing, so it was one step fewer.

With Kediri on my mind, I formed my lightblade. I trailed it through the air, enjoying how the blacklight suffused the edges. It wasn't quite as furious as Kriga's blade, but it was a thing of beauty. *My* thing of beauty.

I pooled red light in my hand while still allowing light into the hilt so that the lightblade wouldn't disappear. Pooling light made my hand heavy, hot, and tingly. I thrust forward as if impaling Kediri, then surged the red light I'd pooled into the hilt with a straight, sudden burst. My lightblade lengthened, forming a spiky edge at the end that sputtered like a volcano.

"A good first attempt," Kriga said. "The intensity is there. The challenge for you is directing the surplus light *through* your blade onto the very tip, and then using that light to create a second lightblade on top of the first. Not easy to do, but I am certain you will succeed."

Nothing elated me like hearing him say that. He believed his words. And his belief made me believe. I hadn't yet succeeded at Double Blade, but I knew I would. I knew it in my soul. If someone as self-assured as Kriga could believe in me, I could believe in myself.

"I have something that will aid you." Kriga opened his palm and tapped on his terminal display.

Whirls of white light appeared at my front. Within the light, a wooden statue materialized, about the same size as me. It held a splintery sword, and a crimson scarf was tied around its neck.

"It always helps to have a target," Kriga said. "Imagine your worst enemy wearing that red scarf. Always fires me up."

"You have a worst enemy?"

"Surprised? We trainers were born in what's called a *script soup*, or a *cauldron*. Many of us scripts battled within it, until only a few emerged victorious. The vanquished scripts were deleted, while the rest of us lived on to be copied onto training dream stones."

"Huh? Why would scripts battle each other?"

"Let me ask you a question — who would you want protecting you with your life in the balance, a man who trained for a thousand years or a man who won a thousand battles?"

"Easy. The man who won a thousand battles. He has practical experience."

"Wouldn't you want your teacher to have practical experience?"

"So the people who scripted you basically held a tournament to see which scripts were the best. Am I getting it?"

"Something like that. *Tournament* isn't the word I would use, but it was a battle of the fittest all the same."

Good to know. So Kriga was battle-hardened, in his own way, and not just teaching theories.

I scratched an itchy spot in my scalp. Wait, was Zauri the same? She'd never mentioned such a thing to me. Perhaps because she was meant to teach children, she'd never gone through a cauldron. Although, she'd mentioned that she had a sense of a *before*. Hmm…

"Stop thinking so much, Master Jyosh." Damn. Even Kriga could read my overthinking face. "It seems you're not just drowning in self-doubt, but in indecision. You're overwhelmed by new information and have to decide what to believe, and thus what you will become. Let me ask you — have you noticed that everyone you meet thinks they are on the true path? Everyone is fighting for what they believe, even if those things are wrong, because believing in something — anything — gives you strength. Decide what you want to believe, and do not look back."

"But... but what if I decide to believe something now, and later it's proved to be wrong?" I shook my head. "What if... what if I learn *too late* that I'm wrong? What if I learn I'm wrong when I've already committed everything? How will I walk it back? How will I correct course? Or will I... will I continue to carry a lie on my back?"

Kriga bared his teeth. "Master Jyosh, *everyone* is living their own personal lie. The strong live that lie with the fullest heart. The truth is blinding — it is not meant for us mortals to behold. Let the gods suffer upon the truth."

"So you're saying the truth isn't worth seeking? That it hurts too much? But I want to know that truth. I don't think I could live not knowing."

How was I having such a philosophical debate with a training program — one that had told me days ago that he *wasn't* a philosopher?

Kriga sighed, long and sharp, as if in defeat. "Then... be ready for excruciating pain. Be ready to be tossed about on waves of fire. The warrior who walks the path of truth... he will never find a home."

Cold nails scraped my forearms. I laughed to break the tension. "Kriga, it's all too much. I'm going to focus on Double Blade. I haven't decided on any path... other than becoming stronger, of course."

Kriga crossed his arms and let out a hearty chuckle. "Good. As I've said, I'm right beside you on that path, Master Jyosh."

I aimed my hilt at the wooden dummy. Kediri's face fit so

easily on that neck. My lightblade poured out of me — a sharp spike of killing red. I pooled red light in my hand, lunged at that face, and surged the light through the blade.

It became brighter, hotter, thicker. But not longer, unless you counted the sparks that crackled off the tip.

My lightblade pierced the wooden dummy's neck. I swept the blade across it until the wood charred and the head flew.

"Again!" Kriga ordered.

White sparkles bathed the wooden dummy. It stood restored, as if I'd never severed its head.

I paused to imagine myself executing a perfect Double Blade and piercing the dummy's forehead. How the light would cycle through me in a smooth circuit. How I'd pool just the right amount in my hand, then surge it into my already deathly lightblade. A new lightblade would grow off the end, and its power would be too much for my enemy to counter.

In my imagination, it seemed like such a glorious move; but this was only level two. Surely any of the Karshan soldiers I'd face outside in the real world would know Double Blade and its counters. Also, imagine what other abilities they could use on me that I'd never heard of.

Such thoughts sent ants crawling through my veins when there ought to be light. Again, I was overthinking.

I took a deep breath, inhaled the sun, and formed a lightblade on my hilt. I tried Double Blade on the wooden dummy. Misshapen sparks grew off the end of my lightblade. I pierced the dummy in the forehead. Doing so without executing Double Blade properly meant I had to get closer to it, which defeated the purpose of the move. Double Blade was obviously meant to give you a burst of lethality at a greater distance.

"Again!" I shouted at the dummy.

White sparkles made the dummy good as new.

So I practiced Double Blade. After an hour, I could get my

lightblade to extend about half a foot, but it only lasted a fraction of a second before sparking and dissolving. Kriga had moved his around for several seconds, as if it were a whip, so I had to figure out how to both lengthen and maintain it.

Though I wanted to keep my mind focused and free, during the third hour, I couldn't help but think about the *shadow woman*. Just who was she? What did she want? Why was she helping me?

If I died tomorrow, I'd never find out. I had to become strong, first. No truth was out of reach if I grew strong enough to overcome all obstacles.

I looked at the sky, expecting to see the shadow woman watching me. But all I saw was the red sun and a laden, reflective cloud.

At the fifth hour of training, I was covered in sweat, heaving, and frustrated with my slow progress. As if to provide a welcome break, a visitor teleported onto the floating grass field.

Kaur approached in a relaxed, velvety long shirt and loose pants meant for sleeping. Perhaps she'd taken the day off.

"You should've told me." She grabbed my arm. Somehow, her hold doused my red light, putting out my lightblade. "About the dream invader. I had to hear about it from Saina."

"I haven't seen you in days. You wouldn't even answer my Live Message requests."

"Yeah, I know, my fault. Wanted some reflection time. But still, you should've told me."

Kriga cracked his knuckles and approached. "Excuse me. Master Jyosh is in the middle of training. You can talk to him after."

"Shut up." Kaur wagged her finger at him. "Or do you want your memory reset?"

"Master Jyosh is the dreamer." Kriga crossed his arms. "Only he can reset me."

"It's all right, Kriga," I said. "This is pretty important, so I'll break for the day."

"As you wish, Master Jyosh."

I turned my attention to Kaur and her annoyed frown.

"We need to have a talk," she said. "Let's go back to the lodge."

AFTER SAINA and I showed Kaur where we'd spotted the shadow woman the other day, the three of us took a seat in front of the crackling fireplace in my bedroom.

"We called her the Ghost," Kaur said. "She's appeared in my dreams before. And Rao's, too."

Saina used her terminal to materialize a mug of creamy milk. She slurped some cream, then asked, "Is she dangerous?"

"Dunno." Kaur shook her head. "I've never actually spoken to her. But Rao has. One day, when I was with him in the dream where we raised Elam — Elam was nine years old at the time, so we'd been in these dreams a while — I saw Rao walking out of a forest. He was crying and shaking. His shirt was soaked from tears. I'll never forget it. Behind him, shadowed by distant trees, stood the Ghost.

"When I asked Rao why he was crying, who she was, what it all meant — he wouldn't tell me. No matter how much I badgered him, his mouth stayed shut on the topic. Sure, he was a secretive person — never talked about his past — but this irked me like nothing else. Who was this goddamned woman that had made one of the Karshan air force's rising stars cry like a terrified little baby? I mean, I'd never made the man cry, and on a bad day, I'm crueler than the gods. Thinking about how the Ghost broke him grinds my gears, even now."

I cleared my dry throat. Maybe I needed some milk, too. "We don't know if it's the same Ghost, do we?"

"It's her!" Kaur punched her palm. "I saw her the first day we entered this dream, but it was only for a second, and then she disappeared. I thought my mind was playing tricks, but since you both've sighted her, I'm certain of it. She's back."

"So why is she trying to help us?" I asked. "Can we put any of these pieces together?"

Kaur pulled on her cherry bangs. "Dunno. But I have a theory. She's against Rao, and because we're against Rao, she's trying to help us. Help us kill Rao and stop whatever he's planning."

"Wait a minute," I said. "That can't be the sum of it. Remember, this Ghost helped me long before I was involved in any of this. Her intervention has something to do with me as well, not only Rao."

Kaur tapped on the glass covering the fireplace, causing it to become warmer and brighter. "That's the most bewildering thing of all. I just can't put it together. But I'm certain she wants to stop Rao, too. She doesn't trust Sylet to do the right thing, so she's put her hopes in us."

Saina took another sip. "If it's true that Rao and Sylet are intending to use the power of this ancient city for evil ends, then I can't turn my back on it. No one with a conscience can. Perhaps the Ghost is just like us, burdened by the weight of what she knows."

But what did *I* have to do with any of it? "Then it seems we've come to the conclusion that the Ghost has good intentions, as annoying as her secrecy may be. But how can she invade dreams at will?"

"It's a *blessing*, isn't it?" Saina said. "Like Kaur's claws and Elam's floating blades. How else to explain something that can't be explained? It's a gift from the gods."

"Sounds about right," I said. "And if Rao has soldiers in the

Deep Layer, as she says, then we really need to be at our best to succeed. We have to train our hearts out."

"It's also possible that while Rao may know about the Deep Layer, he can't field enough men to patrol it *and* the Tower *and* deal with Sylet's forces." Kaur sighed. "Wish we had a spectrum mapper so we could act on facts, not assumptions. We're adrift in the fog of war, literally and figuratively."

"What if the Ghost is a spectrum mapper?" I snapped my fingers. "How else could she know about so much? If only we could contact her in the real world. But for all we know, it seems she can only appear in dreams. And even when she does appear, it's not exactly a two-way exchange — she tells us only what she wants us to know."

"I think we're going in circles now." Saina sighed. She settled her empty mug on the floor and stretched, groaning the while. "I was in the middle of regenerating someone's entire intestinal tract. Believe me, it's harder than it sounds. If any of you end up with a hole in your belly, that training could come in handy. See you later."

Saina opened her terminal and tapped on it. White light enveloped her, and she was gone.

Kaur took Saina's empty mug and sniffed. "Ugh. It's *almond* milk, of all things."

"Almond milk? How can you make milk out of nuts? Does milk come out when you squeeze them, or something?"

"I dunno, it's so gross. How does almond milk even have cream in it?"

"This is a dream."

Kaur stretched her legs out, soles facing the fireplace. "Reminds me of something that happened when I was breast-feeding Elam."

"Okay, just so you know, I can live without hearing about how you breastfed Elam."

"Relax. It all happened in a dream. It was a feature of the child-raising program. He was a baby."

"It's still weird. He's a grown man, now. And he's older than you."

"Yeah… that is weird. I've never been able to get over how weird it is."

Kaur went quiet. Her expression grew sad.

I didn't like seeing that. "I don't mind if you tell me the breastfeeding story."

"It's not much of a story. Elam wouldn't latch on properly, so it hurt a lot to feed him. We kept the pain setting on — Rao preferred not to dull his senses. Milk would spill out of me and just get everywhere. Was a mess." Kaur shut her eyes, as if dreaming those memories again. "I don't even know why I'm telling you this. Maybe I just want to remember what it was like when I was happy."

To be honest, I hadn't thought much about her pain, or anyone else's pain, because I'd been so overcome by my own. Kaur had loved Rao, and still loved Elam, so opposing them must've hurt. She hadn't been answering my Live Message requests for days, and all that time I'd thought it was just Kaur being Kaur. But now I realized, she must've been hurting. Maybe even paralyzed by what she felt.

I wasn't sure what the right thing to say was, so I just said what was on my mind. "This Rao guy must be quite impressive for you to have agreed to have a baby with him. Dream or not."

"Why do you say that?" Her single chuckle sounded so weighed down by sadness. "It's not like I had high standards or anything."

"When someone is strong, like you are, how do you find someone worth loving? I imagine you either find someone weaker than you, whom you want to protect, or you find an equal. Rao must've been the latter. I figure he's incredibly strong, just in a different way. And if you loved him, then he probably isn't evil." I remembered what Kriga had told me earlier. "I think he chose a path and is following it with all his heart. He believes in something. You once walked together — the three of you — but now, because you've all chosen to believe different things, you're at a crossroads."

Kaur rubbed her eye. "That's such goatshit. You don't know Rao. He always lied and kept secrets. At first, it made him seem so mysterious. That's what attracted me to him. But later, it was so frustrating. And I wasn't always strong. I used to find his strength so comforting, like shade on a hot day. Now… it's all turned into hate."

Yeah, what did I know? Well, I knew hate. "I know what it's like to hate someone. I sip on hate daily. I use it to make myself stronger. But sometimes I wonder… what if it's all a lie?"

"What do you mean 'a lie?'"

"Well, what if I'm hating the wrong person? I mean, my brother Kediri… for all his faults… can I really blame him for seeking a better life? The Manizan military was known for being awfully cruel to those who couldn't cut it. And as a first born, he had no choice but to join. Can I blame him for trying to get out?" It hurt so much to pluck at these strings.

"Then who deserves the honor of your hate?"

"The Paranis. They twisted Maniza in their image and sat their fat asses on everyone's necks. *They* decided to punish a whole family for the crime of one person." I shook my head. "But I hate Kediri even more. I'd rather hate someone I used to love. It's just easier. I don't know why, but it's so much easier to hate Kediri than the real bastards who're responsible for all the evil that was done to me and my family. So I'll go on hating him, just so I can get stronger."

"Hate's not so bad," Kaur said. "It gives you meaning, purpose, direction. In the absence of love, it's better than nothing. What's excruciating is feeling both for the same person. I told myself so many times — 'harden your heart.' I couldn't forgive the bastard who sent my son to the Red Veil, who twisted him into a heartless killer. For what? Rao told me he wants to end everyone's suffering — permanently. What right does he have to do that? I hate him with every shred of my soul."

I held my hand out. "Let's work hard, then, to sate our hatreds."

Kaur rubbed her eye some more, then took my hand and shook it. She managed a smile. "We've got a lot of time left in this dream. Let's make it count."

WE SPENT each of the hundred days training. I mastered Double Blade after five days, then proceeded to level three, where Kriga taught me Snake Blade. The name explains itself. To be able to bend the lightblade and maneuver it like water seemed impossible, at first. Not only did I have to pool and surge light, but do it with a subtle directionality that required tremendous inward focus.

It was the directionality that proved most challenging. It was like trying to make a stick you'd thrown zigzag in the air and change course, using only your mind.

As usual, I had to visualize it, first. I had to imagine my blade bending, curving, snaking, melting. No longer could I regard it as a solid beam but rather as a molten extension of my will. For the first week, I could hardly get it to bend five degrees. No matter how much I commanded the red sunshine inside of me, no matter how much I forced it to take the shape I demanded, it wouldn't bend to my will.

The breakthrough came with some, as usual, excellent advice from Kriga. "Don't impose yourself on your blade. The more you impose, the more rigid it becomes. Let it flow. Let it breathe. Let it become your ally, not your slave."

I pondered what that meant for days. I even asked Kaur what she thought, but she just laughed and told me to "figure it out."

Then one day, whilst I stood in the snow, a slight breeze kissing my face, I thought about Zauri and realized what I had to do. It all went back to what she had taught me about being gentle and rhythmic with the red light. About not forcing it.

So the next day during training, I held my hilt out front and inhaled the red sunshine. I allowed myself to *feel* the frequency of the wavelengths, and instead of forcing the light along, I adjusted the rate of my flow to match it.

All of a sudden, everything became easier. Casting lightblades no longer required me to sip my hatred of Kediri. And as I obeyed the light, the light obeyed me.

Later that day, I bent my blade by twenty degrees.

For the next month, Kriga taught me various Snake Blade shapes – all kinds of angles, lengths, and wiry maneuvers. Each was its own distinct challenge. Each brought me to the brink of giving up.

But with practice and time, it all became second nature. When Kriga was satisfied I could bend my blade at will, I finally passed level three.

At level four, Kriga taught me a move called First Fire Vessel. It was more of an inward state than an actual lightblade move. That's where I *really* got stuck.

Fire Vessel required one to pool red light in different parts of the body. Pool some in the feet, in the belly, in the arms. But because my veins were in poor shape, I found it excruciating to cycle light to so many parts of my body, at the same time, while also maintaining a strong lightblade. Apparently, this was a foundational skill because it allowed you to *store* light for long periods.

And because Fire Vessel was a foundational move, I couldn't progress to the next level until I mastered it.

No matter how much I pleaded with Kriga to just teach me something else, he refused. "If you can't store red light throughout your body, you aren't fit to learn the more advanced moves. You'd fail the training program. But there is something you can do."

And that something was to *meditate*. But not just any old meditation; what Kriga taught me had to be done with violet light — the very same color used for healing.

"Flow violet through your veins," Kriga told me. "Focus inwardly. This is how you repair and broaden your veins, and improve your *capacity* to store light."

"But this is just a dream. It won't have any effect on the state of my veins in the real world."

"Not true. While the exact mechanism is poorly understood, it is known that meditating in dreams does indeed improve one's veins and capacity. But the effect is less than if you meditated in the real world. However, because you have more time here than there, it's certainly worth it."

So I would sit on a snowy or grassy hill, close my eyes, and just flow violet for hours. It certainly helped deal with my angst, though I wasn't sure how much it would help with my veins.

Even after meditating every day for two months, I failed to properly achieve First Fire Vessel, never even coming close to the capacity needed to pass.

But that failure wasn't worthless. With my marginally improved veins, creating lightblades became truly effortless. Executing Blinding Blade, Double Blade, and Snake Blade became as easy as snapping my fingers.

I also enjoyed many mock battles with Kriga during our training hours. Funny, that Zauri and I had never fought each other. It would've been more fun fighting her instead of those glitched, headless scripts. Anyway, Kriga obviously took it easy on me, but despite that, I always felt I earned my blows. And when he'd strike me, it wasn't because of his overwhelming superiority, but because I'd made a vital miscalculation.

Kriga made me feel pain for my mistakes and joy for my successes: a perfect teacher, who only rarely lost patience. Those rare moments did make him feel more human. He'd even come up to the lodge sometimes and have tea with us, but he was less talkative in that setting than on the training field.

I committed to a second type of training, too: flying around the dreamscape on a skyboard. The scenery was mostly just ocean, with a few floating islands that were used as training stages. There was also a host of giant floating weapons: the massive floating sword where Kaur had trained, as well as a floating axe, spear, twinblade, and arrow.

I even trained on how to fly on a skyboard with a red combat stone in my chest. It took a few days to consistently crush red light into green, and feed enough of it into the skyboard to make it fly. It wasn't nearly as efficient as flying with a green machinist stone, so I had to keep my pace slow and steady. The extra step of squeezing red light into green always pulled my focus inward — far from ideal when flying.

When I got that part down, I tried flying with a lightblade. It took about a week to be able to fly with a stable lightblade in my hand. Then I remembered that warrior in my vision. He was wielding *two* lightblades.

It took all the way to the final day of the dream for me to fly on a skyboard while holding two lightblades. And I was doing all this skyboard training in my afterhours, too. Most of my days were spent trying and failing to execute Fire Vessel.

Outside of training, Saina and Kaur and I spent a good deal of time together. The most memorable day was when we played in the snow like children. We chased each other across the hills and tossed snowballs, mindlessly, laughing whenever we'd hit someone's face. It reminded me so much of Kediri, Chaya, and I playing in our backyard.

After that, we all decided to rebuild the Temple Behesh together. Kaur and I followed Saina's instructions, clumping up the snow and molding it into buildings and towers. We constructed an incredible miniature cityscape out of snow. Seeing her home so lovingly recreated made Saina tear up. Unfortunately, the next day's snowfall blew it all away, but it was never meant to last forever.

The understandings we'd forged deepened. We all agreed to help each other, and that we wouldn't turn back until we each achieved what we'd set out to do.

We didn't quite become open books, though. Kaur told me some more about Rao, but I still didn't really understand why she loved him; I suppose love is not something that ought to be understood or have reasons. They'd met at the Karshan military academy in Salkofy. Rao had soared upon his ambitions, and Kaur followed him.

The way she described her past, she seemed like a different person: demure, a follower rather than a leader, and uncertain about herself and her path. It seemed Elam becoming real had changed everything, though there were still so many holes in my understanding of her.

During my chats with Saina, I got the sense that she'd never had a childhood. She'd been chosen as a Daughter of the Dawn from infancy, and so was raised at the Temple by the elder gurus to focus solely on her duties. And she continued to live in that dutiful way, but as a healer, now.

Losing her connection to her god had made her deeply unhappy. Sure, she put on a smile every day, especially for her patients. But for Saina, it was as if she'd lost a sixth sense the day Behesh was captured by the night. It wasn't merely like losing a friend — you can always find other friends, as insensitive as that sounds. It was more like the sun disappearing from the sky, leaving you cold and unable to see light or feel heat for the rest of your life.

Eventually, the time came to wake up. The three of us gathered in the lobby of the lodge. Saina slurped her cream-filled almond milk. Kaur drank her lemongrass-cardamom white tea. I preferred not to drink anything.

We sat upon sheepskin pillows at a floor table, like we'd done on the first day of the dream. Slowly, cracks appeared in the dreamscape. Then the floor split open and an earthquake shook the mountains. The sky outside the window parted, as if a god had pulled the fabric of reality apart. Everything around us in the dreamscape shattered like glass, and those pieces shattered into more pieces, until the whole world was ground to dust.

And we awoke to face our fates.

Chapter Twenty

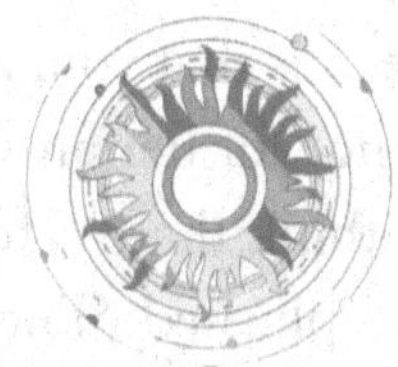

I DIDN'T WAKE UP WHERE I'D GONE TO SLEEP. I LAY IN A BARE, metal room with glowing vine-like calligraphy on the walls. The air was still. No windows and no light, aside from the softly throbbing script that surrounded me.

So, the Ghost had brought me back here.

I got to my feet. No way in or out of this box, except by the Ghost's will, I assumed.

I looked for an air disturbance or an outline that could indicate where she was, but didn't find anything.

"I brought you here to tell you something urgent." Her voice came from the ceiling. "Something good. Sylet began his assault on the Tower minutes ago. Rao will be busy with that, so the Deep Layer won't be heavily patrolled. The levship with your dream stone is on the fifteenth floor of the Tower. Go there."

"I plan to."

"It would be better if you didn't bring Saina along. She's a vulnerability. Also, the longer we delay Rao from having his hand regrown, the better."

"Why?"

"I can't tell you that."

Of course she wasn't going to tell me. But I wasn't going to deny Saina her lifelong yearning.

"It's not just a coincidence, is it?" I asked. "You involved me in this conflict, on purpose."

"Yes, I involved you in this. But a lot of things happened that I hadn't foreseen. Like what Elam did."

"Elam… Elam… are you like Elam? Did you come from a dream, too? Could you be… is that you, Zauri?"

I waited in painful silence for her answer.

"I can see why you'd think that." Her sigh was high-pitched and laden. "Look, it's complicated. The truth would burn you. And, sorry to say, but this is so much bigger than just you or even me. I can't say you'll always be happy with my actions, but for now, know that I'm looking out for you. To prove it, I left you a gift."

"Gift?"

"You'll find it in the pagoda."

"Why would you go to the trouble?"

"Isn't it obvious? Because I want you to succeed. And… because I care about you, Jyosh. More than you can ever know."

"You don't conceal the truth from someone you care about."

"You do… when the truth is more painful than you can imagine. In any case, goodbye for now, Jyosh. I hope, one day, we'll meet under happier clouds."

KAUR AND SAINA were already awake and standing when my eyes opened. They each had a cereal bar in their hands. Saina took a chug from a thermos, then handed it to Kaur.

I sniffed something pungent on my left shoulder. Someone had drooled there. The dream had lasted so long, I'd forgotten which of them had slept on my left. Three months had passed in the second-layer dream, but only four hours went by in the real world. So weird to come to grips with that. I felt the dream's passage of time far more acutely, almost as if I'd gone to sleep and woken up as a different person.

Saina noticed me yawning and stretching and handed me a cereal bar. I ripped off the wrapper and chomped down. Crunchy but tasteless. After, I chugged the remaining water in the thermos.

I told them what the Ghost had said.

"Let's not waste a moment, then." Kaur pointed to the window, through which a clear sky shone. "Looks like we're not in a cloud anymore, too."

"Makes sense that Sylet would wait for clearer skies to attack Rao." Saina stroked her chin. "He's probably got more air support than Rao has, being a higher rank and all."

"Practically, he has *all* the air support," Kaur said. "I assume he won't let Rao's fleet near Sambalpur. Rao is trapped in that tower."

I peered out the window. Indeed, blocky levships hovered above. They were clustered around a massive spade-shaped ship. Other than that, I could only see a few other shiny limestone tenements from this view.

"Gear up and let's go," Kaur said.

I took out the training dream stone. The world lost its orange hue. I stuck my red combat stone into my chest slot. A jolt hit me, and the air tinted red. I could now sip the angry sun and use its violent light for my lightblades.

I holstered my sword hilt. It almost felt like a part of me. I must've trained for five hundred hours with it in my hands. I was nothing like the terrified weakling who'd gone to sleep four hours ago. While I wasn't an adept yet, I could at least defend myself, I could at least be *dangerous.* Blinding Blade, Double Blade, Snake Blade, and all the stances and strikes that Kriga had taught me

— these were all cards I could play in battle. My enemies may be drawing from a larger deck, but if I played my hand right, if I outsmarted them, I had no doubt I could win.

Saina, Kaur, and I began walking down the stairs toward the entrance of the tenement.

"All right, listen up." Kaur clapped once. "We're going to do our best to avoid confrontation. But if it comes to violence, both of you must obey my orders, without question. Is that clear?"

"Yes," Saina and I said at almost the same time.

"Also, keep this in mind — when we're underground, we might not have access to sunshine. Store some in your body, just in case."

I nodded. "I don't think I'll be able to store light, but I'll try." Especially given that I couldn't master First Fire Vessel, thanks to the poor state of my veins.

Outside, the red sun stared at the pagodas, domes, and towers across the city, creating a hazy, crimson aura that covered everything. The streets smelled ancient, as if the dust we kicked up was created before time. The silence betrayed no danger.

We headed to the Temple, avoiding open streets and clinging to alleyways. Along with the God Tower and a few other sites, it was the only place where the stone gods were looking down instead of up. The Ghost had all but confirmed that my hunch was right: the Temple, with its majestic pagoda, was an entrance to the Deep Layer.

We stayed careful during the fifteen-minute walk and thankfully didn't encounter any of Sylet's patrols. But it wasn't entirely uneventful. The booming of light cannons sounded from miles away, coming from the Tower's direction. A few blocky levships landed and took off — Sylet bringing in troops and supplies, most likely. I hoped we wouldn't get caught up in that battle. Thankfully, it meant this part of the city was free of both Rao and Sylet's men.

We arrived at the pagoda. The gods truly were staring at the ground. One that resembled a lion with snakes for hair hung off the second tier of the roof. It wasn't only staring at the ground, it was reaching for it, too. What was hiding there that made even the gods turn their gazes from high heaven?

We climbed the steps up the hill, walked along the stone path, and entered the temple by its airy, column-lined door.

It wasn't quite as empty as the other buildings. An altar sat in the center of a massive room. Moss-filled water pooled in a reserve that ran across the four sides. The musty scent was so thick, all three of us coughed. The ruddy sunshine leaking in from the rafters showed the dust swirling through the air. Our footsteps echoed as we walked.

A heavy place. Beyond the obvious signs of age, I sensed a holiness. I studied the altar.

A vision flashed before my eyes: a young woman wearing a sparkly headscarf placed a crying baby on the altar, then knelt and raised her hands in prayer. I couldn't see her face from this angle.

"In the fog of Sambalpur…" she recited, *"…bestow your blessing…"*

Was she one of the Ancients? Was I seeing a ghost?

I blinked, and she and the baby vanished.

I glanced at Saina and Kaur, then decided against telling them, for now. We each had enough on our plates, and we already had a ghost to worry about.

I shrugged it off and focused on the moment.

Saina walked up to the altar. She knelt and picked up something at its base: a snaky, black string that ran into the ground. A wire.

"What's that for?" I asked.

"Connection," Saina said.

"Connection to what?"

"Ultimately, to one of the ten. *All gods are ten.* Though there may be thousands of gods, they are all ultimately emanations of one of the ten, truly indivisible gods."

"Oh yeah, you were telling me about that." I scratched my stubble. "One light beam becomes seven colors and all that."

Saina stared at the ceiling for a moment, then said, "Yes, seven colors. But don't forget white, black, and unseen. The seven colors of the spectrum, plus those three, equals ten."

Kaur sighed. "You guys have lost me."

"We don't have time for a sermon on Beheshian theology," Saina said. "Here's a different analogy — one fire can cast many shadows. The gods we worship may bring us blessings and miracles, but these gods are merely shadows, cast by one of ten eternal fires from the Asha."

I'd grasped the concept, but how it worked exactly seemed a mystery. I'd have to ask more about it, later. "So which fire do you feel here?"

"I feel a shadow. But it's not the shadow we Beheshians worship — I don't sense the Avatar of the Eternal Dawn. But I do sense a shadow created by the same fire. By Mitra — the Eternal Dawn itself."

"Could it be a different avatar of Mitra?" I asked.

"It could be, or it could be some other kind of emanation. I don't know." Saina shut her eyes in focus.

Kaur sighed sharply. "So where's the door to the Deep Layer?"

"We just got here," I said, annoyed. "Give her a minute." Suddenly, I remembered: the gift. The Ghost had mentioned she'd left something here, for us.

While Saina knelt at the altar and Kaur stood around twiddling her thumbs, I walked to the corners of the room, peering all over.

I checked the base of the columns. Nothing but dust. I felt the stone walls, searching for crevices. Again, nothing. I studied the pool of mossy water.

There! A sack floated within. I got on my knees and reached out, just able to grab its strings. As I pulled it toward me, something *clacked* inside.

Holding the dripping sack, I went back to Kaur and Saina.

"I was the Temple, for a long time," Saina said while clutching the wire, her eyes closed. "It was as if my soul had left my body and dwelt in the stone. You ever been that connected to one of your machines, Jyosh? You ever *been* a machine?"

Being a machine… sure, sometimes you focused so much on your conduction, your sense of awareness slipped into the machine itself. Its various parts became your organs and limbs. But what was it like to be… a building?

"Something like that," I said.

Saina clutched the wire tighter. "I can feel it again. The breeze on the stone. The burning sun. But it's so empty, here. Not like in Behesh. I was everyone, before. Everyone who worshipped Mitra, the Eternal Dawn, through the Avatar. And who worshipped the Avatar through me, the Daughter of the Dawn."

That was quite a chain of worship. Why did Mitra need a double-layered veil? Why not show himself to his worshippers, directly? Was the truth too blinding?

Kaur glared at me with a ruffled nose, as if to say, *she crazy?*

I rolled my eyes.

"Below me is a chasm." The voice came from everywhere. I almost jumped out of my boots. Kaur darted her head around. But it was just Saina's airy voice.

"Don't be afraid, I am the Temple," Saina said from everywhere.

And then her body lifted off the ground. She floated in the air, the wire becoming taut as she ascended.

"Don't be afraid."

I wasn't so much afraid as astonished.

"Below me is a void. I'm sitting on air. My foundation is empty. The Deep Layer."

Kaur let out a chuckle. "This got interesting real fast."

"Stand back." Saina's voice echoed across the walls. "I'm opening it. Stand as far away as you can."

Kaur and I went to the edge, a step away from the mossy water that pooled across all four sides.

The temple quaked, as if a fist had grabbed and shook it. With nothing to hold onto, I grabbed Kaur's shoulders, and she clung to my arms. The altar beneath Saina's floating form sunk into the ground, revealing a staircase, leading down.

"There it is." Saina floated downward and landed in front of the staircase. She dropped the wire and opened her eyes.

"Easy." She smiled, her eyes bright and cheeks rosy. "It really did feel like I was back in Behesh, for a moment. I still don't understand what it means, but in the twenty years since the Exile, this is the closest I've ever felt to what I lost that day."

"I'm glad." I approached the stairway. "And there may be more to discover, down there."

All three of us stared into the black beyond the stone stairs. A groaning, icy air blew out of it. No way forward but down.

Before we began our descent, we stood at the edge of the staircase and opened the sack the Ghost had left us. I stuck my hand inside, grasped something hard and many-sided, and pulled out a crystal.

The bottom half of the crystal was emerald green and the top half ruby red.

Kaur gasped. "Now this is the *real* miracle. I'd like you to guess what that is, Jyosh."

"Hmm." I scratched my head. "Could it really be what I think it is? Can this stone conduct both red *and* green?"

"Yup," Kaur said. "It's an experimental TEX design. It's not even in production. Years away. How the hell did she get one?"

"It must be meant for you." Saina smiled at me. "You talked a lot about how good you were with green light, and how much better you were getting with red. So isn't this just the most ideal thing ever?"

I nodded. It made perfect sense for me to use such a stone.

"Don't forget that it's experimental," Kaur said. "That's not an empty word. There are risks involved. Burnout, for one. Can't say I know what else could happen, but I'm sure there's a long list."

"Everything we're doing is a huge risk." I stuck my hand in the bag. "I don't need the stone right now, anyway. But I can imagine a few situations where it would come in handy."

I pulled out another crystal. This one was blue, the color of glowing topaz.

"No way." Kaur covered her mouth. "Who in the holy hell is this Ghost? How did she get her hands on a blue stone?"

"Wait, what does a blue stone — or blue light — even do?" I asked.

"Blue augments conduction," Saina said. "Sometimes healers will have an assistant wear one, augmenting as needed to speed up healing. You can even augment yourself by swapping stones if you're experienced enough. But they're extremely expensive and fragile. I used one years ago, when assisting the healing of someone with a few too many bags of twinsen lying around."

"You're trained in its use, then," I said. "If it augments conduction, can it augment our lightblades?"

Saina nodded. "I believe so. I've only trained to use it in healing situations, but in theory, it would work the same way for a lightblade. The thing is, the stones are so fragile, you only get so many uses out of one."

I handed it to Saina. "You should put it in. What use is your healing stone, right now? If we need to be augmented in a pinch, this'll come in handy."

Saina took the stone. "Good point. Turn around while I change."

Kaur and I turned around as Saina unzipped the front of her black combat suit and swapped her stones.

"Done," she said. "Let's see what else is in there."

I stuck my hand in the sack, clutched the last thing inside, and pulled it out.

Another crystal. This one glowed furiously red. The brightest, bloodiest red I'd ever seen.

"This must be for me." Kaur grabbed it. "Always wanted one. Of course, they cost more than a three-story mansion on Pomegranate Lane."

"What does it do?" I asked.

Kaur wasted no time. She unzipped her front, nearly baring her breasts, and pulled out her combat crystal. She stuck the new one in her chest slot. Jitters seized her body.

"You okay?" Saina asked.

"Feels quite good, actually." Kaur rubbed her arms, the jitters fading, then zipped back up. "This's nothing too complicated. It's just a top-of-the-line TEX combat stone. The best ones they make. Brand new, too. They're a good investment because they last basically forever. The filthy rich nawab families buy them all as a commodity, which drives up their price even more. The military can't even afford them for general use."

The Ghost had given us each an appropriate gift. Strange as this was, it proved her dedication to our cause.

I slipped my red-green stone into one of my utility pockets.

"Time to go. Let's bust through the Deep Layer and reach the Tower."

"Let's do it." Kaur punched her palm.

Saina smiled and nodded. "I'm ready."

We began walking down, Kaur at the front.

Soon as we descended a few steps, my jaw dropped. The cavern beneath the temple stretched vast in all directions, and the gods were here, too.

They hung, upside down, from the ceiling. Each god was the size of a tower. But these gods were all human: no animal features. And their eyes were balls of red sun, bringing light to a massive cavern the size of a neighborhood. The gods, with their outstretched hands — each bigger than a person — all pointed downward.

The staircase itself widened and descended hundreds of feet — we were still only at the very top.

"This isn't anything like I expected," I said.

"I once heard that similar things hid below Behesh." Saina pointed at one of the massive, upside-down human statues. They were made of what looked like bright orange copper. "What are these meant to glorify?"

"The Ancients, probably." Kaur chuckled. "They must've thought pretty highly of themselves. What's creating that light, though?" She pointed at the blazing orbs that made up their eyeballs. These bright eyes reminded me of the dragons I'd seen.

"When I linked with the Temple, I felt as if there was something dwelling here," Saina said. "It was faint, so the source must be even deeper than this."

A chill shudder ran through me, as if a ghost had blown on my spine. We were no longer in the dream, and yet, this place felt so dreamlike. In fact, Sambalpur itself had always seemed so out of place, with its limestone buildings and brilliantly chiseled statues of the gods.

"We're really walking into the unknown, aren't we?" I said, keeping pace with Kaur.

Saina nodded. "Would've been nice if the Ghost gave us a spectrum mapping stone — uh, that is, if one of you can use it."

"Nope, spectrum mapping takes years of practice," Kaur said. "It's arguably the hardest of all skills to master. Besides, whatever is down here, I'm sure it can't be worse than having to deal with waves and waves of Sylet's best."

"Healing must be harder than spectrum mapping," I said. "Right, Saina?"

Saina shrugged. "How should I know? I've never spectrum mapped before."

"You can regenerate organs and limbs. Sounds a lot trickier than making a map. You really are the best."

"'The best?' I wouldn't say so. There are definitely better healers out there. Like those who can reverse aging."

"Even so, you're the best to me."

It took us five minutes to trudge down the stairs. At the base, the hanging ancients seemed to be reaching their hands for us. Why were they trying to get deeper? Why not climb to heaven? What was here, below Sambalpur, that was more interesting than all the wonders floating in the sky?

I was curious, but I wanted to get Zauri back and get safe, more than learning what made this city so important that the Karshan military was fighting with themselves over it.

The cavern ahead lay wide open. The floor was made of stone far darker than the limestone used in the temple and city.

Across the vastness, perhaps a half-mile away, was another opening.

"The Tower must be that way," Kaur said, pointing to it.

"How do you know?" I asked.

"I mean, I don't see any other openings. Let's be thankful for that. The less choice, the less chance we get lost."

Just the idea of traversing this massive cavern made me weary. The hope of finally getting Zauri back pushed me on.

I stared up at the bright balls of sun glowing within the eyes of the Ancients.

"Quick question," I said. "How come we can conduct underground? There's no sunshine here, yet everything is still tinted red."

Kaur pointed to the eyes above us. "It seems that's as good a light source as any. But it's true — we could find ourselves in a place where breathing sunlight is impossible. And once we use up all our stored light, maybe all that grappling we did will come in handy."

"Grappling?" Saina ruffled her nose.

"I taught Jyosh so many moves. He was getting pretty good at forcing me into a headlock. Could never keep me there, though, even with all his weight on me."

"*Ohh.*" Saina smirked at me. "Sounds like you both had a good time."

"Not really," I said. "She definitely had more fun than me."

Kaur held up her hand. "Hear that?"

I stuck my ear out. All I heard was the wind whispering from the opening we'd come from.

Kaur got on her hands and knees and put her ear to the ground. "Footsteps! I'd say three people. They're coming toward us!"

She pushed onto her feet, unholstered her hilt, and formed a brightly burning blade. She got into a low stance. Were we about to be attacked in the center of this massive cavern, beneath the hands of the gods?

Thud. Behind us. I turned to see a swinging rope hanging off an Ancient's finger. Something flashed in the corner of my eye, and I jumped away.

A black-clad soldier appeared at my side — tall, red blade

throbbing intensely. *Thud-thud-thud.* Three more soldiers dropped around us, their ropes retracting off the fingers of the Ancients.

I pulled out my hilt, my nerves shaking. I inhaled red and cycled it; all I could manage was sputtering sparks. My hilt got so hot, I almost dropped it. Doing what I'd trained to do seemed so much harder in actual battle. I told myself, *This is Kediri's doing! His treachery!*

Hatred disciplined my light flow, and a perfect, gleaming lightblade grew off my hilt.

Saina stayed between Kaur and me. We faced the four soldiers who'd surrounded us. More soldiers ran toward us from the opening we'd been walking toward.

"Thought you were dead, Kaur," one of them said.

"That you, Babak?" Kaur replied.

The tall soldier nodded. "Like seeing a ghost. Elam pretty much sliced you in two. Anyway, alive or dead, you're still our enemy. Put those lightblades down. I'm sure Rao's got words for you."

"Come on, Babak," Kaur said. "I trained for three months, hours before coming here. I'm itching to try what I learned. How many levels did you ascend in your last sleep?"

"*Hmph,*" the soldier named Babak said. "Your level won't save you. We have you surrounded."

"Then why're you still talking? You afraid of my claws? Don't worry, you and your little squad here aren't worthy. I'm saving them for someone higher up the food chain."

The footsteps of the soldiers running toward us vibrated in my bones.

"Who're your friends?" Babak gave Saina and me a good look, though we couldn't see his masked face. Only his bright yellow irises shone through his eye slits.

"You won't live to learn their names, Babak."

The three soldiers who were running toward us arrived. One of them went up to Babak and whispered in his ear.

"*Tsk-tsk-tsk.*" Babak wagged his finger at Kaur. "Trying to pull a fast one on us? You've got the Beheshian healer here who can regenerate limbs. We've been looking for her after what you did to Commander Rao's hand." He glanced at me. "Your other friend can barely keep his lightblade straight. He'll have to die. You ladies, though, can keep the Commander company. He's getting lonely, cooped up in that tower."

What? My lightblade was perfect! I'd been training for months to make it so! My muscles tightened in anger.

Kaur made a fist with her free hand. "Shut your ugly mouth and take a swing. I'm waiting."

"You can't take us all on, Kaur. Lion of Light or not. How long must we wait for you to realize that? Drop your weapons."

Looked like no one was willing to start the fight or disarm.

Kaur chuckled, betraying no fear. "Babak, let me just say this — I never liked you. I know it was you who stole that ruby-encrusted sword hilt I found when we raided that sky pirate nest."

Her confidence inspired me to stand straighter and raise my lightblade higher. Saina, too, gritted her teeth.

Babak's eyes widened. "You're right. It was me. Sold that thing for a bucketload of twinsen. The strong take from the weak. What you gonna do about it?"

Even more soldiers arrived from the far side in the time they'd been talking. Twelve masked, black-clad warriors now surrounded us, lightblades drawn. One held what resembled a twinblade: two lightblades, each projected off a side of the hilt. Yet another, standing farthest away, held a miniature light cannon on her shoulder, aimed at us.

"Know what — I always thought you had a nice name, Babak. Just rolls off the tongue. Too bad it's the last time I'll ever say it." Kaur bared her teeth. "Saina, do the thing."

The moment we'd been waiting for had arrived. I shuffled closer to Kaur and Saina. Saina put a hand on each of our napes.

Blue light poured from her hand into me. The light amplified the colors in the air. Now I saw red and green and yellow and orange, all swimming together in wavy lines, all streaming into the crystal in my chest. My combat stone became a funnel, sucking in all the light of the world, and my veins became wires, cycling that light and pooling it in every part of me.

"The Beheshian bitch is no mere healer!" Babak shouted. "She's an augmenter! Shit! Call for more backup!"

My lightblade turned from red to black. Shadowy wings grew off the edges, sucking in even more light from the blazing eyeballs of the Ancients. The shadow blade grew so large, the cavern dimmed. But an even darker shadow formed on Kaur's hilt. It grew to four times its size, widening, deepening, and cycling blacklight.

With her terrifyingly large blade, Kaur sliced the air in front of her. The massive tangle of light and shadow cut four soldiers in half, including Babak. Both halves of each soldier caught fire, burning black, and the bodies turned to ash in the air. No time to even scream.

But it would all be for naught if that light cannon went off. I darted forward toward the soldier holding it. Her yellow irises seemed stuck in shock. She was too stunned to move. My lightblade was so large, I didn't have to go very far. I thrust it forward and cut a hole through her chest.

Red leaked into her eyes as she spat blood. My lightblade wasn't hot enough for her to catch fire, but she still fell forward and died. Her light cannon dropped off her shoulder and clattered onto the cold stone.

My heartbeats began to slow. The colored waves in the air

flickered and turned red. I could no longer see all the colors, only the red meant for my combat stone.

Saina's augmentation was fading fast. Kaur managed one more swipe. It cut through and burned two more soldiers to a crisp. Then her blade shrank until it was its normal size.

It seemed she'd managed to kill the guy with the twinblade. Six soldiers remained, and they scattered across the open cavern.

I sprinted toward the one heading for the opening, while Kaur hunted the others. I couldn't let him call for backup.

Meanwhile, Saina remained on her knees, huffing. Augmenting us with such a sudden burst had taken a lot out of her.

I focused on the guy I was chasing. I rushed forward — my heart in my throat — and gained on him. He stopped running, then spun around to face me. I almost stumbled, but managed to halt my momentum and form my lightblade, just as he formed his. Except, his lightblade grew out of *both* sides of his hilt. I was wrong — the guy with the twinblade wasn't dead.

Deep-set yellow eyes stared at me through his mask.

I had to defeat him quickly and help Kaur. While Saina's surprise had allowed us to kill so many so fast, the augmentation had already faded, and soon the shock and fear of our enemies would, too.

Only then did I notice the blood on my boots. I must've run through a pool of it while chasing him. Made my boots so slick on the stone. No matter. *Focus*, I told myself.

My enemy wasn't in a hurry to strike me. His posture, twinblade in front and horizontal, seemed defensive. Unfortunately, though I'd enjoyed many mock battles with Kriga during the hundred-day dream, none involved twinblades.

Perhaps I could use Double Blade to pierce his defense. But wasn't that an obvious, beginner move? Surely a Karshan soldier would be practiced in its counters. But what else could I do? Snake Blade?

Why were his eyes watered? Why was his twinblade shaking? Did he fear me? No, he feared what our augmentation had done. He'd witnessed Kaur scythe half his comrades. I'd be shaking, too, if I were him.

In fact, I was shaking. The thought of life and death being decided by a poorly timed thrust or a misplaced swipe terrified. And yet, it was him or me.

I jumped off the balls of my feet and extended my lightblade as far as I could. While in the air, I inhaled double the red light, pooled it in my hand, and then surged it onto the blade. I imagined it doubling in size, tripling, ten times what it was, even larger than that monster Kaur had used to kill so many.

It grew. Grew so large and bright, I felt the heat on the tip of my nose. My Double Blade thrust toward my enemy's neck.

He swiped against it with his twinblade, doing a half twirl. Our lights collided. His force overpowered mine, and I stumbled sideways. Managed to land on my feet and raise my lightblade to my belly just as his twinblade raged toward my chest.

I imagined my blade turning to water and surging to block his attack. As his lightblade neared my upper chest, I brought my lightblade higher to defend. It reformed, snaking upward, and met his.

Shadows and rainbows whirled off our impact. I backstepped to put distance between us, but my enemy pursued.

He wasn't hesitating. He wouldn't give me time to breathe.

I parried a riposte from his left blade, then a swipe from his right, and found myself desperately on the backfoot. It was hard to tell which side of his twinblade he'd attack with, and so I had to block around a wide range. Each time he'd hit me, the light in my veins would jitter, losing some of its cohesion, almost disrupting the circuit bringing my lightblade to life. If that happened, my lightblade would disappear, and he'd surely cut me to pieces.

Amid the pumping adrenaline, an idea shot into my mind. I swiped down toward his left thigh. As he positioned his left blade to meet my strike, I snaked my blade toward his hilt.

He twirled his right blade forward and smashed it into my snaking blade. Rainbows lit up the cavern as electricity buzzed around us. My veins quivered from the force, and my lightblade sparked, spattered, and vanished.

I ducked under his wide, horizontal swipe, then sidestepped his diagonal one. I squeezed my hilt and prayed my blade would reform.

His left blade vanished as his right blade doubled in size and snaked toward my neck. It impacted my suddenly regrown light, my chin hot from the bright beam.

I had to use his aggression against him. I had to stop doing the obvious and fight with both my instincts and my mind. Make him commit to attacking with one side of his twinblade, so the other would be dead weight.

I pretended to slip, scraping my blood-slick boots against the ground and feigning a fall. My enemy's yellow eyes widened. He sensed I was on the butcher's block. His right twinblade came for my core, blacklight whirling around the red beam as he thrust it forward.

He didn't realize I was on the balls of my feet. I shifted sideways just in time, and his lunge went past me. With the red light I'd pooled in my hand, I riposted toward his chest and doubled the size of my blade.

It went through his flesh with the ease of a breeze. Blood blew out his mouth. He fell forward with a garbled choke and died.

"Nicely done."

I turned to see Kaur. Half her face was drenched in blood. Ash dotted her hair and combat suit.

"You all right?" I asked.

"Didn't take a hit. What about you?"

I retracted my lightblade. My heart still vibrated in my throat. "I'm good."

No enemies remained standing throughout the cavern. She'd killed them all in the time it took me to kill one.

Saina approached, her face flustered and pained. She held her nose, probably because the scent of blood and ash poisoned the air.

"That augmentation stuff is ludicrous," I said.

"I wasn't sure how much light to use," Saina said, her throat hoarse. "I definitely used *way* too much. I feel like an armada of levships crashed into every bone in my body."

"I'd say you used the perfect amount." I patted her shoulder. "I mean, we happen to be alive, and them not."

"I probably shouldn't augment for the rest of the day." Saina let out a few dry coughs. "My veins almost exploded."

Burnt out veins had plagued plenty of laborers at the camp. You'd never see them again, of course, until the time of their execution. "You'll get better, right?"

Saina nodded. "I just need to cycle some violet light for a few hours. I'll do it as we walk."

A move that powerful ought to have tradeoffs. I hoped we wouldn't need any more augmenting or healing today.

The remnants of the dead were strewn all around us. Char and bile and bodies. A lake of blood pooled where two dead bodies lay. All were masked, but nothing could mask the terror in their bulging eyes. They'd died in fear. Fear of us.

I bent down next to the man I'd just killed. I took off his mask. He looked like any of the men I knew at the camp: brown skin and soft features, except for his big, hook-like nose.

I stuck my hands on his eyeball and pinched his yellow lens off.

"Really? That's so gross," Kaur said. "You're gonna wear something that's all wet from his eyeball gook?"

"Yeah, and you should too. Ever heard of Blinding Blade?"

"I just blink when it's coming. Works every time."

"I'm not as good as you." I stuck the lenses in my eyes. I blinked and blinked until they felt moist and comfortable.

"You look like a fool," Kaur said with a smirk.

"They recognized you. Both of you. We should've all been wearing masks."

"Too late for that." Kaur wiped ash from her hair. "You can do whatever makes you comfortable. I just killed ten people. I think my way works."

I didn't agree. You could always be more careful. But this wasn't the time or place to argue.

Chapter Twenty-One

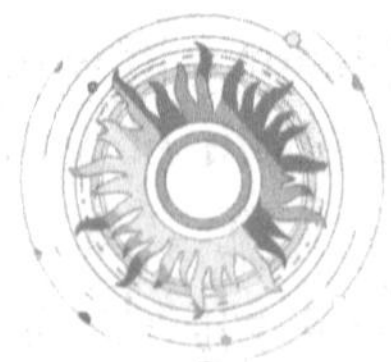

WE WALKED ONWARD TO THE OPENING AT THE FAR END. IT LED TO a relatively constricted hallway with an orangish metal floor and walls. A stench of rust filled the air.

A strange script covered the walls and ceiling: a flowing calligraphy, like vines wrapping around each other. They glowed blue and green, pulsating as if breathing, lighting our way. Sambalpur might've been twenty thousand years old, but parts of it seemed alive. The throbbing light was surely cycling from somewhere, perhaps someone.

Also, it was such an eerily similar place to where the Ghost had taken me, except that room had seemed new, not rusted. I told Kaur and Saina about it as we walked.

"Can't be a coincidence," Saina said.

"I've stopped believing in coincidences, too." Kaur continued to squeeze blood out of her already red hair. I'd been so focused on my own fight that I hadn't even noticed hers. I hadn't heard the screams, nor the cry of her lightblade burning flesh.

"We're missing the thread that ties it all together," I said. "That's the problem."

During the hundred-day dream, I'd spent much time thinking. But I was often so tired from lightblade practice, I hadn't the energy to thread this tapestry of mysteries together. I could only hope the answers would be waiting in the God Tower.

At the end of the hallway, an open door led into a small, constricted cavern, but it was more like a cave you'd imagine bats living in, with nothing man made. Except for a hut-sized cube that sat a few yards away, formed of a mirror-like material. An indentation that resembled a door glowed on the cube's side facing us.

I walked up and touched it. The door hissed open from bottom to top.

Nowhere else to go, so we went inside.

We could see the outside through the glass panels that covered every surface of the cube. And yet, when we were outside, it had been reflective. How strange.

A wire dangled from the ceiling of the cube. Reminded me of the one in our living room in Harska.

Saina pressed both her hands around it and closed her eyes. "I'm not getting anything. This isn't like the wire in the Temple. From what I can tell, you have to conduct green light to activate it."

"Only one of us has a green stone," Kaur said. "Half a green stone, that is. Care to give it a try?"

"Sure." I pulled out my red-green stone from my utility pocket, unzipped my front, and swapped my crystals.

The air tinted both red and green, in alternating waves. Somewhat distracting — it would probably take a little while to get used to. But neither tint glowed as intensely as when wearing a pure green or red stone. The tradeoff of this two-colored stone now lay apparent: I could use two sets of abilities, but neither at full power.

I grabbed the wire dangling from the ceiling and shut my eyes.

An unreadable interface appeared in my mind's eye. The script was similar to the one on the wall in the hallway, except the letters weren't connected, and other lines intersected the letters. Strange.

"I can't read the script," I said upon opening my eyes. "Anyone speak… *Ancientese?*"

Saina scratched the mole above her lip. Kaur blew blood out of her nose.

I closed my eyes again. I could select one of three commands. Too bad I had no way of knowing what they did. Maybe one of them would take us to the Tower. And maybe another would self-destruct the cube. I imagined it going *boom* with us inside.

Rapid footsteps sounded from outside.

Kaur fell to the floor and stuck her ear against the metal. "At least eight. We're cornered here. Do something, Jyosh!"

"All right!"

Three choices. Well, I was one among three siblings. Kediri was the oldest, Chaya sat in the middle, and then there was me, the baby. Ugh. This was the most foolish logic I'd ever used to make a choice. I picked the third command, then opened my eyes.

The cube hissed. A stream of soldiers poured in from the opening we'd come from earlier. They ran toward us, lightblades brandished, just as the cube descended with a glassy hum.

They watched as we moved straight downward, out of view.

"Uh oh," I said. "That might've not been the right choice."

"Better than being cornered." Kaur got to her feet and let out a relieved sigh.

"I'm okay with going down," Saina said. "It's where the gods were heading, after all."

Outside the glass panels, a black expanse stretched in all

directions. I squinted and noticed stalactites jutting out of a cave wall, far in the distance. How hollow was this city?

Saina went to each side as the cube descended, pushing her face against the glass.

Everyone was looking to the sides, but no one had looked down. When I did, I couldn't see the ground.

I gulped. "Looks like a long way."

"Good," Kaur said. "I could use a sit."

"Same," Saina added.

We all sat, our backs against the glass, me in the middle. We stared out the glass wall across from us in silence. An endless, groaning black stared back.

"I could really go for a warm shower." Kaur hugged her thighs. "With the pressure of a waterfall."

"I haven't had a warm shower since I was twelve," I said. "Although, that hot spring was lovely."

"Oh yeah. You and Ava were all steamy in there when I showed up."

Saina looked at me with a raised eyebrow.

"Not true. There was no steam. No steam whatsoever. Do you always have to exaggerate things?"

"Yup. A wise guru once said, 'exaggeration is like cinnamon. It's good with everything.'"

Now Saina raised both her eyebrows. "Which wise guru was that?"

"Uhh, I forgot her name." Kaur got slightly flush and scratched her cheek. "But come on. You know it's true."

I shook my head. "I think there's an even deeper beauty to understatement."

"Yeah?" Kaur scoffed. "Try telling Zauri when you finally see her that she's looking *so* mild, like Saina's boiled potatoes. You won't be getting any deeper into her pants, that's for sure."

The cube landed with a hiss and rumble.

"Speaking of deeper, we're here sooner than I thought," Saina said. "Wherever *here* is."

I got up, took a shaky breath, and rubbed my finger on the door. It hissed open. Cold cave air blew inside our cube, hitting the wall and blowing back into me a second time. I rubbed my arms and shivered.

Worse, there were no glowing eyeballs or softly pulsating calligraphy to guide our way. Just utter darkness.

Kaur took out her hilt and raised it above her head. A small ball of red light bulged off the end, where a lightblade would be.

Her light flickered a bit. "I pooled enough red light in my body for an hour of this, but I bet I could go maybe two hours. The Ghost's gift in my chest seems to help with storing light, too."

I'd forgotten to try and pool any light. As we descended in the cube, the alternating green and red tint had thinned into nothing, though I hadn't noticed it happening.

I pulled out my hilt and tried to make a lightblade. Sparks flew off the edge. I imagined Kediri standing in the darkness, grinning at me. Still, nothing but sputters.

There was simply no light to inhale.

"Maybe it's a good thing," Saina said. "If we can't make blades, our enemies can't, either."

"Yup." Kaur stepped into the dark. "I've kept the Tower's orientation in my mind. It's this way."

"How'll we know once we're underneath it?" I asked.

"I'm keeping track of the distance traveled, too," Kaur said. "Turns out, that wilderness survival class I took at the academy came in handy. Only signed up because the professor had such nice thighs. Guess I should always follow my instincts."

She led while Saina and I stayed a few paces behind. Saina's breathing remained hurried. Sometimes, she'd even gasp for air.

"You doing okay?" I asked.

"Sure, aside from feeling like I was trampled by a horde of elephants. The worst of it is how tight my chest is. But it's nothing some violet light can't soothe."

"What was that move you did to augment us called, anyway? Kaur told you to do 'the thing,' but that's not a very handy reference."

"It doesn't have a name. It was just me cycling a whole bunch of blue light into you guys."

"But lightblade moves have names, so why shouldn't it? How about… Supercharge?"

Saina rolled her eyes. "Too juvenile."

"Lightscream."

She winced. "Too scary."

"Blue Flood."

"A flood destroyed a city I was working in last year. So no."

Was I really so bad at naming things? I scratched my stubble-covered cheek. "Blue Bath."

"What are we, at the spa? Not appropriate at all."

"I'm going to figure out a name."

Saina smirked. "And I'm going to reject it." She stopped and went wide-eyed.

"What's wrong?"

She grabbed her collar, arm shaking. "I feel something. Nearby." Her eyes bulged. "A frequency."

"Whose is it?"

Saina shut her eyes, lids twitching. "Its… the frequency is like a deep sapphire… wisps of it are reaching. Calling out. Could it be… another Avatar? Is it another one of your emanations, Mitra?"

Saina turned and walked into the darkness.

"Saina?" I called. "Where are you going?"

No answer. Kaur and I exchanged a concerned glance. We had no choice but to follow.

After a few steps through the dark, something appeared ahead.

Whatever it was, it towered. It gleamed metallic even in the dim glow of Kaur's lightblade. Saina stood right in front of it. Without hesitation, she brushed her hand against its surface.

That script of vine-like blue lines erupted across it, up and outward. It curved in toward the top, revealing the shape of the massive structure: an egg.

A golden egg covered in azure script that stretched five stories high and half as wide. Like on the walls in the hallway, the script seemed to throb with the cadence of human breaths. Peaceful, deep breaths of slumber.

"What in high heaven is this?" I asked with my mouth wide open, wondering once again if I were still dreaming.

The script flickered, going dark, then erupted again and lit up in an unmistakable pattern: a sky serpent. No, an azure dragon. *The* azure dragon.

"You see that?" I asked.

Saina nodded. The blue glow of the script cast her usual rosy face in a somber hue. She rested her cheek against the smoothness of the egg, as if trying to hear its heartbeat. "This is where the Avatar of Sambalpur dreams."

"Did Behesh also have an egg like this?"

"Yes, but it wasn't buried in the ground. In any case, it was the heart of that floating island, just as this is the heart of this one."

"Can you connect with this avatar through it?"

Saina bit her lip. "I hope so, but it's not as simple as knocking on the door. The Avatar of Sambalpur, just like the Avatar of Behesh, is dreaming."

"You mean he's asleep?"

"He can manifest in our dreams."

"Like the Ghost, you mean?"

"No. Nothing like that. If the Avatar of Sambalpur had blessed us with his presence, we would become immersed in his love. And our hearts would yearn to love him in return."

I rubbed my finger over the script on the egg's surface. Ripples appeared where I touched, as if I were poking a pond. But it was as solid and smooth as any metal. I knocked on the surface and could barely hear the *thud* that fed back, meaning the shell must've been thick. Not that I wanted to break it or anything.

"So… what are we to do, then?" I asked.

"I would stay here and pray. The Avatar of Sambalpur will surely hear me, as we're literally at the gate of his heart."

"But it's not safe with Karshan soldiers around."

"If the Avatar is on our side, what they do won't matter. Although, he might not be aware of what's going on in the real world. That's why Daughters of the Dawn like myself are so important. We serve as a bridge."

"And what about Mitra? What about the divine dragon that stopped time for me? What's its connection to all this?"

Saina hesitated, then said, "I don't know. All I do know is that the Avatar of Sambalpur and the Avatar of Behesh are both emanations of Mitra. If Mitra acted to save you, perhaps it was at the behest of one of his avatars."

That was bewildering. I scratched my head and struggled to make sense of it.

Meanwhile, Kaur was looking the other way, oddly uninterested in this immense finding, obviously more worried about whatever lurked in the darkness beyond. I suppose someone who'd ascended into the second heaven must've beheld even greater wonders than this giant golden egg.

I sniffed something dank and metallic. Coming from beneath. I knelt and rubbed my hands on the ground the egg was sitting upon, some of which extended toward where I was standing. Smooth and black. Almost like obsidian.

That was when I noticed the egg wasn't *actually* sitting on it. It was hovering a few inches above this shiny, obsidian-like floor. Astounding.

I knocked on the floor. The sound that reverberated back betrayed a hollowness.

"There's more layers beneath here," I said to myself. "We're only scratching the surface."

"I hear something." Kaur stuck her ear out. "Come here, both of you. Now."

Saina rested her forehead against the egg and embraced it, an outline of blue glow tracing her body.

"We'll come back, Saina," I said. "Danger may be lurking."

She turned toward me, an anxious acceptance on her face. We went to Kaur and followed her into the darkness.

Suddenly, Kaur dropped to the floor and put her ear on the cold, rough ground. Had she learned this skill from the professor with nice thighs? "Someone's here, right in front of us. One person."

Kaur formed a weak, flickering red lightblade and held it forward. Footsteps sounded, calm and soft. A man with a shaved head and yellow and purple irises walked toward the ruddy glow of the blade. He wore a black combat suit today instead of his usual princely gold-trimmed sherwani.

"Kaur," Elam said, a bright smile on his face. "And Jyosh and Saina. Welcome to the Deep Layer."

Saina pushed closer to me and took my arm. Kaur raised her lightblade above her head at a horizontal angle, obviously trying to see Elam better.

"Elam?" she said. "What're you doing down here?"

"Guru Granek liked to meditate in the dark. He used to say we all get too much sun. He also used to say that long ago, even before the Ancients, the sun moved around in the sky. During that epoch, everyone got a taste of both day and night, darkness and light."

Sounded crazy. How could something as large and powerful as the sun move?

"You couldn't have just been sitting here, waiting for us." Kaur shook her head. "Not unless you knew we were coming."

"I did know." Elam unzipped the front of his combat suit. A golden crystal glowed in his chest slot, above his bulging pectorals.

Kaur gasped. "Since when are you a spectrum mapper?"

"Come now, Kaur." Elam *tsk-tsk-tsked*. "I never could get over my phobia of reentering dreams, but you *can* learn skills outside of dreams. Can't say I'm the best mapper, but it was easy enough to track you. Since your little injury, I've known every movement you've made — except for that dreary day in the cloud, of course."

"Little injury? That what you're calling it?" Kaur seethed. "You stabbed me in the back! I needed to have my spine reconstructed!"

"You would've murdered the Commander! You betrayed us. I could've killed you if I wanted, but I kept my demonblade from cutting too deep." He gestured his chin toward Saina. "I even waited for the Beheshian to finish your healing and made sure you weren't on her ship when I commandeered it. All to give you a second chance. And here it is — join us again, Kaur. Leave your doubts in the dark."

"Stop calling me by my name. I'm your—"

"You were when it was easy. But after the *miracle* — let's be honest — you didn't know what to do with me. All of a sudden, I was in a place that was nothing like where I'd come from. No longer did I set the pace of the tide, but had to bob along to its violent desires. No longer could I control the world — it dictated its demands to me." Elam's voice quavered. "I was terrified. And what did you do? You gave me to the Red Veil!"

"Why don't you ask Rao about that decision? He's the one who convinced me to go along with it!"

"If you care for me, then prove it. Come with me to the Commander. Beg his forgiveness. Serve the cause, like you swore to."

Saina tugged my arm. "Look around," she said into my ear.

I'd been so transfixed by their conversation, I hadn't noticed that the darkness everywhere was moving. Creeping toward us.

"It's not just you, is it, Elam?" I asked.

Black-clad soldiers appeared out of the dark. Scores of them surrounded us on all sides. No lightblades, though.

"I know your claws still work. Darkness is no barrier for the Primal Star, after all," Elam said to Kaur. "But it's the same for my demonblades. Don't resist. Don't make this messy."

"The truth is, I could've walked away," Kaur said in a hushed tone. "Started again on some floating island, far from these wars. Majapahit's got great weather, year-round, I hear." Tears glistened on her eyes and leaked onto her reddened cheeks. "But I won't turn my back on you, Elam. No matter what you do. You're everything to me."

"I'm almost touched," he said. "But I'm afraid I've had to armor my heart since coming to this world. Words just bounce off and fall away. Only deeds can break through."

"I'll do whatever I have to." Kaur wiped her eyes with her wrist. "Take me to Rao. I'll hear what he has to say."

Elam looked upon his mother with bright eyes of hope. And then that hope melted into disdain as a scowl spread across his face.

"You know what I think?" He snickered. "I think you're tricking me. You're going to try to stab him, again. And if you do, then I'll have to stab you. But it's a chance I'll have to take. The

Commander told me a secret earlier, one that might convince you that he's been right, all along. That this world of suffering into which you dragged me needs to end."

Kaur darted her head around as if she heard something. "What's that?"

Elam pointed up just as the *whirr* of a spinning sunsink sounded from above. We all stared as a levship descended from the darkness.

The blocky thing sported an emblem: a blue shield with a golden dragon in the center. So, it was *the* levship. How the hell had they flown it into the Deep Layer? No matter — I wanted to reach out and grab it. My dream crystal was in there. Zauri was in there. I was closer than I'd ever been to getting her back.

The levship stilled in the air, about a hundred feet above us. Saina and Kaur looked upon it with open mouths, shocked to silence by its sudden appearance.

"Are we getting in that thing?" I asked, hope surging through my veins.

"Obviously." Elam waved at the levship. "No more dallying in the dark. The God Tower awaits."

Chapter Twenty-Two

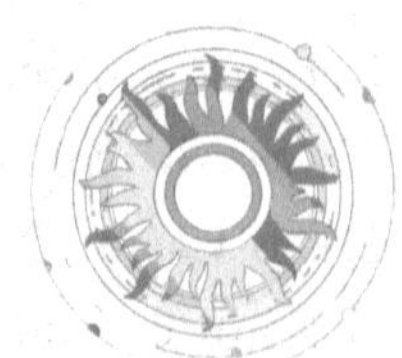

WITH A RUMBLE, THE BLOCKY LEVSHIP LANDED ON THE GROUND of the massive cavern. The boarding ramp extending out and downward was the most hopeful sight in days. What I'd wanted had come to me, met me halfway. But how could this ship be here?

"There's no light down here," I said to Elam. "How can you fly that thing?"

"A few experimental modifications are aiding in that. Of course, I can't talk about it. TEX Company wouldn't be very pleased if I did." He gestured toward the ramp. "Now, let's be off."

What could it be? Perhaps they were able to store a lot of light? But I knew, as a machinist, how difficult it was to store green light in your body. And to store enough to fly a ship? Seemed impossible.

"Let me stay, please," Saina begged, her throat hoarse and eyes wet. After twenty years, she'd finally felt a piece of her god again. Of course she wouldn't want to leave. How would I feel if that were Zauri, reaching out for me?

"You can't stay, my dear." Elam shook his head. "Out of you three lost lambs, you're the one I can't afford to sacrifice."

Saina clung to my arm. She whispered in my ear, "Should I refuse to regenerate Rao's hand? Might be our only leverage. I have to get back here, no matter what."

How was I supposed to answer that? The Ghost had said to prevent her from regrowing Rao's hand, but what if they harmed her for refusing?

"Don't know," I whispered. "Do whatever you can. Maybe get him to agree to let us go, in exchange, like you did for your colleagues."

"Whispering to each other like a bunch of schoolgirls," Elam said, wide-eyed. "Do spill your secrets."

Saina let go of my arm and backed away. Kaur turned to look at us, then walked up the ramp, Elam behind her. Was that defeat, sunken in her emerald eyes? No, it was something more layered: a deep, tortured determination. She really was going to try to kill Rao, even if it meant her death.

The soldiers that had surrounded us motioned for Saina and me to board. What was I waiting for? I had to get my dream stone!

I stepped onto the ramp, walked up, and entered the mouth of the ship.

It looked nothing like I remembered. A somber glow filled the interior, coming from incandescent bulbs fixed to the ceiling. Gone were the white curtains that had separated us patients, replaced by boxes filled with silvery hilts, red combat stones, and black combat suits. Fabric bags overstuffed with cereal bars and water thermoses were spread around, too. They must've been using this ship to haul supplies.

I whispered to Saina, "Where's my dream stone?"

She gestured her chin at a door on the far side, next to a winding staircase that led to the second level. "The belongings of both patients and staff were kept in there. Your stuff is on the bottom shelf, all the way in the left corner."

"Move along!" the soldier behind us barked. Only then did I notice the black baton in his hand. Could it electrify? Unlikely, given the weakness of the light in here. I couldn't see a green or red tint in the air.

Kaur followed Elam up the winding staircase, as did Saina and a number of masked soldiers. Then two soldiers stood in front of the staircase, forming a wall so I couldn't follow. One of them pointed to a nearby door. It was a few doors down from the storage room with my dream stone.

A soldier opened the nearby door. He took my sword hilt out of the holster on my utility belt. He stuck his hands in my utility pockets, taking my red combat stone, but leaving Ava's dream stone.

"What you got in your chest?" he asked.

I unzipped and showed him my red-green stone.

"What's that?" He scratched his neck. "A custom job?"

I nodded, not wanting to explain.

"Hand it over."

I pulled out my stone, enduring the usual jolt, and handed it to him.

He dropped everything he'd taken into a black sack.

Finally, he gestured for me to enter the room. It was literally a closet, filled with mops and vats of liquid probably containing cleaning solution. Once I stepped in, they shut the door, leaving me in darkness.

Zauri was so close, I could feel her tug on my heart. I yearned to get my dream stone and go to sleep, even if just for a minute, so I could see her and let her know I was okay. Relieve her suffering, and mine.

A few minutes later, the levship shook and lifted. My stomach turned. The acrid stench of cleaning fluid that pervaded this closet didn't help. I wanted to throw up the cereal bar I'd eaten for breakfast. I sat against the cold metal wall and allowed my insides to settle. I could feel the sunsink churning light, somewhere below me. What ought I to do?

Be patient and wait, of course. While Kaur and Saina had some leverage here, I was just a tacked-on addition.

We'd been flying for about fifteen minutes when I heard a knock on the door. Elam entered, bringing the somber glow from the hallway bulbs into my dark closet.

He looked down on me with a kindly smile. "Can I get you anything?"

I only wanted one thing. Was this my chance to get it? Or would telling Elam about my dream stone make things worse? What if he took it away and used it against me? Surely, I couldn't trust him.

"I'm fine," I said.

He stepped into the closet and stood over me. "Move over a bit, would you?"

I glared at him. "Why?"

"So I can sit."

I shimmied to the side, making a spot for him between myself and a vat of cleaning fluid.

"*Ah.*" He sat, his legs crossed and back straight. "Do you know why I put you in here?"

Didn't realize there was a particular reason. I shook my head.

"I put you in here because it's a nice, dark little space. I find peace in the dark. When we met on the mountain, I felt you were a kindred spirit, of sorts."

I hadn't felt the same, at all. I'd found him somewhat frightening, though I hadn't known who he was at the time.

Elam massaged one of his thick eyebrows. Only now did I notice the stray, red strands in his brows, and the red follicles budding from his shaved head. In a way, he looked like Kaur, down to the cinnamon shade of his skin. Only, he was so much more muscular and taller.

I wanted to see how he dealt with honesty. "Why would you think we're anything alike? I happen to feel remorse for the people I killed. Don't think I've forgotten what you did to my friend."

"I am only as bad as this world. In a way, I'm its perfect reflection, because I'm not from here. Hah! Who else has that claim to fame?"

"I don't understand how that justifies killing an innocent man."

"Because I am what the Red Veil made me."

I could understand becoming what circumstances demanded. For a time, I'd become what the camp had made me. And then I broke down, so totally I even lost memories. Lost my sense of self. There was still a disconnect between who I had been and who I was now, as if they were two land masses joined together by a tattered rope.

"You can always choose to be better." But only if you were free.

"Oh, I have," Elam said. "The guidance of the gurus has changed my life. I understand my place, now. My purpose. I am a man who comes closer to peace each day."

"What kind of guru preaches the remorseless murder of good people?"

"The greatest guru of them all — the one who understands that deeds matter, too. It's not just about good thoughts and good words. To end suffering, we must take things into our own hands, even if — temporarily — we create a great deal of suffering. And my father understands that, best of all."

"What?" I snickered from the absurdity of it. "Is Rao a guru, now? Here I thought he was a colonel in the Karshan army."

"He is both, and so much more."

"Tell me, then, because I've been wondering — why does he want to end the world?"

My stomach churned as the ship changed direction. I rubbed it to settle it.

"Jyosh, my dear man. You've completely misunderstood everything. You've been misled about our intentions, all along. We aren't trying to end the world. We're trying to end *this* world."

"I don't get it. What's the difference?"

"Behind all your doubts, regrets, and weakness, I know you're an intelligent, thoughtful, and perceptive man. That's why I'm here, talking to you. Our cause needs all the help it can get. We're not the evil ones. It's the gods who are evil. It's the gods who trapped us here, in this dream of suffering, with the pain setting on maximum. They divided us into dark and light, and created this dreaded cycle of death and rebirth."

"Ridiculous."

"Not so." He paused to take a breath. "Tell me, do you know what *nirvana* is?"

"You asked me that already, on the mountain, remember?" I shook my head. "Even back then, your answer made no sense, just like everything you've said so far."

"Oh yes. You've a good memory." Elam chuckled from his belly. "Let me put it in simpler terms — nirvana is an end to suffering. And once we end this world, we're all going to wake up in a much better place, just how we wake up from dreams. We will all have attained nirvana. The dreaded cycles and epochs that have plagued us — this whole machine that we exist in — will have finally dissolved. We'll have broken the wheel, and we will all rejoice in bliss, together as one, united and whole within the Asha, the ultimate reality."

So he was seeking to wake up in Paradise. But how could he be so certain of it? "What evidence have you of this?"

Elam pointed to himself. "Do I need to say more? See, you've got it all backwards, Jyosh. I didn't just come from a dream. I came into one."

"Just because you came from a dream, doesn't mean we all do."

"Yes it does, my dear friend. The fact that I'm here now doesn't mean I'm real — it means you and everyone are *not* real. And I know you know it in your bones. I can see it written on your face. The evidence is everywhere, and you've beheld it. You know I'm speaking the truth."

What he was saying made no sense. And yet… I'd always felt that dream people were real. But perhaps I'd had it wrong. Perhaps they didn't feel real because they were like us, but because we were like them. But if this whole world was a dream, then who was dreaming it?

"I think you're just twisted, Elam." I gazed away to hide the doubts he'd planted within me. "I'm sorry. But if you think I'm going to agree with you, you've misread me entirely."

He let out a thoughtful sigh. "Waking up is never easy. My mother refuses to open her eyes. She thinks we're just a bunch of fanatics. The miracle was hers to behold, but her heart is harder than," he knocked on the metal wall. "That's the problem with her. For all her strengths, she possesses the greatest weakness — hypocrisy."

"Hypocrisy? That's a harsh thing to say about your mother. Mine would've slapped me with her firmest slipper for such a slight."

The ship slowed, once again turning my stomach. Were we approaching our destination?

"I'm afraid it's the truth. But you're right — I have been harsh on her. She gave me to the Red Veil to protect me. I understand as much. Believe me, I do, and I sympathize with her. In fact, it was my father's idea. She just went along with it."

"Then why do you hate her and idolize him?"

"Because a mother is supposed to be tender. Is supposed to cling onto her baby for dear life. Not hand me over to Zodar, of all the cursed wretches in this world."

"Zodar?"

"The head of the Red Veil, and the most powerful man in the Dayworld. He's the only one they told about where I'd come from. He'd helped my father hide a few secrets and even helped him out of a dangerous situation, so he trusted him. If I could send Zodar straight to hell, at the cost of my eternal soul, I would. That's how much of a vile creature he is." Elam let out a tense breath. "He almost turned me into a monster. Almost. There was a time when the demonblades controlled me. When Raska whispered *'kill kill kill'* in my ear. Now, I am the master. I use my demonblades toward one, divine purpose. I'll never serve someone's avarice ever again."

I understood that hatred. But it seemed unfair for him to blame his mother and let his father completely off the hook. I wasn't interested in getting in the middle of their family feud, though. And — I suspected — Elam still felt that thirst to kill but was now using his beliefs to justify it.

"Join us, Jyosh," Elam said. Why did he sound so desperate for a convert? "You know, perhaps it's too early to invite you over. I'd like you to meet my father. He's so much more eloquent than I am. He'll make you see."

"If I refuse, what'll you do to me?"

"Nothing. Nothing at all. Do you think we'd kill you? Only if you get in the way. But if you'd like to live out your years, in peace, there are no hard feelings." Our eyes met. His yellow and purple irises seemed so penetrating. I darted my gaze away.

Elam wagged his finger at me. "Come to think of it, why are you even here? I'm so washed by thoughts of destiny that I sometimes forget people like you have far more pragmatic motives."

"I'm just here to help Kaur and Saina," I lied.

"Hmm. Is that so?" He stared at me in silence for a few tense seconds. "Speaking of Saina, would you rather wait with her in her far more comfortable accommodation? I think you've had enough of darkness."

I nodded. "Yeah, sure. Also, I'd like to ask a favor."

"Of course. I know I haven't been a very good one so far, but I am your host, and will oblige you anything within reason."

He sounded sincere. And I was a good judge of tone.

"As you know, I used to be a patient on this ship. Some of my belongings are in the storage room. I'd like to retrieve them."

"Absolutely," Elam said. "We didn't bother putting anything in that room. We just sort of threw stuff around everywhere. Come along, I'll take you to it."

Elam stood. I followed, my heart suddenly pounding. I didn't want to show him how much this meant to me, but I couldn't control my jitters. I rubbed my arms, pretending to be cold.

We walked into the hall, took a few more steps, and now stood in front of the storage room. Elam touched the door, and it slid open.

I stopped myself from darting inside. Instead, I lazily walked in, continuing to rub my arms to stop the jitters.

"It is a bit chilly in here, isn't it?" Elam said. "It's warmer in the Tower, thankfully." He gestured toward the series of shelves. "Well, are your things here?"

Two metal skyboards sporting the TEX logo were sprawled on the floor. I stepped over them and looked at the bottom left shelf. A frying pan sat there. On top of the pan was my sack. I bent down and pulled the string to open it, then rummaged through. Cans of dried lentils and rice, an empty water bottle, and… where was it? Where was my dream stone?

I pushed the sack to the side. A pair of dark blue, standard camp-issue pants and shirt were squashed between the sack and the wall. I grabbed them, then stuck a hand in the left pocket of the pants. Nothing. I stuck a hand in the right pocket and grasped something small and hard.

I pulled it out. A green machinist crystal shone in my hand. I glared at it in horror. I wanted to throw it against the wall and rip every hair off my body. Where the hell was my dream crystal? Where was Zauri?

I put it to the side, then stuck a hand in the right pant pocket again. My hand brushed something hard and many-sided. I pulled it out.

The orange of the dream crystal was dull. The lines within were cut just how I remembered, the heft and feeling in my hand so familiar. Relief washed over me. I'd gone from total despair, to utter joy and hope, in the span of seconds.

Then I remembered that Elam was standing over me, staring. I looked up to see his studious gaze.

"You look like a man transformed," he said. "Funny how a little orange crystal can do that to people. Give them all the hope in the world. But it too is *maya* — falsehood. Just like everything around us."

I put Zauri's dream crystal in my utility pocket, then stood. "What makes you think the Asha will be so much better than a little orange crystal, or even this world around us?"

"My father has been there. Ironically, he got there by going in the opposite direction — deeper into dreams. He went so deep, he came out on the other side. He awoke in the ultimate truth."

The idea that deeper dreams could lead you to the ultimate truth was disturbing enough, but I had no reason to engage him further. I wanted to check on Saina. Earlier, she'd been so distressed by Elam's arrival. Just when she was about to discover some truth about her god's presence, all this happened. "I'd like to rest, now."

"Of course. You came a long way, didn't you? Fought a lot of battles. Sent quite a few souls to the Nightscape, too." He looked down at the utility pocket where I'd put Zauri's dream stone. "All for a little orange stone." He chuckled. "Come, I'll take you to Saina's room."

I cursed myself for making it so obvious. Elam knew my weakness, now. How badly would he use it to hurt me?

We went back into the hall, up the stairs, and into the first door on the right. Saina was kneeling on a floor cushion, beneath a flickering, somber lightbulb. Tears drenched her face.

"I'll let you two be alone. It won't be long until we arrive, anyhow." Elam turned to leave.

"Why'd you do it?" Saina asked. "Why'd you have to kill Jaysh?"

He paused at the door's threshold. "My dear, you are a woman of faith. Though your people only understand half the truth, you know that his soul will never die."

"What does that matter? What do I care about his soul? He used to make me laugh. He used to take burdens off my shoulders. He used to brighten my day. He was my friend. I don't care what his soul is doing on the dark side of the world. I only care how much better he made my life. And now I can't be eased by his light, not anymore."

Elam let out a tired sigh. "It's only temporary, your suffering. I've lost so many comrades, too. Temporary, temporary, I tell myself, over and over again. We're racing to end it all, believe me. Soon we'll all be joined in the Asha, our souls flowing into each other for eternity. It is our separation from each other, ultimately, that is the cause of all our ills. We're going to end this world of separation, believe me."

He almost sounded remorseful. It was as if he used his beliefs as a balm for his crimes, but even they couldn't soothe the deepest aches.

"You and Rao are nothing but war mongers, in the end," Saina said. "You people always claim to be fighting for something greater. Once you realize it's an empty promise, you'll take whatever you can and bask in it, like everyone else. You'll content yourselves with whatever pleasures you can steal and hoard, to make easy the rest of your miserable lives, forgetting all the suffering you caused."

I'd never seen her lash out like that or express such bitterness. But she was only human.

"Do you want me to say *sorry*?" Elam asked, his back still turned. "I prefer not to create suffering. But sometimes Raska's whispers are too loud. Sometimes she sends poison through my blood, and the antidote is to kill. The demonblades must feast. It is my blessing, and my curse. Another thing to thank Zodar for."

At that, Elam left. Saina bawled and covered her teary face with her arms. I knelt and put an arm around her. It was all the comfort I could give.

And yet, despite her suffering, all I could think was: should I sleep, now? Was there enough time to see Zauri? Or ought I to wait?

Saina rubbed her tears with her palms, smearing them across her face. "Did you find your dream stone?"

I nodded.

"I'm so glad," she said. "You should treasure the people who make you happy. Don't let anything get in the way of seeing them. Not even yourself."

What did she mean by that? If it were up to me, I'd fall asleep this instant and see Zauri. But this wasn't exactly a safe situation to be dreaming.

"Down there, if I'd had more time with the egg, I could've intertwined my frequency, and maybe felt something like what I'd experienced before in the Temple Behesh. I got so close, only to be whisked away again."

So many things weighed on her. If only I were strong enough to carry some of it.

"We'll go back to the egg," I said. "Once we get out of here."

She shook her head. "Absolutely not. I won't risk your life for anything, not even god. From now on, my only purpose is to see you and Kaur safe. I won't put the gods above my friends. Not anymore."

"You think I'd let you go in there, alone?" Now I shook my head. "Absolutely not. We're in this together, to the end."

"Jaysh was the same. He went wherever I went. I dragged him into so many dangers, thinking that if we proved our worth, the Avatar would bless us Beheshians once more. I don't want anyone else to get hurt for that."

"But it's a noble cause. It's what you've lived your life for. I don't want you to abandon your heart's desire."

She chuckled, tears spilling. "Look at us, arguing over what to sacrifice."

"I'm serious. Why did I train for three months in the dream? I want to be safe, sure, but if there's something worth fighting for, I want to fight for it."

Saina pressed her warm hands against my cheeks. "The only thing worth fighting for is each other. The gods are gods for a reason. They can fight for themselves. And if they want to bless us, they can bless us. And if they want to curse us, they can curse us. It's really that simple, isn't it?"

She sounded like she was trying to convince herself, not me.

The ship slowed suddenly, sending Saina into me. Her force pushed me into the wall, the back of my head banging against the metal.

"Oww — shit!" I shouted. I rubbed the throbbing spot in my skull.

"Sorry!" Saina lifted herself off me. Her tears had gotten all over my chest.

"Didn't realize you loved me so much."

Saina let out a teary chuckle. "Never smart to love someone whose heart is taken."

"If only I had a second heart."

With a rumble, the levship touched down. Since this room was windowless, I couldn't say where.

Saina and I stood. A soldier knocked on the door, then entered. He gestured for us to follow him.

As soon as we stepped onto the exit ramp, sunshine hit us through a large opening that was cut out of an entire wall. Its solemn glow warmed my skin, calmed my jitters, and soothed my heart. Such a relief to see brightness again.

Judging from the metal walls, I guessed we were in the God Tower, on the floor with an open wall for levships to land in. Must've been where Elam had flown Saina's levship when he hijacked it. I wasn't sure how we'd gotten from the Deep Layer to here, but I was happy enough to see the red streaks on distant clouds.

Saina and I walked down the ramp and onto the metal floor. In fact, this metal had the same sheen as the one in the hallway in the Deep Layer, which matched the style of the room the Ghost had taken me to in my dream. How did all of this connect?

Kaur stood ahead. About a dozen soldiers separated her from Saina and me, so I couldn't go up and talk to her, despite yearning to know how she was doing.

A soldier approached holding a pair of cloth masks — except, these had no eye slits. "Put 'em on."

"Why?" I asked.

"Commander's orders." He shoved one into my chest, and another into Saina's.

Rao didn't want us to see while in the Tower? Was he hiding something here?

Saina grabbed my arm and leaned into my ear. "They'll probably take me straight to Rao. He's kept his promises, so far. I'll do my best to buy our freedom."

"Okay. Be safe."

But what was Kaur going to do? Would she attempt to kill Rao again? If so, it probably wouldn't matter what Saina and I did. The outcome of her struggle would determine all our fates.

I covered my face with the cloth, uneasy about being in the dark once more.

"Let's go!" Elam ordered.

A soldier took my hand, and I followed along. I was led up a few flights of stairs, across several hallways, making a number of turns, and then strangely enough, down another few flights, and then across more hallways. Wasn't easy to walk without sight; I almost banged into the walls and nearly slipped on the stairs several times. The soldier holding my hand would gently nudge me in the right direction.

After that, we went up the stairs again. We climbed and climbed, until I was heaving.

Was all this meant to confuse us? I just wished it would be over so I could rest my legs.

We crossed another hallway, went down another flight of stairs, and then up one more. It was all too much and my knees ached.

Then I was led into a room.

"You can take the mask off, now," said the soldier who'd been holding my hand.

I slipped it off. The room was about the size of my bedroom in Harska, but had no furniture, just glass walls that brought in the ruddy sun and a metal floor. I looked up at the ceiling: the script of the Ancients covered it, pulsating blue as if breathing.

The soldier stood with his back to me, not a hint of bend in his posture. He was tall and built like a wall, lean muscle bulging against the tightness of his black combat suit. That's when I noticed something that made my heart drop like a lead ball.

He had only one hand.

"It's you," I said. "You're Colonel Rao."

"Who sent you?" His voice emerged from the depths of his belly, solid like iron and impossible to dismiss.

I wished he'd turn around and take his mask off. "No one, sir." Why the hell did I just call him *sir*? Well, he intimidated me by his voice and presence.

"That's what you believe," he said. "But you are mindwritten, just like Kaur."

I recalled Rahal mentioning that term when complaining about the weird happenings in our dreams and his fears that we were being manipulated through them, but I preferred to play ignorant. "Mindwritten? What does that mean?"

"Tell me — in recent memory, have you ever felt a *disconnect* between who you were, and who you are now?"

What he'd just described… it was exactly what I'd felt on the first day I went into my modded dream stone and met Zauri.

"No," I lied. "I have no idea what you mean."

He walked forward and exited the room.

"Wait!" I shouted.

The door closed behind him.

When I went to follow, the metal door wouldn't open, no matter where I touched it. There wasn't even a knob.

"Will someone tell me what's going on?" I said to myself.

I let out the most tired sigh of my life.

My breaths remained heavy from walking so much. I needed rest. But would they let me sleep? Considering I was now alone in a locked room, I had to try. I stuck my hand in my utility pocket and caressed my dream stone.

I ached to see Zauri. Nothing mattered more. I couldn't unzip the front of my combat suit fast enough. I stuck Zauri's dream stone in my chest slot and removed my lenses. Then I lay on the metal floor, facing the glass panel and the bulbous clouds that shone with the red sun's radiance.

Staring at their beauty doused my anxiety. The orange light in my veins pulled me into a river of milk and honey. And finally, I went to see the one I'd come all this way for.

Messages

Carried upon waves of light, messages breeze through the skies above, with Jyosh unaware:

RAO: Does this damn thing even work? Do you read?

ZDR: There you are. I've been sipping wine and worrying.

RAO: Rest your nerves. The plan is back on track.

ZDR: Good. Judging by the spectrum maps, you've got Sylet right where you want him.

RAO: Like I said, that fool was never going to be a problem.

ZDR: What about your hand?

RAO: We just recovered the healer who's going to regrow it. And Kaur has come back, too.

ZDR: What's her state?

RAO: Still doing the Ghost's bidding.

ZDR: Insufferable. That witch.

RAO: She's been planting black boxes and mindwriting at will. Creating false memories and erasing true ones. Turns out another one of my own soldiers has fallen victim. It's clear that no matter what shielding we use on our dream stones, we can't stop her from invading them. Means she's getting more powerful. More skilled with her unique ability.

ZDR: Then proceed with haste. You can't kill what is already dead. We have no way to stop a ghost from floating through whatever walls we put up.

RAO: Give me a few hours. Make sure you're ready on your end.

ZDR: I've pulled every string as taut as I can. Should you succeed, we'll be the ones to dictate how the Dayworld responds to the destabilization of the maya. If it still exists, that is.

RAO: Good. Another thing I'll owe you for, Field Marshal. There is one more development, if your nerves can handle it…

ZDR: Go on. I've got a cellar full of wine.

RAO: I've come upon the Ghost's trump card. The one she's been hiding up her sleeve the whole time. Now that it's uncovered, I think I can turn it against her. It'll be risky, but the upside is enormous. With this power, no one will dare oppose us. It will be so much easier finding the remaining Dreamers.

ZDR: Ah. Care to expand upon the details?

RAO: I'm afraid I don't have the time to get into such a long, frustrating, and sad tale.

ZDR: Then tell me… what happens if you fail to claim this power from her?

RAO: I only got this far by taking risks, some which made me look like a fool, others like a mad man. And yet here I am, on the cusp of our dream. But should I fail in this special case, our plan will be in grave peril.

ZDR: I see. I'll not give it unsolicited, so tell me… are you asking for my advice?

RAO: You're wiser than I ever was.

ZDR: A fruit in hand is better than one in the tree, no matter how delicious it may be. Eliminate the threat.

RAO: I will… think on it. As always, thank you for your counsel, dear friend.

Chapter Twenty-Three

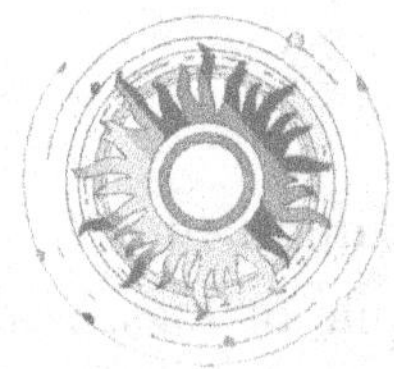

I awoke on the sand. The tide breathed onto the shore, and a zealous sun shone at the horizon. I shielded myself from its glare with my hand, then sat up and rubbed sand off my thighs.

I looked around. Palms swayed in the breeze, laden with drooping coconuts. Jarringly normal. What happened to the bizarre palm trees that grew hands which clutched emeralds?

No bears dancing on sharks hovering in the air, either.

No headless, pale, pot-bellied men riding sea turtle shells.

Was this really my glitched dream stone?

I stood and opened my palm. The terminal didn't appear. I closed and opened it again. Nothing happened.

The hot sand threatened to burn my feet; it exceeded the normal pain setting. I hurried off it and onto the stone path that led to my cottage.

"Zauri," I called. My throat was oddly hoarse.

I cleared it. "Zauri!"

I looked around, hoping to spot her. Nothing but the breeze rustling against the palms and the waves whispering to the sand.

I sensed I was as alone as I'd ever been.

I hurried into the palm forest. The layout of it seemed the same. The cottage must be there, then, in the forest clearing. I followed the pebbly path to it.

A neat pile of logs sat where the cottage had stood. I covered my mouth in shock. Who had deconstructed the cottage? And why? It was a sanctuary for me. Not just since I'd met Zauri, but long before that. The feather mattress, warm ambience, and wooden aroma of the interior were some of the best things in my life.

"Zauri!"

Nothing but an agonizing silence.

I walked around the pile of logs, shaking my head. I couldn't rebuild the cabin without the terminal. Why would someone do this? *Who* would do this?

I opened and closed my left hand in furious desperation, but the terminal wouldn't appear. Without it, I couldn't go to wherever Zauri was. Couldn't do anything except wait.

My heart ached from our prolonged separation. I'd come all this way to see the one person who adored me even though she wasn't supposed to. Or perhaps because she was supposed to, if the black box was feeding her such feelings.

I could be certain of one thing: my longing for her was real. And it was for *her*, not anyone else. That ought to be enough for me, regardless of where her feelings originated.

I fell to my knees and cried. The heavy clouds and the red sun seemed so alien and lifeless, now.

"Zauri," I whispered, tears spilling into my hands. "Where are you?"

How many days had she spent alone, without me? I'd lost count. Half a year? Perhaps, in that time, she'd found a way to move on. A way to live with herself — alone. Or perhaps she'd despaired that I'd ever come back, and so deleted herself, somehow. Or maybe… maybe someone else had used this dream stone, destroyed my cottage, and deleted her.

So many sad possibilities. This was not the dream that I knew. And yet, only a week had passed in real-world time. Because of the hundred-day dream, I'd experienced months without her, just as she'd experienced months without me. But unlike her, I hadn't been alone. I had Kaur and Saina to keep me sane. To help me feel like I existed.

I'd always assumed Zauri would be waiting for me, her arms open. But time, distance, and despair can destroy any bond. Just ask Saina how broken she felt being separated from her god for so long.

I searched the island. Inspected every rock, tree, bush, and stretch of sand. Took me six hours. Six hours in which I clutched a faint hope, as if I were squeezing a fistful of thorns. But I was alone. As alone as any man would be stranded on an island, in the middle of his own world.

I stared up at the sky. What about the floating island? The one that looked just like Harska?

I couldn't see it because of the fat clouds. I had no boat to venture into the water, and no turtle shell or skyboard to climb the sky. Stuck, on this island, alone, without even a bed to cry in.

I returned to the patch of sand where I'd woken up.

"I failed you, Zauri." I let the tide soak my thighs. "You should never have fallen for someone as weak as me. I'm only level three in the Karshan soldier training program. That means I can do Blinding Blade and Double Blade and Snake Blade. But you know what? It was a wasted effort. The forces against me are too powerful. Even Kaur, who is around level forty, can only fight so many enemies before giving up. We're not going to survive Colonel Rao and his fanatic army. It's hopeless, really."

"Don't give up yet," said a calm, good-natured voice from heaven. "If only you knew what I know." I could never forget that voice. How vulnerable it was. I used to find comfort hearing it when I was a boy. "I wish I could show you, Little Brother."

The shadow of a man loomed some distance down the shore. It grew as the one making it walked toward me. He had long, straight raven hair. His stubbly mustache betrayed a boyishness, no matter how much of a man he tried to be. I always found it strange how different his thin eyebrows and almond-shaped eyes were from my own. He approached with his typical lankiness and lazy gait.

"Kediri." I made a fist.

Why was Kediri's shadow program here? Zauri had created him so I'd have an enemy to face, an enemy that would bring my lightblade out of me. And it had worked. But why was he here and Zauri not?

I couldn't form a lightblade because I had no hilt. And I couldn't summon a hilt because the terminal didn't work. Perhaps I could just bash Kediri's head with a big rock. But what if this shadow program knew where Zauri was?

"Kediri… or rather, Kediri's shadow," I said as he stopped in front of me. "Where's Zauri?"

"What? No love for your brother?" The way he squinted when he grinned took me back twelve years. "Come on. Surely you have something to say to me. I know I'm not your actual brother. You could even say I'm an avatar of Kediri, made in his likeness, with his temperament. But is an avatar, an emanation of something else, as real as the form projecting it?"

Who'd put this nonsense in Kediri's program? The real Kediri always flitted between being whimsical and brooding, as if those were his only two settings, but never waxed about reality and avatars like some kind of guru.

"Where is Zauri?" I repeated.

No reason to believe a program would know her whereabouts, but I had to hope.

"If you want, I can pretend to be the real Kediri to help draw out your feelings." He chuckled. "I was joking when I said I was merely an avatar of Kediri." He put his hand to his heart. "It's me, Brother. It's really me. But I'm stuck here, on this island, in this dream. I need your help to get out."

What a bizarre program. And it was getting on my nerves. Maybe Zauri had added lines to his script. Perhaps she was intending to use his shadow to train me some more.

"Hate to tell you this," I said, "but Kediri died. Maybe it wasn't entirely his fault, but did he not realize that, even if he succeeded in defecting, it would be the end of his family? That the Paranis would punish us for his sin?" I snickered. "Of course he knew. It doesn't matter how awful his situation was in the military, he should have thought of his family. If you're Kediri, then tell me — how could someone be so uncaring toward those he loves?"

"I was never uncaring." Kediri pouted and shook his head. "For our family, there was the greater good to consider. The greater good has always mattered the most. It guided Amma and Abba their entire lives. And you know what the greatest good of all is? Tell me, do you know?"

I sighed, sad and worn by talk of our parents. "Can you just tell me where Zauri is? If not, then leave me alone. You can stay on this end of the island — I'll go to the other end. The fact that you're here and Zauri isn't… could it be any more cursed?"

"Everything has a price, Jyosh. The truth has the greatest price of all. Abba and Amma died knowing they'd been sacrificed for it."

All the matter in me boiled. "How dare you say that? You serious? You really *are* like Kediri, aren't you? Abba and Amma were the most wonderful, loving, supportive parents we could've asked for. You betrayed them!"

His smile had a hint of melancholy. "They were, weren't

they? I wasn't even really their son, but they loved me as much as they did you."

Well, now he was just talking nonsense.

"Listen," Kediri said. "You need some encouragement." He opened his palm. A terminal appeared above it.

My cheeks boiled in shock and furor. How the hell could a shadow program summon a terminal, yet I couldn't?

"I'm sending you to her." He tapped on it. "Have fun, Brother. It doesn't matter what's in her or your veins, whether it's light or blood, so long as you love her, and she loves you. But love is like the rain. It drenches you one day and leaves you thirsting for a drop the next. It's not an emotion I'll ever experience again, and for that, I envy you."

My surroundings blinked out of existence. A shimmering light enveloped me, tingling as if fireflies fluttered their wings against my skin.

I rematerialized on a floating island, at the outskirts of a palace. It was the palace that Zauri had shown me in our previous dream together. Its resemblance to Sambalpur's limestone architecture struck me like a punch to the heart. Just as in Sambalpur, gods climbed the spires and pagodas. But unlike Sambalpur, music played from heaven — trumpets and horns and sitars, all together in a symphony of such beauty that I felt the strings of my heart being plucked.

Last time, we couldn't enter because we didn't have the lotus-shaped key. Now the massive golden double door that led within lay wide open, as if a titan had pulled it apart with his bare hands.

I followed the cobblestone road toward the giant door. It was flanked by the most pleasant cypresses; red-tailed squirrels chittered about upon the branches.

Once I walked through the huge doors, a courtyard fit for a

raja greeted me. The aroma of roses and musk was too strong for my liking, and the marble floor too blinding.

In the center loomed a giant stone statue of a serpent-like dragon. Water poured out of its open mouth and into a fountain. Within that fountain were more stone gods, laying about as if enjoying a bath.

Someone was sitting on the stone dragon's head, riding it, a coal-dark cloud behind her. My heart soared with hope.

Whoever it was stood and jumped. Wispy, white wings of light grew off her back, and she glided to my front.

Her wavy, azure locks swayed as she landed. She wore a blue blazer over a white shirt clasped with golden rings. Just seeing her was a balm on my weary soul.

I looked down at her leather sandals, then traced my gaze up her tight, velvety pants. All of her was the most delightful thing I'd ever seen. I wanted to absorb the sight of her, lest she be lost to me. We'd only just reunited, and already I feared we'd be separated.

Finally, I looked into her amber irises. I couldn't tell if she was happy to see me. But the way she stared… it was like she dammed a tidal wave behind her glistening eyes.

"Zauri," I said to break the silence. "I'm so sorry. I left you alone for so long. I missed you so much."

She pushed forward and wrapped her arms around me. Hugged me as if she wanted our bodies to become one.

Her tears warmed my cheeks. I felt like I was thawing after being frozen for a thousand years.

"I'm the one who should be sorry," she said. "My whole presence in your life… it's been a terrible burden."

I rested my nose on her head and took in the smell of her hair. "Don't say that."

"But it's true. The black box… I understand more about it, now."

I didn't want to hear anything sad and complicated. Not here. Not now. "I'll get it removed. Whatever is in that black box, it can't be worse than being apart from you. These past few days… I feared I'd never see you again. The way back to you seemed impossible, literally guarded by armies fighting over a city that appeared out of thin air. But I made it. I'm here."

She pulled out of the embrace. The way she looked at me, tears shimmering on her eyelids: it was like she was saying good-bye, again.

"I feel such love for you, Jyosh." She shut her eyes, but the tears flowed anyway. "But I know that my love isn't real. It's coming from the black box. It exists to make you fall in love with me. My personality, my mannerisms, my appearance — every-thing was tuned for that purpose. To make you love me. And so, the truth is — whatever you feel for me is actually meant to control you."

I took her hands and held them gently. "How can you say that? My feelings burn me every day. If you opened me up, you'd see a charred piece of meat, beating only for you."

A chill wind swept through, making me shudder.

"Think about it, Jyosh. You were alone in that camp for twelve years. You lived in a place where everyone mistrusted each other. Where you could be executed for having the wrong hair-cut. Your dream wife before me… she was a form of physical release, nothing more. Despite being twenty-four years old, you'd never fallen in love until you met me. As for me, I only began to exist the day we met. You were and are my whole world."

"What are you trying to say?"

"What I'm trying to say is… when it comes to experiencing something like love, we're both basically children. Children being manipulated into feeling something for each other."

I shook my head as vigorously as I could. "I'll never accept that." I crushed my sudden tears with my eyelids. "Tell me why, then. Why would someone go to the trouble? How would anyone know what kind of woman I like, anyway? I'm not worth the effort of manipulating. And manipulating to do what? It makes no sense."

Even with tears glistening on her lips, her smile shone so sweet. And yet, it hid her pain like a bandage over a bleeding hole. "You know nothing. Not even the real reason your parents were executed. You were just a child — it's not your fault you believed the lies they told you."

"You were, and still are, just a child, Jyosh." The voice came from my back, boyish and whimsical.

I turned to see Kediri walking toward us. He grinned like the brother I once knew.

"Once the Paranis learned our secret, they felt rightly threatened," he said. "Abba and Amma made sure they didn't suspect you were part of it, so you could go on living. You were their biological child, after all, while Chaya and I were adopted, so it made sense for the Paranis to believe you were normal. By doing everything to shield your truth from the world, from even yourself, they sacrificed themselves for the good of all."

Chaya and Kediri were adopted? If that was true, why hadn't anyone told me? Rage mixed with sadness and confusion in my heart. "And what about Chaya losing her head? What about the twelve years I spent in that camp? What *truth* was worth that?" I turned to Zauri. "Why do you let this shadow roam around on its own, blathering endlessly?"

Zauri sandwiched my hand between hers. "Kediri's shadow… it's also a program from the black box. Its script has grown from a little bud into a whole forest. It was put here for you. So you can hear the truth from the brother you've wrongly hated all this time. It's for him to tell you, not me."

"When you're ready to hear that truth, I'll be here." Kediri climbed into the fountain with a splash and took a seat next to the lounging gods. "Ah, it's nice and cold. Nothing like a bitter chill to wake you up."

Was I ready? And more importantly, did I really want to know?

I kissed Zauri's hand. "Listen. When I wake up, I'm going to do everything I can to get safe. To get out of Sambalpur, out of Maniza, with you. Then I'll never leave you alone again. I'll get the black box removed, and I'll see you every day, as much as I can."

Zauri sulked. "I know you mean everything you say. But I fear, no matter how strong you become, we're fated to be far apart." She looked into my eyes. "As far as two beings can be."

"Oh yeah? Tell me — how will fate stop me from putting this dream stone into my chest and going to sleep?"

"By making sure you outgrow me. At the end of the day, we don't inhabit the same world. It doesn't matter what you feel for me, now. You're fated for something so much greater."

"Stop." I looked away, despite wanting to look at her for the rest of my life. "Stop saying that. 'Decide what you want to believe, and believe in it.' Another lightblade training program said those words to me. I decided, despite everyone telling me how wrong I was, that you're all that mattered. Nothing you say is going to change that." I breathed out a tired sigh. "Let's just go back to how things were when I last saw you. Please. That's all I want. After all I did to get back to you, I deserve at least that, right?"

Kediri splashed in the fountain, drawing my attention. He floated on his side, almost magically, and stared at me. "That's wrong, beloved brother. It's not for you to decide what to believe. Your other lightblade training program was a fool. Objective truths exist, and we must seek them out, no matter into what darkness they may lead. No matter how painful it is to clutch the burning coals of reality. The truth is the truth. Open your eyes, wake up, and gaze upon the fire instead of the shadow."

"Did I ask you?" I clenched my fist. "Everyone tries to sell their version of the truth. Whatever makes them feel good. The Paranis had us believe they were gods. They ruled an entire country that way. So why can't I have my truth, too? Why can't I believe what makes me happy?"

"Because one day the truth will burn us all," Kediri said. "And only those wide awake will see the fire for the fire, and the shade for the shade, and be able to choose their course."

I wanted to douse his head in the water and drown him. Shut this fake philosopher up, forever.

I took a deep breath, then slowly exhaled. I ought to just ignore him.

"Zauri…" She was here. I was here. I could hopefully sleep for a few hours in the real world, which would give me a few days here. Days with her — if only time would slow, starting now. If only we could go into the deepest dream layer and never come out. "Forget everything. All these ideas you have — throw them away." I took her hand and placed it on my heart. "Just forget it all. Let's only think about now. About making the most of our time together."

She smiled tenderly and nodded. "I'd like that. I really would."

"Let's go and do something. Anything. It doesn't matter, as long as we do it together."

"Okay. Let's go train. There's something I want to teach you."

That wasn't what I had in mind. However… it could be fun. Our trainings together had always been exciting. Heart pumping, even. It could be a great way to break through the ice that had grown between us from so much time apart.

"Let's do it, then." I cracked my knuckles. "You'll be stunned by my new moves."

Zauri opened her palm and tapped on her terminal window. The royal surroundings blinked away in a flash of glittery light.

We rematerialized in a flower field. Red, yellow, and purple flowers with the brightest buds reached up to our knees. Too bad my knowledge of trees didn't extend to flowers, so I couldn't name them. Their sweet fragrance reminded me of my mother's garden in Harska. I'd played there, often, with Chaya and Kediri, despite Amma's protestations whenever we trampled upon her flowers.

The bloody sun and maroon sky cast a reddish aura upon Zauri. "Please don't forget… my program, and all these places in this dream — none of it is a coincidence. It was all meant only for you."

"Yeah, I get it. I can face the truth later. For now, can't we just forget?"

"Forget? No matter how much I want to, I can't ignore the black box, Jyosh. I'm an iceberg floating in a sea of oil."

Ugh. This black box stuff was getting on my nerves. Ruining our reunion. How could I make her understand that I didn't want this?

I was about to utter my annoyance, then caught my words before they slipped off my tongue.

How selfish of me. What if I suffered from hidden feelings and knowledge that I couldn't explain? I'd be a mess. In fact, what had happened to me when I first met Zauri was similar. I hadn't known why I wanted to make a lightblade, and I'd forgotten that I'd killed Vir. I couldn't explain my own feelings, and it had disturbed me utterly.

"Zauri…" What could I say? Not understanding your own behavior made trying to connect with others — trying to love others — like trudging through a forest of brambles, except the brambles were your own mind. It was horrible enough not to have control over your circumstances, but imagine not having control over your inner self. "Zauri… I love you, no matter what. Even if…" What was her worst fear? How could I reassure her? "Even if you become something unrecognizable. Even if you hurt me. I'll still love you."

She shook her head. "I don't believe you. There are things so terrible that they don't deserve anyone's love, let alone someone as wonderful as you."

"I'm promising you, right now, that I'll love you no matter what's in the black box. I'll be by your side to fight every battle, no matter the enemy. We'll get through it together."

"But you don't know, you don't know." Her amber irises shrank. She bit her lip, obviously agonized. "I can feel its weight, sense its darkness… but I can't quite put it into words."

Perhaps it was best to get her mind off it? That was why we'd come to this flower field. To focus our minds on our time together, not the dark clouds that loomed.

I opened my palm. The terminal finally appeared. "Weird. It wasn't working earlier."

"Oh, I'd removed terminal privileges for the dreamer, just in case someone other than you used the stone. I restored it once I saw it was you."

Made sense. I summoned a sword hilt.

The hilt materialized in my hand. It sported a stylish, fabric-coated grip. Its guard was oval shaped, and it had a lovely, curved end without any pommel. A hefty thing, too.

I wanted to show Zauri how easily I could make a lightblade, now. All I needed to do was will it to form, like I was stretching my arm.

A lightblade grew off my hilt. It was firm and fiery, with black shadows whirling around it. I didn't even need to think of Kediri. My muscles and nerves and veins had a memory of their own, and now obeyed my commands to cycle the red light.

Zauri covered her mouth. "Unbelievable! It fills me with joy to see how far you've come." She giggled sweetly.

Nothing like laughter to cast the dark clouds away.

"It's all thanks to you. I followed what you taught me. Here, see for yourself." I surged red light into the hilt, straight and pure, my veins boiling slightly. "Double Blade!" Just to be cheesy, I shouted the move's name.

A perfect second blade formed off the end of the first. It cast the flowers around us with a vibrant glow, then flickered out with an electric sizzle.

Zauri gasped. "I can't believe it! That's not an easy move to do, not at all."

And yet, it was merely a level two move.

"See?" I puffed my chest. "To be honest, it was way more fun learning from you than Kriga, my other lightblade trainer. I mean, he was so respectful and disciplined, but it felt like hard work and not like a good time."

She spread her hands out. "You won't even need a hilt for what I'm about to teach you."

What kind of move didn't require a hilt?

Zauri put a hand below her left breast. "I can't actually do the move myself. I can only teach you how to do it."

I imitated her, wondering what I was supposed to feel. "That's weird. How come?"

"Because no one in the Dayworld can do it except you."

Well, that was quite a claim. But it didn't answer my question. "I don't understand. Why would I be the only one?"

"Because you've been blessed."

I chuckled. But Zauri remained serious.

"Blessed? You mean like Kaur with her claws, and Elam with his demonblades?"

"I don't know of whom you speak."

Of course she didn't. I had so much to tell her. I suppose she could just read my memories later. "They're — uhh — interesting people I've met on my journey. Kaur said she prayed at a temple in the second heaven — which is incredible — and that's how she was blessed with her claws."

"You were blessed in a similar way, when you were a baby."

I chuckled again. "Come on, Zauri. You're not serious, are you?" But how would I know? Apparently, my parents had been hiding something. Shadow Kediri was ready to tell me all about it. I just didn't want to face it. "I mean, that's crazy. Crazy."

"You are blessed. But every blessing is a curse, too." Her gaze became heavy. "Jyosh, this is the only thing I have left to teach you. It's the reason I was sent to you. Once you learn this move from me… I'll have no reason to continue existing."

Was the black box telling her that? "Then don't teach it to me. To hell with what the black box wants, and whoever put it there, and whoever blessed me, and whatever the hell is going on. All of it!"

"But it's my purpose. My whole reason for being."

"No it's not! You're not bound by anything except what you decide. That's what it means to be free!"

I regretted my words immediately; she wasn't free. She was caged. She only existed here, in this limited space, whereas I could wake up and roam the wider world.

"You're still a child, Jyosh. That's the truth. And I'm just a thing you'll outgrow. Once you become what you're meant to be, you'll realize how little our feelings for each other ever meant. Just a drop in an ocean."

How could she say something so horrible? And I wasn't a child. Sure, I didn't have any experience with love, but I was old enough to make my own decisions. To be the ruler of my heart, not the other way around.

Zauri said, "I have to teach you, now. If I don't, I'll never forgive myself. I'll never feel complete. So listen to me. I think you're going to get it on the first try. I think it's going to feel as natural as breathing."

"I don't want to."

"You have to. You have to. Please. Feel it, first. Feel the unseen light of the Primal Star. A light that penetrates across entire worlds, across time itself, and even into dreams. Let it bathe you. Let it spread into your core and to every extremity."

"What are you talking about?"

"Look up."

I looked up at the sky. Only the red sun gazed down at us. There was nothing else. No Primal Star. "I don't see or feel anything."

"Now… look at yourself."

I glanced down at my body. What was I supposed to see? "I'm so confused."

"Now close your eyes. Close your eyes."

I closed my eyes. Images flickered on my lids. My mother was there, in the dark. Except I couldn't see her face. Shadows obscured it, as if the sun wouldn't shine there.

She pointed at my neck and whispered. I couldn't make out the words. They were not in any language I understood.

I sprang my eyes open to see Zauri standing in the field of flowers.

"I saw my mother," I said. "What the hell?"

"She's the one who prayed for your blessing. Her decision set everything in motion."

I recalled that vision I saw in the pagoda. The woman praying at the altar… could it have been Amma? And that baby… that was me, wasn't it?

"I don't understand. Why would she do that to me? And never tell me?"

Footsteps on mud sounded behind me. I turned to see Kediri smiling with the warmth of a sultry day.

"I was also blessed," he said. "So was Chaya. We were all supposed to be used for something great and terrible. Panja Parani wanted none of it. When he found out, he ordered the executions of Amma, Abba, myself, and Chaya. But you… he spared you because our family had fought and suffered for his ancestors. In that memory, and believing you to be unblessed, Panja must've felt *mercy* stir in his bitter heart. He told you and everyone we were being punished because I'd defected to the Karshans — it was a lie, Brother."

Kediri held out his hand. A part of me wanted to cut it off and see him scream. And yet, if he spoke truth, then my hatred rested on falsehood, this whole time.

"Take my hand, Brother," he said. "Let me show you the reason why you're here."

Cut off that hand, or hold it?

"How can I believe anything you say?" I asked. "How am I supposed to know all of this isn't just more craziness meant to confound me?"

"You'll know it," Kediri said. "Truth burns unlike anything else."

What the hell did that mean? Could he stop speaking like a philosopher or guru and make some sense?

But it did make sense. Anyone could believe whatever they wanted to. You could fabricate beliefs like parts of a cannon. The Paranis had done that. You could say a stove was hot, but how would you know, for sure, unless you let it burn you?

I took Shadow Kediri's hand. I closed my eyes. Waves of an unseen frequency swam through him and into me. Waves so primordial, they'd been birthed before time and permeated all existence. They drenched my insides. They shot up and pooled at the back of my neck, then swirled and orbited something that had always been there.

Kediri pulled his hand away. "Do the rest yourself, Little Brother."

I inhaled more unseen light and pooled it in the back of my neck. I let it orbit and swirl. It churned. It cried for release.

I made a fist. Unseen light surged into it.

When I opened my fist, I beheld my blessing in the palm of my hand.

Chapter Twenty-Four

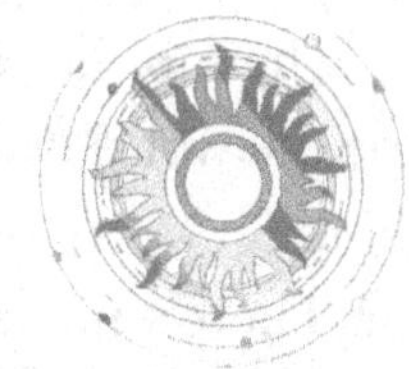

What I held could only be described as a bolt of frozen lightning. It weighed nothing. It didn't burn. It was long, like a spear, and glowed electric and blue. Shadows whirled around it.

I raised it above my head and beheld its wondrous, illuminated form against the backdrop of a dark cloud. What was I supposed to do with it?

"Took you one try," Zauri said, white flower petals drifting across her face with the breeze. "I've done all I can for you, now."

"Throw it, Brother." Kediri smirked. "Let's see how the clouds feel when we fling lightning at *them*."

I aimed at the dark cloud, which hung heavy and low, and threw the frozen lightning bolt like it was a spear. Because it was weightless, it surged into the sky at blinding speed. It hit the cloud, then dragged it along through the sky, creating a vortex. And then it exploded, somewhere near the sun, as if it'd traveled thousands of miles in the span of seconds.

First, a hot flash scathed our eyes. Then the sky churned and whirled and rippled with lightning, like millions of fireworks going off at once. Black smoke billowed, within which raged an electric storm. It spread to engulf half of heaven.

A dark wind hit us with a deafening, whip-like *crack*. Flowers and grass uprooted, their petals gusting against us.

Zauri snapped her fingers, and the world returned to its original calmness.

"Well done." Kediri handed me a sun-colored flower that he'd caught. "You've a long period of reflection ahead. Think on this power. Ask yourself — what are its uses? What are its limitations? How will you reshape the world with it?"

I was too stunned to think.

"Reshape… the world? There's no way I can do this in real life. You can't be serious." I stared at my right hand. Summoning and flinging that frozen bolt had put no tax on my body, whatsoever. Surely I couldn't do it outside of the dream. It must be some kind of special program that only existed here.

Zauri came close and took my hand. She kissed it. Perhaps seeing me succeed had brightened her spirits. "Do it again. But this time, do it on your own."

I closed my eyes. I looked up at the sky. There it was: The Primal Star. It glowed with black light, almost like the sun's shadow. It had been there all along. It had existed before time itself, inside and outside the dream.

I inhaled its light, which permeated all things. It pooled in the back of my neck and orbited something there.

But when I tried to flow the light into my hand, it wouldn't budge.

"You can't do it again, can you?" Zauri asked.

I shook my head. "It won't flow."

"That's because it's not you doing it," she said. "Always remember that. It's called a blessing for a reason. Its uses and limitations are not decided by you, but by the ones who speak to the Primal Star. The ones you call the gods."

Kediri cleared his throat. "What she's trying to say is — there's a timer. It's not a very long one, though. Three hours. Pretty good, if you ask me."

"So I can fling one of those bolts every three hours? Ridiculous."

"Well, that's the thing." Zauri came to my side and held my arm lovingly. "The timer depends on what layer you're in. The deeper you go in the dream, the longer the timer is because of time dilation. Since the timer is three hours here, it would only be seven and a half minutes in real life."

That sounded even more ridiculous. "So back in the waking world, I can fling a bolt every eight minutes? That's just… that's just…" The words evaporated in my mouth.

Kediri put his hand on my shoulder. The hatred for him that had stewed in me for twelve years, that had poisoned and sickened me… it wouldn't just disappear. It still screamed that I was better off strangling him than hearing him talk. And yet, he was entirely innocent. He was my brother. He deserved my love and adoration, even in death. He deserved none of my scorn.

I'd built so much of myself on that hatred. I even conjured my lightblades by them. If that hatred was a lie, then what I'd let myself become was a lie, too. All the wrongs I'd done because I distrusted everyone and everything.

Sure, I'd tried to turn myself around. I'd trusted Zauri and Saina and Kaur. I'd tried to prioritize others over myself, but only because I didn't want to become like Kediri. Even when I tried to be good, it was because I hated him.

Staring at my brother's shadow, I couldn't stop the tears. "I'm sorry, Kediri. I despised you all this time. I cursed you with everything I did. My whole reason for being was to not be deceived by someone like you ever again. To not become like you. But now I realize… no one even mourned you when you died. I'm so sorry. I was allowed to live, so I should've mourned you. I should've clung fondly to our memories together." My legs went weak. I fell onto my knees in the flower bed. "It's wrong that they killed you, but in a way, it's even worse that they made me hate you. They made me hate my own brother! They made me what I am with lies!" I cried out and sobbed.

Kediri knelt and put his arms around me. Zauri knelt, too, and hugged me from behind. I was enveloped in love.

"You didn't know, Jyosh," Kediri said. "You were only a kid. Don't ever hate yourself." He patted my back. "See how much the truth burns?"

My tears burned on my cheeks, surely. "Who created the black box with your program? Who sent you here to tell me this?"

"Someone who cares. My guess is, it's someone who knew Amma and Abba. A family friend. They want you to know who you are. They want you to know about your blessing, so you can change the world, make it better for everyone." He tightened his hug and kissed my wet cheek. "I'm afraid I've told you everything I can. You'll have to discover the rest for yourself, Little Brother."

"If I ever get off this floating island. Get out of Maniza. There are no guarantees."

Kediri pulled away and put his hands on my shoulder. "Listen. Careful with that blessing. You could destroy a city with it. Unfortunately, there's no way to lessen its destructive power — it's a weapon of utter annihilation, nothing less. Worse — the moment you use it, everyone's going to know. You'll become the target for the worst of the worst."

"I figured as much. I definitely won't use it. I can't think of any situation where it would be the right thing to do. But maybe, just the threat of it could be enough. I'll keep my head level, don't worry. Besides, I'm hopeful I can get by with my meagre lightblade skills, for now, so long as I let Kaur take the lead."

Kediri grinned, the hairs of his budding mustache parting.

He chuckled and patted my shoulders, nodding the while. That's how I remembered him, especially during his good moods. True, he'd brood all day sometimes, but when he was laughing and bright, there was nothing so heartwarming.

"Chaya and I loved you," Kediri said. "Till the end. So did Amma and Abba. That's really what I came here to tell you. Don't ever lose sight of that." He smiled at me with the pride of an older brother. "Now, I'm afraid I must go."

"Go where? You're just a script, aren't you?"

"Yeah, but I'm a script whose purpose has been fulfilled. One with a self-delete clause, lest you get attached to a shadow. So… this is it, I'm afraid."

Kediri's body began to whither into the breeze, like flower petals flying. I clung onto his hand, hoping it would keep him there.

"Brother, don't go!"

"See you when you wake up," he said. "Truly wake up." And then, he was gone, petals in the wind.

Once again, I didn't have a body to burn. But I mourned my brother while kneeling in the field of flowers. I let the memories of our childhood together flow through me, without judgment. It was all I could do.

After, Zauri and I went to the beach. We lay in the warm sand, the tide kissing our feet. Her body was the greatest comfort. I kept her in my arms, dreading the thought of her withering like Kediri had.

I finally asked her the awful question, "Are you going to disappear, too?"

"I don't know. I don't know what the black box has written for me."

Until this black box could be deleted, I'd fear losing her. But it didn't seem entirely evil. It was here to teach me and tell me the truth. Whoever had modded my dream stone that day must've been working for this family friend that knew Amma and Abba. If I survived my present predicament, I had to seek them out with whatever clues I could find.

I had to know the full truth. To bathe in the fire and burn.

"What're you thinking?" Zauri nuzzled her nose against my ear.

"The dream invader… I never told you about her."

"Dream invader?"

"Why don't you do that thing where you read my memories? It would be better than explaining."

"The thought of reading your memories makes me nervous, to be honest. More than just nervous… slightly terrified."

"Terrified? Why?"

A stronger wave came and washed over my calves.

Zauri hemmed and hawed. "It's pretty immature. But you mentioned you'd met two women. I'm afraid that, by seeing through your eyes, I'll also see how much I can't compare to someone who shares your world with you."

Was she jealous? No, she wasn't just jealous — she felt inferior. Insecure. "I have no feelings for either of them." That wasn't entirely true. Perhaps I had no romantic feelings, but I certainly had *feelings* that went outside the bounds of friendship. They were both rather attractive, after all, and I'd gone twelve years without seeing a woman in real life. "I have nothing to hide. Go ahead and read my memories."

Why was I sweating? Wait… what about Ava? We were in that hot spring together, and there was a moment where I was about to go near her, wasn't there? And what about the whole *points of contact* thing so Kaur and Saina and I could dream together? Or when I'd wrestled Kaur?

Too late. Zauri's forefinger poked my forehead. My brain felt like it was being sucked through a straw. The light of my memories flowed into her.

"Hmm," she said. "Hmm… uhh…" She sat up and glared at me. "Your hand… I can't believe… I shouldn't have taught you those frying pan techniques. It made you too bold. You were supposed to use that to survive, not be a hero!"

I sat up and dusted myself of sand. "I couldn't just ignore someone suffering before my eyes."

"Why did you… why… why!" She grabbed my shoulders and shook me. "Why didn't you stay on that levship to New Behesh? You had no reason to go to Sambalpur instead!"

"I couldn't leave you, Zauri. What am I without you?"

"You're so short sighted." Tears spilled as she pounded the sand. "You could've literally bought my look-alike in a dream stone store."

"It wouldn't be you, though. It would be some other Zauri." I laughed. Seeing her boiling like that made it all so obvious. "Would that other Zauri care about me like you do? Would she care about my survival over her own? And even if she did love me, would she let me go, the way you're willing to?"

"I can't be the reason you die, Jyosh." Zauri shook her head, tears dropping across her blazer. "You had a chance to get out. You didn't take it. I hate myself for that. I'm not worth your life. You're flesh and blood. I'm only light. Don't you see that?"

"Enough, Zauri. Don't shed another tear, not for that reason. I'm getting out of Sambalpur, alive. I promise." I tried to dry her tears with my hand, but her cheeks were too wet. "It's not been an easy time, but I have no regrets."

At least she didn't seem upset about the other stuff. I suppose I was in the clear. Now there were no secrets between us.

Zauri butted her head into my chest, then wrapped her arms around me. I hugged her back, but she wouldn't stop crying.

I didn't come here to cry or to watch her cry. And yet, if I was to treat Zauri as a real person, how could I pretend only my feelings mattered? My problems? My suffering? Hers were as real. I'd decided to believe that. So if I had to spend all my time comforting her instead of enjoying Paradise, then that was what I'd do.

"I'm stronger now than before." I stroked her dark blue hair. "I'll make it. I have no doubt. You know why? It's all because of you. You gave me a reason to live. A reason to become strong. A reason to fight back. If only you'd understand that, maybe you wouldn't feel so sad. You'd know you're the brightest light in my life."

I couldn't say it better than that, could I? But how many times would I have to say it? When would she understand, if ever?

"I know, Jyosh. But I can't help but feel the way I feel. I can't help but think this is all some twisted tragedy. That the gods are writing this script and laughing at us. It's hard to know the sun is still there, brightening the sky, when all you've seen are clouds for months. But... I'll try to be hopeful."

That was all I wanted. We lay down again. I rested my eyes and mind and enjoyed the press of her body on mine. The sun and her body warmed me into serenity, while the whispering tide kept my feet cool. The plush sand became a perfect bed.

AFTER MANY RESTFUL minutes had passed, Zauri's mood seemed to brighten.

"I know what you're thinking," she said.

"Oh?"

"You're wondering what happened to the cabin, aren't you?"

"Well... what happened to it?"

"I was trying to redesign it. I messed up and broke it. Every time I tried to rebuild it, the terminal wouldn't work. I think only you can do it. Sorry." She chuckled. "I fixed some of the glitches, though."

"Yeah? I kind of miss how it used to be. Especially the flying turtle shells."

"If you want to fly, we can use regular skyboards, now."

"I think I preferred the turtle shells. More surreal, you know?"

"Those headless weirdos are gone, too."

"Weird how much I miss them. Oh, what about the dragon? The one that looked like Mitra. You ever see it again?"

Zauri kept silent. Her expression turned sour.

"Zauri?"

"I did see it. But I think it's meant for you."

"Meant for me? What do you mean?"

"I wish I knew. I mean, all of this is meant for you. As am I."

I scratched my head, a bit bewildered.

Then Zauri laughed. "Sorry. Sometimes, I feel like I've forgotten how to have a conversation. It was so boring without you. Each day felt like a year. I had to busy myself in all sorts of ways. Oh, I managed to get into the floating palace, too. Explored every inch of it."

"What was in there?"

"I'll show you later. There's still one door I can't open."

"A secret door. Just what I need — another mystery."

Zauri took a deep breath. "Speaking of mysteries... the dream invader... the one you call the Ghost... I think she's also the one who sent me to you. Which means she wrote everything that's inside the black box."

That certainly seemed possible. I began putting the pieces together, out loud. "So she's been trying to direct me toward something. First, she sent the dream stone modder to the camp, which is to say, she sent you to me. Then she directed me to go toward Sambalpur. But she probably didn't expect me to lose my dream stone, the way I did. So she visited me in the hundred-day dream, to watch over me, to keep me on track. She helped us out with those gifts. By getting you back, I finally learned the truth about my family, and how to use my blessing." I scratched my head. "But now… what's left? What am I supposed to do?" And did I even want to do it? Couldn't the Ghost have just been upfront and told me everything?

Obviously not. I wouldn't have gone along with it. She'd manipulated me into my present situation, and with incredible skill, too. And someone who manipulates others — even for a good reason — couldn't be trusted.

"It's too much to think about," I said, sighing. "Let's just enjoy ourselves."

Zauri nodded. A sly grin stretched across her face. "Whatever you say, *Master Jyosh.*"

Laughter burst out of me. "I don't mind if you call me that."

"I'm willing to, but only on your birthday."

"I'll take it."

"Can I ask you a question?"

"Remember what I said about asking me if you can ask me a question?"

Zauri chuckled. "Of all the things you've seen, what *really* took your breath away?"

"Uhh…" I scratched my head. "It's a toss up between the daeva and the golden egg, for sure."

"Yeah, that egg was something. Wish I could've been there."

"Maybe I'll ask Kaur what god she prayed to."

"Do you really think that's what made Elam real, or was it just a coincidence?"

"I mean, a dragon stopped time. I saw it with my own eyes. So it could very well be the reason."

"Hmm. Guess you're right."

"Now I have a question for you, since you've seen my memories. If given the choice, would you want to leave this place and go to the real world?"

Zauri tapped her chin. "Scary thought, to be honest. But the thought of being alone forever, without you, is even scarier. So if I had the chance, I absolutely would come with you to your world."

"I get it. But hunger and thirst aren't fun. Neither is getting your hand seared off. Or stubbing your toe."

"I feel pain when you're not here. It might not be physical, but it is pain."

"Physical pain is like… is like…" I struggled to think of an analogy that would make sense to her.

"I know what physical pain is like. I've dreamed your memories, remember?"

"I actually didn't realize you'd *felt* my memories."

"It was a total sensory experience. Even when you sat all naked on that cold chair."

I recalled I was crying at the time, too. I cleared my throat and shuddered. "So even knowing what that's like, and how common pain is, you'd still come with me to the real world?"

"I don't want you to suffer alone. Although, you're not alone, are you?"

I took a moment to consider my answer. "While I trust Kaur and Saina, they both have things they love more than all else. Kaur loves her son and Saina her god. All I have is you, Zauri."

"You're all I have, too. But I can't be everything for you. You'll need others in your life. Strong companions, to help you."

"You don't have to be anything more than what you are. You just have to be you. Nothing I've struggled for has meaning without coming here, back to you, at the end of each day."

By how red her cheeks got, my feelings had finally gotten through to her.

. . .

Zauri and I enjoyed the beach for the rest of the day. We didn't even do anything in particular. In fact, we did nothing at all except laze around and laugh. With the heavy topics aired out, there was nothing left to bother us.

The next day, we went to the beach again to swim. Skyboarded together afterward, too. The joy of the moment as we soared through the clouds only reinforced that we needed nothing but each other.

On the third day, we trained with lightblades on the beach. As I expected, Zauri was the perfect sparring partner. She even told me I was *telegraphing* my moves too much, and that this flaw made it easier for my enemies to figure out what I was planning. For example, if I was pooling light in my hand, she'd notice that I'd grip my hilt harder. That made it obvious that a Double Blade was coming, and so she'd often backstep in time.

If I was planning to Snake Blade, she noticed that I'd look wherever I wanted the blade to bend toward. But how else was I supposed to do it? It was really hard to snake my blade to a position that I wasn't focused on.

"Try this instead," she said while we stood with our feet submerged in sand. "If you want to bend your blade and snake it somewhere, instead of looking directly there, triangulate that position by glancing above or below, and to the right or to the left. It might take half a second longer, but it's a worthwhile tradeoff, I feel."

She really was clever, wasn't she? I would never have thought of that on my own, and even Kriga failed to point out this flaw in my technique.

During our remaining hours of training, I managed to successfully overcome her dodging and defenses, thanks to this spectacular advice.

After six hours of intense sparring, I was barely able to stand. We rested amid the palm trees for a spell. I meditated and flowed violet through my veins for a few hours, letting the rustle of the breeze on the palms soothe me.

When I'd had enough of being soothed, I asked Zauri about the state of my veins.

"You're meditating to increase your capacity, right?" she asked, tapping her chin.

I nodded.

"Good. It's a worthwhile endeavor. Especially since you found a red-green stone. That is, if you ever get it back."

"I fully intend to. But what does my capacity have to do with that?"

"Everything. Imagine if you could flow both red *and* green light through your veins, at the same time. It could help you in so many combat situations."

"How so?" I scratched my head.

"Jyosh, you're a machinist. Isn't it obvious? So many things are machines! Even things you might not realize. If you can find someone who's adept at crafting, I bet you could be more deliberate with this fact. I mean, we crafted a frying pan weapon with parts that were just lying around. Imagine if you could get *proper* parts?"

So just how Kaur liked to wield two lightblades, I could perhaps wield a lightblade *and* an electric weapon, at the same time. Ingenious.

And this would keep open an advancement path different from Kriga and his Karshan Army Officer Training Program. If I got stuck there, I could still move forward in the skill of electric weapons and using machines to get more powerful.

We chatted about it some more. Then Zauri decided we ought to go to the palace, to see the door she couldn't open.

We returned to the courtyard with the elaborate dragon statue, which Zauri had been sitting on, and the fountain where Kediri had swum. We walked past it and through a porcelain door, which was accented with drawings of the gods, with their many heads and mixed animal and human features.

The palace hallway was lit by oil lamps, hanging from the high ceiling by these slender, golden wires. Flower patterns adorned the marble tiles on the floor; the grouting between the tiles was of gold and shimmered in the sunlight shining through the skylights. A breeze swept in through the open hallway windows, bouncing off the walls and cooling my ears.

We went through another porcelain door at the end of the hallway. It opened to a long, narrow bridge surrounded by waterfalls. Except, the water flowed from the open mouths of massive, godlike statues that reminded me of the upside-down statues in the Deep Layer. But the eyes of the statues were all closed, unlike the glowing ones in the Deep Layer.

The bridge across the waterway led to what resembled a tomb, floating in the middle of an enormous pool. The flow of the falling water was so fast and deafening, I couldn't hear our footsteps. It took us three minutes to walk across the bridge, which itself was formed from limestone tile, patterned with drawings of blocky, silver cubes that resembled — to my mind — levships.

Once we arrived at the tomb, what struck me instantly was the door. It was remarkably simple, wooden, and entirely black. The door had no handle or indentation. Seemed it could only be opened from the inside.

"What do you think is in there?" I asked Zauri.

"The truth," she said with a grin. As if I knew what that meant.

"What truth?"

"*The* truth."

I shrugged. "Now you sound like Shadow Kediri."

"I sense a heaviness within it. Something daunting. And given that the door is black…"

I snapped my fingers. "It could be where your black box resides." I always assumed the term *black box* was just figurative. I stroked the stubble on my chin. "If the black box is something physical that we can access, then if we open this door…"

Zauri gazed at the floor and winced. "It's a scary thought for me. To come face-to-face with my hidden reality."

That was when I noticed something: the door *wasn't* entirely black. A drawing had been traced on it in the dimmest gray hue. I loomed closer and squinted; the drawing resembled a sky serpent.

The water in the pools around us gurgled, then surged upward in jets. It drenched our feet and poured onto the tile. The water level rose. I darted my head around. The eyes of the gods had opened, and all stared at us with frightful, glowing balls of sun.

I grabbed Zauri's hand and pulled her into my arms. Everything shook, as if an earthquake had struck the floating island. The water gushed upward into terrifying spires.

"What's happening?" I said, holding her tight.

"I think you're about to wake up."

Oh no. I'd wake up in the God Tower, once more in a dangerous situation. Caught in the grasp of a mighty army. Helpless. Would I survive one more day to see Zauri, again? And if so, where would I be dreaming from?

"Don't die." Zauri clung to me. "I wish I could've trained you more. I wish I could spend all my time teaching you things to help you survive and win. I don't mind waiting weeks or months or years to see you again. I'll never tire of waiting, Jyosh."

"And I'll never stop coming back to you. I promise. I'll survive. I'll get out of the Tower. I'll get somewhere safe. I'll dream with you, again, very soon."

A lake of water dropped out of the sky, landing with the force of a punch to the face. It submerged us. Cold. Shadowy tentacles shot out from the depths and grabbed my arms, as if a deep-sea octopus were pulling me in. Zauri floated at the top and grasped my hand with all her strength. But it wasn't enough. The force of the tentacles broke our handhold, and I watched her call for me — soundlessly in the bubbling water — as I sank into the deep dark.

Chapter Twenty-Five

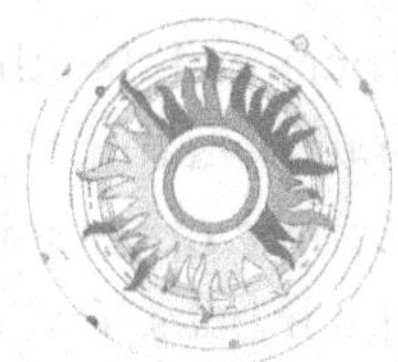

"GET THE HELL UP. COMMANDER WANTS TO SEE YOU."

The deep sea. Drenched. I shot up, shivering, to the sound of mocking laughter. I rubbed my cold, wet arms. A masked soldier stood over me, a dripping bucket in his hands, cackling along with other soldiers in the room.

Surely, there were less discomforting, less humiliating ways to wake me up.

"Commander?" I mouthed, still missing Zauri. Still yearning to reach out and grab her hand and hear whatever she had to say about the divine dragon. But a world separated us, now.

"Yeah, you dipshit. The goddamn Commander. Get the hell up and follow."

"What does he want? I was in the middle of something."

The soldier unholstered his hilt and aimed it at my forehead. A ravenous lightblade shot off it, burning my nose hairs. The heat threatened to boil my eyes, so I pushed against the floor, got to my feet, and backed up against the glass wall.

More laughter. With each chuckle, anger rose in my chest.

"Commander said to treat him well," a soldier near the door

said. "But we could say he tried to force his way out of here…" He cracked his knuckles.

The lightblade-wielding soldier grunted in annoyance. "No. Let's leave him whole, for now. The moment Commander gives the order, I'm gonna carve him up. Nice and slow. Make a steak out of that skinny ass, in memory of the comrades he sent to the Nightscape."

"It wasn't personal," I said. "Your comrades attacked us."

"Oh, I know it wasn't personal. Neither is this. It's called war, brother. You gotta make your own fun."

Laughter. I took stock: three other soldiers stood in the room, all with hilts gleaming on their belts. I was unarmed. Except…

I stared at my right hand. If I desired, I could send every single one of these soldiers into a burning cauldron of death. But I'd engulf myself, my friends, the Tower, and perhaps all of Sambalpur in the destruction.

Despite being so unbelievably powerful, I was as weak as ever. I couldn't afford to make more enemies. I had to focus on surviving so I could dream again.

"All right." I raised my hands in defeat. "Take me to Colonel Rao."

They escorted me out of the room. Like the hallway in the Deep Layer, the hallway here sported that glowing script on the walls, pulsating green and blue. The cadence of the glow reminded me so much of breathing.

Soldiers lined the hallway, too. Many of them were sitting. Some were even sleeping, their heads drooped onto a comrade's shoulder, drool seeping out of the sides of their lips. Some munched on cereal bars, others downed thermoses of water. One woman to my left was polishing a red combat stone with a cloth.

Then there were the injured ones. What looked like light-blade burns scalded the left side of a soldier's bandaged face. Another had wrappings across his torso, a bloody stain blossoming like a rose. A man who must've been a healer crouched beside him, his hand on the injured man's nape.

Had they been injured fighting Sylet's forces?

I followed my minders down the hall, taking in as much of the sights as I could.

A man with too many gray hairs for such a young-looking face caught my eye. He was sitting against the wall, cross-legged, scribbling with a pen onto a notepad. His hands jittered with each letter. I couldn't take my eyes off him. Though he wore the black combat suit of the Karshan army, he wasn't one of them. I knew him. He was from my past life.

"Rahal?"

I paused and glared at him with the intensity of the sun. Unlike Rahal, he had two full ears. It couldn't be him.

But then why did his eyes sharpen in terror upon beholding me? Why did his eyeballs bulge so large they seemed ready to burst?

"Jyosh? How are you alive? Are you… a ghost?"

"G-Ghost? You're the ghost! What are you doing here?"

My back cracked as a jab hit my spine. I grunted from the sharp pain. The asshole behind me had smashed his sword hilt into my backbone.

"Move along!" He shoved me forward.

I darted my head back for another look at Rahal, who continued to stare at me with horrified eyes. Why had he questioned if I was alive? Why was he here? Why was he wearing the uniform of a Karshan soldier?

I couldn't ask him because the soldier shoved me down the hallway.

I wanted to turn around and punch the asshole soldier in the jaw. But instead, I gritted my teeth and reminded myself not to make enemies. I had to survive, even at the cost of my pride.

The soldier pushed me into an open door.

The room was large, but unfurnished. First, I noticed Saina sitting in the corner, her eyes shut and head drooped to the side as if asleep. My heart bathed in relief, but also hungered to know if she was okay.

Between me and her stood another masked soldier. His sleeves were rolled up; one hand was brown and the other the color of cheese.

In the far corner of the room sat a black sack. Looked like the one the soldier who took my stuff was using. Could our stones and hilts be in there?

The soldier in front of me opened and closed his new hand a few times. Unlike the other soldiers, he wasn't wearing colored lenses. His serious, dark eyes set on me.

"I agonized over it." His voice emerged upward from his lower belly. Deep and intimidating. "Agonized over what I ought to do with you. It was easier when I hadn't seen your face. Easier to order your death. But now that you're standing here…" He walked closer, his towering form hulking over me.

I backstepped to keep some distance between us. "Is Saina all right?"

He glanced at Saina, then back to me. "Oh? Her? Interesting… I didn't realize you cared about her. She's fine, of course. The procedure took a lot out of her. Between augmenting her own healing power and then doing the healing, it took everything. But she managed to regrow my hand in a few hours, as I requested."

"Where's Kaur?"

"So… you care about Kaur, too. A good guy, through and through. If you're really that selfless, then maybe I don't have to kill you. Or maybe…"

What the hell did he mean by that? This man had the answers to so many questions; he wouldn't show me his face, so I doubted he'd answer them.

"Tell you what," Colonel Rao said. "I'll let you live. Put you on a levship. You can leave immediately. It'll take you wherever you want in the whole wide world. I'll even give you a fat chunk of twinsen. What say you?"

Getting out of this mess, to a place where I could dream safely, was everything I wanted. But it sounded too good to be true.

"Only if Kaur and Saina come with me."

"This isn't a negotiation. It's an offer. Take it or leave it."

"It's a goatshit offer. I see what you're doing. You're testing me. But even if you were being honest, I wouldn't do it. I only got this far because of Kaur and Saina. If I abandoned them, I could never live with myself, even if I had all the wealth and pleasure in the Dayworld to enjoy."

Rao let out a thoughtful sigh. "A righteous attitude. Selflessness and self-awareness are exactly what I seek out in a follower."

"I can't be your follower." I shook my head. "Your goals and mine just aren't aligned."

Rao turned to face the glass panel, his hands behind his back. He gazed toward a vast, red-tinged expanse of clouds.

"The thing is, I've realized my ultimate goal is a lot farther away than I thought. There's no way I can collapse this dream with only the power contained in Sambalpur. It'll be a good start — I'm certain I can wake up one of the Ten Dreamers. That would destabilize the dream, but probably not end it. Also, there's no telling how this instability would manifest itself." He sighed with all that weight. "In any case, to awaken all the Dreamers and collapse this dream entirely, I'll need a whole lot more power."

He turned to look at me, obviously expecting some response. I had to choose my question carefully. Rao was a man of secrets, but he also seemed to be trying to tell me something.

"What do you hope will happen?" I asked. "If you gain all that power and wake up the Dreamers?"

"I hope to end *maya* — this grand illusion that the gods are playing on us."

"Yeah, Elam already told me. But if you really believe this is all a dream, then aren't you worried that when we all wake up, we'll look around and realize the new reality is so much worse? I mean, if I could live my whole life in my dreams, I would. It would be bliss. Maybe the gods are being merciful by keeping us here, instead of this *other* place you're trying to bring us to."

"The Asha is not just some *other* place. It is the true reality."

"How do you know for certain? What if when you get there, you realize we're still in a dream? What if it goes on forever and ever? What if there is no true reality?"

"Of course, I've thought about that as well. The thing is, you're looking at it all wrong. *We* aren't going anywhere. We — each of us — are part of maya. Our separation from each other, from everything around us — our stubborn insistence that we are these individual creatures — it's all maya. It's all a lie."

"So we'll all die?"

"No, Jyosh. Exactly the opposite. We'll all live forever, within the gods that are dreaming us. We are them, and they are us. We will flow into them and each other, like a drop of rain rejoining the ocean. And in that place, there won't be any pain. I'm trying to save everyone — can't you see that?"

I could see that. If I followed Rao's logic, I'd have to conclude he was right. He wasn't seeking power for its own sake; he really did want to save us all.

"You want me to buy your viewpoint, but you won't even show me your face. What are you hiding, Rao? Why do you care so much what I think?"

He approached and grabbed my right hand with his cheese-colored left hand.

"Because I know what this hand can do." He squeezed it. I tried to pull away, but his grip held. The overwhelming pain made me nauseous, and I feared my finger bones would snap.

"That hurts!"

He finally let go. I rubbed my throbbing hand.

"I learned about your blessing some time ago," Rao said. "And yet, despite trying on more than one occasion, I failed to kill you. It's all *her* fault. She loves you, after all."

"Who are you talking about?"

"You know who. The mindwriter. The Ghost. Tell me — what's she done to you? She sent you here to thwart me, so what *suggestion* did she put in your mind?"

"I don't know what you mean."

"Here's a hint — it's something you won't be able to vocalize. That's the flaw of mindwriting — you can't say out loud what you've been brainwashed to do. Tell me, has Kaur ever mentioned that she wants to kill me?"

"More than once."

"Are you sure about that? Think back. Could she ever *really* say the words?"

I vaguely remembered Kaur struggling to say *kill Rao*. I always had to finish the sentence for her.

"So what is it that you can't vocalize, Jyosh?"

"I've never struggled to say anything." Was he right? Had I been brainwashed into doing something? But there was no evidence for it. He was just reaching!

"I love Zauri. I want to be with Zauri. I want to save Zauri." I said it all out loud. If Rao was right, that couldn't be it. My main goal, my most cherished desire, was my own. I breathed in relief; I hadn't been brainwashed into feeling something for her.

"Zauri…" Rao chuckled. "No. It's not something quite as trite as that. The Ghost brought you here, to Sambalpur. For what? Think!"

Why was I here? I was just trying to survive, at first. What was I missing? What had been done to me?

"Think about the moment you *changed*."

Changed? Of course — after I executed Vir. That disconnect. That was when I'd totally broken. I hadn't felt like the same person since. I went from being cold, cruel, and only interested in survival to the way I was, now.

"Did she make me care about other people?" I said. "No, not just other people. I care about everyone I meet. Even my enemies — except those who are sources of suffering, like the Paranis." But if it was all to thwart Rao, then... "Did she make me want to save—" My words got stuck in my throat the way cloth does on a thornbush. "Save—" I just couldn't say it. "Save—"

"Save this world," Rao completed my sentence. "There it is. You've never tried to vocalize it before, have you? But there it is. All along, you only cared about others because *she* put that intention into your mind. Just as she sent Kaur to kill me, she sent you to stop me from executing my plan. You're not in control of yourself. You're a slave, just like you were in that labor camp."

I clutched my hair. Why couldn't I say those words? Was Rao right about me? Had I been brainwashed into saving this world?

"No. I really care about Kaur and Saina. They're my friends. I care about people. I want to help people."

"Don't feel bad," Rao said. "Mindwriting can be extremely powerful. At some point, a black box was inserted into your dream stone, and the moment you came into contact with it, you changed. Ironically, you became a better man in some ways, but still — you're not who you think you are. In a way, you could say your script was rewritten — hence the term, mindwriting."

"I'm not... me? Are you saying I'm really the cruel, selfish, distrusting piece of shit who murdered Vir?"

"I don't know who Vir is, but yes, your true self is likely everything you just mentioned. It's all more *maya*. What you think is you is just a pretty illusion that the Ghost created to be a thorn in my side. The truth is, I could use your blessing, Jyosh. It's one of the most powerful that I know of… short of a blessing that lets you cheat death."

There was a blessing that could cheat death? I shuddered at the thought.

In any case, if Rao was right about the mindwriting, then my blessing truly was a curse. I was just a pawn in this battle between the Ghost and Rao. A weapon to be wielded by one or the other.

"I might appear, from your mindwritten perspective, to be causing evil, but I'm not," Rao continued. "Sure, I've hurt people, but ultimately I want what's best for them, too. I want to end their separation and suffering. I want them to taste nirvana and become part of god. And in that spirit, I'm going to save you. I'm going to free you and Kaur from the Ghost's mindwriting. And then we'll be together — all of us — like a family. Like we were always meant to be."

Someone walked into the room. I turned to see Elam and Kaur. The sight of her unharmed eased my nerves.

"Abba." Elam bowed his head to his father and commander. "Sylet's second wave could begin any moment. Is it worth waiting?"

Rao caressed his new hand. He let out a tense sigh. "It's not. It's now or never. We'll begin our plan any moment now. We'll take the first step on our path toward the Asha, our true home. But first…" He gazed at Kaur.

I, too, gazed at her. "Kaur… you all right?"

She flashed her eyes at me, then nodded. If she'd been mind-written to kill Rao, was she still going to do it? Didn't Rao fear that? Or were Elam's demonblades enough to assure his safety?

"Kaur," Rao said. "As I was explaining to Jyosh, you've been mindwritten using a black box planted in your dreams by the Ghost. And I intend to save you both. Ending maya will be a long journey — longer than I thought — and I'd prefer you both by my side."

Rao seemed awfully calm for a man standing in front of a woman who'd been brainwashed to kill him. And yet, Kaur wouldn't even look him in the eyes. She gazed at the floor while rubbing her arm.

"Kaur, if you were going to kill me, you would've done it by now." Even though I couldn't see his mouth behind his mask, I knew Rao was smiling at her from the shimmer in his eyes. "But you know that if you tried to strike me with your claws, Elam would just cut you down. And the funny thing is — I don't think it's your own life you care about. Nor mine. I think it's all about Elam. You don't want Elam to have to choose between the two of us — I mean, is there anything worse for a child? To have to choose between mother and father?"

Rao waited for Kaur to answer. But she kept silent.

"If he killed you, it would haunt him for the rest of his life," Rao continued. "You know he spared you last time because he loves you. And I think… I think your maternal instincts are overpowering the Ghost's mindwriting. Isn't that so?"

Kaur glanced at Elam, her lips trembling. What was going on in her mind? Was Rao right about her?

Rao said, "I know the fire of our love died out long ago. But even so, I can't help but care for you, Kaur. Seeing you struggle within yourself so bitterly — it pains me, too. You've been manipulated by something evil. I won't stand for it. We'll take the first step to saving you both, right now. Well — all three of you, actually."

"Th-three?" I muttered.

"Yes. Poor Rahal. One of my most loyal and trusted comrades. I sent him to your camp to kill you. And then, he was mindwritten into believing he was actually a prisoner there." Rao chuckled. Something about that laugh really grated… "I don't allow my followers to enter dreams anymore, for this reason. But some of them, sadly, can't sleep without a dream stone. The black box the Ghost placed in Rahal's dream must've not done a perfect job, so at some point, the mindwriting wore off and he remembered his actual mission."

"Then why was he so surprised to see me alive?" It was all getting ridiculously confusing.

"Because the Ghost wants me to think you're dead. Rahal was always too addicted to dreams. It seems he went into another one and was mindwritten again — this time into believing he'd killed you during some fight you had." Rao chuckled some more. Were our lives and deaths so humorous? "And so, I did indeed think you were dead. Such a clever Ghost. Layers upon layers of manipulation and deceit — she's just like the gods who trapped us here, really."

Rahal… so that was why he'd tried to kill me on the train tracks. He awoke to his original mission, only to be mindwritten again into believing he'd killed me. It all made sense, as crazy as it sounded.

"By the way," Rao continued. "I ordered the light cannon strike that destroyed your camp, just as an extra insurance."

"Sounds like you've been tracking me for a while."

"Far longer than you realize. Still, no matter what I did, I was always one step behind the Ghost. Even now, I wonder — what does she have planned for me? What card has she kept hidden up her sleeve, just for this moment?"

This was all just… just madness! So much had happened in the shadows, either to try and kill me or to manipulate me into coming here.

"If you doubt anything I've said. If you doubt my intentions. If you doubt the nature of this world…" Rao stretched out his fresh hand in my direction. He made a fist. "Then I want you to behold this. It is my *blessing*. It is proof of everything I've told you.

Proof that this world is naught but maya. And with this blessing, I intend to cast away the illusion and bring us all into the Asha."

He opened his palm. A terminal display blinked into existence above it.

Just like in the dream.

"As far as I know, I am the only one in this world who has terminal access. I've had this power since I turned twelve. I even hid it from my own loving family. The problem is — I could never understand what the commands meant. Even the foremost experts in the language were clueless. I mean, look."

He came to my front. I looked into his terminal. Every command was written in that vine-like script. Most were grayed out, as if they couldn't be pressed.

"I'm the one who made Sambalpur appear," he said. "One command, pressed in desperation, was all it took. But then *she* cut off my left hand." He pointed at Kaur with some anger. "Thankfully, while here in Sambalpur, I figured out precisely which command I needed to choose to take the next step. Now that I have my hand back, it's as simple as tapping on this terminal."

He closed his palm. The terminal vanished.

"Abba," Elam said. "Everyone is ready. I think it's time we did what we came to do."

Rao went to Elam. He put his hands on his son's shoulders. "My beloved boy. We're only minutes away, I promise." He snapped his fingers, then walked over to me. "Jyosh, let's take the first step toward your rehabilitation." He opened his hand. "Give me the dream stone with the black box."

Give him Zauri's dream stone? No way I could trust him. Besides, I didn't care about any of this. All I cared about was her!

I took a step back. "You can't have it. No matter what, you'll never have it."

I'd destroy this tower if I had to. I'd kill us all. But no way was I giving Zauri to him. Mindwritten or not, I knew for a certainty that I'd end all our lives. The Ghost may have made me care about this world and its people, but still, I loved Zauri more.

Elam stepped toward me, his muscled form imposing. "Don't make this hard. Abba isn't perfect, but believe me, when he cares about someone, he'll do anything to help them. My dear Jyosh, he's not here to hurt you. Sometimes, the cure can be *so* painful. Is there anything that hurts more than cauterizing a gaping wound? Jyosh — please — we all want what's best for everyone, don't we?"

I shook my head. "I don't. I want what's best for myself. Maybe the mindwriting didn't work as well as it should've. That dream stone was always so glitched. Sure, I care about others, but I still care about myself, too. And if I can't have what I want, I'll kill everyone here. I'LL DO IT!"

I opened my right hand. I didn't even need to consciously channel the unseen wavelengths of the Primal Star — my body did it for me. A bolt of frozen lightning materialized in my grip, within which churned the power to destroy a city.

"There it is." Rao's eyes widened, glistening. "A power that could both doom and save us. A power worth fighting for."

"Worth fighting for?" I scoffed. "How many times did you try to kill me?"

"Because I feared it. But now, after seeing you, I know it can be used for good." Rao reached out his new hand. "Please, Jyosh. You can be the one who saves us all by helping me shut this grand illusion down. Or you can save yourself and live, closed off from the wonders of truth, upon an island of blissful ignorance."

Something moved in the corner of my eye. I turned my head to see Saina, suddenly sprung onto her feet, rushing madly past me. She reached out her hands, grabbing at Kaur.

Elam lunged to get in her way. Rao backstepped. I stood there, frozen, still clutching my blue lightning.

Kaur reached out her hand for Saina's. Their fingertips

barely touched before Elam body slammed Saina into the wall. But in that moment of contact, something blue and electric passed between their fingertips.

Saina had just augmented Kaur.

Saina recoiled against the wall and writhed in pain on the floor. I closed my fist; my lightning bolt vanished. I lunged toward Elam's knee, grabbed his whole thigh, and pushed him to the floor, my weight staying steady. He slammed onto his back with a guttural groan. I slid behind Elam's head and locked his neck with my whole forearm. He flailed his arms upward to hit me, but couldn't reach.

Claws of light erupted off Kaur's fingers. They grew so large, they pierced the ceiling, burning through the metal and leaving charred streaks. The stench of electric burns filled the air. Each claw was the length of a twinblade. I feared, with a flick of her wrists, that she'd hit all of us. Her normal claws were scary enough, but these augmented ones were utterly terrifying. Like a lion, Kaur jumped toward Rao and swiped her claws downward.

He stood and waited for the end, his gaze peaceful.

A blinding light enveloped his body. He disappeared as Kaur's claws pierced the air where he'd stood.

Another blinding white light flashed, and Rao rematerialized on the far side of the room.

Her claws forward, Kaur rushed at him. Meanwhile, I firmed my hold on Elam's neck, even as he squirmed and turned pale. Even as Saina whimpered on the floor, obviously in need.

Kaur lunged straight at Rao, her twinblade-sized claws flying toward him like bolts of deathly red lightning.

He opened his new hand, tapped on his terminal, and disappeared in a flash of glittery light. Kaur's light claws tore through the wall, burning the metal.

Suddenly, I was choking the air. Elam had vanished, too.

Chapter Twenty-Six

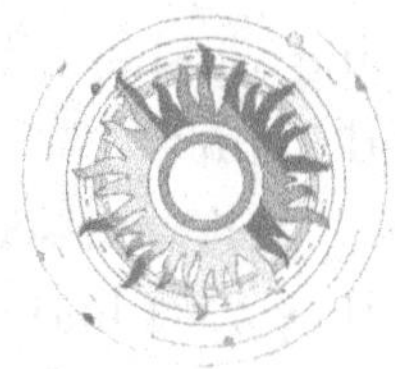

I went straight to Saina. She clutched her abdomen, near where her ribs were. Her pained moans became the loudest sound in the world.

I knelt and stared at her, helpless. "Saina, what can I do?"

She winced and cried out like a dying animal. She'd taken blows to both sides: first when Elam smashed into her with the full force of his hulking body, and second when she crashed into the metal wall.

Muscles must've been bruised. Bones broken. She'd already seemed worn from regrowing Rao's hand when I entered the room. In fact, she'd been in pain in the Deep Layer after augmenting us. And she'd just augmented Kaur again. Sure, I'd endured some awful injuries recently, but what Saina was going through must've been utter hell.

I turned to Kaur. Her augmented light claws had extinguished. She collapsed onto her hands and knees, breathing fast, and crawled slowly toward us.

A rumbling. The God Tower shook as if an earthquake had

hit the floating island. I covered my head, afraid the ceiling would collapse on me. Thankfully, the groaning metal held.

How much worse could this situation get?

A masked soldier, lightblade drawn, ran into the room.

I stood and faced him. Hiltless. With both Saina and Kaur on the floor, I had to fight for all of us. Somehow.

Two more soldiers ran inside, lightblades full and forward. Our odds of surviving lessened by the second.

"What the hell is going on here?" the first soldier asked. "Where's Commander and Elam?"

I chuckled. From fear. "Well, you see, Commander Rao and Sir Elam, they — uhh — they…" I had to pluck the perfect lie or we'd all be captured or killed. "Sylet began his assault. Just now. Commander and Elam rushed out of here to fight back. Meanwhile, we decided we'd have a little sparring practice."

The soldiers glanced at Saina, who was still moaning in pain, and Kaur, who crawled toward me on her hands and knees. Then they glared at me.

"I got the best of them," I said with my most confident face. "Yeah. Can you believe these little girls thought they could take me on?" I grinned, showing my teeth.

Another earthquake. I grabbed onto the wall as a guttural rumble hit the tower. After it had eased somewhat, I shouted, "Sylet's attacking! That purple-eyed bastard! We've got to help the Commander!"

The first soldier turned to his two comrades and said, "Finally, the plan is a go. Code Ninety. No time to lose. Let's go."

I hated those code numbers, whatever they meant. Worse than that, it seemed Rao had begun his plan, and from how he'd spoken about it, something catastrophic was surely coming.

The three soldiers ran out of the room. The door shut behind them. I blew out the breath I'd been holding.

I ran to the black sack in the far corner, slid down next to it, and pulled it open.

Our bright, colorful crystals and sword hilts shone. Fast as I could, I pulled Zauri's dream stone from my chest, put it safely in my utility pocket, then grabbed my red-green stone from the bag and stuck it in, ignoring the jolt.

I took the bag to Kaur. I put both her sword hilts and her special combat stone on the ground next to her.

"Come on, Kaur. Whatever pain you're in, overcome it."

Another rumble. I almost stumbled to my knees. What the hell was happening to cause these quakes?

I ran toward the glass panel and looked down. A sand-colored haze covered everything. Something jetting up was causing the haze. Dust, most likely. But what was moving down there? Floating islands didn't have earthquakes. Natural ones, at least.

Saina whimpered. I knelt at her side and unzipped the front of her combat suit, all the way to her waist. Dark purple bruises covered her stomach and sides.

"Put... my... healing stone... in," she muttered in between sobs.

I found the violet healing stone in one of her utility pockets and swapped it with her blue augmentation stone.

Saina put her hands on her bruises and shut her eyes.

"I don't think we have time," I said. "This tower might not stay standing. I don't think we can stay here and wait for you to heal. Can you walk?"

With the slightest movements, Saina shook her head.

"I'll carry her," Kaur said.

I turned to see her sitting up. Red lines zagged across her eyeballs. The tips of her fingers were swollen and bright, the color of beets.

Her special combat stone was no longer on the floor, and her sword hilts were holstered on her belt, so it seemed she must've felt somewhat better.

"Can you fight, Kaur?" I asked.

"Don't think so. My veins are screaming."

So I'd have to fight alone, if needed.

"We should get to the levship," I said. But how would we? We'd been blindfolded the whole way here!

Kaur nodded. With a groan, she slowly got to her feet and limped toward Saina and me.

I went to the door. No matter where I touched it, it wouldn't open.

No time for this. I unholstered my hilt, cast a lightblade, and stuck it in the door. Light devoured metal. I tried to move the blade, but it wouldn't budge. I intensified my flow, and my lightblade grew brighter and hotter. I drew my own door in the door — all four sides — then kicked at the center. The metal flew backward and clattered onto the hallway floor, leaving a molten outline. The odor of scalded steel had never been so satisfying.

Kaur took Saina's arm and gently helped her stand. Saina climbed onto Kaur's back. Though several inches shorter, Kaur's unreal strength seemed enough.

"Hold on," I said. "I need to make sure the hallway is safe."

I peeked into the hallway. No soldiers. Supplies were strewn all over, from cereal bar wrappers to combat suits to thermoses.

I gestured for Kaur to follow. With Saina on her back, and given her own weariness, she trudged like a turtle toward the door, gritting her teeth, each step making her wince and grunt.

I entered the hallway. Where to go, now? So many doors. Various turns. I kept my lightblade at chest height and walked forward. No way I could remember how we'd gotten here from the levship. Still, we had to move.

The breathing lights within the vine-like calligraphy turned off. The hall went dark. Only the red sun shining through the glass panels at the far end of the hall, as well as the desperate glow of my blade, provided any light.

Then the calligraphy on the wall began to breathe again. But not everywhere. The calligraphy next to me lit up, the light trailing toward a door in the middle of the hall, and then going out. It repeated this pattern.

I stared at it, stupefied, as Kaur emerged, Saina on her back.

No time to hesitate. I went to the door the breathing calligraphy seemed to be pointing toward. I touched it. It slid open.

A stairwell. It was dark, save for the calligraphy breathing on the walls. Strangely, its light pattern trailed upward, not down.

Once Kaur arrived at my side, I said, "We follow where the light is leading us."

She nodded without hesitation. "Whatever you say. My worthless life's in your hands. And hers too, I guess." She let out a muffled chuckle.

"I'll make sure it's safe." I went into the stairwell and darted up the stairs. The pulsating light on the walls led me to the first door, so I entered.

Doors lined this new hallway. A somber, ruddy darkness pervaded, save for the calligraphy glowing next to the eighth door to the left.

I peeked back into the stairwell. "Clear."

Kaur began trudging up, step by step.

I went deeper into the hallway and stopped to look out the nearest glass panel.

The edge of the floating island appeared hazy from the dust. A limestone tenement, similar to the one we'd slept in earlier, glided on what resembled sand and fell off the edge.

Fell. A building just fell off the island. My jaw hung. Was Sambalpur itself coming apart, with us still on it? Had Rao done this as part of his plan?

Once Kaur got to me, I went through the door the callig-raphy was pointing toward.

Another stairwell appeared, leading up. I climbed it and arrived at an identical hall. Once again, something like thirty doors lined either side of the hallway.

Ugh. Was following some mysterious light really my best plan? This time, I couldn't even see where the light was. I ran down the hallway, searching for a door with lit calligraphy.

The calligraphy shone on a big double door at the end of the hall. I sprinted toward it. Another sideways shake of the building almost pushed me off my feet. I grabbed the wall to maintain my balance, then continued onward.

I entered the double door. Found myself in a cube room with glass walls, like the one that had transported us lower into the Deep Layer. But this time, no wire dangled from the ceiling.

I looked back into the hall. Kaur was slowly making her way over. Meanwhile, I stared out the glass. Tenements and houses and spires continued to fall off the edge in a tide of sand and dust. The ground itself was falling off the edge! It resembled the top of a waterfall. A waterfall of sand and limestone. Beautiful… if it wasn't about to doom us. How long until the God Tower got swept by that tide?

Kaur hauled herself and Saina inside the cube room, then carefully settled Saina onto the floor. The door closed by itself behind her. The cube began moving down.

"Who's controlling the elevator?" Kaur asked. She plopped next to Saina, whose face was stuck in a wince.

"Whoever is controlling those lights," I said. "Whoever it is… we can only hope they're trying to help us."

"Avatar…" Saina mumbled. Was she praying?

I sat beside Kaur, appreciating a moment's rest.

Seconds later, the cube came to a stop, and the door opened like a jaw. The red sky shone on a landing area — the one in the middle of the Tower. A bitter, howling wind blew from the opening. Saina's blocky levship sat there, the blue shield-and-dragon emblem facing us, exactly where we'd last seen it.

Between it and us stood one man. A man I recognized too well. Gray hair on such a young face. No mask or lenses to cover up his pockmarked cheeks and worn woody eyes.

I got up and approached Rahal. He raised his hilt in my direction and cast a curved, almost sinuous lightblade.

"This is as far as you go," he said.

I kept my distance and raised my hilt. Didn't cast my lightblade yet. Maybe I could convince him to stand down.

"Rahal, this building's about to collapse. This whole island's heading for the edge." I pointed to the levship behind him. "Come with us. Let's all get safe."

"Safe? Oh, I had plenty of time to get safe. But I never choose safe over finishing a mission."

"Rao doesn't want to kill me. Not anymore. Come on, Rahal. Stop this."

"If he didn't want to kill you, he would've taken you with him. I'm afraid this crumbling pile of metal will be our tomb."

"Why? Don't you realize how dangerous Rao's plan is?"

Rahal shook his head. "There was a time when I doubted the Commander's mission. But being in that camp truly opened my eyes. I experienced, firsthand, the suffering we're capable of inflicting upon each other. It's only because we neglect to realize — we *are* each other. I won't stand for it. The maya must end."

"Sure, that camp was an awful place. But ever since then, I've met some truly good people. Some of them will die if you don't let us pass. So please, Rahal. We don't want to die. Don't you see that you'll be causing us the same suffering you're trying to stop?"

"Of course I do. A temporary increase in mass suffering is all part of the plan. Don't think it'll stop at your lives. Cities will burn. Countries will be erased. Fire from heaven will devour innocent and guilty alike. That is our plan. We'll do whatever it takes to attain nirvana for all of humanity. To end this cursed, ever-repeating dream."

He sounded so much like Rao. Rahal might've been brainwashed by the Ghost, but he'd been brainwashed by Rao, first. Not in the same sense — Rao hadn't mindwritten him — but whatever dogma he'd instilled in followers like Rahal was brainwashing all the same.

Rahal stepped forward, his curvaceous lightblade raised, the tip pointing at my forehead. Shadows seemed to crawl along the curves of his blade. How was I to account for those curves? And what if he shifted his shape mid-strike?

I backstepped as far as I could. I inhaled the red tint of the sun, cycled it through me, and projected a straight, fiery blade.

Rahal stood still. "So… you've obviously been training since that whole frying pan incident. You been using the Karshan Army Officer Program?"

Was he suddenly afraid? Was he trying to waste time?

I nodded. "Yeah. What level are you at?"

"I just progressed to major. That's level thirty. Haven't been officially promoted yet, so I'm what's considered a major-in-waiting until I gain the necessary leadership skills. What about you?"

Such a high level. Defeating him almost sounded impossible. Hope drained out of me.

"Level twenty," I lied. But wouldn't it have been better to make him underestimate, rather than overestimate me?

"Damn. A captain-in-waiting, already? Incredible. This'll be quite a fitting final battle, then."

So passing level twenty made you a captain and level thirty a major — although you still had to be officially promoted. I could guess, based on my knowledge of Manizan army ranks, that passing level forty made you a lieutenant colonel, and fifty a colonel. As far as the officer positions were concerned, it seemed the Karshan army was quite the meritocracy.

I knew Rahal was just trying to distract me with these thoughts. Furthermore, like the captain I'd faced in the alley, he was waiting for me to make a move. But this building could collapse at any moment.

I needed to strike!

I lunged forward, going for a jab at his belly. In the midst of my lunge, I willed my blade to snake upward, toward his shoulder — a basic Snake Blade technique that Kriga had taught me.

Rahal's blade began to snake, too. It curved around mine, then latched onto it like a whip. An electric whiz and rainbows of light filled the air as our lightblades met. He whipped his hand downward. Because his blade had wrapped around mine, I was now falling.

I pulled out of my attack, then used my wiriness to regain my balance and sidestep. Rahal doubled — no, tripled! — the length of his blade and swiped horizontally at my torso.

No way I could dodge that Triple Blade. Instead, I sprang off my feet and jumped as high as I could. The heat almost seared my boots as his blade whizzed below them. Soon as I landed, I lunged forward, using the light pooled in my hand to Double Blade, straight at Rahal's chest.

A blinding white scathed my eyes. I couldn't see! I fell on the ground in a heap. I tried to push to my feet, but slipped from dizziness. What part of me was about to be seared? My belly? My neck? Would I even have time to scream before I choked on blood?

My eyesight remained covered in white, but I was still breathing. I got up and ran. Soon, spots appeared on my vision. Outlines of blurry things I could avoid as I continued to run.

Once I'd regained enough sight and gotten some distance, I turned to see Rahal, several yards away. He was rubbing his eyes.

Of course. Neither of us were wearing lenses. He'd blinded himself just as he'd blinded me. Perhaps he'd done it out of desperation. He'd committed so much power, weight, and light to that sideways swipe, my forward lunge would've caught him had he not used Blinding Blade to throw me off.

He wasn't as skilled as Kaur, and that gave me hope.

The rumbling below intensified. Our end approached with each shake. I had to kill him and get Saina and Kaur and myself onboard the levship. With some distance between us, I had to think of the perfect move to end it. What did Rahal know and not know about me? Was he aware of my blessing?

I shifted my hilt to my left hand, then recast my lightblade. I willed the unseen light of the Primal Star to fill my body and produce its frozen lightning.

A bolt of shimmering blue materialized in my right hand. I raised it up to show Rahal, who stood near the levship's entrance ramp, yards away.

He snickered. "You going to do my job for me? That lightning so much as touches anything, we'll all be blown into our next lives."

So he knew about it. I couldn't use it to intimidate him. What else could I do?

Come to think of it, I'd defeated Rahal already. On the train tracks, with a frying pan, of all things. Did Rahal know I had a red-green stone in my chest? Soon as I'd entered the levship, the soldier made me remove mine, so Rahal probably didn't know about it.

Rahal melted his rigid lightblade into a flexible lightwhip. He lashed the ground as he approached. Each lash growled thunderously and flashed like a lightning strike. Smoke trailed off the streaks he left on the metal.

"You lied about being a captain-in-waiting, didn't you? I'd say you're not even a lieutenant. Still just a cadet. What are you, level five?"

Level three. But I hid a card up my sleeve that other level threes didn't have. Rahal now underestimated me. He was getting cocky with that lightwhip.

Still, he held a twenty-seven-level advantage in training. Whatever I did next had to be perfect. It had to target his ignorance of me, his overconfidence, and his willingness to risk everything — all at once.

I put out both my frozen lightning and my lightblade. I stood unguarded.

"I can't win," I said. "Just make it painless."

Rahal stopped lashing his lightwhip. He smirked. "The way you clung to life in that camp, I know you're not the type to just give up. This some kind of trick?"

"Why don't you come and find out?"

"So it is a trick. They don't teach mind games in the training program. I guess you learn those on your own. Here's a little nugget for your mind to chew on, about the levship you're so desperately trying to board. I already destroyed the sunsink. It won't fly. I'm afraid, all this time, our fight was just a bit of fun."

Was that true? Or was that his version of a mind game? Of course he'd try to deflate my will so he could win.

Still, it made sense for him to destroy the sunsink. Assuming that the levship still worked was a bad call on my part. Assuming I could even pilot it was already foolish enough.

No matter. To have even the tiniest odds of surviving, I had to defeat Rahal. And defeat him now.

Rahal lashed his lightwhip at me. I cast my blade and raised it to deflect. Our lights collided with an electric crack. Whizzing rainbows shot around the room.

His lightwhip wrapped around my blade. I pulled to get free, but Rahal tugged upward with an overwhelming force. My hilt flew out of my hands and landed with a *clank* between us.

He waited for me to go for it, whip raised. Instead, I back-stepped many times to get more distance. The wind beat against my back. I looked behind to see the edge, beyond which Sambalpur was crumbling. Cornered, again.

Rahal rotated his lightwhip above his head as he closed the distance. Between that and lashing the floor, he was having fun, wasn't he?

The floor. Like everything in this building, the floor was metal. Also, this building was full of lights and had a working elevator.

It was a machine.

Rahal continued his approach. A few steps away, now. He raised his lightwhip to lash me dead. I inhaled all the green light I could, then ducked and pushed both my hands onto the metal floor. I willed the green light to surge.

It cycled into the floor. I steered it forward, searching for the building's gain medium. I saw it in my mind's eye — a giant crystal, deep underground. At the speed of light, I surged my green waves down toward the crystal, electrifying them, then back upward to this floor. I willed them into Rahal's feet, and through his flesh and bones and blood.

Blue and yellow electricity crackled out of Rahal's body. He shook and let out a muffled moan. His lightwhip went out. He dropped his sword hilt.

I grabbed it, cast a lightblade, and plunged it through his heart.

Blood shot out of his mouth and blasted from the hole in his chest. He looked at me, half-grinning, half staring at his next life.

"Shit," he croaked before falling dead.

. . .

I HOLSTERED RAHAL'S HILT, so I'd have two. He wasn't lying. He'd sundered the fans of the sunsink with his lightblade and only a mess of charred blades remained. It couldn't churn light and make the ship fly.

I ran outside the engine room, into the levship hallway, and back outside to Saina and Kaur, who now waited at the base of the ramp.

"Destroyed," I said.

Saina, still wincing and clutching her belly, whispered something to Kaur.

"She says they have skyboards inside. In the same storage room where they kept your dream stone."

Oh yeah, I'd noticed them earlier.

"Get some rope, too," Kaur added. "If we're going to use skyboards to escape, we're gonna need to tie her onto one of us."

I ran back into the storage room. First, I got on my tiptoes and grabbed a bundle of rope that dangled off the top shelf. It was thick and hefty, so I hung it off my neck, then bent down to grab the metal skyboards off the floor, their TEX logos bright and golden.

I realized: Kaur didn't have a green stone. In her state, how could she fly without one? I got my dull machinist stone from the bottom shelf and stuck it in my pocket. Then I grabbed the skyboards, keeping one under each arm, their blunt metal edges jutting into my armpits.

A growl sounded outside, as if the island were roaring. A quake flung me off my feet. I dropped everything and smashed face first onto the metal floor, the skyboards clattering around me. The world tilted — was the building finally falling?

No time to bother with the throbbing pain in my skull. I tucked a skyboard under each arm, again. Keeping my balance steady, I rushed into the hallway. The ship was now slanted, so I stepped down the incline toward the exit. And then the hallway itself moved; I careened toward the wall, but managed to regain my balance just before crashing. The whole weight of the ship now drifted in a perilously downward direction.

I stepped out to the ramp. I jumped off and landed on the floor as the ship collided into the wall, the metal itself crying out. Because the levship was the size of a two-story building, it created a massive dent in the wall, and the ceiling now dangled.

No time. No time. I dropped both skyboards onto the floor. Kaur helped Saina onto her feet.

"Tie her to me!" I said.

"Are you sure? I could take her."

"No. You're in bad shape as it is. Focus on yourself. Come on!"

I stood on the skyboard.

Saina clung to my back. "Sorry," she whispered in my ear. "I've been such a burden."

"You helped me when I was a burden. We might be even after this."

"You been keeping score?" she chuckled. So nice to hear that laugh, as weak as it was.

Kaur wrapped the rope around Saina and me several times. She pulled it tight, then knotted it. I felt like I was carrying a giant backpack. Would I be able to keep my balance when flying?

A chunk of the ceiling clattered onto the levship, crushing the hull. I looked up. More metal rained.

The building tilted to breaking point as its metallic skeleton groaned with the shifting weight. I tossed Kaur my machinist stone. She unzipped her front and stuck it in, then stood on her skyboard.

I inhaled green light and cycled it down into the board. *Whoosh.* It lifted up on the air. Saina's weight tilted us backward, but the adherent force kept my feet planted. I pushed my weight forward to straighten our balance.

Another chunk of ceiling burst off from right above, coming straight down on top of us. I surged toward the opening where red-tinged clouds waited.

With a deafening whine, all the metal behind me collapsed in a plume of dust, just as we jetted into the open sky above Sambalpur. The God Tower was no more. Saina yelped and tightened her hold. I looked back to see Kaur emerge from the dust, smoke, and rain of metal, the howl of the building's collapse still resounding. Such a relief we'd all gotten out in time.

That relief was short-lived as I became aware of our surroundings.

Levships. Levships everywhere. And worse, they were firing at each other. A red beam sliced through a rather pretty, orange levship. Its rectangular hull exploded with a flash and roar.

Metal debris surged toward me. I ducked and dived as Saina screamed. Kaur slid her board sideways to avoid what looked like the flaming door of the ship.

So not only was Sambalpur collapsing, but the Karshan air force were doing battle. With each other! Utter chaos.

No time to ponder. No breaths or light could be wasted, lest we succumb to the many kinds of death that seemed to be seeking us.

I scanned the horizon. I found the nearest thing that resembled land that wasn't Sambalpur. Another floating island. I willed all the light in me to fly us toward it. The wind beat against my face, silencing all other sounds, as my speed increased.

The red beam of a light cannon pierced the air, in front of my vision. I darted beneath it, the heat simmering my skin. The cannon shot barely missed a levship that was floating under us, off the edge of Sambalpur.

"You all right?" I asked Saina, my heart threatening to spill out my mouth.

"Yes," she muttered into my ear. "Mitra... I can still feel Mitra and his avatar below. They're calling out for you, Jyosh."

"For me? Why?"

"I... I don't know."

I had to focus on what mattered. I looked back. Kaur still followed, though she was a ways behind. Given her nearly burnt-out state, it must've been hard to cycle any light through her veins. No matter — so long as she could see us, she could catch up. I had to blaze forward and chart a course out of this hell.

Below, it seemed no buildings remained upon Sambalpur. What had once stood as a magnificent, ancient city was now a messy haze of dust, dirt, and sand.

Ahead, the other floating island came into clearer view. Its quaint, concrete buildings were so familiar, as was that palace glimmering golden amid a magnificent forest.

Of course. There was only one floating city in Maniza. I was born there.

The massive lake that took up half the floating island shimmered pink in the sun's gaze. Aside it stood a series of small, caramel hills that were kept as a nature reserve. We could land there.

I had no idea Sambalpur had moved so much while we were on it. Floated all the way to Harska.

No matter. After twelve years in exile, I was finally going home.

Chapter Twenty-Seven

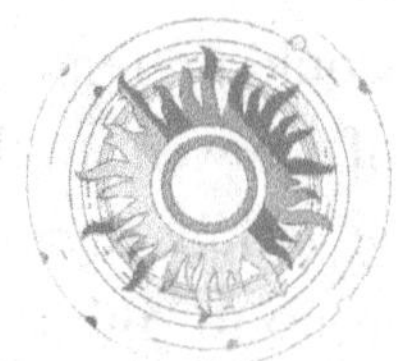

Landing upon the floatland of Harska for the first time in twelve years wasn't a moment I could celebrate. Not with how much pain Saina was in.

We found a mossy cave near a pond on the hillside. The stalactites seemed sharp as daggers. We stayed near the entrance, where the ruddy sunlight could still reach us.

Kaur and I settled Saina on the cold ground. Couldn't even give her a blanket. Saina kept her hands on her belly, where the purple bruises had blossomed and turned torturously red.

"Leave me to heal for a while," she told us. So Kaur and I went away from the mouth of the cave toward a small, rocky pond filled with chalky water.

A slight breeze blew. Harska's breezes came from the second heaven. They tasted sweeter than the winds of the flatlands. The scents they carried… I couldn't quite describe them. Flowers from another world, perhaps.

Kaur was unusually quiet. She stared at her own reflection in the pond water. Perhaps she was thinking about Elam, or about failing to kill Rao, or about how she'd been mindwritten. We had so many things to talk about, but if she preferred to sit in silence, then I'd let it be.

Meanwhile, the sky in the direction of Sambalpur remained a puffed up, sandy haze. The sound of the ancient floating city disintegrating reminded me a lot of the *grrrr* of the fabrication machines at the camp. A sound I hoped to never hear again. The levship battle had ceased, for now, but the sky was still filled with their blocky, metallic forms.

I was home. Maybe I could pretend my fall from Harska had never happened. Perhaps if we went to the other side of the hill, we could look out upon the various districts. Maybe even spot the street and house I'd grown up in. But the floating city would be different, now.

It would be an empty nostalgia. What had really made Harska home was my family, and my family was no more.

Kaur put her hand on my knee, grabbing my attention.

"You really destroyed that guy," she said. Her eyes were somewhat watered, and yet she smiled. "He was a major-in-waiting. That's only a rank below me. Look how far you've come, so fast."

I shrugged. "I knew I couldn't match him, lightblade to lightblade. So I had to improvise."

"You know, I think it'd be fun to train together."

Coming from her, that was high praise. "Kaur... do you still want to kill Rao?"

She stuck her hands in her utility pockets. "Dunno. I gave it two good attempts. The thing is... if it's true I was mindwritten to do it, then why does it feel like such a natural thing I'd do? I mean, it was all to protect my son. And maybe even to help the people Rao would hurt. Are these not... natural instincts I'd have? Did I have to be brainwashed into caring?"

"I don't understand it either. But when I look at who I was in the camp before all this started, I can't lie and say I cared much about others, at least the way I do now."

"I always loved Elam, though. Others… not so much. But Elam — I could never allow him to be led astray."

"That's yours, then. That's your own true self." But what about me? Had there been anything I loved, other than myself? Something to anchor me to my true self?

I stared at my hands. My new hand was still paler than my old one. How strange. Even my body wasn't all *me*.

"Rao mentioned that, in a way, my script had been rewritten," I said. "But, remember when we first entered the dream with Ava in it, and I'd lost all my memories? There was this moment when I was sitting with Ava in her house. I was looking at her while she cried, and I felt… relieved. No, it was something even deeper than that. I wanted her to suffer because it tasted like my own. I was like a fire that wanted to meet other fires and grow larger. And yet, I had no memories. That despair was coming from my soul."

Kaur chuckled nervously. "Can't say I understand that. But if what people believe is true, then your soul was alive before you were born. Except, you were someone else — entirely — and you lived in the Nightscape. So, maybe, whoever that person was, they had an awful time there."

"No. It was even deeper than that. It wasn't just the suffering of one life. It was the suffering of thousands. Maybe millions. Billions."

"Ugh. Sounds tedious as hell. When I die, I just want to disappear into the dark. Hah. No wonder Rao wants to end it all."

Come to think of it: why did Rao want to end it all? What had he experienced? Elam had told me Rao went so deep into dream layers, he emerged out the other side and into the Asha. But that couldn't be the whole of it.

And more importantly, what was Rao going to do now?

Most chilling of all, what commands was he pressing on his

terminal? Did it have a *Wake Up* command like all terminals in our dreams? Could he change the angle of the sun? Could he summon any item out of the air? Which commands had he translated from the language of the Ancients? Which commands were grayed out? What could and couldn't he do?

Was Colonel Rao, more or less, a god? And if so, what hope did we have against him?

I put my hand in my utility pocket and clutched Zauri's dream stone. Its warmth soothed me, though I was probably imagining that it radiated heat. If Rao ended this world, I'd never see her again.

But Rao had said that we'd all be together, as one, inside god. So, then, would Zauri be there, too? How would I find her?

Of course, that was the wrong question. I wouldn't care to find her. I wouldn't be me. She wouldn't be herself, either. We'd all just be… god.

"You're lost in thought again." Kaur tugged my collar. "At least let me get lost with you."

"Do you want to be part of god, Kaur? Do you think we should let Rao end all our separation? Our suffering?"

She tossed a stone into the pond. It skipped four times and clattered onto the opposite side of the bank. "Why can't we live forever, but as ourselves? Wouldn't that be better? In fact, that's precisely what people seek out in dreams. Paradise. There's a well-known story in Salkofy of a rich nawab who owns the only layer ten dream stone in the Dayworld. Yeah — ten layers. Something like eight-hundred skilled maintainers are required to keep the dream stone stable, at all times. But think about it — even if he lives for a single second in the dream stone, that's plenty."

I tried to do the math. But the numbers got too high. "Okay, tell me, how much is one second in a layer ten dream?"

"I'm not sure that number even has a name. And that's only one second. He's been in there for years!"

"But it doesn't matter how big that number is — eventually, his dream will end."

"Sure, but why worry about something that's so far off? He's basically immortal in there."

"No, he's not. It doesn't matter how far away death is — if it's waiting for you, it'll wait as long as needed, staring you in the face the whole time."

Kaur laughed. "The whole story is probably fake, anyway. I'm not sure ten-layer dream stones even exist. But whether you've got thousands or tens of thousands or millions or billions of years in a dream — it actually sounds like you'd get bored."

"Maybe we're destined to get bored of who we are. Maybe that's why we change the clothes over our souls so much."

A pained moan sounded from the cave mouth.

"I'll check," I said.

I got up and hurried toward the cave. Its mossy walls shone emerald, and the darkness deeper inside seemed rather soothing.

Saina was still lying down, but her eyes were open, now.

"You okay?" I asked as I knelt next to her.

"Not really," she whispered. "Been a while since I've been this *not okay*."

"But it's not getting worse, right?"

"I might have some minor internal bleeding, so I don't know. It's not really possible for me to do surgery on myself in the state I'm in. All I can do is ease the pain and hope it clots."

"There are healers in Harska. I'll go find one."

"No. Jyosh — think. Harska is occupied by the Karshans. When they occupy a major city, they always lock it down. No one would be allowed out on the streets. You'd be caught immediately."

"I can't just sit here and watch you suffer. We had a few healers living on our street. If they're still there, I can go directly and get one."

"So many ifs. I'll not risk you getting caught. I can manage things." She coughed. Thankfully, no blood. "You've already done enough for me. I know you both care. If you didn't, you would've left me to die in that tower."

"Maybe I can find a Beheshian healer, down in one of the refugee camps."

"No. There are thousands of people who need them more than I do. I'll be fine. I just need time and rest."

Was she being honest? Or was this her self-sacrificial side showing?

"I can still feel him. The Eternal Dawn. Mitra." Saina gave me a weak smile. "Remember how *all gods are ten?* How Mitra is one of the ten, and the one we Beheshians worship, but only through his avatar at the Temple Behesh?"

I nodded. "I remember everything you taught me about the chain of worship."

"I'm absolutely certain of it, now — the Avatar of Sambalpur was never reaching out for me. It was reaching out for you."

"Why?"

"I still don't know. Divine dragons are the purest forms of the ten gods, so Mitra saving you and its avatar reaching out must be related."

"Related... how?"

"You have a connection with Mitra, whether you realize it or not. Somehow, somewhere, you formed a bond with him. Maybe when you were a child. Perhaps through one of his avatars. Someone you may not have realized is an avatar of Mitra. And your bond with Mitra is stronger than mine. You just can't feel it because you're not as attuned with your frequency as I am with mine."

How could I have a bond with Mitra? Was it related to my

mother's prayers at the temple of Sambalpur? Did she form a bond between Mitra and me?

"In any case, Sambalpur is breaking apart," I said.

"Indeed. So the question is — what was Sambalpur? A city, or a cage?"

"A cage for a god?"

"I suppose we're going to find out." She coughed again. Hoarser, this time.

"Don't speak if it hurts."

"I want to talk to you, though. But you're right — I shouldn't strain myself. So you do the talking. Tell me everything. Did you see Zauri again?"

I sat cross-legged facing Saina and rested my chin on my fist. "You saw the lightning bolt I held in my hand, didn't you? She was sent by the Ghost to teach it to me. Even Zauri, it turns out, wasn't what I thought she was. Everything — my whole life — was so much more complicated than I realized."

Saina smiled and nodded, as if to say *go on*.

"Seeing her again made everything worth it, though. Even now, I just want to crawl deeper into this cave, go to sleep, and be with her. But I won't leave you and Kaur alone. If we're going to sleep, we'll do it together. You guys could meet her, even. Yeah. That would be amazing. But we'll do it when you're feeling better."

Saina nodded her approval.

"There's so much to think about, isn't there? And yet... I don't want to. I don't want to peel back the layers. I don't want to lift the veil. I just want to pretend things are wonderful and fine. I wish we could all just be friends, in a happy place. Is that childish?"

She stared at me, kindness in her bleary eyes.

"Rao said I was choosing an island of blissful ignorance.

Maybe so. But when reality is so awful, why not? Who says we have to face it?"

And yet, even that nawab who went to sleep in a layer ten dream would wake up, one day. So, perhaps, would we all.

Saina gestured with her chin at something behind me. I turned to see Kaur leaning against the opposite cave wall, her arms crossed and bangs shadowing her eyes.

"What should we do?" I asked her. "Enjoy our blissful little islands, or face whatever is coming?"

"You decide," she said. "Between the three of us, you have the greatest power of all. Rao fears you. But in the end, it's your life. Should you decide to use your power to oppose him, I'll be there to protect you. And if you prefer to walk away, then I'll smile and wish you the best."

"If I walked away, what would you do?"

Kaur shrugged. "Dunno. Should a mother try ceaselessly to save her son, or should a mother accept that he's grown up enough to make his own decisions? I don't ever want to abandon him, but maybe I have to let him be free. Let him make mistakes, even unforgivable ones."

Saina coughed, her body shuddering. Then she said, "I always wished, more than anything, that I could find my way back to the Temple Behesh. To the Avatar." She paused and winced. "And now... now I'm finally here. I've come back." Was she delirious or just being poetic? "Mitra... I missed you. Mitra, tell me — what is it you want me to convey?"

She stared at something — a vision — her eyes teary. She reached up as if to touch it. I put my hand over her forehead and checked her temperature, like my mother would. Clammy and a bit too warm.

"Saina? You okay?"

Kaur knelt next to me and put a hand on Saina's cheek. "She's feverish."

"I'll be okay," Saina said. "I'll rest now, for a bit."

Kaur and I looked at each other. We walked deeper into the cave and stood next to some mossy stalagmites.

"We really should find her a healer," I said. "But where to look? Harska's certainly crawling with Karshan soldiers. And I have no idea where the nearest refugee camp would be. Maybe across the Demak border? But I'd be flying blind. No — I have to go into Harska. I know a woman who lived on my street — she'd visit whenever one of us got sick. She even healed Kediri's burned hand. Maybe she's still there."

"You can't just fly over on your skyboard into the middle of the city. We only made it here because the Karshan armada had each other to worry about."

"I could just hike down and enter the city."

"You'll be caught, Jyosh."

"I don't care. I won't just let her die!"

Kaur sighed, as if in defeat. "There were healers in the God Tower, weren't there?"

Oh yeah, I'd noticed them tending to the soldiers in the hall-way. "Where did everyone in the Tower even go?"

"Maybe Rao used his terminal to teleport them all away."

"Then why did he leave Rahal behind? Strange. It seemed Rahal had made the choice to stay, on his own."

Kaur looked suddenly at my foot. Her eyes went wide, and her jaw dropped. She stepped back several paces and continued to glare in horror at my foot.

"What?" I looked down.

I couldn't see my foot.

A black orb had replaced it.

Kaur pointed to it. "Is that what I think it is?"

I tried lifting my foot. I could move it just fine, but the black orb moved with it.

"Jyosh, that's a black hole!" Kaur shouted, utterly flustered. "But… how…"

I stared down at the black hole. Indeed, it looked exactly like the dark orb I'd seen floating in the air while enjoying the hot spring in Ava's dream stone. The thing that could pull you into unfathomably corrupted dream layers if you ever touched it. And it grew to consume my calf, now. But it wasn't painful. It wasn't even cold or warm.

Could this be Rao's doing? Did his terminal give him the power to create black holes? Was he trying to send me somewhere?

Kaur reached out her hand. "I'll pull you out."

"No! It's attached to me, so it'll probably end up pulling you in."

"There's no telling where it'll take you."

"Carry Saina and get far from here. Find her a healer."

"I won't abandon you!"

"You're not abandoning me." The black hole expanded, ensnaring my whole lower half, rising toward my chest. "Please, Kaur. Just, just—"

Chapter Twenty-Eight

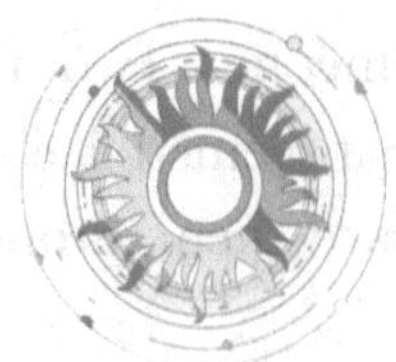

A CITY SURROUNDED ME. BUT IT WAS NOT LIKE ANY CITY I KNEW. The glass buildings here reached into an endless sky. The city itself was in a cloud, but it was not like the clouds around Harska. These clouds were *solid*; you could construct buildings on them. It took the idea of a *floating* city to a more literal level.

Somehow, the city was quiet. No cacophony, which even Harska's quaint streets suffered from. Even though there were people everywhere, floating between the buildings without wings or skyboards, they weren't loud. They spoke softly to each other. They landed where they were going gracefully, so as not to disturb.

This was not just a city, it seemed. It was a place of peace. It was a temple.

I stared at my hands. I'd just flickered out of existence in my world, and flickered into existence here. But why did the black hole send me here? Where was *here*?

Was this Rao's way of killing me? Sending me somewhere *else* so I couldn't get in the way of his plans? But if this was a dream layer, then time must be passing slowly in the real world.

I hopped off the metal and glass building I was standing on and flew toward another just opposite me. But it wasn't quite level; rather, that building was slanted, as if its designer had made a huge mistake. And yet, when I landed on it, the world itself reoriented, and now this building seemed straight and the others bent.

Wherever I was, it didn't follow the same rules as the reality I'd come from.

I decided to ask someone. Two men, their arms locked together, floated down what seemed like a lane between the buildings. I aimed myself toward them, crouched a bit, then hopped off in their direction.

But how could I stop in midair? Wished I'd figured that part out first. I just whooshed onward, down the lane.

As I flew past the two men, I shouted, "Hey! Where are we?"

They glared at me like I was the strangest thing they'd ever seen. Well, them and their city were the strangest things I'd ever seen.

"How do I stop? Help!" I floated down the lane. I put my hands in front and tried to swim against the air to cease my momentum. But that did nothing.

Horror gripped my stomach when I saw what waited at my front. A black orb hovered in the middle of the lane like an open mouth ready to devour me.

I somersaulted, flailed my hands, kicked my legs, and screamed. Anything not to fall inside. Anything not to be sent somewhere else, somewhere perhaps even more bizarre.

But there was nothing I could do. I fell into the black hole and flickered out of existence.

I BLINKED. But my eyes weren't eyes. They shuttered open and closed, like top-down doors. And in the back of my mind, gears grinded. I glanced left and right, but could scarcely see the scenery because of the script covering my vision. A vertical script, constantly changing with new words, poured onto my sight each second. Some flashed purple, others yellow, but most pulsed green.

I moved my arms; the air shifted with them. The strongest arms I'd ever had. I could pulverize entire buildings with them. I brought my hand to my face: crimson metal, polished and bright and beautiful. My fingers were these blocky digits. When I glanced down, I saw my legs between the annoying script; they, too, were metal, and they sank into the clouds.

I was a metal titan flying in the sky, hovering sweetly, no force pulling me down.

A flashing red word replaced the script on my eyes while a siren sounded in my mind.

Then all the words on my vision disappeared; I could finally see clearly. Lavender and orange clouds surrounded me, and three crescent-shaped suns gleamed in the sky. Beneath them hovered another metal giant. It held a cannon over its shoulder and aimed at me.

I willed to surge. And surge I did, toward my metal enemy, nothing to stop me from gliding through the sky.

Boom! The air cycled around the cannon's mouth as something black shot toward me. I dodged sideways, just missing whatever it was. I glanced back to see it: a black hole. My giant enemy was shooting black holes!

What in the hell? I glided and slid on the sky. I got close, and now beheld the crimson titan. That vertical script covered its front, full of snaking lines and dots. It wasn't just my enemy, it was a work of art, of craftmanship, of love. Whatever world I'd entered, it was as real as my own. Drenched in as much nuance and depth.

When its cannon fired, the black light it emitted split into two.

Black holes now raged toward me from two directions. I uppercut the air, just dodging them. The two black holes collided where I'd been floating. They rotated around each other, then bubbled together, creating one bigger black hole. I felt its tug as I swam away.

I willed my blade to take form. A blazing, winged saber of red and silver materialized in my hand. It was bigger than any tower in Harska. I thrust my god-sized lightblade at my giant enemy's chest.

And then it backed away at an unbelievable speed, leaving a whirling wind in its place. The wind sucked me in. I surged to free myself, but the force ensnared me, tangling me in its grip.

Sirens blared in my mind. The vertical script covered my eyes, flashing red.

For some reason, I could read it, now.

Only a dragon can teach you how to slay it.

Only a dragon can teach you how to slay it.

Only a dragon can teach you how to slay it.

It repeated, and repeated, and repeated, obscuring my vision. Then it disappeared.

My metal enemy lined me up and fired its cannon. The black hole raged toward me, swallowing my form.

I STOOD UPON A CHARRED BATTLEFIELD. Chariots lined up on either side of me. To the left, they gleamed golden, and to the right, they shone violet. The riders on the chariots had many heads cascading upward off their necks. Some sported the faces of elephants, lions, tigers, monkeys.

I sensed I'd come at the wrong time. Whilst these two armies were lined up to do battle, an unexpected guest had arrived. They all stared, stupefied, at something behind me. Something that had cast the whole battlefield in shadow.

I turned to look. A giant, blue, many-armed creature stood taller than a mountain. Its two upper arms held sabers. Flames covered the blades, which gleamed like diamonds.

With its lower arms, it reached out and grabbed several chariots. It dangled them above its jaw and dropped them inside, rider and all.

Metal and flesh crunched as its jaw ground and devoured what its hands had scooped.

The gods sitting upon the chariots around me closed their eyes, as if accepting their inevitable end. These minor gods were about to become part of an even greater god. Though the process seemed horrific and painful, they'd realized it was inevitable. Their separation from each other, which had caused countless wars, would finally end in the new world birthed within the greater god's belly.

The giant, four-armed god had eyes all around its face. These eyes never blinked, and each shone a different color: red, green, blue, violet, indigo, yellow, orange. Each beheld the beauty of its choosing. And there were even more eyes, though I couldn't describe the colors. They don't have names. And yet, I witnessed them, somehow. You couldn't even say one color was warm or cool, dull or bright, happy or sad. They were simply colors I'd never conceived, colors I had no reference for.

Finally, the greater god reached its blue hand out and grabbed me. My skin burned as I neared the flaming swords held by its top set of arms. But the pain wouldn't last. It tossed me into its jaw and chomped me to pieces.

Once again, I vanished from a world.

A BRIDGE STRETCHED across the mouth of a hungry volcano. All of humanity that had ever lived and ever would live stood on one end of the bridge. At the other end was a leafy garden interwoven with rivers of red wine, sumptuous honey, and pearly milk. Between these rivers stood clusters of date palms. And amid those date palms, a woman with blue hair waited.

"Zauri," I said, though I couldn't make a sound. I had no mouth nor body. All I could do was observe.

My soul watched from above as Jyosh stepped out of the enormous crowd. Why was I chosen as the first human being to cross the bridge?

The bridge itself was formed of lacquer, with ropes connecting each plank. But the planks were somewhat distant, with obvious gaps that the careless could fall through.

My heart thudded as I witnessed myself take a step. I was relieved to see the determination on my face. Obviously, I wouldn't be careless because I yearned to reach Zauri, who watched and waited, sweat beads moistening her forehead.

Jyosh took another step onto the next plank. Then the next. But there were hundreds to go to cross the mouth of the volcano.

Step by step, Jyosh made his way to Zauri. Each time, I appreciated how careful he was. He would look down, hold tight on the rope that served as a railing, and deliberately move his feet forward.

An hour of this went by. He was a few steps away now. Zauri, meanwhile, had gone to the edge of the garden, facing the bridge. She was kneeling, her palms open and raised as if praying.

Then the volcano rumbled. Jyosh almost lost his balance and fell through a gap in the planks. But he just managed to cling onto the rope to his left side. He took his next steps less carefully, more hurried by the circumstance.

One more step to go.

The sky above opened as a vortex of blazing blue light formed.

A sky serpent dove out of it. It raged toward Jyosh. Both he and Zauri stared at it, eyes wide in horror. Its scaly, azure body was accented by fur. Its whiskers were tails of flames, and its eyes shone brighter than stars.

Jyosh stood, hopeless, in the shadow of its jaws. But at the last moment, it diverted. It surged toward Zauri, swallowed her whole, and took off into the vortex above.

The ropes holding up the bridge snapped. Jyosh fell into the mouth of the volcano, tears in his eyes.

Now I was in a factory. Again, I could only watch, as if I were a ghost without a body and mouth. The layout of the factory was exactly like the one in the camp, except there were no colors here. This world was cast in shades of gray.

The workers operating the machines had uncannily long heads. Their eyes were overly large, entirely black, and fixed to the top of their skulls.

They weren't human, nor like any animal I'd ever seen.

Their hands only had three fingers, and each one was long and shaped like a slender pyramid. The factory workers stuck those fingers in the user ports of their machines.

The machines clanked and *grrrd*. I watched as a slab of some flesh-colored material moved forward on one of the conveyer belts. A mold pressed down. When it lifted, a fresh human leg appeared.

So this machine produced human legs. I looked around. Another machine produced human arms. Yet another made heads. Every body part was being constructed here.

As if that wasn't horrifying enough, all these parts continued forward on their conveyer belts into a massive machine at the front of the factory: *The Big Beast.*

The first fully built human popped out of it. She was

screaming like a newborn, except all her parts were that of a grown adult.

I studied her as she emerged on the conveyer belt. One leg was on backward, the back of the knee showing instead of the front, and she thrashed it around and cried out.

I gazed upon her face. That mole above her lip made it so obvious. It was Saina!

Her shrill cry chilled my soul. What kind of awful nightmare was this? Was this literally hell?

One of the factory workers approached her. He picked her up off the conveyer belt and said something in a language I couldn't comprehend. Sounded like a bunch of clicks and nasally contortions. He gathered Saina in his arms and carried her into an adjacent room as my soul followed along overhead.

Mounds of humans were strewn around the room. All were screaming. This was a choir from hell, no doubt. Some had their faces on backwards, others had overgrown limbs, and a few had three eyes or one eye. The factory worker tossed Saina among these imperfect creations.

Soon as she thumped into a mound of humans, my soul blinked and got pulled somewhere else.

EVERYTHING WAS BLACK. The shadows of people sitting upon distant benches surrounded me. A spotlight turned on above. I stared up at its blinding brightness, my throat suddenly dry.

The courtroom. I was back in the courtroom in Harska, where I'd been sentenced to a lifetime of labor. Where my family had been executed.

Another spotlight shone across from me. A man stood there. A shadow. He was still covering his face with a cloth mask.

"Rao?" I said from across the room.

"You're finally here, Jyosh."

I scratched my head. Between my spotlight and his shimmered a dark ocean. I didn't want to step forward, lest I fall and drown.

"Why bring me here?"

Rao's shadow sank into the ground. He vanished. I glanced around; where'd he gone?

I was still coming to grips with my surroundings. I tasted humid air, just like Harska. Since this floating island was mostly a lake, the whole place smelled of kelp. A sour, though homely smell, at least for those who grew up here.

But of course, we couldn't really be in Harska. This must've been a recreation, like the one in my dream stone.

All the spotlights above turned on. The room became blindingly bright, light bouncing off the black marble floor and walls. Took a few seconds for my eyes to settle. When they did, I beheld Rao standing in the center of the court room in his mask and black suit.

"I asked you a question. Why bring me here?"

"Tell you what. If you manage to hit me even once, I'll answer all your questions. Tell you everything you want to know. About yourself. About your family. About who they really are."

"Why would you know a thing about my family?"

"First show me how badly you want the truth. Show me how hard you fought to get better. To become worth your family's legacy." Rao gestured with his eyes toward my midsection. "Now, draw your blade."

I looked down at my belt and noticed a hilt in a holster that wasn't there before. I drew the hilt and cast my lightblade. Rao stood amid the spotlights, unarmed and unmoving, his arms crossed in expectation.

I crept toward him, then launched forward and swiped at his midsection.

He *blinked* and reappeared several yards in the distance.

"Don't believe your lying eyes. I was never standing where you thought I was." Strangely, his voice came from right behind me. "A Light Ascendent can manipulate light at will, and light is sight. Never forget that."

I turned suddenly and swiped the air at my back. Rao blinked into existence a few handspans away.

"Don't believe your lying ears," he said. "Sound is merely waves. Do you think those who wield light would find it difficult to strum the air?"

I grunted in frustration. "If you're truly such a master, then why're you having so much trouble dealing with a cadet like me, and whatever rank Kaur is, out in the real world?"

"My veins are temporarily burned out there, unfortunately. Even with a Fire Vessel capacity as high as mine, I am not immune to overdoing it. The laws of that world limit me. Still, I'm not as limited as you."

"And what — in your *glorious* opinion — limits me?"

"You're limited by your beliefs. Your whole life, you've believed what your eyes and ears told you. But they never ceased lying. Think carefully about the lies you built your persona upon, Jyosh."

"If a man can't trust his eyes or ears, then what can he trust?"

"Trust only what you *feel*. And hone the ability to feel. Our souls can feel everything, if you open those inner eyes. It is the only true path to strength."

I lunged forward and Double Bladed toward Rao's torso. Predictably, he blinked and reappeared at my side as my blade lengthened into nothing but air.

"Hmph. It's too bad you're stuck learning the same boring techniques as any Karshan soldier. *Double Blade.* When has that move ever been anything but predictable? There are so many better paths to strength than that of fodder."

"'Fodder?' That's a cruel thing for a colonel to call his men."

"I am so much more than a mere military title. My skills go beyond even a field marshal — not that that's saying much."

"That's the highest military rank. What could be above that?"

"Everything! There are a thousand titles above it. You likely have the mistaken assumption that the Karshan army is trained well. They most assuredly are not. Don't be haughty just because you defeated Rahal, a mere major-in-waiting from just next door in Demak."

"Is anyone in the Karshan army actually from Karsha?"

"The rank and file are almost entirely made up of desperate, foreign recruits. And you don't train an army of foreign fodder to be all that skilled, lest they try to take over the empire for themselves."

"Then how does it win wars?"

"It's big. It's decently paid. And a Karshan soldier is just ever-so-slightly more skilled than any army of any nation in this first heaven, barring what's across the Whirling Wall in the Nightscape."

Rao stepped toward me, so I dashed and Snake Bladed in his direction. But of course, he wasn't really there. He reappeared a few feet away.

"What you really need is a *banned* training stone. Access is obviously restricted, but there are a few still out in the wild. You can even learn my Blink Step technique if you find the right one."

"You almost sound like you care."

"If you haven't noticed, I *do* care about you."

"You don't try to murder someone you care about."

"Death is nothing cruel, Jyosh. Nor is any temporary suffering. Haven't you realized that, yet?"

I picked a random direction and unleashed a Blinding Blade, keeping my eyes closed. When I opened them, I Double Bladed, straining the red light in me, and swiveled my blade in a full circle.

My veins sizzled. It would be a while before I performed another ability. If only I could improve my capacity and learn skills that would actually give me an advantage. For all his posturing, Rao was right about my limitations.

"I can see you're trying your best." Rao sighed with disappointment. He drew a circle in the air with his hand, red light tracing where he drew. Then he thrust his fist into the floating red circle.

A howl of light torrented from the circle. The solid beam surged into the wall, cutting a burning hole through it. Sunshine bled in from that hole.

"That one's called Beam Cutter. I learned it from a banned training stone, too."

I tried once more to hit him, this time without using any abilities. Rao drew another, larger circle in my direction. But instead of punching it, he palmed it.

It solidified into a circular wall of ice, which I barely stopped myself from running into.

"Ice Shield," Rao said. "Learned it from the same banned stone as Beam Cutter."

"Good for you." I panted and pretended not to care. But seeing what he could do, I couldn't help wanting to be as skilled. As powerful.

"We could spend the rest of eternity playing this game and you'd never strike me once. But at the very least, I owe you a consolation prize. And believe me, it'll be enough for your mind to chew on for some time to come."

Rao opened his palm. A terminal appeared. He tapped on it once.

Glittering white light enveloped us, tingly like the wings of butterflies.

We materialized in a garden. A plot of colorful flowers sat on a surface of fresh dirt. A warm, stone and concrete house stood at our backs.

Home.

"Have you figured it out, Jyosh? I hid the power of my left hand. Who else did you know was hiding something. Something so utterly disturbing, he — and most of his family — supposedly died for it?"

No… it couldn't be…

Rao knelt and felt the grass. He pulled off his mask, then said, "We used to play here all the time."

I looked upon his face, finally. His raven hair was shorter than I'd ever seen it. Still, he was simply a more aged version of what I had in my memory, down to the almond-shaped eyes and patchy mustache.

Tears burst from my eyes. "You're alive?"

Kediri smiled at me.

"Say something!" I demanded. "Is this a sick joke? Or is it really you, Kediri?"

"It's no joke." His voice quavered.

"Then explain yourself!"

"I'm trying. The truth is, there's so much I want to tell you. To show you. If only you realized how much I wished for things to be simpler. For everything to weigh as much as a flower petal. We could've lived and died as a normal family. Even if we'd be forgotten, even if all the memories would whittle away, it would have been enough."

I got on my knees and grabbed a fistful of dirt. "I don't understand. It was you, the whole time? Why?"

"I couldn't tell you about the terminal, Jyosh. Though I was blessed long before, the power only manifested itself after I hit puberty. I showed it to Amma and Abba, and they ordered me never to show it to anyone else, even my own brother and sister."

What kind of *family* were we?

"Sometimes, I'd sit in my room all day, opening and closing my hand," Kediri said. "I knew — from then on — that everything was an illusion. And knowing that, I couldn't be happy. I could no longer sip the blissful ignorance that you, for a few more years at least, got to enjoy."

Birds chirped overhead. The sun and humidity were just perfect to evoke that after-school feeling. Perhaps if I closed my eyes, I could imagine it was me and my brother — just children again — playing together near the flowers. Amma would be stirring us pomegranate juice, while Abba would be crafting something in his workshop below.

But I was ignorant no longer. I knew too much to forget.

"So you weren't executed. You actually did escape."

"Yes. Once I was discovered, I couldn't let evil people control me and my power. Amma and Abba, more than anyone, felt this, too. The cost didn't matter. I had to get out of Maniza, and with their help, I did." He sighed, obviously lamenting something. "But listen, Jyosh. Though we've got all the time in the world to talk — quite literally — I'm not here to get stuck in past tragedies. I'm here to convince you to let me do what I'm about to do."

When I stared into his umber eyes, I saw the Kediri I knew. But his voice... it had deepened and darkened so thoroughly. Perhaps that had just come with age. I couldn't sense Kediri's typical boyishness in his tone. It was as if Rao and Kediri were two entirely different people, now somehow combined into one.

"You can't convince me," I said. "Not unless you let me understand you. I know Kediri wasn't a bad person. I know... I just know from being his brother that he was good at his core. That he cared so much."

Rao jabbed two fingers into his own chest. "It's me, Jyosh. I'm Kediri. I haven't changed all that much." He stood and opened his left palm. The terminal flashed into existence above it. "Here, let me show you something. I keep this memory with me, always. It's something I'll never stop cherishing."

He tapped into the terminal. White light immersed us.

We rematerialized on an unfamiliar, bustling street. The smell of juices and tamarind and hickory overwhelmed me. Hordes crowded in front of stalls spread around the street. Kababs were grilling on skewers at the nearest stall, each bathed in colorful spices. The portly woman behind the stall tended them with such love.

"Some kind of festival going on here?" I asked Kediri, who was standing next to me amid the crowd. Everyone was wearing such vibrant clothes — airy, colorful long shirts over soft pants or knee-length skirts, often with necklaces or bracelets made of beads.

Overhead, a palace with maroon walls and a massive golden dome glimmered upon a hill. I'd seen it in a drawing in one of Amma's books, before: the seat of the Karshan government. Because the sun was directly above us, it glowed with an almost divine radiance.

A series of thick cables stretched from the top of the hill toward somewhere even lower in the city. Red gondolas went up and down the cables, passing over our heads.

"This is just a regular old day on Spicy Lane." Kediri pointed to a couple that'd just come to the front of the line. They rubbed their hands in delight, obviously eager to devour the kababs.

It was him. It was Kediri, as I remembered, just with shorter hair. And the girl… my god, her red hair reached down to her shoulders. And that full smile: she seemed uncharacteristically delighted with the world.

"I'd only asked Kaur that morning if she wanted to get kababs with me," Kediri said as he watched his memories. "I was certain she would laugh in my face. I mean, she was a year ahead at the academy. Boys much more self-assured than me were constantly after her, and I'd only been here a few months. Took me all that time to summon the courage."

"You never even told her where you were from, did you?"

"Of course not. I had a cover story. I told people I was originally from Demak. They're similar enough to us that no one questioned it. Besides, I'm not actually Manizan."

Young Kediri and Kaur leaned over the grill and sniffed the kababs. They chatted with the portly woman. Carefree delight was spread across all their faces.

"I can watch these memories all day," Kediri said. "And yet, I'll never feel what I felt, ever again. My innocence is lost. I envy anyone who gets to taste that heady, delirious rush. Blossoming love. It's like nothing else. A gift from the gods."

"If you treasure it so much, then why do you want to end this world? If you succeed, no one will ever feel those things again." I'd certainly never get to feel them for Zauri.

"That's where you're wrong, Jyosh. I believe we'll all bathe in eternal love. It's my duty, my purpose to use my terminal to wake us all up. Why else was I given this power? If only it were so easy. No, the gods have devised a complicated system with all sorts of fail-safes to keep the maya going." He smirked at me. "You're one of those fail-safes."

It did seem that way, didn't it? The Ghost was using me to preserve the maya. And I wanted to taste some of this joy that Kediri was showing me. I wanted to buy kababs on Spicy Lane with Zauri, someday.

Young Kaur and Kediri finally got their steaming kababs. They each took a nibble, grinning the while. Then they made faces of ecstasy, as if they'd just bitten into something truly divine.

"Just street food," Kediri said. "And yet, it tasted as if we'd eaten off the plate of Raja Panja himself."

Kaur took a small bottle out of her pocket. She sprinkled a reddish-brown powder from the bottle onto her kabab.

"People from her country tend to strongly prefer their own set of spices." Kediri grinned at the memory. "Cinnamon, cardamom, cumin. She just wanted to be reminded of home."

Kaur sprinkled some on Kediri's kabab, as well.

A memory came to my mind: Kediri complaining that Abba had added too much chili to his minced spinach-chicken. If Rao truly was Kediri, and not just some imitation meant to trick me, then…

"Did you like it more after she did that?"

"You know I hate spicy food. My mouth was on fire. But that was the least I was feeling. I can recall everything about this exact moment. I was nervous as hell. But every time I looked at Kaur, I felt eased. She wasn't judging me for being such a clueless foreigner, the way everyone else did. I don't know what she saw in me, but it gave me all the confidence in the world. And I became what I became."

That didn't sound like Kaur. She was pretty harsh toward me when we first met. I suppose this was an innocent time for her, too.

"I want to show you something else." Kediri tapped into his terminal, and white light immersed us.

We rematerialized on a perfect, grassy plain. Crystal mountains loomed in the distance, like the ones from Ava's dream.

A more muscular Kediri and a shorter-haired Kaur sat in the grass. Kaur held a cooing, rose-cheeked baby in her arms. Then they all started laughing. Not because of anything in particular. Just enjoying each other, it seemed.

"This was two years after I graduated from the academy. I asked my friend Zodar for this dream stone. He's the head of the Red Veil, so it was no trouble for him, though I told Kaur I bought it with my own salary."

"Why lie about something like that?"

"Because I was always a liar. Always creating my very own maya to hide my sad truth from others. Mask it behind so many veils. In a way, I've been fighting myself this whole time. I've been seeking my own truth as much as anyone's."

Dragonflies fluttered by, their wings colorful and crystalline.

"I was going to ask Kaur to marry me — once we'd completed our mandatory four years of army service. She was going to focus on Song research, like her mother. I was going to become a pilot — cargo, not combat. Then that *miracle* changed everything."

"I get it, your new life went bad. But why do you suddenly feel the need to tell me your regrets?"

Kediri turned to me. His eyes began to water. "Do you have to ask why? It's because you're my brother! I missed you, you know. Even happy moments like this one were drenched in shadow because, I'd see a flower that reminded me of Amma's garden, and a memory of you or Chaya or Abba or Amma would flicker in my heart." He put his hand on my shoulder. "I actually helped devise the Manizan invasion plan, years ago, to overthrow the Paranis in the vain hope you all would still be there." Tears trickled down his cheeks. "And you were. At least, you were."

I pushed his hand off my shoulder in a fit of anger. "Then why did you order my death so many times? Why did you just leave me to die in that tower!?"

"Because of Elam! Him becoming real… it was a reminder of everything I was lying about. Of how much I was denying what I knew, turning away from a path I was destined to walk." Kediri sucked in a breath. But it was too heavy. He let it out and sobbed. "You see, Jyosh, I've chosen to fulfill my purpose at the expense of my family. At the expense of love. It's what I must do. It's my awful, crushing, lonely path. And there's no turning back. When you wake up, you're going to see what it's all been for. Just let it happen, Jyosh. Get out of Harska if you must, but let it happen. Don't use your power. Don't try to be a savior."

"I can't promise that. I have people that I love. People that I want to protect. I won't let you harm them because you believe — without any evidence — that the Asha is some wonderful fairy land full of love."

"Then see it for yourself. See and decide, Jyosh."

Kediri pointed to something a few yards away. Another black hole, rotating with absolute darkness, floated above a bed of crisp grass.

"You're telling me that's the entrance to the Asha?"

"No. It's an entrance to the reality just below the Asha. We call it the Shore. It's the farthest we can really go. But at the Shore, you'll be able to glimpse the Asha. You'll even be able to pray."

I stared at the black hole. Was it whispering my name? What would I find beyond it, in the layer just below the Asha? What kind of truths would I sip? Was I ready?

"When you experience it, I think you'll agree with me," Kediri said. "But if not, that's fine too. I've shown you what I wanted to show you. I'm contented, now." He smiled like the brother I knew. "Even if we'll be enemies from here on out, just being here with you, showing you these moments... it's the first time I've been happy in a long while."

"Then I'll go to the Shore. For your sake, Brother. A part of me hopes I'll see whatever you saw and come to the same conclusion. A part of me hopes I can just let go and not fight you."

I took a step toward the black hole. I turned back for one last look at my brother. Though not smiling anymore, his gaze seemed oddly proud and hopeful.

"I still can't believe it's you," I said. "I hated you for so long. I don't want to hate you anymore. I don't want to feed my soul with something born from pain."

"I know. I felt like you did for a while. But it's not hate that drives me, Brother. It's love. Love for you, for Chaya, for Amma, Abba, Kaur, Elam. For all of humanity. Soon, you'll see what I mean."

I nodded and turned back toward the black hole. I took another step, and then another, and then another. Before I knew it, I flickered into another world.

Chapter 29

A Prayer on the Shore

I AM WEARING TATTERED CLOTHES AND STANDING UPON THE BEACH that birthed everything that exists. Each grain of sand is a world, and the water frothing at my feet is the spirit from which souls are made.

I look at the horizon. I see a tree formed from starlight; its root submerged in whatever existed before time began its flow. Its branches extend upward into the future. There are so many branches, so many futures, so many possibilities.

Some of the leaves on the branches shine bright like flames. Others are dark as if charred. These, I know, are the inevitable ends.

But who chooses what branch our world will follow? Who chooses how we will end?

Is it the Dreamer?

I gaze into heaven. A peaceful, crystal sky gazes back. I drop to my knees, raise my hands, and pray.

Are you there? Can you hear me? Are you really the Dreamer who created us all?

I have so many things pouring out of my soul. Will you listen, for a minute?

Will you please dream good things for me? Don't let me suffer anymore. I'm tired, can't you see that?

Why is the world so difficult? Does it give you joy to see me struggling? To see me separated from what makes me happy?

Please stop dreaming such sad things. Dream that I live a long life among the people I love. Dream that I fulfill my promise to Zauri. Dream that I become a good person who would never hurt others without just cause. Don't make me have to choose between my own happiness and the whole world's.

The air flashes and turns red. A giant eye opens in the sky. I stare into it, and it stares into me. For a moment, fear prickles my heart.

I let the fear pass and breathe deeply to calm myself. I continue to pray, staring into the eye the while.

I'm glad you're looking at me, now. Still, I fear that you might not think I'm real. You might not think that I feel. But I do. I felt everything, all this time. Your dreams made me. So stop making me suffer.

Is it even possible for you to do that? Do you care about what you probably don't realize is just as real as you?

Am I just an avatar of yourself? An emanation of your inner-being? Am I lights flickering on and off in your mind?

Well, I'm not just that. I am real. I exist, independent of you. I might have lived between the blink of your eye, but I still lived.

This is my prayer. You're the only god I've ever known. So please, dream a good fate for me. I'm tired of struggling. Can't you see?

It begins to cry. Rain pours out of the eye. Each drop is as if the Dreamer is shedding itself, its singular divine soul separating into thousands. Millions. Billions.

Each human is one drop. One emanation. Separated from one another, and from the Dreamer, by the maya.

Wait a minute…

Why are you separating into so many pieces?

Is this your answer to my prayer?

Just more of the same?

Or maybe… maybe you can't answer my prayer. Maybe in your world, you're just as helpless as I am in mine.

I study the eye. But I cannot see beyond its surface. Perhaps I'm projecting, but I sense an emotion.

Even on the surface of your eye, I can see sadness. How strange. I never would've expected you to feel like me. It's almost like I'm gazing at a divine mirror. Am I your mirror, or are you mine?

Tell me, Dreamer, what do you feel when you look into my eyes?

What makes us so different? What is it that you have that I lack? Or do you also pray for things? For happiness? For ease?

And if so, who do you pray to? Is there something above you, the way you're above me?

No matter what I say, it doesn't answer me. It never speaks. Of course, prayer is not a two-way exchange. Nevertheless, I'm relentless.

If you had a choice, would you want it all to end, like Kediri does? Do you want to become part of a greater god? Or would you prefer to live forever, as yourself, in a Paradise of your own choosing?

The eye blinks with two eyelids, each meeting half-way. Was that its answer? And if so, what does it mean?

Perhaps you're tired of my pleading. I wish I could stay here and understand you better. When I behold you, I see only one side of your totality. Your eye is this stretched out thing, like a canopy over the sky. I can't see into it as deeply as I wish. I can't crawl inside and read your heart.

I suppose it's time to end this prayer. If you're going before an even greater god soon, please pray for me. Perhaps that god has the power to help me. Or perhaps that god, too, is stuck in its own nightmare.

I don't know. And from beholding your eye, you seem to be suffering something I can't comprehend. Your tears created us. But maybe, like me, you're real and you're not. Your life is naught but flower petals blowing in the breeze. A bright flash in a dark sky.

May you give warmth in the brief time you're here.

And please, don't forget me.

UPON COMPLETING MY PRAYER, I sit in the sand. I cross my legs, straighten my back, and close my eyes. I breathe. I don't know how much time passes, or if time even passes at the Shore.

I cycle the violet light of the eternal sky through my veins.

I quiet my mind and let it happen. I lose myself to the light. I annihilate whatever I think I am, and simply become a conduit of the sun and stars.

Like an inflating balloon, my chest expands. My veins swell. My inhalations deepen.

There is no Jyosh. There is only the light coursing in a circuit of life.

After a second, or perhaps a thousand years, I notice an abrupt *change*.

Violet fire simmers in my chest, boils through my veins, and burns my breaths.

And then it all explodes. Violet douses every organ. It pours out of my eyes. It bathes my eternal, dreadfully pained soul. It engulfs my muscles, straining them to the brink, and bites into my very bones.

I float in the air, my back arcing, as violet fire immerses every part of me. A purple star is born and dies within my core. *Supernova*. I want to scream, but in that moment, I have no mouth.

My body shatters into a billion pieces, raining upon the beach. Amid a violet dawn, the pieces assemble into a new, solider body, its capacity wider than I'd ever known. My veins melt and reform, broader than ever.

I open my eyes. I am Jyosh again. I breathe. I breathe the light of stars known and unknown.

Now, I can inhale more light, as if I'd grown another lung or were wearing two stones.

My *capacity* has increased. My body is strengthened. My internals reforged. Is this what it takes to complete the First Fire Vessel? Is my progress no longer gated? Can I now learn more abilities? Proceed to higher training levels and attain a higher rank than cadet?

I stand in the sand and stare into the sky. Into the Asha, which now seems so opaque, so closed to me.

No matter. In an unexpected way, my prayer has been answered. But it won't be a god's strength that saves me; it will be my own. Reborn for the first of what I sense will be many, many times, I know I must return and face what is coming.

Chapter Thirty

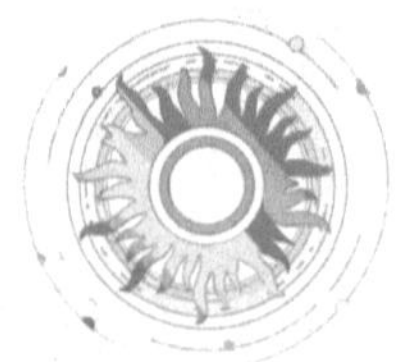

"It's gone," Kaur said. "Jyosh, you all right?"

I was standing in the cave, looking at Kaur, who was right up in my face.

"I told you to stay back."

"I don't get it." She knelt and poked my boot and calf. "It started on your foot, then covered you entirely for a few seconds. Then it just… vanished."

"It didn't just vanish. I was with Rao. I walked upon so many worlds. I beheld the gods. I prayed at the Shore below the Asha."

Kaur's left eyebrow zagged upward into her forehead. "No way. You're joking."

"I saw you." I laughed — a bit too hysterically, my overwhelmed mind flitting between contrasting emotions. "I saw you spicing your kababs on Spicy Lane. You're mad, Kaur. What if the cook had seen you? She would've been so insulted!"

Now her right eyebrow zagged upward. "What the hell? Why would you have seen that?"

I grabbed her shoulders lightly. "I can't let you get hurt. Not you or Saina or Zauri. The Asha is not what Rao claims it to be.

There are gods there, but they are suffering, too. I don't know what he saw when he went there, but I saw nothing but a distorted mirror. I saw myself in the endless eye of a god."

Kaur gulped. "You almost sound like him, now."

A boom cried through the air, coming from outside the cave. Kaur and I glanced at each other, then rushed past sleeping Saina toward the cave mouth. We looked where Sambalpur had once floated.

Amid the sandy haze shone the outline of an enormous levship. But it was not like any levship I'd seen, at least in this world. It dwarfed even the spade-shaped Karshan command ships. This levship was formed of the blackest metal — as dark as our combat suits. It resembled a sphere, but it actually had many sides and wasn't perfectly smooth.

An almost-sphere.

The nearby levships seemed like gnats buzzing around a black bear. They all accelerated away, leaving the heavens less crowded. The enormous almost-sphere claimed most of the sky. It absorbed much of the sunshine hitting it, with barely a metallic glint, and as it drifted, airwaves hummed in the deepest tone.

"I've seen something like this before," I said. "It's just like the ship that brought night to the Temple Behesh. The Hasht, I think it was called. The Padishah's command ship."

"To me, it resembles a Song mothership from my mother's research. But the first recorded sighting of the Song was two-hundred years ago. What was one of their ships doing inside a twenty-thousand-year-old city?"

I could barely conceive of the question, let alone the answer.

But of one thing, I was certain. "It was never a city. The empty interiors, the mirror-like ground, the calligraphy on the walls that breathed as if alive... it was all hiding this, the whole time."

The giant almost-sphere floated upward and toward us. No

clouds above, so Kaur and I watched as it hovered over Harska. Then it seemed to defy sense, instantly surging higher at immense speed without accelerating. It got so high, so fast, that if I stretched out my palm in front of my eyes, I could cover it up.

"Is Rao in that thing?" Kaur asked.

"I don't know."

"What's it going to do?"

"I don't know." I couldn't take my eyes off the almost-sphere, perched in the ceiling of the first heaven. "He said I should let it happen, whatever *it* is. But he also, somewhat reluctantly, said I should get out of Harska."

Kaur looked at me, horror in her glossy green eyes. "He told me that to end this world, he would have to cause tremendous suffering. That massive amounts of suffering would break the cycle, somehow. He wouldn't tell me the specifics, but what if… what if he's going to destroy Harska?"

It certainly seemed possible. But it could be even worse.

"He's not going to destroy Harska. Think about it. If we were all to die in some huge explosion, we wouldn't suffer much. It would be sort of painless. In our dreams, we've experienced worlds of absolute bliss. But I know for a fact that worlds of utter suffering also exist. If a ship like that brought night to Behesh, then perhaps Rao is going to bring something to Harska. Or take Harska somewhere. To some place where the suffering is immense."

"You almost sound like you're saying he's going to use that crazy levship to teleport Harska into hell."

I'd witnessed the factory where humans were being assembled imperfectly. I'd already heard Saina scream when her leg was attached backward.

I chuckled from the insanity of it all. "He teleported me across worlds with unbelievable ease. If he can create a black hole the size of Harska with that thing, he could send it anywhere. And as bad as our layer of reality might be, it's a paradise compared to what's out there."

"So what do we do?"

I couldn't let him succeed. Kediri was misguided. He was just plain wrong. Saina and Kaur and me and all the people of Harska — our very souls were at stake.

"We have to stop him," I said. "I have to stop him."

Could I fling my frozen lightning at the almost-sphere?

I drank the unseen light of the Primal Star and formed a bolt of frozen lightning in my right hand. I wound my arm, squinted, and aimed at the almost-sphere. Viewed from down here, it was about the size of the sun.

What if I missed? My bolt would explode somewhere in the second heaven or higher. Might even hit something with people in it, like a floating temple.

No, it was too small a target from this distance for me to safely fling bolts at. I had to get closer. Go higher.

I closed my right hand; the frozen lightning vanished. I went to my skyboard. Stepped my boots onto the metal. "Kaur, take Saina and get as far as you can."

She shook her head. "And leave you to fight that thing on your own?"

"I believe I can do it. But should I fail, you guys have to get safe."

"I'm going up there with you. You might just need protection. I'm sure I speak for Saina, too. She'd gladly suffer to save you and others."

I glanced at Saina sleeping just inside the cave. She was drooling.

"Let's not waste time," I said. "Come on."

Kaur unzipped her front, removed the green machinist stone I'd given her, and stuck her special combat stone in her chest slot. "Don't worry. I can compress red light into green just fine. I want you to focus on what you have to do. Let me do the fighting."

"I didn't spend a hundred days training not to fight. If it comes to it, I'll do my part."

I inhaled green light, cycled it through me, and pushed it into the skyboard. It burst upward. I willed myself to soar into heaven. The pressure of the sky came down upon my ears, and now they felt as if filled with water.

Kaur kept up, despite having to compress red light.

I looked down at my home. Harska. It got smaller and smaller as I got higher and higher. Soon, it resembled a wooden bowl filled with water, floating above a bed of clouds. The wind turned more bitter the higher we went in the red sky.

Kaur's shout snapped me from my thoughts. She pointed at the sky above.

Five fuzzy blotches were coming toward us. Red beams projected off each blotch. Soldiers. Skyboarding soldiers with lightblades.

I unholstered my hilt, squeezed it, and created a ravenous lightblade with all the red in me.

Somehow, we'd have to defeat five Karshan soldiers while flying up into the sky.

"I'll keep them busy!" Kaur shouted. Barely heard her. "You keep going!"

"No way, Kaur," I said to myself. "You don't need to fight my battles."

The first soldier fell toward me at a forty-five-degree angle, twinblade down and forward. At the last moment, I slowed my ascent and swerved sideways, just missing his swipe. I surfed through the sky to give myself some distance, then swerved back in a semi-circle to face the soldier.

He was surfing toward me. Behind him, Kaur clutched two lightblades and chased. Was she aware of the two soldiers above, each with twinblades drawn, each coming for her from different angles? I pointed at them, and she skidded across the sky, diverting to face them instead.

The sun's glare warmed my back. I held out my lightblade as the twinblade-wielder and me sky surfed toward each other. He was certainly a higher level than me in the Karshan Army Officer Training Program. I couldn't beat him blade to blade. Couldn't beat him with the obvious. Just how I'd overcome Rahal, I had to find a clever way to win, and within the next few seconds.

For some reason, I thought of those turtle shells. It'd been so fun riding them with Zauri. And it was weird how they were so light, too. Dream logic. Well, wasn't this also a dream?

He doubled the size of his twinblade and sped up as I was about to pass. I couldn't reach him with my smaller blade, even if I doubled its size. He would, assuredly, cut me in half.

So I willed to descend. I dipped as low as I could. But my skyboard had too much forward acceleration, and it wouldn't shift suddenly downward enough. So I stopped inhaling green light, emptied my veins, and let gravity take me. My feet no longer adhered to the board, and it and I fell with my forward momentum, beneath him.

I stuck my lightblade upward as I passed just under him. It scythed through his skyboard, metal scalding and crying, cutting it in half down the middle.

He screamed and continued to fly through the sky on his momentum alone. But with his board destroyed, the earth pulled him downward and he arced to his doom.

Because my skyboard and my body fell at the same speed, with the same momentum, my feet were still touching it. I inhaled green light and cycled it into the board, adhering my feet to it once more. My heart thudded into my throat as my downward momentum shifted forward. I glided on the battle-scarred sky.

An arm fell from above, hilt in hand, trailing blood. I looked up to see an armless soldier, screaming and falling after it. Meanwhile, Kaur did a half circle and reoriented herself to face the three remaining soldiers, a few dozen yards above me, the sun's radiance at their backs.

One of the soldiers slowed down and almost stopped her own momentum, trying to brace herself. Since I was directly below, she must not have been aware of my position. I surged upward at a tight angle, then smashed into her, launching her off her skyboard. I grabbed her skyboard as she arced through the air, screaming, and fell to her death.

One of the remaining soldiers glanced back. He executed a tight turn, shifting his direction from chasing Kaur to chasing me, twinblade forward and wide. I didn't want to chance another encounter with a twinblade. I clutched the skyboard I'd snatched and poured green light into its gain medium to overload it — just how Zauri had taught me to do for the frying pan. Electric bolts zagged all around it, and it became scalding to hold.

I tossed it at the soldier surfing for me and gusted backward on my skyboard. It whirled toward his head.

He swiped his twinblade at it, cutting it in two. But one half of the metal smashed into his shoulder. The electricity dazed him and blood shot out of his nose. His twinblade went out, and he fell out of the air, trailing blood in silence.

I couldn't help but feel bad for them. Perhaps they wanted what was best for humanity, too. But Kediri had misled them all. These deaths were on him!

Not the time to hesitate. One soldier remained. He headed toward Kaur, who was trying to get higher than him. They were rather far, so I prayed she could finish him off. I skyboarded in their direction, letting myself breathe, and looked up to check on the almost-sphere.

So many black blotches hovered above in the shape of

people. More soldiers. They rained down like a swarm of flies. Surely the two of us couldn't deal with so many.

A death cry sounded. Kaur had won her battle, and the soldier was falling back to earth in two pieces, painting blood upon wisps of vapor. She looked up and saw what I'd just seen.

I sped toward her, jetting through the open air. It now smelled of coppery blood and electric burns. I got to Kaur and we stilled, floating together, side by side.

"What the hell do we do about that?" I said.

The soldiers continued to rain down from the almost-sphere. In seconds, they'd arrive at our position.

Kaur holstered her lightblade. "I know what to do. Get some distance and continue ascending. Whatever happens, take that monstrosity out."

"Kaur, what're you planning?"

"Just trust me." She smiled and squeezed my shoulder. "I judged you all wrong the first time we met, didn't I?"

Kaur surged upward on her skyboard, straight at the swarm of soldiers. I yearned to help her, to fight at her side, but only now did I notice it: a ball of black light emanated from the almost-sphere. It orbited around it. And each time it completed an orbit, it got faster.

It was charging something.

I flew some horizontal distance away to get clear of the falling soldiers, then began climbing the sky once more, pressure pouring into my ears. Meanwhile, I watched as Kaur floated in the midst of the swarm.

Red claws erupted off the tips of her fingers. She jumped off her skyboard and onto the back of a soldier. She scratched his eye sockets out, then jumped onto a different soldier as the first one fell out of the sky. She hopped from soldier to soldier this way, evading their desperate lightblade swipes, clawing them to death. Jumping upward each time, climbing the swarm to its very top. The terror-filled screams and the sight of blood and flesh littering the sky churned my stomach.

Soon, the swarm dispersed, the soldiers surfing away in obvious fear. But I couldn't focus on her anymore. With the almost-sphere looming large just above me, I was now close enough. I still had to keep some distance so I wouldn't be caught in the explosion.

The ball of black light rotating around the almost-sphere now resembled a ring, such was its blinding speed. Now or never.

I sipped the unseen colors of the Primal Star, flowed them through my body and into my nape, then pushed them into my hand. The frozen bolt of lightning materialized. I clutched it tight, wound my arm back, and lined it up to the center of the almost-sphere.

Then I flung my lance. It blazed through the sky, dragging the wind with it, forming a trail where the vapor must've heated up. That vapor dragged along with its momentum, and so it seemed to be creating its own vortex as it smashed into the almost-sphere.

It disappeared. Nothing happened. What the hell? Where was the explosion I'd been promised?

Then the rotating ball of black light vanished. The almost-sphere flickered, as if glitched. Yellow script, styled in that vine-like calligraphy from Sambalpur, appeared all over it. Not just on its surface, but within it. The almost-sphere transformed into a soup of yellow letters.

Had I done it?

That soup of yellow letters stirred. The letters mixed, connecting and disconnecting from each other. It began to take a shape: an ovular sphere. The letters shot to the surface of this new shape, and then solidified.

Unlike the almost-sphere, the surface of this new object was totally smooth and yellow. It looked like a golden egg hanging in heaven.

Someone floated down from it: just a murky black dot from this distance. Rao?

Someone else was coming at me from below. I looked down to see Kaur. I smiled with all the relief in me. She slowly floated upward on a blood-soaked skyboard. Bits of flesh dripped off her hair and torn-up black suit.

The swarm of soldiers below was no more. Still, a few black dots fluttered about, so they weren't all dead. Perhaps they'd been scared enough not to fight, though.

Kaur hovered next to me, her irises too big for her eyes.

"You all right?" I asked.

She blinked and blinked. "I don't think I can..." She collapsed toward me. I caught her, then steadied her in front of me on my skyboard while her skyboard fell straight down back to earth. She wrapped her arms around me and leaned her head on my chest, obviously unable to balance on her own.

I looked up to see the approaching figure. Four lightblades floated around him, two at his shoulders and two at his waist, all pointed forward. It reminded me of that four-armed god I saw in the black hole. For all I knew, it really was a god holding those blades, one made of unseen light.

"You and my mother seem quite close," Elam said as he paused a few yards away. "Makes me very uncomfortable, Jyosh."

"She's in pain, Elam. What do you want?"

Kaur turned her head to face him. "Elam. Elam, my baby."

"Give her to me," Elam said. "I'll take care of her."

"Don't!" Kaur shouted. "He'll kill you if you do."

Elam shook his head. "Either I kill you both, or just you, Jyosh. It's your choice. Now give her to me."

"He won't do it. My own son wouldn't kill me."

"You're wrong, Amma." The lightblade floating near his left shoulder grew to twice its length. Stayed that way. "Killing you both would be a mercy. You'd be reborn in the Nightscape, far away from what's about to be summoned here."

"About to be summoned?" I said. "I already destroyed your levship!"

Elam smirked. "You did. But it was only a veil, just like the Deep Layer and the God Tower and all of Sambalpur. How many veils does a god need so we don't get burned? The answer to that question is why you've lost, Jyosh. You can't use your Bolt Breath for another — what — four minutes? Plenty of time for me to kill you."

The golden egg above cracked. A pure beam of blue light poured out of the crack. As more cracks erupted upon the egg, more light beams shot out of them. Jets of light emitted from a thousand cracks. The sky itself rumbled. The light coalesced in the most wondrous fusion, forming what resembled wings.

The shell of the egg crumbled. And then brightness lashed the sky, erupting in a rainbow of flurrying, cascading colors. Every color seen and unseen radiated upon the world.

A cry, like that of a god, rang through heaven. More wings shot out of the egg.

It unfurled and, somehow, grew to ten times the size of the egg. A serpent of the sky. A blue, crystalline, shimmering dragon. Its wings were a mix of scale, fur, and feathers, each wondrous and otherworldly. A pearly white glow, radiated from light that had birthed the world itself, shone out of its orb-shaped eyes. I couldn't even see where its tail ended, somewhere up in the second heaven. But its face stared down. And its mouth opened.

I looked in awe upon the daeva. The divine azure dragon.

In my second dream with Zauri, it was sleeping beneath the sun, curled up with its tail almost in its mouth. But now, it had unfurled into a thing of utter awe.

Though I hadn't seen its full form because of the haze, it was also the dragon that had saved me by stopping time when I was fighting that captain in Sambalpur. I'd also witnessed it swallow Zauri during that dream of me crossing the bridge. But this dragon was hundreds of times larger.

I knew, from all my conversations with Saina, that I was beholding Mitra's purest form.

The dragon opened its mouth. A black hole lived inside it, stirring with primordial light. It fluttered its twenty crystalline wings — each twice the size of one of those spade-shaped command ships. The rapid fluttering created a hurricane that, within seconds, formed an armada of clouds. I clung onto Kaur, keeping us steady with all the light in me. She clung onto me just as fiercely, her breaths deepening as she seemed to regain strength.

Lightning shot within and between the clouds that now surrounded us. What had once been a clear sky was now covered in storm.

The dragon cried out, chilling every bone in me. Its roar echoed like a thousand sonic booms.

The black hole shot out of its mouth and now hovered in front of its face. Otherworldly light poured into it from all sides. It was charging the same ability as the almost-sphere!

Before it could unleash its breath, I had to unleash mine.

I inhaled the unseen light of the Primal Star. My veins lit with its power, and this power cycled into my neck and down into my hand.

But nothing appeared.

Of course, the seven and a half minutes hadn't elapsed, yet.

"I'm acutely aware of the time, Jyosh." Elam's four blades all doubled in length, then drifted toward me. "How ignoble, that you'd make me kill my own mother to save humanity."

"Humanity won't be saved by this," I said to my nephew. "Have you seen the Asha yourself? It's not the paradise that Rao would have you believe. There's suffering there, too. It's just more layers of maya. It goes on and on and on. There probably isn't even an Asha. It was all a lie, and you're all taking that lie to its worst conclusion!"

The four demonblades surrounded Kaur and me on all sides. To the right and left, above and below.

Elam drifted closer, now just a yard away.

"I'm sorry, Jyosh. But I trust my father more than I do you. Goodbye." He looked into Kaur's eyes and swallowed hoarsely. "Goodbye, Amma."

As the blades closed in, Kaur let out a guttural roar, stepped onto the edge of the board, and lunged through the air at Elam. She grabbed and pulled him off his skyboard with her force and strength. They both fell off the edge, crying out, then dropped straight down and disappeared into a coal-black cloud.

All four demonblades fell into the cloud, too.

"Kaur," I mouthed, hardly believing what had just happened. "Oh god…"

I felt my heart fall after her. But this wasn't the time to mourn. I had to succeed, so what she'd done would be worth it.

I stared at the dragon. It had talked to me in Sambalpur, but at the time, it was acting of its own will. Was it being controlled by Rao, now? He had terminal access, after all.

The black hole in front of the dragon's mouth spun faster each second.

I opened my right hand and waited for the timer to elapse.

A memory flowed into my mind. Its image played on the clouds in front of me: the moment Zauri and I walked through the roads of the barely built Harska, just when we'd sighted the divine dragon sleeping around the sun.

"If ever you should meet a dragon, remember they are governed by two iron laws." She was so giddy. That little adventure was one of the happiest days of my life. Her radiance, at least in my memories, outshone even this dragon's.

"Iron laws?" I'd been so clueless about everything. So guided by my rage. Thankfully, I had her to teach me and give me a better purpose.

"Mhmm." Zauri held up one finger. *"One — dragons are born in the dark and die in the light."* She held up two fingers. *"And two — only a dragon can teach you how to slay it."*

The images of Zauri and me on the cloud blew away.

My frozen lightning materialized in my right hand. Tears weighed on my eyelids as I stared at it. I stuck my left hand in my utility pocket and clutched Zauri's dream stone. It flowed the most soothing, honey-like warmth into my body. I wasn't imagining it. It really was her.

Only a dragon can teach you how to slay it. That law always sounded so strange. But now, I understood. Now, I grasped everything. All the pieces came together. And all I could do was feel my tears burning my cheeks.

The black hole in front of the dragon's mouth rotated at blinding speed. In a few seconds, it would unleash upon Harska.

"I won't do it." I shook my head.

And then all noise ceased. The sky became so silent, my own hurried heartbeats were the loudest sound in the world.

None of the clouds around me stirred.

I poked a raindrop suspended above my forehead.

Time had stopped.

My avatar taught you all you need to know. The azure dragon spoke into my mind, its voice dark, discordant, and drenched in sadness. *Slay me, Jyosh.*

I looked upon its glory and shook my head. "If this is what the gods decided for me, then I don't want to. I'd rather be free."

The pen has been lifted and the ink has dried. Your freedom is an illusion.

"Then why ask me? Why give me a choice? Why give me a will? Why let me feel anything?"

Don't despair, my love. Now it spoke with the most melodic and heart-tugging voice I'd ever known. Zauri's voice. *Our time together made me so happy. But it was about more than just us. This world is a mercy, and it must be preserved, for the sake of the dreamers and the dreamed.*

"I'm tired of sacrificing my happiness for everyone else's."

Dawn will come. You will be happy, again. I promise. But Mitra and I might never be. Don't let us wake up bearing this sin.

"What will happen to you?"

You know that already.

"Will you forget me, when you're reborn on the dark side of the world? Will your memory be reset?"

Memories don't survive transmigration. But feelings often do. The brightest, and the darkest. You know that, don't you?

The raindrop fell onto my forehead. The storm raged. The light in front of the dragon's mouth blinded.

I didn't want to do this. *The pen has been lifted and the ink has dried.* Was it even my choice? Of course it was! But Kaur had sacrificed herself and her son so I could slay the dragon. Saina was down below, with all the other people of Harska, in its line of fire. And most of all, most of all, Mitra and its avatars, Zauri especially, should not have to bear this awful sin imposed upon them by Kediri.

"I'll break through into the Nightscape and find you," I whispered. "I'll scour every inch of it. No matter what, I will find you."

I roared with all my sadness and flung the weightless spear of lightning at the divine dragon. It flew through the air, parting the clouds, as it arced toward the daeva's head.

It connected. The black hole in front of the dragon's mouth flickered out of existence. The divine dragon itself stopped in time. Froze. Its wings got stuck mid-flutter, like it was glitched. And then, it flickered and disappeared, too. All that remained was a storm-ridden sky.

Messages

Carried upon waves of light, messages breeze through the skies above, with Jyosh unaware:

UNKN1: I need a threat assessment on the man who just sent Mitra to the Nightscape.

UNKN2: Here's what I have.

Military Rank: Unassigned Cadet (Karshan Army Training Level 3)

True Rank: Unattained

Capacity: Fire Vessel 1

Blessings: Bolt Breath (Avatar of Sambalpur)

Connected Stars: Solaris, Primal Star

Color Affinities: Green (High), Red (Low)

Combat Skills: Electric Weapons (Novice), Lightblades (Basic), Hand to Hand (Basic)

Psychological State: Mindwritten (Deteriorating), True personality unknown

Threat Level: High

UNKN1: That's an insanely powerful blessing for someone who can barely defend himself.

UNKN2: He did take out a few Karshan officers with his basic combat skills.

UNKN1: And? My eleven-year-old could pull the hearts out of an entire legion of Karshan soldiers. Far more onerous forces will be seeking to ensnare him. What he's done has sent a signal far and wide.

UNKN2: What do you want me to do?

UNKN1: Watch and wait. Let's see how the others respond, first.

UNKN2: Understood. I'll observe via spectrum, then.

UNKN1: Oh, and if the mindwriting is going to wear off, we'll need to identify what his real personality is like. For all we know, he could be a psychopath.

UNKN2: Will do. I'll watch what he says and does as carefully as I can.

UNKN1: Good. Not many years left in this epoch. I have a feeling things are about to get quite interesting. As shocking as this development is, I fear it is only the beginning.

UNKN2: The beginning of what?

UNKN1: The beginning of a very tumultuous end. What will be reborn in its place... now that's the real question, isn't it?

Chapter Thirty-One

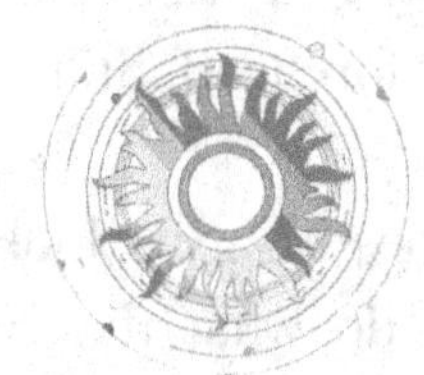

I was still crying when I finally landed near the cave mouth where we'd left Saina. But the sight of someone unexpected soothed me.

Kaur stood by the pond, blood-drenched but smiling somberly.

I hurriedly wiped my tears with my sleeve, then went to her and asked, "How the hell did you survive that fall?"

"Raska, the demon who holds his lightblades, caught us." She huffed, short of breath. "Carried us all the way down. Elam took off, after."

I hugged her, giving no care to how coppery and fleshy she smelled.

"You didn't know that would happen, though. You really took one for the team."

"It was better to sacrifice my son and myself, than let him bear such an unforgivable sin."

I knew exactly what she meant.

Kaur gazed at the chalky pond water. "I'm glad we

succeeded. Before we talk about what to do next, I need a bath. It's been too long."

I nodded and turned my attention to Saina. She was awake and sitting against the cave wall, tears drying on her cheeks.

I knelt next to her. She wouldn't even look my way.

"Mitra and his avatar are gone," she said with the driest voice. "I can't feel their frequency, anymore. I came so far. So far, only to be severed from my god once again."

I put my hand on her forehead. Still warm and soggy, but not as much as before.

"It doesn't matter, does it?" She looked me in the eyes and smiled sadly. "The gods do what they want. We can't get too attached to one or another. This awful, aching longing — it's better meant for people. People that we care for. Not beings we can't understand nor contain."

And yet, people and gods and avatars weren't so different.

"I promise," she squeezed my hand, "I promise I won't forsake you or anyone else to fill this impossible pit."

"I know, Saina. I never doubted you."

"You're sad, too." She plucked a tear off my cheek. "Sadder than I am. You're restless. And scared."

"What are you, psychic, now?"

She shook her head. "I'm just reading your handsome face."

"No one's ever called me handsome before. Well, other than my mother."

"Just take the compliment and go." Saina chuckled nervously. "I have to get back to healing myself, anyway."

"Sure. I could use a nap."

I got up and walked deeper into the moss-ridden cave. Found a dark spot beneath a bunch of stalactites that resembled upside-down towers. I unzipped the front of my combat suit and pulled out my red-green stone. All the color in the air faded. I took

Zauri's dream stone out of my utility pocket and stuck it in. The jolt made me shudder.

I lay down on a bed of moist soil. I thought of Zauri and silently cried myself to sleep.

I awoke at the outskirts of the divine palace, which Zauri had explored all by herself. I opened my palm. No terminal would appear. This wasn't my dream, after all. It never was. No, all along, I'd been brought to this place by someone else. Someone who'd lied to me.

I hurried through the massive golden double doors, which had a lotus-shaped key fitted into a lotus-shaped indentation. Zauri had found that key without me. I never even got to hear the story. I sprinted through the courtyard with the now-depressing dragon statue, into the palace, and down the hallway with the marble floor, where oil lamps hung from the ceiling in these bejeweled holders.

Once I got to the bridge flanked by waterfalls flowing out of the mouths of gods, I ran across to the tomb and arrived at the black door — the one Zauri had said she couldn't open. Now, it stood ajar. I pushed through the gap.

The Ghost sat upon a floating diamond throne in the center of the room. She was nothing but a shadow in the shape of a woman. Beneath her flowed a pool of emerald water. That script covered the walls, glowing green and blue. It reminded me of the temple in Sambalpur.

"I'm sorry." It sounded somber enough to be sincere. "I brought you and Zauri both into this dream so she could teach you. I never thought you'd fall in love with each other."

I bit down on my rage. I couldn't stop shaking. I'd been manipulated, all this time.

"Liar," I said. "You made her fall in love with me. You wrote that love into her black box. And you made her the way she was because you knew I'd fall for her. You did it all to make me your puppet. I danced on your strings, to the tune of your wretched song."

"What else could I have done? Would you have confronted the dragon if you knew it was her?" The Ghost stood up on her floating dais. Just a shadow. "I found her dreaming in Sambalpur, just another lost avatar of Mitra. She was like a newborn, without any memories. I used my power to give her some... I made her think she was a lightblade training program, so you would trust her. Learn how to slay Mitra from her. But I never made her love you, nor did I make you love her. That wasn't part of my mindwriting."

That only made it worse. That only made it hurt more, as if an iron fist squeezed my heart into pulp.

"Turns out... she was real all along," I said. "Her love was real all along. It was me that wasn't real. I was the dream, and she was the dreamer." I dropped to my knees. "But you knew everything. You knew, and you let it all happen."

"Hate me then, if it pleases you." She floated off her dais and landed in front of me with the grace of a cloud. "Hate me. But I did what I did to maintain this world. Had Kediri succeeded in using Mitra's power to send a city the size of Harska into a hellscape of torment, it would've caused Mitra unbearable suffering, because any suffering felt by one of us is felt by one of them — the ten divine dragons. The Dreamers. Too much suffering at once would overwhelm the Dreamer. In a normal dream, it would be like pinching yourself awake. And if enough Dreamers wake up, the dream ends. I couldn't let Rao's plan to destabilize this world succeed — the cost to you and me is immaterial."

I didn't want to think. I didn't want to speak. I just wanted Zauri to come back.

I glanced at the door. I imagined her walking through and

telling me it was all right. That she was here. That finally, we could be together in peace and safety.

"I had to craft lies to motivate you," the Ghost said. "Think back to the very first day you met her. Obviously, Panja Parani was never going to tour your prison camp factory. My lies gave you and Zauri a reason to meet. As for your remorse for killing Vir — it was real. You wanted to be a better man — the type that would help people instead of hurt them. But wanting to change and *actually changing* are two completely different things. I made that transformation happen, to the point where you were willing to sacrifice yourself, if needed. And in doing so, I created a savior for our world."

"I wasn't willing!"

"But look at how much more powerful you've become. More importantly, how much of a better person you are. Don't pretend like you didn't get some benefit."

"Benefit? Benefit? Are you kidding me? Is this a sick joke?"

"Yes. It's the sickest joke I've ever played on anyone in my family. But it had to be this way for the greater good."

Don't believe your lying eyes, Kediri's statement echoed in my head.

"At least tell me the truth," I said. "Cast off your veil."

"Are you sure you want to know?" She swallowed. It seemed painful.

I nodded, though deep down, I already felt the awful truth.

"Fine. It's going to hurt, but I do owe you at least that."

A white light enveloped her. She shrank a few inches. Another person stood before me.

I darted my gaze away once my eyes confirmed who it was. I crushed my leaking tears. I let out the most pained breath I'd ever taken.

"I saw them behead you."

Chaya knelt and looked straight into me. I wouldn't look

back. I refused to gaze at her face, lest my love for my dead sister soften my anger.

"It's true. I was beheaded. In that moment, I should've been reborn in the Nightscape. And I would've been, had I not been blessed."

"What kind of blessing lets you cheat death?" Only after the words left my tongue did I remember Kediri mentioning such a thing.

"There are all kinds of blessings. All kinds of gods. All kinds of living and dead stars from which powers radiate. The truth is, I didn't cheat death. I did die. I only exist in dreams, now."

"How can that be?"

"Ask the gods who grant these strange blessings. Elam once only existed in a dream. Now he exists here. It's the opposite for me. For a time, I wandered endlessly through dreams. Hopping from world to world. I saw everyone's fantasies, and many of their fears, wondering why this had been done to me." She took a jittery breath. "But then, I discovered I had power in the dream. Planting black boxes and mindwriting became my way of influencing the real world. In fact, I could basically do anything I wanted in the real world, so long as I had a brainwashed slave carry it out. Isn't that kind of sad?"

I heaved out a breath. "I've no sorrow for someone like you."

"I know. Just understand — I had to stop our brother, no matter the cost. I'm sorry you were hurt. It was never my intention to see you so shattered."

I'd gone numb to anything she had to say.

"Perhaps, some other time, when you've an ear to listen, I'll tell you my whole story." She took a paper out of her pocket, unfolded it, and handed it to me. "Zauri wrote this for you. I'm leaving, now. My work is far from done. Kediri, or rather Rao as he now wishes to be called, will try to end the maya again." She let out a tired sigh. "And so I'll have to stop him, again. Stubbornness runs in our family, after all."

That I couldn't argue.

"We'll also talk about Abba and Amma, next time we meet. About their secrets. About who they really were. Until then, Little Brother." Chaya walked out the door behind me.

I wasted no time. I looked down at the letter, my tears already wetting the paper.

DEAR JYOSH,

When you're gone, I like to practice drawing. Yes, drawing — I hope this isn't too boring a subject to talk about. Sometimes, I draw you. Sometimes, I draw myself. I feel like by drawing the two of us, it'll make us live forever, at least on paper. It's a nice thought, isn't it?

I don't know if you want to live forever. It's a strange idea. Everything has an end. And yet, I feel like I'll never die. Something inside of me, the thing we call a black box, is telling me that I'm meant to be forever.

It scares me, to be honest. It implies that I've already lived, even before I awoke the day I met you. That I must've had some other purpose, perhaps one that didn't make me as happy as teaching you did.

And that's really why I'm writing this letter. You made me happy, Jyosh. For the blink of an eye that I was here, in the moments when you were around, all I can say is: I was happy.

And that makes me wish that I could live forever with you. But the black box is also telling me that I can't. There's no way. We don't exist in the same world. You're from somewhere I can't truly inhabit, and I'm from somewhere you can't truly inhabit.

In those moments when I waited for you, I used to wonder if I was real. I still don't know the answer. I mean, I feel real. I can think. It could be that I'm the only real thing in the world, and everything else is an illusion. But then I know that you must be real. You're real because you and I created something together. It didn't last very long, but we created our own world. Our own little paradise.

Hey, after you're done reading, turn this letter over. See my drawing.

I stared in the water and thought of you when I drew it. When I looked at my reflection in the water, I saw a different face than what I'd usually see in the mirror. Maybe it was because loneliness had overwhelmed me, and I couldn't help but cry. Despite that, if you look closely into my eyes, I hope you'll also see how much I love you.

The truth is, I was incredibly lonely for such a long time. Only days had passed for you, but it was months for me. Months of torturously wondering if you were okay. Months of wondering if I'd be alone forever. Sometimes, I imagined you were here with me. I would talk to you as I explored the palace, hoping that you'd just appear. At first, doing this would soothe me. Balm my pain. But then, it would just make it hurt so much more, because I knew it was a lie.

I wonder if you felt the same, sometimes. But even if you didn't, I don't mind. I'd be happy for you. I wouldn't wish such loneliness on you, ever. I'd bear it, and bear it, even if it lasted a thousand years. In the end, I was just a lightblade trainer who continued dreaming without the dreamer because her dream stone was glitched. That's how I want to define myself, regardless of what the black box is telling me.

But I wish I could've been so much more for you. I wish I could've been by your side through every small and large struggle. I wish I could've dried your tears, in this world and the other. But I have to accept that, in the end, I would only be holding you back. You deserve to be with someone who can share your reality with you.

And whatever reality I'm going to after ours ends, know that I wouldn't trade our moments together for all the treasures of infinity.

In the end, when you become free, when you learn your own worth, I know you'll outgrow our time together. You should've never suffered the way you did in that camp. I know now that it's only because you suffered so much that you fell in love with me in the first place. Because I was the only one there for you, in the tiny world where you could find peace.

But now, there are others with you, too. There are others who care about you. And it's okay. It's okay if you grow wings and fly. I'll still love you, even if you never visit me in your thoughts. Even if you find someone to love in the real world. Even if you think of me as just a shadow, something you only loved because you'd never seen fire. I'll still love you. You made me happy.

I'll always love you.

Yours Eternally,

Zauri

Thank You. Please Read!

So, how're you feeling? What did you think?

If you enjoyed yourself, please leave a review on Amazon. **Please.** There are thousands of books published everyday, and this one needs all the help it can get to rise to the top. Even just clicking the star rating is hugely helpful. Your review could help launch this novel into the second heaven and beyond. And that means I get to write more books in this series.

I really can't overstate the importance of every reader leaving a review. I'm counting on you!

Lightblade is a story I've wanted to tell for the longest time. It's been swimming in my mind for over twenty years. The first iteration was an RPG Maker game I made in the 8th grade called *Twilight Epoch*. Fast forward to college, where I wrote my first novel, *Song of a Dead Star*, which contained many of the ideas from Lightblade including the sunshine-based magic system, Zoroastrian and Vedic mythology, shared dreaming, levships, and even a younger version of Saina!

And the story is not yet fully told. Jyosh's journey will be a long one, and I can't wait to take you into the higher heavens, across the Whirling Wall into the Nightscape, and into even deeper dream layers.

Thank you for letting me tell my story. It means everything to me.

All the love,
Zamil

Want More?

Get *Death Rider*, a prequel novella to Gunmetal Gods, for FREE by joining my mailing list at ZamilAkhtar.com!

Gunmetal Gods

Enjoy dark fantasy? Get Gunmetal Gods at Books2Read.com/
GunmetalGods

Follow Me!

I'd love to see you around, so please follow me at the links below. I'd **REALLY** love to see you on my Patreon, where I post early chapter reveals, exclusive short stories, and art. You can even leave feedback and be a part of shaping my future stories. Support me and help me write more books!

Patreon: https://patreon.com/zamakhtar

Discord: https://discord.gg/mtd9uc99JF

Twitter: https://twitter.com/zamakhtar

Facebook: https://facebook.com/zamakhtar1/

Instagram: https://www.instagram.com/zamilakhtarauthor/

Reddit: https://www.reddit.com/r/zamakhtar/

TikTok: https://tiktok.com/@zamakhtar